BITT

"You're so beautiful," he murmured huskily. "I want you, Sharla."

His confession was thrilling, and she adored him so completely that she interpreted his words to please herself. Her love was indeed working miracles.

Trusting him, she pressed her lips to his and wound her arms about his neck, presenting him her body, heart and undying loyalty.

"I've never met anyone like you," he whispered. "But I know I've been waiting for you all my life."

"I feel the same way," she answered. "Maybe it's destiny."

"If that's true, then it's the first time destiny has rewarded me." His kissed her, his mouth taking hers with breathless urgency.

Sharla responded fully, wishing this moment could last forever. "I love you, darling," she murmured as his lips left hers. Soon she was consumed by passion, never realizing until later that he never uttered the three words she wanted so desperately to hear . . .

ROMANCE FROM JO BEVERLY

Destiny

Rochelle Wayne

Zebra Books
Kensington Publishing Corp.
http://www.zebrabooks.com

ZEBRA BOOKS are published by

Kensington Publishing Corp.
850 Third Avenue
New York, NY 10022

First Printing: March, 1998
10 9 8 7 6 5 4 3 2 1

Printed in the United States of America

One

James Rayfield, poised in front of his full-length mirror, admired his naked physique. The master bedroom's elaborate decor provided an expensive background, as though he were posing for a portrait that not only revealed his naked masculinity, but his great wealth as well.

"Come back to bed, love," a woman's voice beckoned. She drew back the covers, exposing her own naked flesh.

Her body was firm and voluptuous and too tempting for the average man not to gaze upon, but James was no longer interested. She had served her purpose—his sexual needs had been temporarily satisfied. His eyes remained on the mirror as he continued his self-examination. He was well pleased with his reflection. Despite his forty-odd years, he still had a young man's body. He thought his sinewy frame perfectly proportioned; not an ounce of fat dared mar such excellence. His eyes scaled up his body until he met his own gaze, which stared back at him from the mirror. His admiration didn't end with his physique, for he found his face strikingly handsome.

James Rayfield was indeed attractive. His dark-brown hair was still as thick as it had been in his youth; a touch of gray at the temples lent him a distinguished air. A full, carefully groomed mustache complemented his good looks.

"It's still early, love. Come back to bed," the woman repeated, her tone soft but persistent.

Her words placed an impatient frown on James's brow, but he didn't bother to turn away from the mirror as he voiced his irritation, "Good God, Claudia. You sound like a whining whore. Can't you get enough? What does it take to satisfy you?"

"You satisfy me, love," she was quick to reply. "I only want to hold you in my arms a little longer."

He reluctantly turned away from his reflection and cast a cold gaze upon Claudia, who was watching him through love-glazed eyes. "Get up, put on your clothes, and go downstairs," he said testily.

His brusque dismissal didn't dim the love that burned within Claudia, for she was accustomed to Rayfield's moods. She felt she knew all his faults, and she loved him in spite of them. She also believed that James shared her amorous feelings and that someday he would marry her. That marriage, however, would have to wait at least a year, since Rayfield's wife had died only a month ago and a decent period of mourning must be upheld. After all, James was a prominent citizen and he had an image to protect.

She got out of bed regretfully, for she did indeed want James back in her arms. Only when they were together did she really feel alive. She lived solely for their stolen moments; everything in between was only a means of existence until they could be together again.

She dressed slowly, in no hurry to leave. Each minute spent with James was heavenly. Even when his mood was foul—sometimes even abusive—she truly worshiped him.

James slipped into a silk robe and turned to Claudia. "When you go downstairs, order me a bath," he said.

She finished dressing in her drab uniform. Rayfield insisted that his domestic servants dress according to standard—dark gowns and white aprons for the women, and black suits for the men.

Claudia had now worked for Rayfield for nearly a year. Last spring one of his maids left to get married, and he advertised for a replacement. Several women, including Claudia, applied for the position. James conducted the interviews, for his wife was bedridden. The other applicants' references were far superior to Claudia's, but Claudia was the only young and attractive one; therefore, she was hired. Within days, James had her in his bed.

Claudia approached her employer hesitantly, for she was uncertain of his mood. She stood in front of him and gazed imploringly into his face. "Do you want me to come back to your bed tonight? Please say that you do."

He didn't hide his annoyance. "When I want you again, I'll let you know! I can't stand it when you beg!"

"I just love you so much that I want to be with you as often as possible."

He arched a sharp brow. "Are you going to order my bath, or do you intend to carry on with this foolishness until I lose my temper?"

She turned away and moved quickly to the door. But she couldn't leave without pursuing one more time. "Later, I'll bathe and sprinkle myself with lilac talcum in case you decide to send for me." With that, she left hurriedly, closing the door.

"I'll send for you all right, but not for the reason you think," James uttered to the absent Claudia. It was time to fire the woman; she was getting on his nerves.

Moving across the carpeted floor, he went to his dresser and picked up a silver cheroot case. He lit his smoke, returned to the bed and sat on the edge. As he awaited the hot water for his bath, his thoughts drifted to his wife's ward, Sharla. He brought her lovely image to mind, and the vision revived his sexual hunger. Claudia had appeased his passion, but his voracious appetite for Sharla was never sated. Such desire had materialized gradually. As Sharla's maturity bloomed, so did his hunger. Now, having her was an obsession he could barely control. As long as his wife was alive, holding his lust in check was necessary. If Olivia had known of his desire for Sharla, she would certainly have divorced him. She had loved her ward as though she were her own daughter, and no mother could have been more protective. But none of that mattered anymore; Olivia was dead and Sharla was now his responsibility. She would soon be twenty-one and would come into her inheritance, but until then she was completely dependent on him. A deep scowl hardened James's face as he thought about Sharla's inheritance. She would soon be a very wealthy young woman, and he begrudged her every inherited penny. If not for Sharla, his wife's entire fortune would be his.

Soon his scowl disappeared. He intended to marry Sharla, and then he would have it all: his wife's entire fortune and her lovely ward as well.

He went to his wardrobe and withdrew a tailor-made suit. Tonight, at dinner, he would subtly begin his romantic pursuit. Considering Sharla an innocent, he was sure he could lay a trap, capture her, and win her love. He knew he had to move slowly and carefully; after all, he was supposed to be in mourning. But he felt he had all the time in the world. He didn't foresee Sharla leaving, for this was her home. She was not romantically involved with anyone, therefore, there would be no sudden engagement to interfere with his plans.

A wide smile crossed his face. He was confident that everything would work out splendidly.

As James was thinking about Sharla, she was in her bedroom thinking about him. However, her thoughts were far from complimentary. She didn't like James and never understood why Olivia had married him. She supposed Olivia had been blinded by his dashing good looks and winsome charms. Men like James Rayfield were irresistible to most women; Sharla was one of the exceptions. She never had a tangible reason for disliking James; her feelings were instinctive. Nevertheless, she had to give him credit where credit was due. He had been a doting husband to Olivia for the duration of their six-year marriage. But then, why shouldn't he be doting? He was penniless when Olivia married him. She made him a rich man, and Sharla suspected James loved money as much as he idolized himself.

Sharla got up from her vanity and walked to a bedroom window. Her room faced the back of the house, and, pulling aside the heavy drapes, she glanced absently down at the immaculately trimmed grounds surrounded by a high iron fence. Behind the iron barricade a few widely spaced trees separated the private grounds from the noisy, bustling streets of St. Louis. The sounds of moving carriages, people's voices, and the general hubbub of city life carried faintly through the bedroom window. The sounds were not disturbing, for they seemed a natural part of home. She had moved into this bedroom at the age of three, and the distant city sounds were as familiar to her as the room itself.

She turned away from the window, and her gaze swept across the spacious room as though seeing it for the first time. A Queen Anne bed occupied the center; the canopy, covered in a bright fabric, matched the spread and the floor-length drapes. In one corner stood a high chest of drawers. The stunning piece was made of maple and pine with sported raised gilt figures that rested on a tortoiseshell background. Streaks of red vermilion added a final touch. The huge room easily accommodated several pieces of furniture: a delicate vanity, a writing table, two wardrobes, three armchairs, and a plush settee.

However, as Sharla perused the room, she was remem-

bering when it sufficed as a nursery. Later, it had become
a young girl's room, then, on her sixteenth birthday, Olivia
had brought in professional decorators and the room had
been transformed to its present status. Sharla was well
pleased with the decor, but in a reminiscent mood, she
recalled the day she had first walked into this room, which
was also her first clear memory from childhood. Although
she had been only three years old, she could still recall
the day with uncanny clarity. In her mind, she saw herself
coming into the room with Olivia. She had been a little
scared and overwhelmed by her rich surroundings. She
had held tightly to Olivia's hand, the beautiful woman's
touch giving her a feeling of security. The nursery, done
all in pink, had been a wondrous sight to the young Sharla.
She felt as though she were dreaming and that she would
surely wake at any moment and find the nursery had vanished like a puff of smoke. But it was no dream; she was
really going to live in this grand house and sleep in the
pink nursery. Olivia had taken her from the dreary orphanage and brought her here to grow up surrounded by
opportunity and wealth. Sharla had been certain that
Olivia was an angel from heaven.

A warm smile touched Sharla's lips as her reverie continued. She soon learned that Olivia was her guardian,
and not an angel. When Sharla was old enough to understand, Olivia explained that she couldn't adopt her because she was a widow. The law didn't allow such a privilege
to a woman alone. She was, however, her authorized guardian, which made Sharla her legal ward.

Sharla was the center of Olivia's life until she became
involved with James Rayfield. She remained a nurturing
and considerate guardian, but falling in love changed
Olivia. She had been a widow for eleven years when Rayfield suddenly came into her life. Olivia fell in love quickly,
and, following a whirlwind courtship, she and James were
married. Sharla was only fourteen at the time, but despite

her tender age, she sensed a coldness in Rayfield that completely eluded Olivia. Despite Sharla's reservations, Rayfield seemed to make Olivia happy, and that was all that really mattered, for Sharla loved her guardian totally and unselfishly.

Moving away from the window, Sharla went back to her vanity and sat down. Dinner would be served soon, and she knew she should dress for the occasion. James always insisted on dinner being a formal affair, whether they had guests or not. Tonight, though, there would be a guest—Dexter Rayfield. He was James's younger brother. Sharla didn't especially like Dexter. She found him arrogant, conceited, and manipulative. He was a successful business tycoon—thanks to Olivia's generosity. Wanting to help her brother-in-law prosper, she backed him in several investments, which had paid off handsomely. Dexter, like James, had Olivia to thank for his prosperity and security.

Sharla sighed deeply. She also owed everything she had to Olivia. But she somehow felt that the Rayfields weren't sincerely grateful; she, on the other hand, was more grateful than words could express. A trace of tears dampened her eyes, for she had loved Olivia. The weeks following her guardian's death were healing ones for Sharla, and she was beginning to deal with her grief. Olivia had been seriously ill for an extended period, and there had been plenty of time for Sharla to mentally prepare herself for Olivia's impending death.

She picked up a hairbrush and began running it briskly through her long, honey-colored tresses. A moment of dread coursed through her, and she stopped brushing for a few seconds as she considered the best way to bring up her announcement at dinner. She wanted to go away for a while. She thought about it, decided the best approach was a direct one, then went back to grooming her hair. She had a feeling James would insist she remain here. But this house held too many memories of Olivia, and she

wanted desperately to leave. She also wanted to put distance between herself and James Rayfield. James, however,
controlled her inheritance, and it galled her that she had
to ask him for money that was rightfully hers. But Olivia's
will stipulated that James be in charge of Sharla's finances
until her twenty-first birthday, which was still six months
away.

She did, however, have a little money of her own. Olivia,
knowing a young lady needed some independence, had
given Sharla an allowance. She had managed to save a tidy
sum, but it wasn't nearly enough to pay for a European
tour, which was what she had her heart set on. She intended to stay away for six months, come home after she
turned twenty-one, claim her inheritance, then move out
West and buy a cattle ranch.

She put down her brush, gazed intently at her reflection,
and mumbled aloud, "Sharla Matthews, if I didn't know
you better, I'd say you're out of your mind. A cattle ranch?
You know absolutely nothing about operating a ranch."
But living in the West had been a dream of Sharla's since
childhood. A look of determination crossed her fine features. She would buy that ranch and make it a success; all
she needed was money and confidence. She would soon
have the money, but she wasn't so sure about the confidence. But such a doubt was not a deterrent; she was determined to learn everything she needed to know, and
through learning she was certain her confidence would
grow.

Going to one of the wardrobes, she looked through a
row of gowns, decided on one in particular and placed it
on the bed. She then added undergarments from the chest
of drawers and dressed as quickly as possible. The delicate
gown, white silk trimmed with deep-blue velvet, gracefully
draped Sharla's slender frame. She slipped her feet into
a pair of blue velvet slippers, then returned to the chest
of drawers, opened one of her many jewelry boxes and

took out a sapphire necklace with matching earrings. She sat at the vanity and adorned herself with the expensive gems. The sapphires, as dark blue as her eyes, had a stunning effect.

She again brushed her blond tresses, then drew the long locks away from her face and secured them with two combs embellished with painted violets. Studying her reflection, she decided she was properly dressed for dinner; the lovely image looking back at her completely escaped her vanity.

Sharla Matthews was exquisite; her honey-colored tresses fell past her shoulders in silky curls, her eyes, accentuated with sharply arched brows and thick lashes, were strikingly blue. High cheekbones, a delicate nose, and full-shaped lips were as beautiful as though sculpted by an artist demanding perfection; but character was in her countenance as well as beauty.

She left the room, moved quickly down the long hallway and descended the marble staircase. She paid no attention to her home's elaborate furnishings and expensive objects of art as she made her way to the kitchen, for the house's costly decor was a part of her everyday life.

In the huge kitchen, she found Agnes the cook, Claudia, and another maid putting the final touches to dinner.

The matronly cook, large-boned and extremely overweight, turned away from the stove to greet her young mistress. "Evenin', Miss Sharla. You look mighty pretty." Sharla's presence didn't surprise the cook, for she was used to the young mistress spending time in the kitchen. Ever since she was a child, she had often come to the kitchen, seeking the cook's company.

"Good evening, Agnes," Sharla said with a genuinely warm smile. She drew out a chair and sat at the table. "Do you have time to join me for coffee?"

Agnes said that she did, and she quickly poured two cups and settled her large frame into a kitchen chair that

seemed too flimsy to support her weight, however, it was stronger than it appeared.

"You seem a little troubled," Agnes observed, looking closely at Sharla. "Is there something on your mind?"

She smiled hesitantly. "No. I mean, yes."

The woman chuckled good-naturedly. "Don't you know?"

"Agnes, I want to take a European tour—an extended one."

"Exactly how long is extended?"

"At least six months. That way, I'll be twenty-one when I return."

"But why do you want to leave your home?"

"This house holds too many memories of Olivia. I need to get away."

"But those memories will still be here when you get back," the cook reminded her gently.

"Yes, but I don't intend to live here. I plan to collect my inheritance, move away, and build a life for myself."

Agnes was taken aback. "Miss Sharla, you're talking nonsense! This is your home! Furthermore, where would you go?"

"Out West; probably Texas. I want to buy a cattle ranch."

"You don't know anything about running a ranch."

"I can learn."

"Women don't run ranches; that's a man's job."

"This is the 1880's, and it's about time women demanded their independence. Just because I'm a woman doesn't mean I can't take care of myself."

Agnes shook her head, and emphasized her disapproval by clucking her tongue against the roof of her mouth. "Running off to Europe is bad enough, but moving to Texas is the craziest thing I ever heard. Miss Sharla, you know Miss Olivia would never have approved."

"I'm not staying in this house any longer," Sharla said firmly. "If James won't give me the money to tour Europe,

then I'll go someplace I can afford until my twenty-first birthday."

"Why are you so determined to leave here?"

"I told you—this house holds too many memories."

"It's more than that," Agnes replied keenly.

Sharla paused, debating if she should confide in Agnes, then decided to proceed. "I'm uneasy living here without Olivia. I don't think I can trust James. It's the way he looks at me."

Claudia was now working in the pantry, but she could overhear the conversation between Sharla and Agnes. The pantry was very close to the kitchen table, and their voices carried clearly.

"What do you mean—the way he looks at you?" Agnes was asking.

"Like he wants to take me to bed."

Her answer didn't surprise Agnes, for she was extraordinarily perceptive and had seen through James Rayfield from the beginning. She had tried to warn Olivia not to trust him, but the woman reacted so angrily that Agnes never again said anything against James in Olivia's presence; it was hopeless, for she was blindly in love. Agnes's impression of James proved to be true when she learned that he was having an affair with Claudia. Nothing in the household escaped Agnes for very long, and she soon spotted Claudia sneaking into the master's bedroom. She didn't let the maid know that she was wise to the liaison, nor did she tell Olivia. Her husband's philandering would have broken her heart. Agnes had a feeling that James had been unfaithful to his wife from the very start. She had doubted his nocturnal outings were spent playing cards at his club, but were most likely a cover for licentious encounters.

Agnes reached across the table and placed a comforting hand on Sharla's. "Mr. Rayfield might be a scoundrel, but he's also a gentleman. Although he finds you desirable, he wouldn't compromise you. There's no need for you to run away." Agnes truly believed her words; a man could be a philanderer and still be a gentleman. James had never done or said anything to make Agnes think otherwise, for he had carefully guarded his infidelities from Olivia. In Agnes's opinion, that made him very considerate and protective of Olivia's feelings. She didn't like him, but she nonetheless credited him as a gentleman. After all, a lot of husbands stray.

The butler, an elderly man with snow-white hair and a matching handlebar mustache, stepped into the kitchen. "Miss, your guest has arrived," he said to Sharla. "I showed him into the parlor."

"Is James with him?"

"No, ma'am. Mr. Rayfield hasn't come downstairs yet."

"In that case, I suppose I should see to our guest." She rose from her chair reluctantly, for she wasn't looking forward to entertaining Dexter.

Claudia left the pantry, and her eyes followed Sharla as she walked out of the kitchen. Jealousy swarmed through her violently, for she knew Sharla had spoken the truth. James did look at her as though he wanted to take her to bed. She had seen James bestow that look upon Sharla, and each time it had inflamed her jealousy. She would kill James before letting him leave her for Sharla or any other woman!

Two

Dexter was at the liquor cabinet when Sharla came into the parlor. He gave her a disinterested glance, then returned to pouring himself a drink.

"Would you like a sherry?" he asked.

"No, thank you," she replied, going to sit on the sofa.

He moved to a chair across from Sharla, and toyed with the glass in his hands as though he wasn't really interested in drinking. Sharla watched him; he always consumed brandy in the same fashion—his fingers would caress the sniffer a minute or so, then he'd take a tiny sip, place the drink aside, and light a cheroot.

Dexter was a younger version of his brother. Like James, his hair was dark brown, and he sported a luxuriant mustache. He was tall, slender, and very handsome. His resemblance to James was not only physical; Dexter was also conceited and arrogant. Sharla suspected he considered himself quite a ladies' man; after all, he was one of the most eligible bachelors in St. Louis. Dexter was her guardian's brother-in-law, which made him a frequent visitor, and most of the young ladies in Sharla's social circle envied her her close ties to him. Sharla, however, did not consider herself fortunate, for she could barely tolerate Dexter. On her twentieth birthday, a gala affair that had filled the ballroom with dancers and a complete orchestra, Dexter, under false pretenses, had taken her onto the terrace, where he had made romantic overtures. She had firmly squelched his un-wanted advances. Weeks later, he was still trying to win her over, but to no avail. Finally, accepting defeat, he ended his romantic pursuit. He was now impersonal and somewhat aloof, which was fine with Sharla.

Dexter took a long drag off his cheroot, blew the smoke out slowly, then looked at Sharla as though her company was tiresome. "How have you been?" he asked, his tone flat. He was evidently trying to make conversation, for the silence between them was uncomfortable.

"I still miss Olivia, but otherwise I'm fine."

"Olivia," he murmured, feigning sadness. "I can hardly believe she's gone."

Sharla doubted his sincerity.

"Poor James," Dexter continued. "He absolutely adored Olivia. It'll take a long time for him to get over her death."

"I hardly think so," Sharla remarked, unable to suppress her feelings.

"Why do you say that?"

"James adores no one but himself. He'll get over Olivia with extraordinary ease."

"I didn't know you were so bitter."

"I'm not bitter. I just know your brother."

"But I think you *are* bitter." He scooted to the edge of his chair, and leaned closer to Sharla. His eyes bored coldly into hers. "You resent my brother, don't you? If Olivia hadn't married him, you would have inherited her full estate. Well, my dear, just remember this—James has more right to her fortune than you have. He was her husband and her next of kin. You were merely her ward—a waif she rescued from the orphanage because she was a lonely widow. So don't you dare pass judgment on my brother, for you are the freeloader."

Sharla bounded angrily to her feet. "I loved Olivia as though she were my mother!"

"What's going on in here?" James suddenly asked, coming into the room.

Dexter leaned back in his chair, took a calming sip of brandy, and replied, "Sharla and I have a difference of opinion, that's all."

James didn't pursue the matter. "Dinner is ready," he said, moving to Sharla and offering her his arm. She accepted his gentlemanly gesture. Dexter, taking his brandy with him, followed them into the formal dining room.

James sat at the head of the table; Sharla was seated on his right and Dexter on his left. No one said anything as Claudia served the soup, but the moment she left the room, Sharla turned to James and said with a confidence she didn't truly feel, "I need an advancement on my inheritance. I want to take a European tour."

James was about to taste his soup, but he lowered his spoon as though he had suddenly developed an aversion to food. "A European tour?" he exclaimed. "That's out of the question!"

"Why?" Sharla demanded. "I've never been to Europe. It's not as though I'm a child. I'm old enough to make my own decisions. And I certainly don't intend to travel alone. I'll hire a companion."

Anger flared in James's eyes. "I said, it's out of the question!"

She met his anger without a flinch. "And I said, I'm old enough to make my own decisions."

"You might be old enough, but haven't you forgotten something very important?"

"What's that?"

"You don't have any money."

"I have money, all right."

"But I control it."

"Only for six more months."

"Then your tour will have to wait six months." He wasn't

about to let her leave. In six months' time, he was sure he could charm her as easily as he had charmed Olivia.

Sharla stared at him defiantly. "Is there anything I can say that will change your mind?"

"No, there isn't." His tone softened, as though he were trying to pacify a child. "Sharla, I'd be neglecting my responsibilities if I allowed you to go to Europe. Young ladies do not travel abroad without a proper escort—a father, brother, or husband."

"In that case, I'll go to New York. Olivia's aunt lives there, and I'll stay with her. I'll return in six months."

James started to speak, but she held up a silencing hand.

"I don't have to ask you for money," she explained. "I have enough to travel to New York."

"Why are you so determined to leave?"

"I don't want to live in this house without Olivia."

"That's ridiculous!"

"Is it?" she countered. "I don't think so. I'll return after my twenty-first birthday and claim my inheritance." She eyed him threateningly. "Don't you dare find some legal loophole that will hold up my inheritance." She didn't trust James at all and considered him devious.

"Hold up your inheritance?" he asked, a brow arched sharply. "That wouldn't be too difficult. I question if you're legally competent. You aren't acting very rationally, and I have Dexter as a witness."

"Legally competent?" she said fiercely. "You dare to question my state of mind?"

"You're becoming more irrational by the minute," James uttered. He turned to his brother and asked, "Don't you think so, Dexter?"

Dexter smiled smugly. "Maybe grief has made her a little unhinged. I've heard of that happening."

"Yes, so have I," James said, as though in full agreement. "Losing Olivia has taken its toll on poor Sharla." He turned back to his charge, who was eyeing him furiously.

"Don't worry, my dear. With proper rest and quiet, you'll soon be as good as new. And I, of course, will see that you're well taken care of."

"Your threats don't scare me! I'm going to New York, and when I return, I will claim my inheritance. Legally incompetent, indeed! If you try something like that I will . . . I will . . ."

"You will, what?" James taunted. "Kill me?"

"I'd be mad enough to kill you!" she raged, knowing full well that she could never commit such a horrendous crime. Her appetite had vanished. She left the table and stormed out of the room.

James was too upset to eat his soup, and he pushed the bowl aside. "Damn!" he cursed softly. "I can't let her go to New York."

"Why not?" Dexter asked, doing justice to his soup. The scene hadn't diminished his appetite. "Why should you care if she leaves?"

"I want her here where she belongs!"

Dexter raised a suspicious brow. "Surely you don't have marriage on your mind."

"I might," he admitted.

"You can't be serious! The girl's a waif. God only knows who her parents were. Hell, insanity might indeed run in her family."

"If you feel that way, then why did you pursue her? And don't deny it; I knew what you were doing."

"Oh, I don't deny it. But I didn't want to marry her for God's sake! I only had sex on my mind. The Rayfield blood is untainted, and I intend to keep it that way. Thieves, murderers, and mental incompetents might run rampant in Sharla's family. I mean, who the hell knows? I wouldn't want her as the mother of my children."

"I never thought of it that way. But, damn it, you're right. What could I have been thinking? I can't marry Sharla. Thanks to Olivia, she's so well polished and educated that I never really considered the circumstances surrounding her birth." A lewd glint suddenly came to his eyes. "But I can still have her."

"Sure, as a mistress. Besides, in the long run you'll be doing her a favor. Otherwise, she'll become a dried-up spinster or marry a common laborer. No man from a decent family is going to ask her to marry him. Bloodline is too important. But Sharla is very willful and stubborn. She won't succumb easily."

"I beg to differ with you," James remarked confidently. "When she finds herself impoverished and completely dependent on me, she won't be so willful and stubborn. Since she was three years old, she's had all the advantages of wealth. She couldn't begin to make it on her own, penniless, and branded mentally unbalanced."

"Then you plan to have her claimed incompetent?"

"I most assuredly do, and I intend to start immediately. After dinner, I want you to fetch Doctor Eastman and bring him here. Tell him that Sharla has been behaving quite irrationally and that I'm very concerned about her." James leaned back in his chair, smiled complacently, and continued, "Sharla's family is a mystery, and it should be easy to plant the notion in Eastman's head that she might have inherited a mental imbalance. With your testimony and the doctor's, there won't be a problem having Sharla declared legally incompetent. Furthermore, in all honesty, Sharla has always been a mite strange."

Dexter cast him a questioning look.

"She doesn't behave like most well-raised ladies," James explained. "For instance, when we visit the stables, she refuses to ride sidesaddle, but uses that western saddle she ordered and rides astride as though she were a man. Such disgraceful behavior was very embarrassing for Olivia and me. Our friends were abashed, and poor Olivia could barely face them. Then, last year, Olivia learned that Sharla was spending her allowance on shooting lessons. Why would any lady in her right mind want to be a marksman? When Olivia questioned her, she said that someday she intends to live out West and own a cattle ranch, therefore, it was important that she know how to defend herself. A cattle ranch? Can you imagine that? The girl has always been eccentric. Now, she wants to run off to Europe without a proper escort. Having her declared incompetent won't be a problem. I'll visit my lawyer in the morning and sign the necessary papers. He will expedite the procedure and the papers will have a judge's signature on them before the end of the week. Then Sharla will do as I say, for I'll have full control of her inheritance . . . indefinitely."

Dexter grinned expansively. "You shrewd devil; I'm proud to have you for a brother."

James returned Dexter's smile with deep affection. The conniving Rayfields did genuinely care about each other. Despite the ten years separating their ages, they were close friends, as well as devoted brothers.

Born to rich, aristocratic parents, they had grown up surrounded by wealth and all its privileges. However, their father was a poor manager of money, and he squandered his inheritance on gambling, women, and numerous bad investments. The brothers were not aware of this until after their father's demise; their mother had died three years before. After the reading of the will, they found themselves in dire distress. James, being the oldest, tried diligently to restore their wealth, but his efforts barely kept them from declaring bankruptcy. Five years following their father's death, they were still living one step away from poverty. James's social activities seldom coincided with Olivia's, but on a few occasions they both attended the same function. A polite greeting was all that passed between them. Then one night, at a masked ball, they found themselves standing side by side. A waltz was playing, and James asked Olivia to dance. That was the beginning of their whirlwind romance. For Olivia it was love at first sight, for she was truly seeing James for the first time. She had never really looked at him as a woman looks at a man. James, however, viewed their romance quite differently. Although he found Olivia very attractive, it was her money that he loved.

Now, as he relished having Olivia's full estate, along with a humbled Sharla, he said to Dexter, "You're right, I am a shrewd devil." With a wide sweep of his arm, which indicated his surrounding wealth, he added with a sly smile, "But look where being shrewd has gotten me."

At that moment, Claudia, along with the butler, came into the dining room with the main course. James welcomed their intrusion, for his appetite had suddenly returned.

Dexter, planning to visit Dr. Eastman, left shortly after dinner. James sent word to Claudia that he wanted to see her in his study. He was seated behind his desk when she came into the room. Not bothering to get up, he gestured tersely to the chair across from him.

She sat in the indicated chair, gazed adoringly at him across the span of the desktop, and asked, "Why did you want me to come here instead of your bedroom?"

James settled his elbows on the desk and steepled his fingers. His piercingly blue eyes were icy cold. "Claudia," he began sternly, "I want you out of here first thing tomorrow morning. I'll compensate you generously. Spend your money wisely, and you'll have no financial worries as you look for new employment. I'll also write you a letter of recommendation. You'll have no problem finding another position."

Claudia sat unresponsive, as though James had spoken in a foreign language and she hadn't comprehended a word. But the shock didn't last long, and her mind suddenly digested everything he said. She bounded quickly to her feet, stared at him with crazed eyes, and screeched, "You can't do this to me. I love you! I won't leave! I won't let you throw me out like this. Do you hear me?"

"Hear you? My God, you're screeching like a damn shrew. Lower your voice, or I'll lower it for you." He rose slowly, moved around the desk and stood before his distraught lover. He glowered down into her face like an enraged god. "You stupid wench! You can't defy me! Why, I should throw you into the streets without a dime."

"Money!" she cried angrily. "Do you think I care about the money? I love *you,* and I don't want to live without you!" She clutched his arms desperately, her fingers grasping his coat sleeves like a lobster's curling claws. "You love me, James! I know you do! Please don't send me away! Please! Must I get down on my knees and beg you?"

He grabbed her hands and forcefully flung them aside. "Touch me again, and I'll knock you to the floor!"

His threat stunned her into a moment of rationality, and as she stared into his cold eyes, she faced the truth. He didn't love her; he had never loved her. He had selfishly used her for his own pleasure; never once did he consider her feelings. Claudia's reasoning, which was eerily calm, didn't remain that way very long. Ironically, James did indeed have an unbalanced woman in his household, but it wasn't Sharla. Claudia had always been emotionally unsound, and James's cruel rejection was enough to send her over the edge.

Her features twisted into a demented leer, and her voice dropped an octave lower, as though it were controlled by an inner demon, "I'll get even with you for this! I swear I will!" As she continued ranting, her voice resumed its natural pitch, though her next words came in a screech. "Just because you have lots of money and live like a king, you think you can treat women any way you please! Well, you can't treat me like dirt and get by with it! Are you throwing me out because of Miss Sharla? I've seen the way you look at her. You want to take her to bed, don't you?"

He couldn't stand her screeching any longer; it rubbed his nerves raw, like fingernails raking a blackboard. "Shut up!" he bellowed. "Open your mouth again, and I'll throw you into the streets! In the morning, I'll have your money and a written recommendation. Now, leave this room before I decide to fire you without compensation."

Claudia's anger dissolved into heartbreak. She lived solely for James; she couldn't imagine living without him. He would find another lover, of course. If not Sharla, then someone else. A vision of him in bed with another woman flashed fleetingly before her eyes; it aroused insane jealousy. She felt she'd rather see him dead.

"Damn it!" James suddenly yelled. "I told you to get out! My God, woman, are you daft?"

Tears flooded her eyes, and she let them roll down her face unabated. "James . . . please . . ."

His patience snapped, and, grabbing her arm in a vise-like grip, he forced her to the door, opened it, and flung her out of the room. Her balance was precarious, and she tottered for a moment before turning back to look at him with pleading eyes.

He slammed the door in her face.

Claudia had gotten no farther than the stairway, and was sitting on the bottom step crying as Sharla, on her way to the kitchen for dinner, started downstairs. The servant's distress quickened her descent.

"Claudia?" she said with concern. "What's wrong?"

She partially restrained her sobs. "Mr. Rayfield fired me."

"Fired you?" Sharla exclaimed. "But why?"

She shrugged her shoulders. "I don't know why."

Sharla, unaware of Claudia's liaison with James, had always considered her a reliable and hard-working employee. That James should dismiss her was puzzling. She felt sorry for Claudia, who was obviously very upset.

"I'll talk to Mr. Rayfield," she told Claudia, hoping to lift her spirits. "I'm sure this has all been a misunderstanding. But don't worry, you won't be without a job. If Mr. Rayfield won't change his mind, I'll take you to New York with me."

"New York?" Claudia questioned, wiping tears from her eyes. "I didn't know you were going to New York."

"The decision came up quite suddenly. I intend to leave within the week. Where is Mr. Rayfield?"

"In the study."

Claudia's eyes followed Sharla as she left to talk to James. She didn't want to go to New York, and Sharla's offer had no effect on her troubled emotions, which were again working themselves into a frenzy. She leapt from the bottom step with the quickness of a jack-in-the-box, and hurried to the study door to eavesdrop. She wanted to hear what James had to say about her. She stealthily turned the knob and opened the door a mere crack. She could now hear the voices inside easily.

James and Sharla were standing in the center of the room, which was decorated with a man in mind, for the high-priced furnishings and ornaments were totally masculine.

"Why did you dismiss Claudia?" Sharla demanded.

"I just fired her a few minutes ago. How did you hear about it so soon?"

"I found her crying."

"Crying?" he questioned. "The girl has no reason to be so upset. I promised her compensation and a written reference."

"Why was she dismissed?"

"Sharla, I am the head of this household. The hiring

and the dismissal of employees is my responsibility. I do not have to answer to you."

"It doesn't really matter, for I no longer consider this house my home. I'll take Claudia to New York with me."

Anger flashed in his eyes. "You aren't going to New York!"

"You can't stop me!"

"The hell I can't!"

She came back with a defiant flare. "How do you intend to stop me? Are you planning to lock me in my room?"

"I have a much better way to keep you here." The anger was gone from his eyes, replaced with unmistakable desire. Now that Dexter had convinced him that marriage to Sharla was out of the question, he saw no reason to subtly pursue her. He intended to have her declared legally incompetent; cajoling her was no longer necessary. She would soon come to him, humbled and totally dependent. He would then buy his way into her bed.

She recognized the desire in his eyes; she had seen it too many times before. "Stop looking at me as though you can see through my clothes," she uttered angrily.

He moved so close to her that she could smell cigar smoke and brandy on his breath. "I'm going to enjoy bringing you down to size. You so easily forget who you really are."

"What do you mean by that?"

"Most likely, my dear, you are a bastard. Why else would your mother have deserted you? She left you at the orphanage because you were conceived in sin. Olivia's taking pity on you and raising you in this home does not make you legitimate. A leopard doesn't change its spots."

Moving with the quickness of a striking snake, he grasped her shoulders and drew her against him. "It would be in your best interest to be nicer to me. After all, your future is in my hands." His lips swooped down on hers, their assault passionate and demanding.

Struggling forcefully, she managed to break free. She darted to the desk and grabbed the letter opener that James always kept positioned beside his mail.

"Don't you dare lay a hand on me again or try to kiss me!" she threatened, holding the razor-sharp opener defensively.

He chuckled harshly. "Do you think I'm scared of that letter opener? Besides, you don't have the nerve to use it." As though to prove his point, he started toward her with determined strides.

Three

"Don't come a step closer," Sharla warned, brandishing the letter opener as though it were a knife.

James wasn't afraid, for he didn't think Sharla capable of such violence. Furthermore, he was confident that he could wrest the letter opener from her hand with ease. A spark of anger flared. How dare the insolent vixen threaten him! Who did she think she was? He relished bringing her down to size. It was time she learned her place.

He advanced unhesitantly, the expression in his eyes lustful, as well as arrogant. When he was within inches of her, he held out his hand and ordered firmly, "Give me the letter opener."

"No!" she replied, taking two steps backward. Her gaze flew to the door, where Claudia was still behind it, listening. That the door was slightly ajar escaped Sharla's notice, for her gaze was too fleeting. Hoping to avoid a confrontation with James, she was considering making a beeline for the door when, all at once, his hand snaked out and grasped her wrist. He squeezed painfully in an effort to force her to drop the letter opener.

Despite the pain, she held tenaciously to the sharp weapon. He suddenly loosened his hold, but his fingers remained curled about her wrist.

"You impertinent little nobody!" Rayfield seethed.

"Drop the opener before I force you into submission. Don't you realize you should be grateful to me? You were living here because of Olivia's charity, and now you're here under mine."

"I don't believe you!" she exclaimed. "You're so wrapped up in self-importance that you think you not only own this house, but me as well!"

"I do own you," he came back, a smug grin on his face. "You'll soon find out that I control you completely." He let go of her wrist and stood before her with an air of confidence.

"What do you mean you'll control me?" she asked, her eyes glaring into his.

"I intend to have you declared legally incompetent. You will live here and obey me, or find yourself in the street without a penny to your name."

Sharla's temper erupted. "You conniving bastard! Take me to court; I'll fight you all the way!"

"Don't curse, my dear," he said, his smug smile expanding. "Such crude language is very unbecoming. Also, my dear, we won't be attending court. This matter will be handled by my lawyer—out of court. I have a lot of influence, and I personally know every judge in this city."

"Why are you doing this to me?" she asked, desperation creeping into her voice. "Does my inheritance mean that much to you? Olivia made you very wealthy. Why do you want my money, too?"

"Your money sweetens the pot, but it certainly isn't the ultimate reward."

She regarded him warily. "Exactly what are you implying?"

"*You* are the ultimate reward. In a few days you will come to me humbled, penniless, and completely dependent on my generosity. I will treat you well, and in return you'll do my bidding."

"Never!" she exclaimed angrily. "I'd rather live in the streets!"

"You say that now, but you won't feel so rebellious when your pockets are empty, you're homeless, and your stomach gnaws with hunger."

At that moment, Claudia, still eavesdropping, detected the butler's footsteps. She hurried down the hall and darted out of sight. Peeking around the corner, she watched as the servant approached the study door.

Sharla's furious outburst greeted the butler, and he stopped in his tracks. Curious, he moved closer to the door and listened.

"I'll never humble myself before you!" Sharla was shouting. "Don't think for one minute that you'll ever lay a hand on me! I despise you, and I'd kill you before letting you touch me!"

"Kill me?" he taunted. "That's twice tonight you've threatened my life. How do you intend to do me in? Do you plan to kill me with that letter opener?"

"With pleasure!" she spat, shocked by her furious retort. She could hardly believe that James's cruelty had provoked her into such a violent response.

"Give me the letter opener," he said calmly. "Hand it over now, before you hurt yourself with it."

"You'll be the one who gets hurt!" she lashed out. She intended to hold on to the weapon until she was safely out of the room. She was too afraid that James would try and kiss her again—but this time he might not stop with a kiss!

Meanwhile, in the hall, the butler was hanging on to their every word. Claudia was growing terribly impatient with him. She was still peeking around the corner, which gave her a clear view of the servant. She moved out of sight, then cleared her throat loudly, hoping the sound would send the nosy butler fleeing. She waited a moment, then looked back around the corner. Her plan had worked. Fearing detection, the butler had hurried away. She quickly returned to the door, where she could again hear everything that was being said.

James's patience had run out. He was through playing Sharla's silly little game. It was time to teach her a lesson. When he was through delivering his punishment, she would never again dare to wield any kind of weapon in his direction.

She was holding the letter opener in her right hand. He reached out and grabbed her right wrist, endeavoring to twist her arm behind her back, his fingers digging deeply into her flesh as he tried to force her to drop the "weapon." To his surprise, she fought back with amazing defiance. She was stronger and more determined than he had thought.

"You damned wildcat!" he uttered between gritted teeth. He drew back his free hand, intending to slap her face soundly. However, she quickly drew up a knee and jammed it into his groin. The pain was so excruciating and unexpected that he suddenly fell forward, as though he planned to collapse into her arms. The letter opener, which was still grasped tightly in Sharla's hand, was pointed upward, its blade as dangerous as a knife's. She tried to evade James's fall, but there wasn't time. His weight fell against her heavily, and the razor-sharp opener plunged into his shoulder. The wound wasn't too serious. However, it was deep, and as Sharla withdrew the blade, blood, spurting like an erupting volcano, splattered her dress.

James dropped weakly to his knees, his hand now clamped over his wound in an effort to blot the stream of blood.

"Dear God!" Sharla cried, dropping the letter opener. She knelt beside him and carefully eased him to the floor. "Lie still; I'll send for the doctor."

She fled across the room and out the door. She didn't see Claudia, who was flush against the wall, grateful Sharla ran in the opposite direction from where she stood. Otherwise, she couldn't have missed seeing her.

Claudia rushed into the study and to James, who had remained on the floor, moaning and writhing with pain. It did her heart good to see him in misery. She wished Sharla had killed him!

James, aware of her presence, snapped irritably, "Don't stand there like an idiot! Get some bandages before I bleed to death."

His insulting tirade rekindled her earlier rage, and, spotting the letter opener, she picked it up stealthily and knelt beside her former lover. Her eyes glazed over with insanity, and her heart beat as powerfully as a drum. At this moment, she hated James Rayfield with a delirious passion. She wanted him dead more than she had ever wanted anything. Driven by a psychotic force too powerful to control, she raised the letter opener and sent it plunging into James's chest, hoping it would penetrate his cold-stone heart. She withdrew the weapon, and stared into his face like a demon from hell, waiting anxiously for him to draw his final breath.

But her assault wasn't fatal, and his arms flailed weakly as he tried vainly to grab the opener, but Claudia was too quick and too strong, and she again stuck the sharp-edged blade into his chest. Working herself into a demented frenzy, she withdrew the knife and stabbed him again and again. He soon stopped squirming, and Claudia was pleased to stare down into a pair of open eyes that were now devoid of life. She quickly dropped the bloody opener beside the body, rose to her feet, and stared down at her victim as though she wasn't quite sure what to make of him.

Her frenzy was supplanted by numbness, and she left the room as though in a daze. As she headed for the servants' rear stairway, her borderline sanity returned and she was suddenly struck with what she had done. Her stomach churned, and, clamping a hand over her mouth to hold back rising bile, she escaped to her room.

In the meantime, Sharla had sent Agnes to tend to James and she was ushering the butler out the front door, telling him to fetch Dr. Eastman without delay. Although James's wound wasn't life-threatening, she knew he needed a physician's care as soon as possible.

The butler was on his way out when Dr. Eastman's enclosed conveyance stopped in front of the house. His driver alighted quickly, and opened the carriage door for his employer and Dexter.

Sharla was so grateful to see the doctor that she didn't wonder why Dexter was with him, or why they had come to her home.

"Doctor Eastman!" she exclaimed. "Thank God you're here! James has been wounded. Hurry. He's in the study."

She waved the physician inside, and as he rushed to his patient, Sharla and Dexter followed close behind.

Agnes, her face ghostly pale, met them at the door. "He's dead!" she gasped, her eyes flitting from Sharla to the doctor.

Eastman went quickly to James.

"Dead?" Sharla cried. "He can't be dead. The wound wasn't that serious."

"Wound?" the doctor questioned gruffly. "Don't you mean wounds? This man was stabbed several times." His accusing eyes traveled over her bloodstained gown.

Dexter went to his brother and stared down into his lifeless face. Dexter's brow was layered with perspiration, yet he felt chilled to the bone. James dead? It was almost more than his shocked mind could grasp.

Sharla followed in Dexter's footsteps. She dreaded seeing James this way, but she had to see for herself that the wounds were many. His blood-soaked jacket and shirt bore several gaping holes. The sight was grotesque.

"I don't understand!" Sharla cried to no one in particular. "I tell you, there was only a shoulder wound. My God, someone came in here and killed him after I left!"

"What kind of fools do you think we are?" Dexter uttered fiercely. "You can't lie your way out of this! You killed James, didn't you?"

"No!" she cried.

"I don't believe you, and I intend to prove you killed him. I'll see you hang from the gallows, so help me God!" The butler was poised in the doorway, and Dexter told him, "Get the constable and bring him here immediately."

The servant, complying, left at once.

Dexter turned back to Sharla. "Go to your room and stay there until I send for you."

She resented his authoritative manner, but was too upset to say anything. Furthermore, she needed to be alone and was more than willing to oblige. She turned to Agnes. "Call me when the constable arrives," she commanded.

She left the study and went upstairs to her room. She paced back and forth, her thoughts racing. Who could have killed James? And why? Why would someone murder him? It had to be one of the servants, for she didn't think anyone had come in off the streets. The front door was locked, and the back door led into the kitchen. Agnes had been in the kitchen all evening.

All at once, Sharla's pacing ceased. Claudia! Good Lord, did Claudia kill James? Was she that upset over being fired?

Maybe there was more to her dismissal, she thought, wondering if Claudia and James had been lovers. Was that why Claudia was so upset when she found her on the stairs crying? Did James fire her because he was through with her, and did his rejection drive her to commit murder?

A shiver ran up Sharla's spine, for she had a chilling suspicion that Claudia might indeed have committed an insane act of violence.

* * *

Sharla entered the parlor, where the constable and Dexter were waiting for her. The law officer, middle-aged and paunchy, met her at the door. He led her to a wing chair and insisted that she sit down. He pulled up an extra chair, placed it across from hers, sat, and studied her with suspicious eyes.

"Tell me exactly what happened between you and Mr. Rayfield," he said.

She explained that they had argued and that James had accidentally fallen against the letter opener. She assured the officer that it had only been a shoulder wound.

"Why did you change your dress?" Dexter interrupted. She had exchanged her blood-spattered gown for a clean one. "Didn't you want the constable to see how much blood was on it?"

Dexter turned to the lawman, whom he was well acquainted with and addressed by his first name. "Tom, her gown had blood all over it; entirely too much blood for a mere shoulder wound."

"I'd like to see this dress," Tom replied.

Stepping to the open doorway, Rayfield called for Agnes. She was nearby and came at once. "Go to Sharla's room," he told her, "and bring down the dress she was wearing."

As Agnes left to carry out Dexter's instructions, Tom said to Sharla, "For now, I have no further questions. But I'll want to talk to you later."

Sharla rose to her feet. "I didn't kill James," she pronounced, looking the constable straight in the eyes.

"I didn't say you did," he replied.

She hesitated, wondering if she should continue claiming her innocence. Would the constable be more apt to believe her if she did? However, his stony visage told her otherwise. She had a feeling she was his prime suspect. She moved across the room, but stopped suddenly and remarked, "I suggest you question Claudia. She's an employee. I think she and James were lovers."

"You think?" the officer questioned.

"I can't prove it. In fact, I didn't even consider it until after James was murdered."

"How convenient for you," Dexter uttered bitterly. "In order to protect yourself, you're willing to place the blame on an innocent servant. You forget, I heard you threaten James."

"What are you saying?"

"At the dinner table, did you or did you not say you'd be mad enough to kill him if he held up your inheritance?"

"Yes, but I didn't mean it."

"Well, James took you very seriously." He spoke directly to the constable. "James was so worried about Sharla's state of mind that he sent me to fetch Doctor Eastman."

"That's absurd!" Sharla said angrily. "There's nothing wrong with my mind. And James knew it! He simply wanted my inheritance and . . . and he wanted me!"

Dexter, still looking at Tom, raised a shrewd brow. "See what I mean? She's unbalanced. Everyone in this city knows James idolized Olivia. He wasn't interested in Sharla or any other woman. He was still in mourning. Losing Olivia broke his heart."

"We'll talk later," Tom said to Sharla, dismissing her with a terse wave of his hand.

She decided to go to her room. Later, when she talked to the constable, she'd insist on Dexter's absence. Maybe he would listen with a more open mind if Dexter wasn't there.

She passed the butler on her way out. She didn't notice that he seemed uncomfortable to suddenly find himself in her presence. He waited until she had climbed the stairs before entering the parlor.

"Mr. Rayfield," the servant said, pausing and nervously shifting his weight from one foot to the other. "I need to talk to you and the constable."

"Very well, Dobbs," Dexter replied.

The butler turned to the officer. "Sir, I think you should know that I overheard Miss Sharla threaten Mr. Rayfield's life."

Tom rose quickly from his chair. "Go on," he encouraged.

"I was on my way to the study. The door was slightly open, and I could hear Miss Sharla and Mr. Rayfield arguing."

At that moment, Agnes entered with the bloodstained dress. Her presence didn't deter the butler, and he continued, "I heard Mr. Rayfield ask her if she intended to kill him with the letter opener, and she said she would do so with pleasure. A moment later, he asked her to hand over the opener before she hurt herself, and she replied that he would be the one to get hurt. I didn't hear any more because I returned to the kitchen. A few minutes later, Miss Sharla came running into the kitchen saying that Mr. Rayfield was accidentally wounded."

"I knew it!" Dexter remarked angrily. "Sharla murdered James! My God, Tom, how much proof do you need? Dobbs heard her threaten to kill him."

"Your brother was a strong man," Tom replied. "It's hard to believe that a woman could get the better of him with a letter opener."

Dexter went to Agnes, jerked the bloodstained dress from her arms and held it up for Tom to see. "Look at this!" he shouted. "Do you honestly believe this much blood came from a shoulder wound?"

"It's possible," he replied. "However, I must admit that Miss Matthews does look mighty guilty. But before I arrest her, I want to talk to all the household help."

He quickly questioned Agnes, but she had no helpful information. She did, however, insist on Sharla's innocence and told him he should question Claudia. She assured the constable that Claudia and James Rayfield were involved.

"That's a lie!" Dexter retorted. Actually, he didn't know if James had bedded the servant or not, and he certainly didn't care. In his mind, Sharla was guilty. He wanted her tried and executed. Furthermore, he was James's only kin, which meant he would inherit his brother's full estate, and he didn't intend to share any of it with Sharla.

"I don't lie!" Agnes huffed, offended. "I saw Claudia sneaking into Mr. Rayfield's bedroom."

"Don't believe her," Dexter told Tom. "She'd say anything to save Sharla. She helped Olivia raise Sharla, and she's as protective of her as a mother."

"Is that true?" Tom asked Agnes. "Do you love Miss Matthews?"

"Yes, I do," she admitted.

"Don't you see what's going on?" Dexter demanded. "Agnes and Sharla concocted this whole story to take the blame from Sharla and place it on Claudia."

"I'd like to talk to Claudia," Tom said. He turned to the butler and asked him to bring her to the parlor.

Within minutes, Dobbs returned with Claudia. She now had her emotions fully under control. She answered the constable's questions calmly and gave a convincing performance. She swore that she and James had not been lovers. Agnes challenged her denial, but she smoothly insinuated that Agnes had never liked her and wouldn't hesitate to spread such a vicious lie in order to save Sharla.

Agnes could see that she had lost the battle, for the constable was obviously leaning toward believing Claudia. In his mind, the circumstantial evidence against Sharla was too incriminating. She asked him if he was through questioning her, and he told her that she could leave. She hurried up the stairs, and without bothering to knock, she barged into Sharla's bedroom.

"You must get away!" Agnes told her.

Sharla was resting on the settee, but she stood quickly and gaped at the woman as though she had lost her mind. "I can't do that! If I run, the constable will think I'm guilty."

"He already thinks you're guilty. You have to hide somewhere until we can find a way to clear your name. If you don't, the law will have you behind bars. God only knows what might happen to you in such a horrible place."

"But where can I go?"

"I know a place. You'll be safe there."

Sharla couldn't imagine where Agnes planned to send her; she could think of no such haven. "What do you have in mind?"

Agnes was suddenly hesitant. "Miss Sharla, you must trust me. I . . . I know what I'm doing. If you remain here, you'll be arrested. The constable, and Mr. Dexter as well, already have you tried and found guilty."

"I don't want to run away, but I realize it's the only way I can find time to clear my name. And, Agnes, I'd trust you with my life. Now, where do you want me to go? Who in this city would be willing to hide me?"

The woman paused, drew a deep breath, then blurted out the name, "Maxine Reynolds."

Sharla gaped at her incredulously. Maxine Reynolds was the most renowned madam in the city. Her house of ill repute was ostentatious, but very popular. Her clientele consisted of some of the most prominent men in St. Louis.

Sharla sank back onto the settee, stared at Agnes, and said somewhat breathlessly, "Maxine Reynolds! I might be inexperienced, but I'm not that naive. I know who that woman is!"

"We don't have time to argue. Come with me, and we'll hurry out back and ask Albert to take you to Maxine's." Albert, the coachman, had worked for Olivia and her first husband. Unlike Dobbs, who had been hired by James, he was very fond of Sharla and completely trustworthy.

Sharla didn't budge. "I can't ask a complete stranger for help! And of all people—Maxine Reynolds?"

"If you won't do it for me, then do it for Olivia."

"I don't understand."

"When Olivia knew she was dying, she told me if you ever got into trouble or needed help, I was to send you to Maxine Reynolds."

"Olivia actually knew this woman?" Sharla gasped.

"Yes, she did."

That Olivia had been acquainted with a prostitute was staggering. It didn't make sense. Sharla began to wonder if she had really known the woman who had taken her into her home and loved her as a mother. Were there other secrets in Olivia's life that she knew nothing about?

Agnes went to her, took her hand and drew her from the settee. "Come. We don't have a minute to waste," she argued gently. She ushered the confused Sharla out the door and down the servants' stairway.

Sharla's thoughts were reeling. Too much had happened in too short a time: First James's murder, then all the evidence pointing at her, and now she was fleeing from the law. But even more mind-boggling, she was running away to a house of ill-repute!

Four

There wasn't time for Albert to prepare the buggy, so he saddled one of the horses and led it to the back door, where Agnes and Sharla were waiting. Agnes had given Sharla a shawl, warning her to keep it wrapped about her head. The shawl, along with the dark night, would help conceal her identity. She had also written a note, which she handed to Albert with instructions to give it only to Maxine Reynolds, or to her housekeeper, Hattie.

Sharla, listening, was even more confused. Hattie? Why did Agnes know the housekeeper's name? Was she friends with the woman? She didn't think such a relationship was plausible. She was about to question Agnes, but before she could, the woman drew her into her arms and hugged her tightly.

"God be with you, child!" Agnes said, tears in her eyes. She released Sharla brusquely and told Albert that they must leave at once.

The coachman, elderly but still physically strong, lifted Sharla onto the horse, then mounted behind her. Sharla placed a halting hand on the reins and looked down at Agnes. "I can't leave like this," she said. "You must tell me why you're sending me to Maxine Reynolds. Also, why are you so familiar with her servant's name."

"There's no time to explain," she answered, gesturing for Albert to leave regardless of Sharla's misgivings.

Kneeing the horse gently, Albert guided it away from the back door, past the house, and to the street. He coaxed the spirited gelding into a brisk trot.

The home where Sharla had lived for seventeen years was soon swallowed up by the dark night. She wondered dismally if she would ever see it again. Surely, she would! After all, she was innocent, but proving her innocence might be an impossible task. She would probably get caught and go to prison for the rest of her life—or else be executed! That possibility was so terrifying that she forcefully thrust it from her mind. She couldn't bear to dwell on it, and she turned her thoughts instead to Maxine Reynolds, which sent her mind swirling with unanswered questions.

Meanwhile, inside the house, the constable was still in the parlor with Dexter. He was finished questioning the servants and had decided to further interrogate Sharla. He wasn't fully convinced of her guilt, but she was none-theless his prime suspect. Twice, she had threatened James's life, and she certainly had the opportunity to kill him. Still, the evidence against her was circumstantial. He shrugged as though resigned. She wouldn't be the first person, nor the last, to be found guilty due to circumstan-tial evidence.

He spoke to Dexter, who was seated on the sofa nursing a glass of brandy. "Will you get Miss Matthews? I want to talk to her again."

Rayfield was eager to oblige. He left the room and hur-ried upstairs. He returned moments later, his face flushed and his words heated. "She isn't in her room! I bet the murdering chit has fled!"

"Maybe she's in the kitchen," Tom suggested.

"If she isn't there, I'll get Dobbs and we'll search the entire house." Dexter rushed into the kitchen, where he found Agnes. She swore that she hadn't seen Sharla.

Rayfield quickly located Dobbs, and they searched every

room, even the servants' quarters. By the time Dexter returned to the parlor, his temper was boiling. He informed Tom that Sharla had indeed run away.

The constable didn't seem too surprised, for it wasn't rare for a prime suspect to flee. "Where do you suppose she went?" he asked Dexter.

"I have no idea."

"Well, don't worry, she'll be found. I'll go to my office and get my men working on it. If you'd like to place a reward, it'll make my job easier."

"I'll place a reward, all right! And it'll be substantial. By this time tomorrow, half of this city will be looking for her! I guarantee it!"

Maxine Reynolds's establishment sat atop a hill at the edge of town, the Mississippi River forming a picturesque background. Steamers, gambling boats, and cotton barges traveled the mighty river, many of them docking within sight of the Reynolds house. The white clapboard two-story home was brightly lit by outside lanterns bordering the winding lane that led to the front door. More lights, enclosed in red lampshades, embellished the long porch. Three hitching rails were installed. At night, they were usually filled, for Maxine ran the most popular place in the city. Her girls were lovely, clean, and experts in their line of work. However, prostitution wasn't the only attraction; a poker room, consisting of several tables and a stocked bar, also drew patrons into her establishment.

As Albert turned the horse onto the meandering lane, Sharla gaped wondrously at the large house standing like a beacon in the night, its bright lights showing the way to the front door. She had never seen the house up close, and had certainly never passed this way at night; therefore, she had no way of knowing that it was so blatantly displayed.

Fortunately, the lane remained empty, and Albert guided the horse to the back of the house without detection. He reined in, dismounted, then assisted Sharla. Here, one gaslight sufficed, and a patch of darkness fell between the house and the river that lay beyond. Lights from several boats, reflected in the rippling water, sparkled like a myriad of stars.

Albert knocked on the back door. A moment later, it was answered by a Negro woman. She was dressed in a black dress adorned with a white apron. She was middle-aged, attractive, and quite tall for a woman.

"What can I do for you?" she asked, regarding the pair warily.

"Is your name Hattie?" Albert asked.

"Yes," the woman replied.

He handed her the note. "Will you give this to Miss Reynolds, and tell her it's from Agnes?"

"Agnes!" the woman repeated, apparently familiar with the name. She waved Sharla and Albert into the kitchen. There was no one inside. "Wait here," she said. Her eyes swept over Sharla, as though there was something different about her. Though intense, her gaze was fleeting. "I'll be right back," she said, hurrying to the side door, which led to the servants' staircase.

Sharla removed her scarf, and looked curiously about the room. The kitchen was cozy, clean, and very much like her own. She silently laughed at herself. Did she think this kitchen would somehow be different?

The voices of prostitutes and their customers carried faintly into the room, their laughter and chatter accompanied by a piano playing a lively tune. Sharla unconsciously tapped her foot to the beat as she awaited Hattie's return.

She didn't have a very long wait. The woman, again using the side door, was back within minutes. She spoke to

Sharla, "Miss Reynolds will see you." She then turned to Albert. "Tell Miss Agnes that Miss Sharla is safe."

The coachman left, and Hattie led Sharla up the staircase and into a well-lit hallway. She warned her to wrap the shawl about her head in case they should encounter a customer. At the end of the hall, Hattie opened a door and ushered Sharla inside.

She found herself in an elaborate, but tastefully decorated bedchamber.

"This is Miss Reynolds's private quarters," Hattie explained. "You'll be safe here." She went to the door, but before leaving, she assured Sharla that Miss Reynolds would be right with her.

Sharla moved to a rose-colored settee, flanked by two overstuffed chairs, removed her shawl and sat down wearily. Her mind was still swirling with unanswered questions, and she felt as though she were lost in a maze that only became more perplexing with each turn.

The door opened and Sharla rose to her feet. Maxine Reynolds, wearing an expensive silk gown, walked into the room with the grace of an elegant lady. Her blond hair was in a stylish chignon, and her face bore only the slightest touch of rouge. Sharla was taken aback, for this woman didn't fit her image of a madam. She wasn't flashy, nor was her face heavily painted.

Sharla stood as though riveted to the floor. As Maxine moved across the room and stood before her, Sharla gazed into a pair of eyes that were as blue as her own.

Maxine's perusal was as intense as Sharla's, and she studied her young companion like an artist scrutinizing a subject she was about to paint.

Sharla, clearing her throat, broke the silence between them. "Miss Reynolds, I don't understand why Agnes sent me here."

Her smile was so warm and loving that it helped ease

Sharla's tension. "She sent you here because she knew I would take care of you."

"But why?" Sharla cried. "You don't know me! I'm nothing to you!"

"Let's just say, I knew Olivia."

"She never mentioned you to me."

She smiled again. "Now, why would she say anything to you about me? She wouldn't want you to know that she was acquainted with someone like me."

"I know now, and it was Olivia's wish that Agnes send me to you. Therefore, there's no reason for further secrecy. Please explain why you and Olivia were friends."

Maxine gestured for her to return to the settee, and she sat beside her. "Olivia and I knew each other as children," she decided to reveal. "Although our lives took different directions, our friendship remained intact. Oh, we didn't visit back and forth, but we did stay in touch. I often told her if she needed my help not to hesitate to ask."

"And Agnes knew about this friendship?"

"Yes; she and Olivia were very close."

"Apparently, Hattie knows, too."

"I have no secrets from Hattie. However, the past doesn't matter. We should be discussing you. Agnes's note wasn't very informative. She only said that you're in serious trouble. Tell me what has happened."

Sharla recounted the night's events in detail. She finished by swearing that she didn't kill James.

It was a long moment before Maxine responded. "You are indeed in serious trouble," she said, reaching over and patting Sharla's hand. "I'm sure you didn't commit murder. But the evidence piled up against you is staggering. I agree with Agnes. You must stay in hiding. The law would surely keep you in jail until your trial. Jail is no place for a young lady. Somehow, we'll have to find a way to prove your innocence. From what you've told me, I think Claudia is the most likely suspect. But how in the world do we get her to confess?"

"I don't think we can, regardless of what we say or do." Sharla sounded terribly depressed.

"We'll deal with Claudia later. First, we must take care of you. Staying here is very risky. Too many people come and go, and eventually someone is liable to spot you. There's also my girls to consider. One of them might talk. I'll have to send you someplace safer."

"But where?"

She sighed heavily. "I don't know. I'll have to think about it. For now, I want you to stay in this room. Hattie and I will tend to you and see that you have everything you need. Don't leave this room under any circumstances. Do you understand?"

"Of course I do. Besides, where would I go?"

"You must be very uncomfortable here. I'm sorry this had to happen. I'll try to make your stay here as easy as possible."

"Please don't apologize! I should be the one apologizing. I'm a terrible inconvenience."

"You could never be an inconvenience," she murmured, a trace of tears misting her eyes. Her emotions came dangerously close to crumbling, but she tentatively took control, feigned a cool composure and said, "Helping you is the least I can do for Olivia." She rose abruptly. She needed time away from Sharla, for she was afraid of her own feelings. It was imperative that she get a tenacious hold on them before returning. "I'll have Hattie bring you a tray. I'm sure you're hungry."

"No, not really," Sharla replied.

"You must eat; you'll need your strength." She headed for the door, assuring Sharla she would be back later.

She hastened down the hall and descended the front staircase. As she made a beeline for her office, she ignored the clientele who were mingling about, most of them waiting for their favorite prostitute to be free, or else entertaining themselves by engaging in frivolous conversations and drinking.

She darted into her office, closed the door, and breathed in deeply, as though she were exhausted. She wasn't surprised to find Hattie waiting for her.

"Are you all right, Miss Maxine?"

She moved to her desk on shaky legs, collapsed into her chair, and moaned, "I'm not sure."

Hattie stood beside her chair, and placed a consoling arm about her shoulders.

Tears gushed from Maxine's eyes. "Oh, Hattie, I wanted so desperately to take Sharla into my arms!"

"Of course you did. It's only natural. She's your baby— your own flesh and blood. Just because you didn't raise her doesn't stop you from bein' her mother."

"Mother!" she repeated harshly. "Thank God, she doesn't know her mother is a whore!"

"Stop talkin' like that!"

"Why? It's the truth!"

"You ain't sold yourself since before Miss Sharla was born."

She used the handkerchief Hattie handed her to wipe her eyes. "I've got to stop thinking about myself and find a way to help Sharla."

"Is she in serious trouble?"

"Yes, very serious." Maxine told her everything that had happened.

"I can't say I'm sorry to hear that Mr. Rayfield is dead. I never liked that man." James was a frequent customer; Hattie and Maxine knew him well.

"I never understood why Olivia married him," Maxine said. "She was much too good for him."

"What are you goin' to do 'bout Miss Sharla?"

"I don't know. I'll have to think about it. Will you take a tray up to her? She should eat something."

Hattie left for the kitchen, and now that she was alone, Maxine surrendered to more tears. She cried until there were no tears left to shed. Being so close to Sharla had completely broken down her defenses. Through the years, she had seen Sharla on several occasions, but never up close. She had often sat hidden in an enclosed carriage, waiting to catch a glimpse of her daughter. She would park by her school, her home, or across the street from a party that she thought Sharla would probably attend. She had secretly watched her grow from a child into a lovely young woman.

A bottle of port was on the desk; an opened envelope was beside it, and it caught her attention as she poured herself a drink. She had left the letter in clear view so she would remember to send a reply. She reached inside the envelope and withdrew a piece of paper. The handwriting was neat, the spelling flawless. She read the letter for a second time, and as her eyes scanned each word, her mind formed a plan so outrageous that she was actually shocked by her own thoughts.

She dropped the letter as though it had suddenly burned her fingers. "No!" she groaned aloud. "Such a plan is too dangerous and too extreme. I must find another way to help Sharla."

A loud knock sounded at the door. Maxine went to answer it reluctantly; she didn't want to be disturbed. She was startled to find Dexter Rayfield.

He brushed past her, entering the office as though it were his own domain.

Dexter, like his brother, was a frequent customer. Maxine eyed him irritably. "How dare you barge into my office!"

He ignored her retort. "My brother was murdered!" he announced angrily.

Maxine pretended surprise. "Murdered? That's terrible!"

"Olivia's ward, Sharla Matthews, killed him! She ran away and is hiding somewhere. In the morning, I plan to post a reward for her capture. I want your permission to display some of the posters here where your customers will be sure to see them."

Maxine started to refuse, but she suddenly realized that wouldn't be wise. "I have no objections. By the way, how big is the reward?"

"Three thousand dollars."

Her knees weakened. "For that much money, everyone in the city will be looking for her!"

"That's the idea!" He went to the door. "I'll be back in the morning with the posters," he said. With that, he left as unexpectedly as he had arrived.

Maxine returned to her desk, refilled her glass, and took a much needed drink. Three thousand dollars! If one of her girls or an employee should spot Sharla, they might turn her in for that huge amount. She had to get Sharla out of here and soon! But where? Where?

Her eyes returned to the letter. It was Sharla's best choice—her only choice! But would she be willing to go through with it? Was she asking more than Sharla was capable of giving?

Taking the letter with her, she went to the kitchen where Hattie was preparing Sharla's tray. "I need to be alone with Sharla for a few minutes," Maxine told her. "Wait awhile before you bring up her food."

Using the servants' stairway, she went upstairs and to her bedchamber. She found Sharla resting on the settee.

"Dexter was here," Maxine said, closing the door and locking it.

Sharla sat up with a start. "Why did he come here?"

"He's posting a reward for your capture. He wants to display some of the posters here."

"A reward?" she gasped. "How much?"

"Three thousand dollars. That much money will draw

rats out of their holes to look for you." She went to Sharla, sat beside her, and continued, "I have a plan. It's shocking, and I don't know if you'll agree. But we must get you out of St. Louis."

"But if I leave, how can I prove I'm innocent?"

"I'll work on it for you. I know how to deal with the Claudias of this world. But it'll take me a while. In the meantime, you've got to get as far away from this city as possible."

"But the police will be watching the depot and any boat that is leaving."

"You might get away if you leave on horseback. The police can't watch every road leading out of this city."

"Where would I go?"

"To San Antonio. I have a friend there. We're in the same business. She used to work for me. I'll send a letter with you."

"You want me to travel horseback to San Antonio by myself? That sounds more dangerous than staying here."

"You won't be alone." She held up the letter. "I received this earlier today by a messenger. It's from a man named Bill Slade. He was in St. Louis a few months back. He fell in love with Trish, a girl who worked for me. He met Trish in the park and didn't know she was a prostitute, and she didn't dare tell him. But when he asked her to marry him, she felt she had to be honest. It was more than he could handle. He withdrew his proposal and returned to his ranch in Texas. Trish was brokenhearted. She fell into a deep depression, and three weeks ago she packed up and left without notice. This letter is to her. Bill wrote that he hasn't stopped loving her and that he still wants to marry her. His cousin, Lance Slade, is in St. Louis. Bill had him bring the letter with him. He's visiting family, and he had the letter delivered here to Trish. He's waiting for a reply. If she still wants to marry Bill, he'll escort her to her future home. This Lance has never seen Trish."

Sharla looked puzzled.

"Don't you understand? You can be Trish. Lance Slade will escort you out of this city and to Texas."

Sharla leapt to her feet. "You want me to pretend I'm a prostitute!" she cried. "My God, considering everything that has happened, I thought I was beyond shock. But this is too much. A prostitute? I couldn't do that! I just couldn't!"

"The alternative is a hangman's noose."

Stunned, Sharla sank back onto the settee. She sat silent for a long moment before summoning a brave smile. "You know, I've always wanted to go to Texas, but I never thought I'd go there masquerading as a prostitute. But then I never thought I'd be a fugitive. I shudder to think what might happen next. I certainly hope this Lance Slade is a gentleman."

"So do I," Maxine murmured, meaning it more deeply than Sharla could possibly realize.

Five

Dexter went straight from Maxine's office to the poker room. There, he informed everyone that Sharla Matthews had murdered his brother, and that he planned to post a three-thousand-dollar reward. The large amount sparked the interest of the greedy and those who needed money. However, they all assured young Rayfield that he had their full cooperation.

Dexter was about to leave when he was stopped by a friend. Robert Granger was not a member of St. Louis's upper crust, but he frequently came to Maxine's, usually to play poker. Although he never attended the same social events as the Rayfields, he often played cards with them. The young man approached Dexter and expressed his condolences.

Rayfield mumbled a polite reply; however, he did so impatiently. He was anxious to be on his way, and was slightly annoyed at Granger for delaying him.

"I'm sure you have a lot to do," Robert said. "I don't want to keep you, but there's something I think you should know."

"What's that?" Dexter asked, mildly interested.

"My parents live next door to Victor Slade and his wife, Betsy. Do you know them?"

"Slade?" Dexter repeated thoughtfully. "The name isn't familiar."

"Victor is a foreman on the docks. He works for Charles Bradford."

"I know Bradford," Rayfield replied, his patience waning. He wished Granger would get to the point.

"I'm acquainted with the Slades. Victor's nephew is in town. Lance Slade. I don't suppose that name means anything to you."

"Should it?"

"Well, it would if you lived out West. He's a bounty hunter, and his reputation's well known. He's leaving soon and will be going back to Texas. If Miss Matthews escapes the city, she's liable to head in that direction. I mean, the West is the ideal place to elude capture. I just thought you might like to meet Lance Slade and ask him to be on the lookout for her. After all, capturing fugitives is what he does for a living."

"Yes, I'd like very much to meet Mr. Slade."

"I'll take you to him."

"Thanks, Robert. I appreciate your help."

"I'm just glad I can be of assistance. If Miss Matthews murdered your brother, then she should pay for her crime."

"*If* she murdered him?" Dexter exclaimed harshly. "She killed him, all right! She's a murdering Jezebel, and I won't rest until she's behind bars!"

"I don't understand," Sharla said to Maxine, who was seated on the settee watching her pace back and forth. "You want me to pretend I'm Trish and leave here with Lance Slade. Yet, earlier you said for me to contact your friend in San Antonio. How am I supposed to do both?"

"Bill's ranch is about fifty miles south of San Antonio. Insist that Lance take you to San Antonio. Once you are there, tell him that you've changed your mind about marrying Bill. He can't force you to marry his cousin, and he'll have no choice but to leave you. My friend, Jenny, will take care of you."

"But what if Bill comes to San Antonio to see Trish? He might want to know why she changed her mind."

"If Bill shows up, Jenny can tell him that Trish moved on and that she doesn't know where she went. Don't worry about that part, Jenny can handle it."

"What if Lance Slade doesn't want to stop in San Antonio?"

"You have to find a way to convince him." Maxine rose from the settee, placed a hand on Sharla's arm and stopped her pacing. "You must part company with Lance at San Antonio."

"I don't know!" she cried desperately.

"You don't know what?"

"I don't know if I can pull this off! Pretend I'm somebody else? How in the world am I supposed to deceive Lance Slade all the way to San Antonio?"

"Lance has never seen Trish. Bill may have described her, but you two are very similar. Trish has blond hair—a shade lighter than yours, but that shouldn't matter. She's about your height, has blue eyes—they are also a shade lighter. Again, I don't see where that poses a problem. You're slimmer than Trish, but if Lance should mention your weight, tell him that losing Bill took away your appetite."

"In other words, I must learn to deceive quickly and convincingly. Lies must pop out of my mouth as though I've done it all my life."

"Your life might very well depend on those lies. I don't like using the Slades any more than you do, but we don't have any other choice. If you stay in St. Louis, you'll get caught. Dexter Rayfield is very influential; he'll make sure that you're convicted of murder. You can't fight someone like him. He's too important, and you are . . . you are . . ."

"An orphan—a waif—a bastard?" Sharla finished for her.

"Don't degrade yourself like that."

"It's true, isn't it? I was an orphan, a waif Olivia took pity on. And I'm most likely a bastard. Why else would my mother have deserted me?"

Maxine grimaced, as though Sharla's words had inflicted physical pain. She didn't know what to say, since Sharla had indeed been born out of wedlock. She wanted desperately to tell Sharla that her mother had loved her very much—had never stopped loving her. But Maxine was trapped in her own web of deceit, and she had every intention of remaining there. She felt she'd rather die than have Sharla learn the truth.

A knock sounded at the door; it was Hattie, and Maxine welcomed the timely interruption. The servant placed the tray on her employer's desk, pulled out a chair, and insisted that Sharla sit down and eat.

Hattie had prepared a tasty fare: fried ham, eggs, biscuits, and strawberry preserves. Sharla hadn't realized she was hungry until she got a whiff of the savory aromas.

Maxine filled Hattie in on their plan for Sharla to impersonate Trish. Initially, Hattie was opposed, but when she realized that Sharla had no other plausible options, she relented with grave reservations. She wasn't alone—her companions' misgivings were just as strong.

Lance Slade sat on his uncle's porch, smoking a cheroot. He was seated in a cane rocker, his long legs resting on the banister in front of him. The lamp shining through the parlor window cast a golden beam across the porch, its saffron glow illuminating the rugged bounty hunter. Lance Slade wasn't classically handsome. His good looks derived from an aura that was as sensual as it was masculine. He was blatantly sexual. Although the muscles in his arms were hard and distinct, his tall physique was slim, lithe, and supple. A well-trimmed mustache, as coal black as his hair, accentuated a pair of gray eyes that were perfect curtains for his thoughts, for they gave nothing away. They were also direct, bold, and seemed capable of totally mesmerizing a woman should she find herself the object of Lance's desire. Whereas, women found him sexually appealing, men found him impressive, as well as intimidating. He carried himself with the grace and the stealth of an Indian. His Peacemaker, strapped low on his hip, was held in a well-oiled holster for a quick draw.

Lance's uncle, Victor, was also on the porch, his large frame filling a cane rocker that was identical to his nephew's. He studied his companion with a cursory perusal. He wondered if Lance was about to withdraw into one of his quiet moods. Victor was familiar with his nephew's periods of silence. However, during this visit Lance's mood had remained pleasant and chipper. He considered that a positive sign. Thank God, Lance was finally learning to deal with his loss. He sighed deeply. It had been a tragic loss for the entire family. At times, his own sorrow was still very real. Five years had eased his grief, but the pain of losing his brother, sister-in-law, and their two children would never completely go away. Considering it was extremely hard for him to accept their deaths, he could only imagine how difficult it was for Lance. He had loved his family very much.

Worried that Lance's thoughts were traveling into the past, he decided to get his mind on something else. "Would you like to go out for a drink? Don't let me keep you. You've been here three days and stayed home every night. There's lots of entertainment in St. Louis, especially for a bachelor."

"I might go out later. I'm expecting a message."

Victor's interest was piqued. "A message? Who from?"

Lance was uncomfortable with the question. He hadn't

told his uncle and aunt that their son was hoping to marry a prostitute and that he was supposed to deliver her. He was slightly perturbed with Bill for not informing his parents of his marital plans. However, he wasn't about to be the one to tell them. He knew Aunt Betsy would be appalled and that Victor would be irate, as well as disappointed. Accepting a prostitute as a daughter-in-law was asking too much of them. Not that they were pious, or considered themselves better than anyone else; they did, however, hold moral values in high esteem. They could never understand why their son wanted to marry a woman who sold her favors. Lance, on the other hand, was fairly sure he had it all figured out. Bill, despite his success, was somewhat naive. He was not a woman chaser, nor did he consider a romp with a whore a night's entertainment. Like his parents, he held tenaciously to his moral values. Therefore, in Lance's opinion, it must have been easy for an experienced woman like Trish to inveigle Bill into marriage. However, he had no way of knowing if she was after his money or just respectability. That she might actually love him did cross his mind, but he didn't give it too much credence. But he was withholding final judgment until he met her; that was, if she still wanted to marry Bill. He sent Bill's letter to her early this morning, and she was taking a long time sending back a reply.

Victor, his curiosity left unsatisfied, asked again, "Who's sending you a message?"

"Sorry, but it's personal," Lance replied, evading the question.

"Does it have to do with your line of work?"

"There's no connection," he murmured.

"Speaking of your job—I wish you'd retire before you get yourself killed. A bounty hunter! Sometimes I still can't believe you chose such a profession."

The expression in Lance's gray eyes suddenly turned as

hard as granite. "When I find the men who murdered my family, then I'll consider retirement."

Victor spoke pleadingly: "Lance, it's been five years—let it go! You're so full of revenge that it's eating you alive. Rebuild your ranch, marry a nice girl, and have some children. You're wasting your life. You may never find the men who killed your family. You're already thirty years old; you should settle down and live a decent, God-fearing life."

"Don't worry about me, Victor. I know what I'm doing."

"Do you? I wonder if you realize you're headed for an early grave. You've hunted, apprehended, and killed cold-blooded murderers for the past five years. Your luck is bound to run out."

"Luck has nothing to do with it."

An enclosed carriage stopped in front of the house, and they looked on as a uniformed driver stepped down from his perch to open the door. That the conveyance belonged to someone with wealth was obvious.

"You never told me you have rich friends," Lance remarked with a smile.

"I don't," Victor replied, rising from his chair.

Lance stood beside him and watched as two men got out of the carriage and started toward the house. He recognized Robert Granger, for his parents had lived next door to the Slades for years.

Victor, recognizing the man with Robert, uttered softly, "Dexter Rayfield." He had never met Dexter or his brother, but he knew them by sight.

"Good evening," Robert said, before making introductions.

"Mr. Slade," Dexter began, speaking to Lance, "I understand you're a bounty hunter." He paused, waiting for some kind of response. He didn't get one, and decided to continue, "Earlier this evening, my brother was murdered."

"James Rayfield is dead?" Victor interrupted.

"He was stabbed to death!" Dexter replied, his voice filled with rage. With a measure of composure, he told the Slades his version of the murder, then spoke directly to Lance. "I've posted a three-thousand-dollar reward for Sharla Matthews's capture. I thought you might be interested in case she heads west. Robert said you're from Texas, and a lot of fugitives flee in that direction."

"Do you have a photograph of her?"

"No, I'm sorry to say. Two years ago, she had her portrait painted, but it's a huge piece. It hangs over the fireplace in the parlor."

"Describe her."

"She has blond hair and blue eyes. She's also very lovely."

"That's not much to go on."

"I'd be glad to show you her portrait."

Lance wasn't really interested. Furthermore, he doubted the woman would head for Texas. "I don't have time to see the portrait," he replied. "I plan to leave at dawn."

"I can show it to you now."

"I can't leave; I'm expecting a message. Mr. Rayfield, seeing her portrait isn't necessary. A woman traveling alone, and a greenhorn at that, will stand out like a sore thumb. I won't have any trouble spotting her. If I do run across her, I'll remember there's a three-thousand-dollar reward."

"You don't sound very interested."

"The money interests me, but I don't intend to spend time looking for Miss Matthews."

"You're against pursing a woman?"

"It's not exactly my line of work."

"Don't let her sex stop you. She's a cold-blooded murderess! Her attack on my brother was brutal and merciless."

"Was your brother sickly or maybe an invalid?"

"No, of course not. Why would you ask that?"

"It's just hard to imagine a woman killing an able-bodied man with a letter opener."

"Somehow, she must have taken him by surprise. I don't know how it happened; I only know that it did."

"I'll keep an eye out for her."

"Thank you, Mr. Slade. If you do run across her, be on your guard. She's shrewd and very calculating."

Lance repressed an amused smile. "I'll keep that in mind."

Dexter and Robert returned to the carriage and were quickly on their way.

"Three thousand dollars!" Victor remarked. "That's a lot of money. Miss Matthews is as good as caught. For that much money someone will turn her in. She'll never make it out of this city."

"Do you think it's possible for a woman to stab a man to death with a letter opener?"

"I guess so, if she took him unawares."

Lance shrugged the incident aside; it didn't really concern him. Moreover, he was tired of waiting for Trish's reply, and had decided to visit Maxine's and speak personally to Trish. He was about to give Victor an excuse for leaving when another carriage approached the house.

"We're getting a lot of visitors tonight," Victor said.

The driver brought the carriage to a stop, descended to the ground and walked up to the porch. "I have a message for Lance Slade," he said, an envelope in his hand.

"I'm Lance Slade."

He handed him the sealed envelope. Opening it, Lance read the short missive, surprised to find that it was from Maxine Reynolds instead of Trish. The message was short. She wanted to see him right away, for she needed to talk to him about Trish.

The driver indicated the carriage. "Miss Reynolds said that I was to drive you."

"Reynolds?" Victor questioned. "Maxine Reynolds?"

"Yes, sir," the driver replied.

Turning to Lance, Victor asked, "What business do you have with Maxine Reynolds?"

"Private business," Lance replied. He stepped inside the house, grabbed his hat, then followed the driver to the waiting carriage. He climbed inside, and expressed his impatience by closing the door harder than necessary. Why did Maxine Reynolds want to talk to him? You'd think Bill had asked for her daughter's hand in matrimony instead of one of her prostitute's. Well, he intended to make this visit short and to the point. If Trish wanted to leave with him, then she'd better be packed and ready at dawn. Otherwise, he'd leave her behind . . . gladly!

After sending her driver to the Slades, Maxine returned to her bedchamber, where she decided something had to be done about Sharla's appearance. She turned to Hattie, who was about to take the dinner tray downstairs.

"That can wait," she told her, indicating the tray. "We must do something about Sharla. I just sent a message to Lance Slade, and he'll be here shortly. He'll expect to see the woman he thinks is Trish. One look at Sharla, and he'll know she isn't a prostitute."

Sharla was still seated at the desk. She pushed back her chair and got to her feet. "Well, I can't change my looks."

"Of course you can," Maxine replied. "Well, maybe not your looks exactly, but you can certainly change your appearance." She turned to Hattie. "Trish left a lot of her things," she said. "Find one of her most revealing gowns and bring it here. Also, find some gaudy jewelry." She turned back to Sharla, and continued, "Sit at the vanity, and I'll see what I can do with your hair."

Sharla cooperated, and Maxine arranged her long tresses into a upsweep style, holding the curls in place with two combs decorated with flashy rhinestones. Hattie arrived with the dress, and Sharla removed her clothes and slipped into her borrowed attire. The low-cut gown was scarlet-red, and it was fashioned to adhere tightly at the hips. There was no petticoat; therefore, the clinging fabric clearly defined Sharla's long, shapely legs.

Maxine hurried to her wardrobe, returned with a pair of red shoes and told Sharla to try them on. They were a perfect fit. She then had Sharla remove her expensive gems and replace them with cheap jewelry.

Maxine stood back and looked Sharla over from head to foot. She was almost satisfied. "You still need face powder and rouge," she decided.

Sharla didn't dare look in the mirror now that she was wearing Trish's seductive gown; she preferred to postpone the shock. She stood with her back facing the vanity as Maxine powdered her face and applied a heavy coat of rouge to her cheeks and lips.

She again looked Sharla over closely, turned to Hattie, and asked for her opinion.

"If I didn't know better," Hattie remarked, "I'd think she was one of your girls."

Maxine placed her hands on Sharla's shoulders, and encouraged her to turn around and look into the mirror.

She did so hesitantly, trying to prepare herself for what she was about to see. Nevertheless, her reflection was startling. Her mouth agape, her eyes wide with astonishment, she blurted out the first words that came to mind, "Merciful heavens! I look like a whore!"

Six

"I'm sorry," Sharla said quickly, turning to Maxine. "I didn't mean to sound judgmental or . . . or as though I think I'm better than the women who work for you."

"There's no need to apologize," Maxine said with a smile. "Besides, in some ways you are better."

"No, I'm not. No one could be nicer than you are."

"Surely, you don't think I still sell my favors?"

"I . . . I don't know."

"I stopped that a long time ago. I run this business, and at my age that's all I do." She spoke to Hattie: "Sharla is slimmer than Trish. You need to take a few tucks in that dress. I'll wait downstairs for Mr. Slade. When you're finished with the alterations, show Sharla to my office."

Maxine left, and moved swiftly down the hall. The marble staircase faced the main entrance, and she was on her way downstairs when her doorman admitted Robert Granger.

"Robert," she said, welcoming him with a smile. "Weren't you here earlier?"

"Yes, I was," he replied.

"Did you return for another game of poker, or for one of my girls?"

"That all depends. If I'm lucky at cards, then I'll spend some of my winnings on bedroom entertainment. Actually,

I wasn't planning on leaving, but I took Dexter Rayfield to meet the Slades."

Maxine's interest heightened. "The Slades?"

"Victor Slade and his wife live next door to my parents. Their nephew is visiting. His name is Lance, and he's a Texas bounty hunter. I introduced him to Dexter in case Miss Matthews heads west. I'm sure you heard that she murdered James."

Lance a bounty hunter! Maxine's knees suddenly weakened, and for a moment she was so light-headed that she thought she might faint. She drew in a deep breath, regained her composure, and asked as calmly as possible, "Why do you think Miss Matthews will go west?"

"A lot of fugitives head in that direction."

"Did Dexter have a photograph of Miss Matthews to show Mr. Slade?"

"No, he just described her to him. There's a portrait of her at the house, but Lance didn't have time to look at it. He said he's leaving at dawn."

Maxine was surprised to learn that Slade was leaving so soon. She wondered how long he had been in town. If he was leaving in the morning, then he probably had been here for quite some time. Why had he waited until the last day to contact Trish?

"Is anything wrong?" Robert asked. "You seem troubled."

She feigned a bright smile, and assured him that everything was fine. Wishing him luck at the card table, she went quickly to her office and poured herself a glass of port. She took a big swallow, and the liquor had a soothing effect on her nerves. Learning that Lance Slade was a bounty hunter was causing her to have second thoughts. Was sending Sharla with Lance the same as delivering an innocent lamb into the jaws of a wolf? She had wanted so desperately to save her daughter and had thought her plan would work. Now, she wasn't so sure. If only Lance Slade was a rancher instead of a bounty hunter!

She sat in her chair, took another drink, and calmed her anxieties. Maybe she was looking at this from the wrong perspective. A bounty hunter was undoubtedly experienced and good with a gun; therefore, he could take care of Sharla. Maxine was sure several dangers could befall two people traveling from St. Louis to Texas. In that respect, his profession was more an asset than a liability. Moreover, there was no reason why he should suspect his traveling companion was really Sharla Matthews. He would simply see her as Trish, the woman he expected to deliver to his cousin's waiting arms.

A knock came at the door; it was Maxine's driver announcing Lance Slade's arrival. He showed Lance inside, then left closing the door behind him.

Maxine rose from her chair, her gaze sweeping intently over her impressive guest as he moved lithely across the room. His dark trousers and blue shirt fit his tall frame flawlessly; a gun, strapped to his hip, gave him a threatening aura. He stopped in front of her desk, removed his black hat, and said with a halfway grin, "Good evening, ma'am."

It was a moment before she could respond, for she was too enthralled. Although dealing with men was her business, it was rare to meet a man so strikingly sensual.

She indicated the chair facing her. "Please sit down, Mr. Slade. Trish will be here soon. May I pour you a drink?"

"No, thanks," he said, sitting and placing his hat on the desk.

She returned to her own chair, summoned a friendly smile, and said in an offhand fashion, "So, you're Bill's cousin. Are you a rancher, too?" She hoped to lead him into discussing his profession.

"No" was his terse reply.

"Do you work for Bill?"

"Miss Reynolds, I didn't come here to talk about myself. If Trish still wants to marry Bill, then I'll take her to him. I plan to leave at dawn."

"Your tone's a little cynical. You're against this marriage, aren't you?"

"It's none of my business."

"How long have you been in town?"

"A few days."

"Why did you wait until the eve before you plan to leave to contact Trish?"

"I had a hard time deciding whether or not I wanted to be responsible for her," Lance answered candidly. "I considered delivering Bill's letter with an attached note from myself, telling her to take public transportation to Texas."

"Why didn't you?"

"I knew it wasn't what Bill wanted."

"You must be very close to your cousin."

"Close enough," he murmured.

A soft knock sounded. "Come in," Maxine called, certain it was Sharla. She held her breath, and her heart picked up speed. Lance's first impression of Sharla was imperative. Her image implanted immediately in his mind as Trish's might stop Lance from growing suspicious at a later time.

Sharla entered the room. Her seductive gown, along with flashy jewelry and heavy makeup, concealed her virginal innocence.

Lance stood, measuring her with his piercing gray eyes. Although his expression was inscrutable, he was quite impressed with the woman he believed to be his cousin's fiancée. He could see that beneath the heavy makeup lay a natural beauty.

"Trish," Maxine began, "this is Lance Slade." She turned to Lance, and continued the introductions, "Mr. Slade, I'd like you to meet Trish Lawrence."

Amusement flashed fleetingly in Lance's eyes. Such social amenities in a whorehouse seemed somewhat ludicrous. If he didn't know better, he'd think he was in a lady's parlor meeting her maiden daughter. But Maxine was a madam, and Trish was a far cry from a maiden. However, he saw no reason to be unnecessarily rude; he bowed slightly from the waist, and said to Sharla, "How do you do, Miss Lawrence."

"I'm fine, thank you," she replied a little breathlessly, for she hadn't expected Lance Slade to be so blatantly attractive. His swarthy good looks and sensuality were overwhelming.

"Mr. Slade wants to leave at dawn," Maxine told Sharla.

"So soon?" she exclaimed.

"Bring only a carpetbag," Lance told her. "The rest of your things can be sent to you." He arched a brow quizzically. "I hope you can ride a horse."

"I manage to stay in the saddle," she replied.

"Do you have a horse and saddle?"

Maxine answered his question. "Don't worry, Mr. Slade. She'll be ready to leave at dawn, and she'll have everything she needs."

"Miss Reynolds, I'd like to talk to Trish alone. Do you mind? I only need a few minutes."

She said that she didn't mind, and as she left the office, she secretly favored Sharla with an encouraging wink.

Lance remained standing beside his chair, and Sharla was poised close to the door. Neither cared to shorten the distance between them.

"Since we have a long way to travel together," Lance began, "I'd like to put my cards on the table."

"By all means," Sharla replied.

"I've never interfered in Bill's life, and I don't intend to start now. But don't misunderstand me; I think he's making a big mistake. However, regardless of my opinion, if you're what he wants, then I'll put up with you until I can hand you over to him."

"Put up with me?" she questioned, finding his attitude offensive.

"I prefer to travel alone. Furthermore, you're city-bred, a greenhorn and a woman. I just hope you don't complain all the way to Bill's ranch."

"Why would I complain?"

"Traveling horseback for days can be tiring for a man, but for a woman . . . ?"

"I assure you, Mr. Slade, that I will not complain."

A flicker of puzzlement creased his brow, and, again, his gaze swept her thoroughly. "There's something different about you."

She was instantly on her guard. "What do you mean?"

"Your poise—the way you express yourself. You don't act or sound like the prostitutes I know."

"Maybe that's because you've never done business with a high-priced one."

"No wonder it was so easy for you to fool Bill."

She looked at him blankly.

"When he met you in the park," Lance explained. "Now I can see why he didn't suspect you were a prostitute."

Sharla didn't say anything. She didn't know what to say.

"Well, I won't keep you any longer. I'm sure you have some last-minute money to earn. I'll come for you at dawn."

She detected the irony in his voice. "Do you really think I intend to spend my last night here working? I plan to get a good night's sleep." She wondered why she bothered to defend herself. But for some reason she couldn't define, she didn't want him imagining her spending the evening entertaining customers.

He picked up his hat, then crossed the span between them. He paused mere inches from her; he was so close she feared he'd hear the erratic pounding of her heart. A starkly sexual grin touched the corners of his lips, lifting his black mustache menacingly. "If you weren't engaged to my cousin, I'd be tempted to pay your high price. It'd be interesting to find out if you drop the lady facade and make love like a whore."

"That's something you'll never find out. Now that Bill and I are engaged, I intend to remain faithful to him."

Lance's grin turned skeptical. "For Bill's sake, I hope you mean what you say." He put on his hat, the dark brim shadowing his face.

"You don't think a woman like me can change, do you?" She wasn't sure why she asked such a question. Why should she care what he thought about women like Trish?

"Change?" he questioned. "That all depends."

"On what?"

"On how much you love Bill." Suddenly, his strong hands gripped her shoulders, drawing her body flush to his. Startled, she stared into his eyes, but the black brim concealed their expression. "If you don't love Bill, then I hope to God you'll do the right thing and stay here. He doesn't deserve to be hurt, manipulated, or lied to."

She pushed him away so strongly that it broke his firm hold. For a moment, she felt as though she were reliving the violent scene between her and James. He had man-handled her in the same fashion. Her anger, fear, and over-wrought nerves erupted fiercely. "Don't ever grab me like that again!" she cried. "Men like you make me sick. You're bullies, and you treat women like they were put on this earth strictly for a man's enjoyment!"

"That's exactly why you're here, isn't it?" he came back. "For a man's enjoyment? Are you about to tell me your profession was forced on you and that you had no other choice?" He held up his hands as though warding off any response. "Well, spare me your hard-luck story. I don't have time to hear it."

"You're a cold-hearted, opinionated jackass!"

"And you, my sweet, are a high-priced"—he arched a brow—"lady of the evening?" Offering a mock bow from the waist, he opened the door. Maxine and her driver were waiting in the hall.

Maxine told Slade that her coachman would drive him back to his uncle's home. She went into the office, locking the door behind her. She was afraid Dexter might unexpectedly barge inside.

Sharla, pacing, was still steaming. "That man is impossible!" she told Maxine. "He treated me as though I was . . . I was a . . ."

"A prostitute?" Maxine completed. "You have to expect that, Sharla."

Suddenly, all the anger drained out of Sharla. She went to the chair and sat down as though she were exhausted. "I don't think I can go through with this," she sighed. "There must be another way." A spark of energy returned, and she spoke with a tinge of excitement. "Maybe I can buy Mr. Slade's services. I have my gems, and they are worth more than the three-thousand-dollar reward."

Maxine, needing a drink, went to her desk. She didn't bother with port. She picked up a brandy bottle, filled two glasses, and offered one to Sharla.

"No, thanks," she said. "I never drink anything stronger than sherry."

Maxine insisted. "Take it; you'll need it." She helped herself to a long drink, sat at her desk, and said, "You can't tell Mr. Slade who you really are. He'd most likely take your gems, then hand you over to Dexter and also collect the three-thousand-dollar reward. You see, he's a bounty hunter."

"A bounty hunter!" Sharla exclaimed, bounding to her feet and almost spilling her brandy. "Good Lord! That changes everything. I must find another way to get to San Antonio."

"Sit down, Sharla, and listen to me."

She complied; she also took a sip of brandy. Maxine was right—she needed it.

"I think we should go through with our plan," Maxine began. "However, you must be very careful not to do or say anything to make Slade suspicious. He knows there's a bounty on Sharla Matthews. Dexter has already contacted him. But there's no reason for him to suspect that you are Sharla, not unless you slip and give him a reason to think that way. You must start thinking and acting like Trish."

"How can I do that? I never knew her."

"It shouldn't be too hard. Like you, she was a orphan. Only she wasn't raised in a good home with a loving guardian. She remained in the orphanage until she was sixteen. At that age, she was considered old enough to take care of herself and was told to leave. She was very naive, and an older woman who pretended to befriend her manipulated her into prostitution."

A chill coursed through Sharla. "If not for Olivia, that could have happened to me."

Maxine knew she would never have let that happen; she would have found some way to prevent it. She couldn't, of course, pass her thoughts on to Sharla. Instead, she changed the subject. "Traveling horseback from St. Louis to Texas could prove to be dangerous. Therefore, you'll be safer with a man like Lance Slade. You can pull this off, Sharla. Just keep reminding yourself that your life might well depend on it. I'm going to send face powder and rouge with you, and I want you to continue using it. Dexter's liable to have an artist paint your face, plaster it on more wanted posters and have them distributed all over the country. Heavy makeup will help conceal your identity."

"I'm not so sure it will, especially from Lance Slade. Did you notice his piercing eyes? I bet they never miss a thing."

"You only have to fool him until you reach San Antonio.

Jenny will find a way to keep you safely hidden. Meantime, I'll be working to prove that you're innocent."

"How do you intend to do that?"

"I have a couple of ideas in mind. But don't you worry about that. You just concentrate on making a safe escape."

Sharla took another drink; the warm liquor was relaxing. "I don't know how to thank you. You've done so much for me."

"No thanks is necessary."

"Of course it's necessary. You must have cared very much for Olivia to risk your own freedom for mine. It's against the law to harbor a fugitive, you know."

"A little risk here and there makes life more interesting." She spoke lightly, but deep inside she was gravely worried; not about herself, her concern was solely for the daughter she had given up so many years ago.

Maxine insisted that Sharla sleep in her bed. The feather mattress was quite comfortable, and the goose-feather pillows were like resting one's head on fluffy clouds of softness. Nevertheless, Sharla couldn't fall asleep. The day's events kept skimming across her mind, causing her to toss and turn as though the bed was floating on a turbulent sea. That she was wanted for James's murder seemed unreal—as though it were only a nightmare from which she would awaken at any moment. She was afraid; she had never been so afraid. That she might go to prison, even the gallows, layered her brow with perspiration and sent her heart thumping. If she stayed in St. Louis, she would surely be apprehended. Lance Slade was her only hope—her best course.

Her thoughts turned to Maxine. The woman had said that she would find a way to prove that she was innocent. Sharla doubted that was possible. Now that she'd had more time to think about it, she was quite certain that Claudia

had killed James. Her innocence could not be proven unless Claudia made a confession. Sharla didn't think Maxine
or anyone else could extract a confession out of her. Why
should she admit to murder?

Sharla's reverie lingered on Maxine, and she was deeply
touched by the woman's generosity and kindness. Her
friendship with Olivia was still puzzling, for Maxine hadn't
given her much information. She had simply said that they
were childhood friends. She wished she had time to question Maxine; she would like to hear more about their relationship.

Knowing sleep was important, Sharla pounded her pillow as though it were somehow to blame for her insomnia.
She lay still, forcing herself to stop tossing and turning.
Tomorrow would be a long, tiresome day, and she should
face it well rested. She certainly didn't want to be so weary
that she might utter a complaint. She set her jaw firmly,
her expression one of determination. She wouldn't under
any circumstances whine, grumble, or protest to Lance
Slade, regardless of how arduous a pace he might set. A
spark of anger quickened her pulse. The man was utterly
impossible! Moreover, he was a rude, pompous cad. She
dreaded their trip to Texas; his curt manner would no
doubt challenge her self-control time and time again.

A deep sigh escaped her lips, and her determined expression softened as though she were thinking about her
lover. Lance Slade was undeniably the most attractive man
she had ever met, and as she brought a vision of him to
mind, her heart shuddered unexpectedly. She quickly
erased his image. She might find him desirable, but he
was about as likable as a skunk! Furthermore, he thought
she was Trish, a prostitute, who, in his opinion, had inveigled his cousin into marriage. He probably disliked her as
much as she disliked him.

"Lord!" Sharla groaned aloud. "How am I supposed to
travel to Texas with a man like him? He despises the

woman he thinks I am, and I have to swallow my pride and pretend I'm her, regardless of what he says." Defiance flashed in her eyes. Well, she'd put up with his insolence, for he was her best means of escape. However, if he pushed her too far, he'd find that she could fight back!

Seven

Maxine entered her bedchamber to awaken Sharla. Standing beside the bed and gazing down at her sleeping daughter, she could see a resemblance between herself and Sharla, but the young woman also bore a likeness to her father. There was, however, a distinct similarity between Sharla and Maxine's mother.

Thinking of her mother sent a pang of melancholy coursing through Maxine. She hadn't seen her mother in nearly thirty years. For a moment she was overwhelmed with self-reproach, but she pushed her guilt aside and reminded herself that love had been the driving force behind the estrangement from her mother, as well as her daughter. She had removed herself from their lives because she had loved them with all her heart.

A pensive smile touched her lips as her full attention returned to Sharla. She liked her as a person; Olivia had evidently done a remarkable job raising her. Despite wealth and all the privileges that came with it, Sharla was unspoiled, caring, and sensitive. Maxine was very proud of her, and terribly grateful to Olivia.

A rooster crowed from somewhere nearby signaling the first rays of dawn. The fowl's raucous call startled Maxine out of her reverie and into action. There was no more time to waste. She lit the bedside lamp, then gave her sleeping daughter's shoulder a gentle shake.

Sharla came awake at once, bolting straight up as though she expected to confront danger. Maxine's face quickly calmed her fear, and managing a shaky smile, she murmured, "I can't recall ever waking so suddenly. Although I was asleep, I guess my nerves were still as tight as a drum."

"At least you were able to get some sleep," Maxine replied.

The neighboring rooster crowed again.

"It must be dawn," Sharla surmised, throwing off the covers. "Is Mr. Slade here yet?"

"No, but Hattie will let us know when he arrives. I packed a carpetbag for you. I also found riding attire. I brought everything in last night while you were asleep." She indicated the settee. "Your clothes are there."

Sharla went over, looked closely at the attire, then turned back to Maxine. "I can't wear these!" she exclaimed.

"You can, and you must."

She held up the blouse. "This is so thin that it's almost transparent."

"The weather's warm; you won't get cold. There's a light jacket in your bag for evenings."

"I'm not concerned with getting cold. This blouse is too provocative."

"That's why I chose it. It's imperative that Mr. Slade continues to see you as a prostitute. People are judged by the clothes they wear."

Sharla took another look at the riding skirt. The style was satisfactory, but the fabric was too bright. A wide-brimmed hat and a pair of boots completed the costume. These she could find no fault with. Maxine had also laid out undergarments that were too lacy and revealing for Sharla's taste.

"While you get dressed," Maxine began, "I'll hurry downstairs and get you a cup of coffee and breakfast."

Sharla started to tell her that she wasn't hungry, but thought better of it. She should eat, for Lance might want to travel a good distance before stopping for lunch. If she got too hungry before then, she might unintentionally utter a complaint. She was still bound and determined not to do or say anything that Lance could interpret as complaining.

When Maxine returned with a tray, Sharla was dressed and considered herself ready to leave. But Maxine didn't agree. She insisted that Sharla paint her face with powder and rouge. She also suggested that she wear flashy earrings. Sharla was opposed to the makeup as well as the earrings; nevertheless, she prudently conceded.

They agreed that she should take her expensive gems, for she might need to sell them for cash. Maxine cut a slit in the carpetbag's lining, inserted the jewelry, then sewed the lining back together. Sharla was finished with the powder and rouge, and she remembered to put the articles into the bag. Maxine handed her a small wad of bills, along with a sealed envelope. Inside was a letter to Jenny. Sharla took the envelope, but was hesitant to accept the money. However, Maxine insisted that she take it, telling her to consider it a loan.

A knock preceded Hattie's arrival. "Mr. Slade's here," she said. "He's in the kitchen."

Taking her carpetbag and hat, Sharla followed her companions down the servants' stairway, which led into the kitchen. Lance and Maxine's coachman were seated at the table, but they stood as the women came into the room.

Lance's steely gaze raked Sharla from head to foot. The lacy chemise was visible beneath the blouse's thin fabric, and the riding skirt clung tightly to her curvaceous hips. Her long hair, unbound, framed her face, which bore entirely too much powder and rouge. A frown knitted Lance's brow, for he strongly disapproved.

"Is something wrong. Mr. Slade?" Sharla asked, noticing his scowl.

"You need to change that blouse, get rid of those earrings, and take off the makeup," he answered candidly.

"Oh? Do you mind telling me why?" She figured she knew why, but she had a role to play.

"There's no reason for you to look that way unless you intend to solicit customers between here and Texas."

"This is the way I prefer to look and dress, Mr. Slade. I don't intend to change my taste because I'm getting married. Bill loves me the way I am, and his opinion is all that matters. What you think of me is irrelevant."

Maxine smiled, for she thought Sharla handled herself very well. She had a feeling her daughter would have no problem holding her own with Lance Slade.

"Fine," Lance mumbled, his tone sarcastic. "If you want to advertise your profession, that's all right with me. But don't expect me to protect your honor when men ask you your price." He waved a hand toward the kitchen door. "Let's go. We're already late. I'd been here sooner if I hadn't been detained."

"Why were you detained?" Maxine queried, hoping it had nothing to do with Dexter Rayfield.

"Do you know Dexter Rayfield?" he asked.

"Yes, I do," she replied, her nerves tightening.

"I suppose you know about his brother."

"I heard he was murdered."

"Rayfield learned I was a bounty hunter. As I was leaving this morning, he showed up with a wanted poster. He thinks the woman who killed his brother might head west. It seems he was busy through the night having an artist paint the woman's picture."

"You mean a likeness of her is on the wanted posters?" Maxine asked, trying to sound mildly interested.

"It's on the one he gave me." Lance reached into his

shirt pocket, withdrew the folded poster and showed it to Maxine.

She took it from his hands and looked at it carefully. The artist had been rushed, and therefore, he hadn't done that good a job. Nevertheless, he had captured a likeness to Sharla. She appeared innocent, almost angelic, certainly not like the heavily painted, seductively dressed woman Sharla was impersonating. She handed the poster to Sharla as though it were a mere afterthought.

She studied it closely, her observation the same as Maxine's. As she gave the poster back to Lance, she knew it was vitally important that she remain powdered and rouged. Beneath all the makeup, lay the innocent face on the poster.

Lance folded the poster and returned it to his pocket. He wasn't really interested in the reward. Pursuing a woman didn't especially appeal to him. Furthermore, he didn't think an eastern-bred lady would head west, but most likely would remain hidden somewhere in the city.

Maxine turned to her coachman. "Is Trish's horse saddled?" she asked. She had taken the man into her confidence, for he could be trusted. He knew she was helping Sharla escape, though, he didn't know why. Totally loyal to his employer, he had carried out her instructions to purchase a sturdy horse and western saddle for Miss Matthews. Not once did he question Maxine's motives.

He told her that the horse was saddled and waiting out back. Lance's horse was also there, and he again waved a hand toward the door. "Let's go, Miss Lawrence."

Sharla put on her hat, then moved outside a little hesitantly. Now that she was actually leaving, second thoughts set in. Was she doing the right thing? Maybe she should stay here and try to prove her innocence. Her common sense quickly dashed that idea. She'd merely get caught and end up in jail.

Maxine followed them outside, and as Lance was putting

Sharla's carpetbag on the horse, she drew Sharla into her arms and held her close. "I'll find a way to clear your name," she whispered. "That's a promise." It felt so wonderful to hold her daughter that she was reluctant to release her, but she knew Sharla must be on her way without further delay.

"Thank you for everything," Sharla said, knowing she could never fully repay Maxine for her help and kindness.

She turned and looked at the horse the coachman had chosen. She was pleased with his choice, for the roan mare seemed healthy and strong. She mounted the horse with ease. She was accustomed to western saddles; she had her own at home. A wistful smile teased her lips as she remembered Olivia's gentle objections when she learned that her ward had bought a western saddle and was riding astride. However, her objections hadn't been quite that gentle when she found out that her ward was also learning to shoot a rifle. But Sharla had stubbornly continued her lessons, for she was determined that someday she would move out West. Suddenly, her whole body went rigid. Well, she was going west—as a fugitive impersonating a prostitute, and traveling with a man she could barely tolerate. It certainly was a far cry from the way she had always imagined it.

Lance mounted his black stallion, and started toward the street. As Sharla followed close behind, she turned and waved a final farewell to Maxine.

Fortunately, Maxine's business sat at the edge of town, negating any reason to travel through the city. The road Lance decided to take was deserted, for it was still too early for most people to be up and about.

As they gradually traveled farther away from the city, Sharla began to breathe a little easier. She had been afraid that they might be stopped by the police. But her relief was short-lived, for up ahead she suddenly spotted a uniformed policeman. Sitting his horse, he waited for them to reach him.

"Morning, folks," he said affably. "On the road kind of early, aren't you?"

"We have a long way to travel," Slade replied. "I believe in early starts."

"Where are you going?"

"Texas," he replied.

The officer's eyes moved from Lance to Sharla. It was clear her disguise was successful, and he figured she was a prostitute.

"Sorry I had to stop you folks," he said. "But there's a fugitive on the loose, and she'll probably try to leave the city." He waved them on their way; his eyes again zeroing in on Sharla. She was a fine-looking woman, and he actually envied the man with her. That she could be the fugitive he was looking for never crossed his mind. He had been told that she was a rich socialite. If he were to find her, he expected to see a panicked female fleeing in expensive clothes. He couldn't imagine a woman like her keeping her cool and eluding the law. Rich socialites were helpless and weak.

This time, Sharla didn't dare breathe easy until they were all the way out of town. But once they were on a rural road without buildings and people, she began to relax. Lance, riding beside her, was uncommunicative. She doubted he had uttered more than four words to her since leaving Maxine's. She had a feeling his aloof manner was going to make this trip seem terribly long and tedious.

"Where do you suppose she is?" Lance suddenly asked.

The question, coming out of the clear, took her by surprise. "Who are you talking about?"

"Sharla Matthews. Where do you suppose she's hiding?"

"How would I know?" Her nerves grew tense, and her heart started pounding. Was he playing cat-and-mouse with her?

"A three-thousand-dollar bounty is a lot of money. If Rayfield sends that wanted poster across the country, every bounty hunter who sees it will be looking for her."

"You included?" she asked, forcing her voice to remain calm.

He grinned devilishly. "Do I look like the kind of man who would hunt down a woman?"

"Yes, if the price was right."

He didn't bother to deny it. "Well, I doubt if she'll head west. A woman like her is probably too helpless to make it out of the city, let alone make it to the West."

She bristled inwardly. "Why do you think that?"

"Most likely, she's been pampered and spoiled all her life. I've never met a lady like that who wasn't a shrinking violet."

"I doubt if you've met very many ladies, rich or poor."

Amused, he flinched as though her words had a physical impact. "Are you implying no decent woman would want me?"

"You're a bounty hunter, and I can't imagine any woman wanting a man who kills for a living."

"What makes you think I'm a killer?"

"Aren't you?"

He chuckled. "Those who live in glass houses . . . ?"

"My profession is a lot different than yours!"

"That's true. I make my living apprehending men, and you make your living bedding them. Maybe we should work together. You could lure them into bed and then I could barge in and apprehend them."

"Your humor is tasteless! Furthermore, I am no longer a prostitute. I told you that I intend to remain faithful to Bill."

He pierced her with his eyes. "On the inside you may have changed, but outwardly you still advertise your profession. If you really cared about Bill, you'd wash off that paint, take off those dangling earrings, and wear a blouse than isn't transparent."

He was right, and she knew it. But she couldn't clean her face; it was her only disguise. She decided her best recourse was to withdraw into silence. Lance didn't try to continue the conversation; he seemed to have nothing more to say. For that, Sharla was grateful.

Sharla and Lance were miles away from St. Louis, and the sun was dipping westward as Maxine's coachman helped Claudia into his employer's carriage. There was no one inside, and she sat alone.

As the conveyance moved away from the Rayfield mansion and down the city streets, Claudia tried to imagine why Miss Reynolds had sent for her. The driver had arrived at the manor house with a note from Maxine, asking for an audience with Claudia. She almost sent the driver back with a firm refusal, but curiosity got the better of her.

The plush interior was impressive, and as Claudia's fingers caressed the rich upholstery, she began to envy Maxine Reynolds. That a prostitute could obtain such wealth seemed incredible. She had never really thought about it before, but riding in the expensive carriage piqued her interest in the profession. If she had chosen prostitution instead of domestic work, she felt that in time she could have risen to Maxine's present status.

Her face suddenly blushed, and her hand covered her mouth as though she had spoken her thoughts aloud. What could she have been thinking? If her mother knew she was even riding in a prostitute's carriage, she'd roll over in her grave.

Claudia's mother, left alone with a five-year-old daughter, had worked as a maid in order to support herself and her child. Claudia had been raised in the servants' quarters of more than one estate. Last year her mother had died of scarlet fever. She hadn't seen or heard from her father since she was a small child.

The curtains inside the carriage were drawn, and Claudia parted them so she could glance outside. They were passing the police station, and she closed the curtains quickly as though she were hiding from the law. But it was guilt and not fear of detection that prompted such a reaction. She felt bad that Sharla was wrongfully accused of murder. She had nothing against Sharla, had even liked her. However, she wasn't about to confess in order to save her. She hoped Sharla would somehow escape, and then the interest in James's murder would die down. People would stop talking about it, the police would concentrate on other crimes, and Dexter would go on with his life.

Tears came to her eyes, and an ache rose in her throat. She missed James and was sorry about killing him. Why had he made her so angry? She was a little afraid of her anger, for it was getting harder and harder for her to control it. She had childhood memories of her father losing his temper, and she wondered if she had inherited her short fuse from him.

She sobbed softly. She had loved James with all her heart. He had been her whole world, her only reason for living. Now that he was gone, she didn't know what to do with her life. He had been the center of her existence. She felt alone, disoriented, and terribly sorry for herself. However, there was no remorse for what she had done. In her deranged mind it was all James's fault. He should never have rejected her!

The carriage turned onto the winding lane leading to Maxine's house. Again, Claudia parted the curtains to look outside. The coachman drove to the back of the house, got down from his seat, and offered Claudia an assisting hand.

Hattie, aware of their arrival, opened the kitchen door, invited Claudia inside, and led her toward Maxine's office.

Claudia's eyes glanced about curiously as she followed the servant. She could hardly believe that she was actually inside such a renowned establishment. To her dismay, closed doors blocked every room she passed, leaving her curiosity hanging.

Hattie knocked softly on the office door, peeked inside and told Maxine her guest had arrived. She then waved Claudia into the room and left.

Maxine was seated behind her desk. She rose to her feet and indicated the chair facing her. "Sit down, please."

Claudia was a little in awe of the famous madam, and she stared openly at her as she made her way across the room. She sat in the chair, her eyes remaining glued to the woman's face. She had expected to see a heavily painted, scantily attired woman, and was taken aback by this lovely and well-dressed person.

Maxine was also measuring Claudia. Her guest was quite attractive, and despite her modest gown, she could see that her figure was seductively curvaceous.

"I'm sorry," Maxine began, "but I'm not aware of your last name."

"Wilkens," Claudia replied. "I'd like to know how you learned my first name."

Maxine lied smoothly. "A week or so ago, I happened to spot you in town. Your exceptional beauty caught my attention."

Claudia was immediately flattered.

"I asked about and learned that your name is Claudia and that you work for James Rayfield. You see, I'm always searching for new girls to work for me."

"Girls to work for you?" Claudia exclaimed, stunned. "You can't be serious!"

"I'm very serious. Now that James Rayfield is dead, I imagine Dexter will close up his house. You'll be unemployed. I'm offering you a very lucrative job. My girls make good money. If you are frugal, within ten years, maybe less, you can save enough money to start your own business. I'm not implying that you should open a house of ill repute, for there are more respectable choices."

Although Claudia was impressed, her mother's strict upbringing demanded that she react accordingly. "I've never been so insulted!" she remarked irritably. "How dare you bring me here for this!"

She didn't fool Maxine, for she had seen Claudia's fleeting interest. "I didn't mean to insult you," she was quick to say. "Please accept my apology. I won't bother you again, Miss Wilkens. However, I think you are making a huge mistake. A maid's wages will keep you poor for the rest of your life. You can't marry into money because rich, successful men do not marry domestic help."

Claudia cringed. James had taught her that lesson.

Maxine continued, "Working for me you can make more money in an hour than you now make in a month. You're a very desirable woman, and my customers will gladly pay top price to be with you." She paused and watched Claudia closely. She had a feeling she was making headway. "My dear," she said gently, "are you still a virgin?"

Such a personal question took Claudia by surprise. "Wh-what?"

"You can tell me. I'll understand one way or the other."

"No," she decided to confide. "I'm not a virgin."

"Do you enjoy men?"

"What kind of question is that?"

"A prostitute who enjoys men excels in her profession, which means more money for her."

Claudia did indeed like men. James wasn't her first lover. "Yes, I enjoy men," she replied.

Maxine decided to end the interview and give Claudia time to think over the advantages she had offered her. She got to her feet, and said crisply, "If you should change your mind about working for me, let me know."

She went abruptly to the door, opened it, and called for the coachman, who was waiting nearby. She told him to drive Miss Wilkens home.

She closed the door behind them, moved to her desk and poured a snifter of brandy. A smile revealed that she was pleased with herself. She was hopeful that Claudia would return. Then, once she was here living under her roof, she would find a way to entrap her. Somehow, someway, she'd get a confession out of her and clear Sharla's name.

Eight

Claudia returned home to find all the servants gathered in the parlor with Dexter. She wasn't surprised; she knew Dexter had to talk to them sooner or later.

"Sit down," Rayfield told her, indicating an empty chair. His eyes followed her, noticing every seductive curve. He wondered if she and James had been lovers. A faint smile curled his mustache. Knowing his brother, he probably had this pretty chit in his bed whenever he desired.

When Claudia was seated, Dexter announced that he intended to close up the house. Considering he was James's next of kin, he took for granted that the house would soon belong to him. He didn't plan to sell it, for when he decided to marry and have a family, he would reopen the house and move in. But for now, he preferred to remain in his own home, which had belonged to his father and his father before him. He would save Olivia's house and present it to his bride as a wedding gift. He had no idea who this bride might be, for he wasn't seriously involved. Furthermore, he wasn't quite ready to make such a commitment. Being a rich, sought-after bachelor was still too much fun.

He gave the servants one week to make other living arrangements, except for Agnes and Albert. He offered them the job of caretakers. Albert could continue to live in the cottage out back. Agnes, however, would live in the house, keeping all rooms closed except for the kitchen and her own quarters. Although Olivia had left Albert and Agnes financially independent, they both agreed to stay on as caretakers. This house was their home, and they had no desire to live elsewhere.

Dexter assured the other servants that he would give them a generous allowance to tide them over until they could find new employment. He also promised them letters of recommendation. He then dismissed everyone, except for Claudia.

She sat stiffly, and nervous perspiration beaded up on her brow as she wondered why Dexter had asked her to remain. Did he suspect she was involved in James's murder? Was she now his prime suspect instead of Sharla?

When he favored her with a warm smile, her nerves settled. If he thought she had killed his brother, his demeanor wouldn't be so affable.

"I have a proposition to offer you," Dexter told her.

She was perplexed. "A proposition, sir?"

"Yes. I want you to move into my home and work for me."

"You need another maid?"

His smiled widened. "Claudia, are you really this naive, or are you simply playing dumb? No, I don't need another maid. However, that will be your title, and I'll expect you to do your fair share of the household chores. But your salary will be higher than that of a maid's, and in return, you'll come to my bed whenever I send for you." He regarded her keenly. "I suspect that's the same arrangement you had with my brother."

She wasn't about to admit the truth. She had sworn to the constable and to Dexter that she and James weren't lovers. If she now admitted to the lie, it might start Dexter suspecting that she had also lied about the murder.

She looked him straight in the eyes, and answered firmly, "I was a maid in this house and nothing more."

He wasn't sure if he believed her or not, but it didn't really matter. A live-in consort appealed to him, and he thought Claudia perfect for the position. "My proposition still stands. Are you interested?"

She was actually considering it. After all, Dexter was extremely attractive, and, even more importantly, he reminded her of James. "You said that my salary will be higher than a maid's? Exactly how high?"

"I'll give you a fifty dollar a month raise."

She felt like laughing in his face. Having visited Maxine, she felt that fifty dollars was an insult. Before today, she might have accepted Dexter's proposal, but she had learned from a successful professional that she was worth much more than a measly fifty-dollar raise. She decided right then and there to accept Maxine's offer.

Filled with newfound confidence, she rose from her chair and looked at Dexter with a touch of arrogance. "I'm not interested in your offer, Mr. Rayfield. Besides, I've already found a job."

"You certainly didn't waste any time. Where is this new job?"

"I intend to work for Maxine Reynolds."

He chuckled. "Being a maid in a whorehouse will be quite a change. I hope you know what you're doing."

"I won't be a maid, Mr. Rayfield."

He was taken aback. "Surely, you aren't implying . . . ?"

"That's exactly what I'm implying," she said, self-importance in her voice. She whirled about haughtily, went to the door, but turned back and said, "My price is not fifty dollars a month, Mr. Rayfield. Try fifty dollars an hour." She wasn't sure if that was a plausible amount, but it sounded good. She left the room and hurried upstairs to pack her clothes.

Dexter, left with his mouth agape, stared at the empty doorway as though he expected Claudia to reappear at any moment. Suddenly, he threw back his head and roared with laughter. He admired Claudia. She'd never get rich working as a maid, or as his consort, but there was a lot of money at Maxine's. She was exceptionally desirable and could demand top price. However, if she wasn't talented in bed, it wouldn't matter if she was pretty or not. He decided the next time he visited Maxine's, he'd pay Claudia's price and find out if she was any good.

However, his lighthearted mood was temporary, and a sense of sadness swept over him. His grief was still over-powering, for he had sincerely loved his brother. Mixed with his grief was rage. He despised Sharla with a violent passion and knew he would not rest until she was behind bars. That she might be innocent never entered his thoughts. She disliked James, had threatened his life, and had the opportunity to kill him. That was all the evidence Dexter needed to convict her.

He wondered where she was hiding. The wanted posters had been distributed this morning. Someone would surely turn her in very soon; if not today, then by tomorrow at the latest. He was confident that his three-thousand-dollar reward would guarantee a quick arrest.

"Where are you?" he mumbled to an absent Sharla. "Where the hell are you?"

Sharla was extremely tired, and dusk was blanketing the landscape when up ahead she spotted a roadside inn. It was a welcoming sight, for Lance had already told her that they would spend the night there.

The one-story building, constructed of logs, was surrounded by farmland. There was a barn, a large stable, a smokehouse, and several other out-buildings. A stagecoach was parked out front; the horses had been unhitched and were inside the corral.

Sharla and Lance reined in at the hitching rail, dismounted, and removed their carpetbags. A sign was nailed to the door, telling customers to knock.

Lance rapped loudly. A moment later, they were admitted by the proprietor, who sported a gray beard and a friendly smile. However, as he got a closer look at Sharla's painted face, his smile wavered. His wife and the lady from the stage would certainly find this woman's presence offensive.

Lance ordered two beds, dinner, plus food and care for their horses. The proprietor came very close to refusing them service, but his monetary needs were too great to turn away paying patrons. His wife and the lady passenger would have to find a way to deal with this woman being here.

He accepted Lance's money, placed their bags in a safe place, then showed them into the dining room, where five customers were seated at a long table with benches on each side. His wife was serving, and he told her to set two more plates. The stagecoach driver and two male passengers were on one side of the table; a middle-aged couple sat across from them. Lance, followed by Sharla, went to the bench occupied by the couple, for there was plenty of room. He stepped back and gestured for Sharla to sit down, which would place her beside the woman.

Sharla, tired and hungry, was about to comply, but before she could, the lady passenger shot the proprietor an angry glance and spat harshly, "I'll not sit at the same table with this harlot!"

For a fleeting moment, Sharla was taken off guard. Harlot? Then she quickly remembered her disguise. How could she have forgotten her painted face, the gaudy earrings, and her sheer blouse?

"Please, ma'am," the proprietor said gently, trying to pacify the irate passenger. "This is a public establishment, and these people paid money for dinner and a place to spend the night."

The woman didn't relent. "I meant what I said! I'll not keep company with the likes of her!"

Her husband intervened on her behalf: "Sir, surely you don't expect my wife to sit at the same table with a woman like that!"

Lance didn't bother to repress a cynical grin. He had little tolerance for pious people who thought themselves better than others. Nevertheless, he was irritated with Sharla, for she had brought this on herself. He had asked her to dress more conservatively, and to wash off the powder and rouge.

The proprietor's wife, who was glaring at her husband, spoke her mind. "I won't let you subject this lady to that . . . that . . . woman's presence!" She turned a sharp gaze to Lance and Sharla and told them, "You two can eat in the kitchen."

"We'd rather eat here," Lance replied calmly, taking Sharla's arm and practically depositing her on the bench. He wisely placed himself between the two women.

The woman's husband came very close to confronting Slade, but there was a threatening aura about him that convinced the man to keep silent. He motioned for his wife to do likewise.

The proprietor, impatient with the whole incident, demanded that his wife set two more plates. She did as she was told, served the meal, then left the diners to themselves.

The stagecoach driver, and the two men sitting with him, didn't mind eating at the same table with Sharla. In fact, they thought her very attractive and could barely keep their eyes off her.

Conversation was somewhat strained, and only sporadic words passed among the men. Sharla and the woman said nothing at all.

Following dinner, the proprietor showed everyone to their rooms. Space was limited, and Lance had to share quarters with the driver and the two male passengers. The married couple were given private accommodations, and Sharla was taken to a room at the end of the hall. It was small and furnished with the bare necessities. Although the room was cold and impersonal, Sharla was grateful to be enclosed within its private walls. She went to the narrow bed and sat on the edge wearily, as though all energy had left her body. She had known that masquerading as a prostitute would be difficult, but it was even worse than she had imagined. She began to wonder if she could really go through with it. However, as the wanted posters came to mind, she drew upon her inner strength and set her jaw firmly. She would indeed go through with it, for the alternative was too risky. Impersonating a prostitute was better than going to jail.

The door suddenly opened; she had forgotten to lock it. The stagecoach driver stepped inside, closing the door behind him. "Pardon me, miss," he said, a lewd glint in his eyes.

She bolted to her feet. "What do you want?"

"Your price," he replied. "How much do you charge? I got some money with me."

"I'm not for sale. Get out!"

The driver, whose frame was burly, moved incredibly fast for his size, grabbed Sharla's arm and pulled her close. "Don't hedge with me, sweetheart. I know your kind; you're holding out for more money than you're worth. I got twenty-five dollars on me. I'd give you more, but it's all I got. I ain't had a woman in a long time, so this ain't gonna take very long."

Trying to pry his hand from her arm, she cried fiercely, "Let me go! How dare you!"

At that moment, Lance opened the door and came inside. He acted as though finding a man in Sharla's bedroom was no reason for alarm. He spoke congenially to the driver. "When you left our room, I had a feeling this was where you were headed. I'll have to ask you to take your hand off the lady. She isn't selling her favors."

The man wasn't about to fight with Lance. He knew a professional gunman when he saw one, and he wasn't going to put his life on the line for a tumble with a whore. He broke his hold on Sharla, stepped back, and said somewhat apologetically, "I didn't know she was your personal property." He offered to shake Lance's hand. "No hard feelings?"

Accepting the driver's proffered hand, he responded affably, "There's no hard feelings."

The driver, feeling as though he had dodged a bullet, went quickly to the door and left without another word.

Sharla turned on Lance angrily. "That man barged into my room, insulted me, and what do you do? You shake hands with him!"

"Would it make you feel better if I had killed him?"

"No, of course not! But you could've been a little more forceful. He's liable to return."

"There's a lock on your door; use it."

"I should've locked the door earlier, but I forgot."

"Forgetting to lock your door is understandable."

"Oh? Why is that?"

"You aren't used to locking men out of your bedroom."

She wasn't sure if he meant that disparagingly or if he was simply making a statement. She thought it over, and decided he was taunting her. "You don't like women of my profession, do you?"

"I like them fine. In fact, I've met some who are very compassionate and trustworthy."

"You don't consider me compassionate and trustworthy?"

"I don't know if you are or not."

"Do you mind telling me why you treat me the way you do?"

"What way is that?"

She steamed inwardly. The man was impossible! "You treat me like . . . like you can barely tolerate my company."

"It's not your company that I have a problem with. It's the way you look and dress. Why the hell do you have to flaunt your profession? That driver is only one of several men who will proposition you between here and Bill's ranch. Not all of them will be as understanding as the driver. What are you trying to do? Get me killed, or make me kill somebody?"

She now understood his anger, and didn't blame him for feeling that way. But she was afraid to remove her disguise; the face on the wanted poster lay beneath the heavy powder and bright rouge. Even if she could convince Lance not to turn her in, there might be others lurking nearby who had seen the posters and would certainly collect the reward. Also, she had a feeling that Lance would not take kindly to her trickery. He struck her as the kind of man who would react angrily to deceit. No, she must hold tenaciously to her disguise, for it was her only defense.

"Well?" Lance grumbled, impatient with her silence. "Is that what you want? Do you want me to kill or be killed?"

"I want you out of my room," she decided to reply. How could she argue with him when she knew he was right?

Taking her by surprise, he reached out a hand and smeared her rouge with his thumb. "Wash that paint off, and keep it off!" With that, he turned on his heel and left.

Sharla quickly locked the door behind him. A water pitcher and basin sat atop the chest of drawers. She hurried over, filled the bowl with water and scrubbed her face until not a residue of paint remained. However, she knew first thing in the morning she would again apply a thick coat of powder and rouge. Dread coursed through her. Lance would certainly be enraged!

* * *

The next morning, Lance was already seated at the dining table when Sharla arrived. Her painted face did indeed spark his wrath. That she could defy him like this was not only enraging, but mind-boggling as well. Why would she intentionally bring attention to her profession? She was going to Texas to get married, not to open a house of pleasure! Her defiance was totally selfish, and he wondered in earnest why Bill had fallen in love with her. Gritting his teeth, he held his temper in check and said nothing to Sharla about her appearance. But he swore to himself that he'd be damned if he'd kill or be killed protecting her honor.

Breakfast was over quickly, and they were soon on their way. They traveled without talking to each other. Lance was worried that he'd lose control and say too much; Sharla, on the other hand, was too troubled to talk. She had seen the anger in Lance's eyes when she walked into the dining room, but she had also seen a look of bewilderment. Apparently, he didn't know how to deal with her brazen defiance.

He was, however, thinking about her defiance, and he came to a decision. Hereafter, they would avoid towns and inns as much as possible. The less men they came into contact with the better. The next few nights would be spent outdoors and away from people.

"There's a town about five miles from here," he told Sharla. "We'll stop and buy a pack mule and supplies."

She suspected his motives. "Are we going to start camping outdoors?"

"I think that's best."

She agreed, but telling him that would only add to his confusion.

"Since you're so determined to flaunt yourself," he continued, his voice edged with resentment, "I intend to avoid as many towns and inns as possible."

"Whatever you say," she conceded.

He had expected her to spar with him, and her cooperation came as quite a surprise. He shook his head with puzzlement. This woman was impossible to figure!

Nine

Lance left Sharla at the town's general store to buy provisions while he went to the livery to see about purchasing a mule. He told her which supplies they needed, and gave her money to cover the cost. She quickly bought the provisions, then, looking through the store's supply of clothing, she found a pair of trousers and a shirt that looked as though they would fit. She knew she had to continue with the powder and rouge, but she had decided to discard the thin blouse and bright-colored skirt. They would be camping out night after night, and she needed more suitable attire. She was about to pay for her purchases when she noticed a gun rack against the far wall. She went over and took down a new Winchester. She was familiar with the weapon, for her instructor in St. Louis had taught her to shoot with the same kind of rifle.

She bought the Winchester, and told the proprietor she wanted a box of shells. She paid for her purchases, loaded her rifle, then waited by the door for Lance to return.

It didn't take long for him to buy a mule, and he was back within thirty minutes. He came into the store and gathered up the supplies. Sharla quickly snatched up her own purchases.

Lance, busy carrying the provisions and loading them on the mule, didn't notice Sharla's new Winchester until he had their provisions secured. She had removed her carpetbag, and was putting her clothes and the box of shells inside. The rifle lay at her feet.

He grinned wryly, indicated the Winchester, and asked, "What do you intend to do with that?"

"Use it, if it becomes necessary," she replied, closing up the carpetbag, then putting it back on the horse.

"I don't have time to teach you to shoot," he said, taking for granted that she knew nothing about using a rifle. "I want to reach Bill's ranch without any delays."

She started to inform him that she was an accurate shot, but his attitude was so irritating that she swallowed the words. She wasn't sure just why she kept the information to herself—maybe for spite, or maybe she hoped for an opportunity to prove her competence, and at the same time crush his male-minded view of her.

"I don't expect you to give me lessons," she decided to say. She picked up the Winchester and turned to her horse, but there was no sheath to hold the rifle.

"There's a saddle shop across the street," Lance told her. "I can go over and get you a scabbard. That is, if you really want to carry that rifle with you. It might be best if you let me put it on the mule."

"A scabbard will do fine, Mr. Slade. I'll give you some money."

He held up a hand. "Don't bother. Consider it a gift from me to you."

"Thank you," she murmured.

He went to the saddle shop, and Sharla waited with the horses. She didn't notice three men coming out of the town's saloon, but they were very aware of her. They lumbered drunkenly in her direction. As they drew closer, her sheer blouse and heavy makeup deepened their interest.

The three men were brothers, and were reputed to be the town's ruffians. They were always drinking and getting into fights. They paused in front of the general store and stared lewdly at Sharla, who was staring back at them.

"Howdy," the oldest brother said. "How about we buy you a drink?"

"Go away," she said sternly.

"There's no reason to be so unfriendly. My brothers and me, we wanna give you a good time."

"I'm not looking for a good time." She was holding her rifle, and was ready to threaten them if they dared to approach her.

At that moment, Lance left the saddle shop and started back across the street. The youngest brother caught sight of him, and nudged the eldest with his elbow. "That's probably her man; he could be trouble," he said. "Let's get the hell out of here."

The oldest sibling wisely summed up Slade as a man to reckon with. He wore his Peacemaker like a professional and moved with the confidence of a gunman. He looked away from Lance and turned his gaze back to Sharla, his eyes traveling over every inch of her. He knew he would be seeing her again. He motioned for his brothers to join him, and they quickly walked back toward the saloon, where they had left their horses tied at the hitching rail.

Sharla watched them for a moment, then turned around to greet Slade.

"What did they want?" he asked gruffly, indicating the brothers with a nod of his head.

"They wanted me to have a drink with them."

He carried a leather scabbard, and, stepping to Sharla's horse, he attached one end to the saddle horn, then latched the other end so that the barrel would rest under the rider's leg. He reached out a hand for her rifle, and she gave it to him. That it was loaded surprised him.

She read his mind, and lied deliberately. "The proprietor was kind enough to load it for me."

He slipped the Winchester into the scabbard. "Loaded guns are dangerous. Don't draw this rifle unless I give you permission."

"Don't worry, I won't accidentally shoot you." She placed emphasis on the word "accidentally."

He picked up on it immediately. He arched a brow, and a halfway grin lifted the corners of his black mustache. The effect was sensual, and Sharla's heart responded. Such sexual awareness was alien, for no man had ever affected her this way.

"Was that a subtle threat?" he asked.

"Whatever do you mean?" she came back, as though totally innocent.

He regarded her with an expression she couldn't construe, and she wondered what was going through his mind. Actually, he was somewhat perplexed, for he found Sharla very hard to understand. She never reacted the way he thought she would. However, she was a mystery he didn't intend to solve, for he didn't want to get involved. She was engaged to his cousin, furthermore. In an effort to shield his own emotions, he told himself that she wasn't his type.

"Let's go," he said tersely. "We're wasting valuable traveling time." More than ever, he was anxious to deliver her to Bill. She was starting to get to him, and he didn't like that feeling at all.

They mounted and rode out of town. The rural road, bordered by trees and shrubbery, remained deserted for the most part; periodically they would pass fellow travelers or farmers going to town to load up their buckboards.

Lance seemed content to keep talk to a minimum, which was fine with Sharla. She was pretending to be someone else, and if she tried to start a conversation, most of what she would say would probably be lies anyhow.

* * *

Maxine was in her office when Dexter arrived unannounced. He simply rapped his knuckles against the closed door, then barged inside as though he owned the place. Maxine found his arrogance infuriating. She was seated at her desk, but bounded to her feet and said sharply, "Twice now you have invited yourself into my office. I hope you don't intend to make this a habit!"

"Pardon my intrusion, Maxine, but I'm so upset that I'm not thinking clearly."

She offered him a drink, then, as he eased into the chair facing her, she returned to her own seat. He downed his brandy as though it were whiskey, retrieved the bottle from her desk, and refilled his glass. This time, he nursed the brandy.

"What's on your mind?" Maxine asked him.

"I'm very worried," he replied. "I had thought by now someone would have turned Sharla in. I can't believe she's still at large."

"What does that have to do with me?"

He looked confused. "What do you mean?"

She spoke slowly, as though he might find her words hard to grasp. "Why are you here, Dexter? If you have a complaint, take it to the constable."

"I'm not here because of Sharla."

He seemed in no hurry to explain, causing Maxine's patience to intensify. "Is there something you want from me?"

"No, not exactly. I came here to talk to you about Claudia. She used to work for James."

"I know who she is."

"Is what she told me true? Did you hire her?"

"Yes, I did."

"As a prostitute?"

"Why not? She's very attractive."

His mouth lifted in a grin of anticipation. "Claudia is why I'm here. I want to buy her for the evening."

"The entire evening?" Maxine stressed.

His smile widened. "That depends on how good she is."

"She just arrived this afternoon. I think it's too soon for her to entertain customers. Come back tomorrow night."

Dexter had no tolerance for rejection. Resentment flashed in his eyes, and his words were forceful, "I don't like to wait. I want the girl tonight! Send for her and tell her that I'm here. I'll wait at the bar."

"I'll send for her," Maxine replied, unmoved by his anger. "But if she'd rather wait until tomorrow night, I'll stand by her decision."

Dexter pushed back his chair and quaffed down his drink. He dropped the empty glass on the desk haphazardly; it fell over and rolled onto the carpeted floor. He didn't bother to pick it up. That Maxine had the gall not to grant him preferential treatment made his blood boil. He wanted to insult her, to bring her down a peg or two, but he knew that wasn't possible. She wielded as much power in this town as he did, maybe even more. Her clientele was too prestigious—judges, bankers, politicians, and other men of important stature. These patrons held Maxine in high esteem, for she protected their infidelities and guarded their reputations. Several of these citizens were permitted to come in through the back door and leave the same way. Their secret access shielded them from eyewitnesses who might publicly destroy their good standing, or resort to blackmail.

Dexter, suppressing his anger, reminded Maxine that he'd wait at the bar. The moment he was gone, Maxine located Hattie and asked her to bring Claudia to the office.

A few minutes later, Hattie brought her in and left the two women alone.

Maxine summoned a warm smile, for she knew it was vital that she win Claudia's trust and friendship. Such intentional deceit went against Maxine's grain, but she was quite certain that Claudia was a murderer who was willing to let Sharla take the blame. Therefore, she set her conscience aside, and carried on with her ploy.

"Are you settled in?" Maxine asked her.

"Yes, I am. My room is much larger and much nicer than I had imagined. At the Rayfields', I slept in a room not much bigger than a broom closet."

"That kind of life is now behind you. From now on, you'll live in grand style, wear silk gowns, dine like a queen, and have servants to wait on you. However, there is a price to pay. You will sleep with several different men, and it's very important that you make each man feel like he's the world's greatest lover. Some of them are so old and worn out that it will require a superb job of acting for you to fool them."

Claudia smiled confidently. "Don't worry about that. When I want to, I can act as well as a professional. I can lie without twitching a muscle."

Maxine didn't doubt it. She was certain that Claudia had lied to the constable and that her performance had been flawless. She leaned back in her chair, and suggested that Claudia tell her about her life.

"There's not much to tell," she replied. "My father deserted Mother and me when I was a small child. My mother became a domestic servant; that was the only way she had to support us. I attended public school until I was sixteen, then I also became a servant. My mother and I were working for the Caldwells when Mother came down with scarlet fever. She passed away, and soon thereafter I went to work for James Rayfield."

"What were your parents' names?"

"Why do you want to know that?"

"I like to know as much as I can about my girls."

Although Claudia thought her inquiry unusual, she saw no harm in cooperating. "My mother's maiden name was

Alice Donaldson, and my father's name was Jacob Wilkens."

"Have you seen your father since he deserted you and your mother?"

"No, I haven't."

"How old are you, Claudia?"

"I'll be twenty-one next month."

Maxine had gotten the information she needed, and she decided to steer the conversation onto another course before such personal questions could arouse Claudia's suspicions.

"Dexter Rayfield is here," she said. "He asked for you. I told him that it might be too early for you to start to work. But he was very persistent. He's waiting at the bar for an answer. If you'd rather wait until tomorrow night . . . ?"

"Dexter came here just to see me?" Claudia exclaimed. She was flattered, but she also got her first taste of sexual power. From the time she had lost her virginity, she had submissively allowed her lovers to use her—especially James. It had never dawned on her that she was selling herself cheap. But Dexter's being here was proof that a man would indeed pay a high price for her. She silently berated herself for being such a fool. For years she had given away what she could have sold! Moreover, if James had been forced to pay for her company, he might have treated her with more respect.

Maxine, watching Claudia speculatively, sensed that she was pleased to learn that she was the object of Dexter's desire. She was quite certain that, until this moment, the girl hadn't realized that she was so sexually attractive.

Claudia met Maxine's gaze without a waver, and her tone was very businesslike, "Give me time to take a bath and slip into something seductive, then send Mr. Rayfield to me." Claudia had been given Trish's room and the clothes she had left behind.

"Very well," Maxine replied. "Dexter's a lucrative customer. Make sure he receives his money's worth."

"Oh, I will," Claudia assured her, rising and walking to the door.

As soon as she was gone, Maxine left the office and went to the poker room, where she found Jerome Bailey, who was the best private detective in town. She drew him aside so they could talk in private.

"I need your services," she told him.

Bailey, handsome and quite charming, said jokingly, "Why, Maxine, servicing you would be an honor. You're still a gorgeous woman, and I'm a hungry male."

She laughed. "That's not what I had in mind."

He pretended dismay. "Don't tell me it's my professional services that you require."

She laughed again. "Jerome Bailey, you're a lovable rogue."

"What can I do for you, Maxine?"

"I need information on a man named Jacob Wilkens. I'm afraid I don't know much about him. His wife's maiden name was Alice Donaldson. They had one child: Claudia. She's almost twenty-one, so they probably married about twenty-two years ago. Jacob deserted his wife and daughter. Alice is now dead, but Jacob's whereabouts are unknown."

"That's not much to go on, but I'll see what I can find."

She thanked him, then left the room. Digging up information on Claudia's father would probably get her nowhere. She wasn't even sure why she was bothering with it. However, she thought it important not to leave any stone unturned. Proving Claudia's guilt and Sharla's innocence would not be easy; in fact, it might be impossible.

No! she thought. *I won't let myself think that way.*

She had promised Sharla that she would clear her name, and she intended to live up to that promise!

* * *

"We'll camp here," Lance told Sharla.

They had ridden a short distance from the road, and the area was surrounded by towering trees and thick foliage.

"I still don't understand why you want to stop now. It won't be full dark until at least another hour." She had voiced these same words moments earlier when Lance had suggested they leave the road to find a place to set up camp.

"I should think you'd want to stop," he said, reining in. "You've got to be tired."

"Of course I'm tired. But like you, Mr. Slade, I'm anxious to get this trip over with."

Dismounting, he replied, "Don't you think it's about time we dropped formalities? Why don't you call me Lance, and since you're going to be a part of my family, I guess I should call you Cousin Trish."

He moved over to give her a hand, but she swung down from the saddle without waiting for assistance. "Cousin Trish, indeed!" she grumbled. "You can call me Miss Lawrence!"

He grinned disarmingly. "I apologize. My manners are usually better than that."

Standing her ground and looking him straight in the eyes, she said firmly, "I'm perfectly aware that you don't approve of me. Well, that goes both ways. I have no use for you! However, for the remainder of this trip, let's try and be civil to each other. We are civilized human beings, and we should be able to complete this journey without too many altercations."

He offered her a mock bow from the waist. "My sentiments exactly. Let's make camp, shall we?"

Within minutes, they had their bedrolls laid out and a fire burning. Sharla was about to start dinner, but Lance stopped her without explaining why.

Puzzled, she watched as he went to his bedroll, stuffed

it with more blankets, then placed his hat at the end. At a glance it would appear as though someone was sleeping there.

"Why did you do that?" Sharla asked, moving to stand beside him.

"Remember those three men who wanted to buy you a drink?"

"Of course I remember them."

"They've been following us since we left town."

"How do you know that?"

"When I'm being followed, I get a tickling at the back of my neck."

She frowned testily. "Please don't talk to me like I'm a child."

"Believe it or not, I do get this tickle. But there is more to it than that."

"For instance?"

"Like a flock of birds behind us taking sudden flight—the wind carrying the scent of horses and men; a smell that my horse always reacts to. Your mare smelled them, too, and if you were as experienced as I am, you'd have sensed the change in her."

Sharla was duly impressed. "It must take years to acquire that kind of knowledge."

"Without it, I'd be dead." He reached out a hand and grasped her arm, drawing her closer. "We don't have much time. That's why I stopped early. I need to confront our visitors before it gets too dark."

"Is there something I should do?"

"Yes, I want you to stand here beside this bedroll and start taking off your clothes."

"Wh-what?" she gasped.

"You heard me; start taking off your clothes! Those three men will be here soon, and I need a diversion so I can slip up behind them."

Her face was aghast.

"Don't look at me as though I'm asking you to do something you haven't done many times before. Undressing in front of men is part of your profession, isn't it?"

Sharla could only stare at him.

Ten

"Why do you keep looking at me like that?" Lance demanded.

Sharla swallowed deeply, drew a calming breath, and replied, "Your request took me by surprise, that's all."

He regarded her thoughtfully. "If I didn't know better, I'd think you were embarrassed."

"What makes you think I'm not?"

"Don't play games with me," he said testily. "You've undressed in front of men before; one more time won't make a difference. Do as I asked, unless you want those three men to ambush us."

"Of course I don't want that!" she spat. "But surely there's another way to stop them."

He waved his arms impatiently. "Damn it, woman! What the hell is your problem? All right, we'll do it your way. I'll take cover, and when they show up, I'll shoot them. They'll shoot back, of course, which means I'll have to kill them. Is that what you want?"

"No; I don't want any bloodshed."

"Then cooperate, so I can slip up behind them and take their guns without anyone getting hurt." His charcoal eyes pierced hers sharply. "If you'd take off that face paint and exchange that blouse for one that you can't see through, in the future we might be able to avoid situations like this one."

She knew he was right; she shouldn't draw that kind of attention to herself. She wished for a plausible excuse, but there wasn't one, at least not one that she could give him.

"Undress slowly and seductively," Lance told her. "They need to be so enthralled with you that I can slip up behind them. But I'm sure you know how to hold a man's attention. After all, you've had a lot of experience."

Experience! She wanted to laugh in his face. Instead, she met his gaze without a flinch. Somehow she'd find the strength to go through with this, despite the humiliation.

"A couple of minutes after I leave, start undressing," Lance told her. He moved away quickly and disappeared into the surrounding shrubbery.

Alone, Sharla gave in to her anxieties and shivered visibly even though the weather was warm. She unconsciously crossed her arms over her breasts, as though she was already exposed to whoever was watching. However, she didn't lose her nerve, for keeping the intruders' eyes on her was too important. She hoped to avoid a shootout; she didn't want to be even indirectly responsible for anybody's death.

She wondered if the men were out there now, watching her. Lance's stallion, tied nearby, suddenly pawed the ground and whinnied softly. Sharla suspected that the threesome had indeed arrived.

She lowered her eyes to the bedroll, as though Lance was there waiting for her to join him. She pretended a seductive smile, then began to unbutton her blouse slowly. She hoped it wouldn't take Lance very long to work his way behind her hidden audience.

She removed the flimsy blouse and let it fall at her feet. It floated almost weightlessly before landing on the ground. Underneath, she wore Trish's lace chemise. It was so skimpy that it barely covered her breasts. Next, she removed the pins from her hair, and allowed the blond tresses to cascade past her shoulders. The effect was more sensual than Sharla could possibly imagine. She unfastened her skirt, drawing it slowly down past her hips, all the time her mind begging Lance to please hurry!

Although she couldn't see the three men, she could sense their eyes on her, and she knew they were out there. Her nerves grew shaky, causing her to step out of the skirt a little awkwardly. If only Maxine had given her long bloomers instead of short pantalets that hardly came past her thighs. She felt almost naked. If Lance didn't do something soon, she wouldn't simply feel naked—she would be standing there without a stitch of clothing on! What was keeping him? She wondered if he was taking his time on purpose. She wouldn't put it past him!

However, before she had to unlace her chemise, the three men came out of the shrubbery. Their hands were high over their heads, for Lance was holding them at gunpoint.

Sharla grabbed her clothes, but instead of putting them on, she covered herself by clutching them in front of her.

Lance ordered the brothers to unbuckle their gun belts, drop them to the ground, then kick them in his direction. They did as they were told.

"Unload their guns and take the extra bullets out of their holsters," Lance told Sharla.

It was impossible for her to carry out his instructions and hold her clothing at the same time. She started to get dressed, but a gruff remark from Lance stopped her.

"Forget the clothes! You can dress later. Once you get their bullets, go into the shrubbery and bring their horses."

She cast him a furious glare, and tossed her head angrily, causing the dangling earrings to jingle. Mumbling a curse beneath her breath, she threw the clothes to the ground. That she might feel practically naked didn't matter to him, for the man didn't have a shred of decency!

She removed the bullets, then hurried into the foliage and returned with the men's horses. Lance had her unload their rifles, then look through their saddlebags for extra shells. She didn't find any.

"Pick up your gun belts, mount up, and get the hell out of here," Lance told the brothers. "Don't try and follow us again. This time, you caught me in a good mood; next time you might not be so lucky. I might be in one of my killing moods."

They grabbed their holsters, hastened to their horses and swung into the saddles. They were still shocked that this man had slipped up on them so easily. He was as quiet as an Indian. The brothers were worthless, but they weren't murderers. They had hoped to restrain the man, enjoy the woman, then be on their way. Now, they realized that they had walked into a trap that could have been deadly. They turned their horses about and galloped away quickly, thankful that they were still alive.

"Do you think they'll be back?" Sharla asked.

"I doubt it," Lance replied, his gaze really noticing her for the first time. Her partial nakedness was breathtaking, and her blond tresses falling in disarray gave a starkly seductive effect. He couldn't help but feel a man's response.

The desire mirrored in his eyes sent sparks of unwanted excitement shooting through Sharla. For a tense moment, they both seemed to be in the process of sexual discovery, their thoughts filled with the physical awareness of each other. Sharla was the first to look away, breaking the tenuous link between them. Disturbed by her vulnerability to him, she quickly reminded herself that he was about as likable as a rattlesnake. She must not let his sensuality interfere with her better judgment. He was not only a gunman, but a rake as well; she wanted nothing to do with him!

Although Lance was very sexually aware of Sharla, he

didn't try to take her into his arms. He believed she was engaged to his cousin, and that was one line he would never cross.

Suddenly, a brisk breeze blew across Sharla's flesh, bringing to mind that she was half-dressed. She hurried to her carpetbag, removed the shirt and trousers she had bought in town, and put them on. She then packed her blouse and skirt.

Her attire met with Lance's approval. He hoped next she would get rid of the powder and rouge.

Claudia, waiting for Dexter, paced her room somewhat anxiously. Now that she was about to entertain her first customer, she began to have second thoughts. Her misgivings had nothing to do with morality; she was worried that she might fail as a lover. After all, she hadn't had that much experience. Before James, she'd had two affairs, and they had been fleeting. Most of what she knew, she had learned from James.

She went to the dresser and looked into the mirror. Her reflection pleased her, and she smiled as she admired herself. Her dark tresses were unbound, and the silky locks flowed in waves around her shoulders. Her face bore only a trace of powder and rouge. Looking through Trish's belongings, she had chosen a blue nightgown that temptingly shadowed her womanly curves. She had never worn a garment so sheer, or one so expensively made, and she loved the feel of the silky fabric against her naked body. She glanced down at her feet; they were bare, for Trish's shoes were too small for her. However, she wasn't too concerned. Maxine would surely see to it that she had shoes to match her wardrobe. Earlier, she had tried on several of Trish's seductive gowns, and they had fit perfectly. Except for their feet, she and Trish were the same size.

She moved away from the mirror, and hurriedly extinguished all the lamps except for two. She wanted the room bathed in a romantic glow.

A knock sounded at the door, and for a moment her heart froze! Dexter had arrived. She went to the door on legs that suddenly felt too weak to support her. She told herself to smile, turned the knob, and admitted her first customer.

Dexter's gaze raked her heatedly as he came inside and closed the door. That he hadn't really noticed her when she worked for James seemed incredulous. How could he have missed this seductive creature? He supposed it was her drab uniform. Also, she had merely been one of many maids, and therefore, she had escaped his roving eye.

"Good evening, Mr. Rayfield," she murmured. The low-burning lamps dimmed his features and cast a shadow upon his face. In the saffron glow, he looked very much like his brother. Claudia's pulse began to race, and her heart pounded erratically. The moment was eerie, and a chill ran up her spine. She felt as though she were staring into the eyes of the man she had murdered.

As Dexter moved farther into the room and out of the shadows, his resemblance to James wasn't quite so striking, causing Claudia's nerves to settle somewhat.

"Why did you decide to become a prostitute?" Dexter asked bluntly.

"For the money," she replied.

His smile was sincere. "Well, you can certainly make more working for Maxine than working as a maid. Do you know how much you're worth?"

"What do you mean?"

"Do you know how much Maxine is charging me?"

She blushed, for she felt foolish. "I . . . I forgot to ask."

He quirked a brow. "Take some good advice—never forget to ask when money is concerned. However, Maxine is honest; you'll get your fair share."

Claudia's interest was piqued. "How much is she charging?"

"I suggest you discuss that with Maxine. However, it's a respectable amount: so much an hour and a flat price for the entire evening."

"How long do you plan to stay?"

"That depends on whether or not you're worth my time and money." He eyed her intently. "Are you?"

"I don't know," she answered truthfully.

"Let's find out, shall we?" He stepped to the bed, sat on the edge, and motioned for Claudia to stand before him. "Undress," he said. "I want to look at you."

She removed her nightgown with a flourish; she wore nothing underneath and posed for Dexter's searching eyes. Her body was firm and voluptuous.

Rayfield actually licked his lips with relish as his gaze roamed over every inch of her. Her large breasts, small waist, and curvaceous thighs aroused his passion. He stood, and drew her into his embrace. He bent his head and kissed her urgently, his tongue darting into her mouth and entwining with hers.

Claudia, pressing her naked body tightly against him, responded unhesitantly. Her desire was almost primitive . . . exciting; her body, alive with passion, yearned for a conqueror. James and the others had never really satisfied her; they had pleased only themselves. She hoped Dexter would be more considerate.

Dexter lifted her into his arms and placed her on the bed. He then removed his clothes, discarding them as though they were on fire and his life depended on exceptional speed. Naked, he lay beside her, and as he kissed her, his hands explored her silken flesh. She writhed with longing, and gladly spread her legs so that his finger could probe the core of her passion. His warm mouth and flickering tongue soon followed the trail his hands had mapped.

No man had ever pleasured Claudia quite this intimately, and she trembled with anticipation as Dexter's head moved ever lower. She cried aloud with joy, for she loved what he was doing to her. She laced her fingers in his hair, and her head tossed back and forth as a feeling of euphoria began to build inside her. Then, suddenly, her passion crested, and uncontrollable tremors shook her body as she experienced total fulfillment.

Dexter's tongue moved upward, traveling over her stomach, breasts, and then into her mouth. He kissed her deeply, aggressively, then rolled to his side.

"No man has ever made me feel this way," Claudia told him, her voice husky with passion.

Her compliment came as no surprise, for he considered himself a superb lover. "Now it's your turn to pleasure me," he said, placing a hand at the back of her head and urging her lips down to his erect manhood.

Claudia had no insecurities about pleasing a man in this fashion, for James had taught her well. That had been his favorite part of making love, so she had a lot of experience. James had never bothered to return such pleasure; he never went further than achieving his own satisfaction.

Remembering James's every instruction, she thrilled Dexter beyond his expectations, bringing him dangerously close to a climax. He roughly forced her onto her back, mounted her, and rammed his hardness deep into her moist depths.

His forceful entry was as exciting to Claudia as it was painful. Until now, she had never realized that pain could be pleasurable. Her other lovers had always penetrated her gently. She smiled wickedly—an aggressive penetration was much better.

She wrapped her legs tightly about his waist, her hips rising to meet each deep thrust. They thrashed wildly upon the bed, reaching, climbing, for that moment of total rapture. Their completion came to them simultaneously, erupting into a fierce climax that left them winded and exhausted.

Withdrawing, Dexter lay flat on his back, his chest rising and falling with each rapid breath.

Claudia leaned over and kissed his lips gently. "You're a wonderful lover," she murmured. "I never had a climax before, but I had two with you."

He liked such flattery; his male prowess meant a great deal to him. "You chose the right profession, Claudia. You'll make a good whore."

She stiffened. "I don't like that word."

"You mean, whore?" he asked.

"Yes. I prefer prostitute. Whores are cheap, but I'm not."

He chuckled lightheartedly. "Have it your way—you'll make a good prostitute. Maxine knew what she was doing when she hired you."

Brushing her fingers across the dark curly hair of his chest, she murmured, "Your hour is almost up. Do you plan to leave?"

She was still leaning over him, and her large breasts hovered inches from his face; he reached out a hand a gently pinched both rose-hued nipples. "I'll leave in the morning," he replied. "I intend to enjoy you over and over again."

Pleased, she assured him, "You'll receive your money's worth." Her fingers moved past his chest, down his stomach and to his limp manhood.

"Not yet," he said, moving her hand aside. "I need a few more minutes to recuperate."

She laid her head on her pillow and giggled huskily. "I'll give you ten minutes," she said, "then I'm coming after you."

"I'll be ready," he replied with a smile.

Silence fell between them, and it hung on for over a

minute before Dexter suddenly asked, "How well do you know Sharla?"

The question took Claudia off guard. "Wh-what?"

"Sharla—how well do you know her?"

"I just worked for her. I wasn't her friend."

"Do you have any idea where she might be hiding?"

"Of course not. Why do you ask?"

He sighed heavily. "I'm merely grasping at straws. I thought you might have heard something. After all, servants know a lot about their employers."

"Sorry, but I can't help you."

"I wonder where she is," he said, desperation creeping into his voice. "Who the hell is hiding her?" His hands doubled into angry fists. "She can't hide forever. She'll get caught, and then I swear to God that I'll see her hang from the gallows!"

Claudia thanked her lucky stars that it was Sharla, and not her, who was the recipient of Dexter's revenge, for she had a feeling that he would not rest until he believed his brother's murderer had paid with her life.

She nestled against Dexter's lean body, and placed a leg intimately across his. Before, she had hoped that Sharla would escape, but now she felt differently. If Sharla was convicted, then James's murder would be solved and the case permanently closed. It would be in her best interest if that was to happen.

"I'll keep my eyes and ears open," she told Dexter. "A lot of people come through here; maybe I'll learn something. Whoever's hiding Sharla might come to Maxine's, drink too much, and say more than he should."

"I appreciate your help. If I find Sharla because of something you learn, the three thousand dollars is yours."

Her sudden smile was filled with greed. "In that case, I'll do everything I can to find her."

"She's somewhere in this city; it's only a matter of time before someone turns her in." He sounded more confident than he felt, for he had an uneasy feeling that Sharla had somehow escaped.

Sharla sat at the campfire and stared into the flickering flames. She and Lance had eaten supper, the dishes had been washed and put away. Lance was now bedding down the horses and the mule.

Sharla couldn't repress a yawn. The day had been long and strenuous, and she dreaded the rest of the journey. Not only was it exhausting, but traveling with Lance was almost intolerable. She felt she had the strength to endure the trip, but she wasn't sure if she could put up with her companion much longer. The man rubbed her the wrong way; she found his conduct rude and arrogant.

The sounds of footsteps drew her attention, and she glanced up as Lance came toward the campfire. His sensuality hit her with an unexpected force. If only he wasn't so disturbingly attractive! She felt it would be easier to dislike him if he wasn't so excitingly masculine. Her gaze returned to the fire.

He sat beside her, and his close proximity made her even more aware of his rugged appeal.

A coffeepot sat atop the flames, and as Lance filled his cup, he asked, "Are you sleepy?"

"I think I'm more tired than sleepy."

He took a sip of coffee. "You know, Bill talks about you all the time."

She wasn't expecting him to bring up Bill. She tensed and her heart picked up speed. She wasn't sure if she could lie her way through a conversation concerning Trish and Bill.

Lance was beginning to feel more congenial toward his traveling companion, for she had handled herself admirably during the incident with the three brothers. Deciding to talk to her as a friend, he continued, "Bill said he told you about my family, and why I became a bounty hunter."

Sharla didn't say anything. She knew nothing about his family or why he was a bounty hunter, therefore, she figured silence was her wisest course. She could feel the power of Lance's gaze on her, but she continued to stare into the flames as though he hadn't said a word.

Lance had certainly expected a response. After all, Bill had told this woman that his family had been murdered, and that his fourteen-year-old sister had been raped before she died. His eyes remained on Sharla as he wondered how she could be so uncaring. He thought she would at least have said that she was sorry. Damn! How could he have thought for one moment that they could be friends?

Sharla wished he would stop staring at her; it was unnerving. She drew her gaze from the fire and forced herself to look at him. Taken aback by the coldness in his eyes, she reacted defensively. "Why are you looking at me like that?" she asked. "What do you want from me?"

"Nothing!" he said angrily. He put down his cup, got to his feet, and went to his bedroll. That Bill could love such an unfeeling woman was more than he could understand. It seemed apparent to Lance that she was totally self-centered and cared about no one but herself!

Sharla, completely confused by his anger, got up and went to her own bedroll, which was across the fire from Lance's. She lay down and covered herself with the top blanket. She considered questioning Lance; perhaps she would learn why he was angry. But she quickly discarded the idea. She would probably slip up and say the wrong thing, and then he'd realize she wasn't Trish.

There was nothing she could do. Furthermore, she reminded herself that she didn't even like him. So why should she care if he was upset? She rolled to her side, closed her eyes and waited for sleep. But it eluded her for a long time, for as hard as she tried, she couldn't dismiss Lance's unexplained anger.

Eleven

The next few days passed uneventfully. Lance and Sharla were civil to each other, and managed to get along. However, Lance had serious misgivings about his cousin's fiancée. He thought Sharla cold and self-centered. That worried him, for she was about to marry a very compassionate man who, undoubtedly, was blind to his fiancée's indifference.

Sharla, on the other hand, was finding the strenuous journey bearable. In fact, she welcomed the exhaustion, for it helped her sleep at night. It wasn't the tiring trip that bothered her; it was the lie she was forced to live. Pretending to be someone else was getting harder and harder for her to cope with. More than once, she was tempted to blurt out the truth, then plead with Lance not to take her back to St. Louis. But his aloofness was a deterrent; she sensed little warmth in him. Considering his profession, she supposed she shouldn't find that surprising. She couldn't imagine a bounty hunter being very sensitive or sympathetic to someone's plight. Otherwise, he wouldn't collect very many bounties.

They were still in Missouri, but were nearing the Arkansas border. The scenery was stunning, for a rainy season had colored the trees' leaves in dark greens, and wildflowers sported the colors of a rainbow. Long blades of grass formed a thick carpet beneath the horses' hooves. Above, rays from the setting sun lanced through the gaps in the trees' branches, as scattered puffs of clouds skimmed across a pewter sky.

"There's a river up ahead," Lance told Sharla. "We'll camp there for the night."

Her spirits were immediately bolstered. She intended to bathe in this river! Immersing herself in a body of water sounded heavenly. She could hardly wait to scrub every inch of her flesh, and wash her hair until it was squeaky clean.

Dusk was cloaking the landscape when they reached the river. Sharla dismounted hastily, went to the pack mule, got an extra blanket, along with a bar of soap, then told Lance that supper could wait—she was taking a bath!

Trees and shrubbery bordered the river, and she didn't have to walk very far downstream to be out of Lance's sight. She removed the flashy earrings and dropped them carelessly. She controlled an urge to smash them into the ground with the heel of her boot; she hated the tasteless jewelry. Undressing quickly, she waded into the narrow river until the water was waist-level. She hummed a happy tune as she ran the soap over her flesh. Once her body was clean, she lathered her long tresses, rinsing away the soap by ducking her head under the water. She remained in the river after her bath and enjoyed the cool water lapping against her naked flesh. She finally made her way to the bank; it wouldn't do for her to stay here too long. Lance might get worried, and come to check on her. That she might be naked wouldn't deter him, after all, she was supposed to be a prostitute, which, in his opinion, staved off modesty.

She wrapped the blanket about her, then, kneeling at the bank, she washed her clothes. Her earrings forgotten, she hurried back to camp, put away the soap, and draped her wet apparel over some bushes. She hoped they would dry by morning.

Lance had a fire burning and was heating a can of stew. The aroma was mouth-watering; Sharla's bath and swim had whetted her appetite. She was about to join Lance at the fire when, suddenly, she remembered that she had forgotten her powder and rouge. How could she have made such a foolish mistake? The prospect of a bath had wiped all caution from her mind. She could hardly believe that she had left her disguise behind in her saddlebags. She wanted to make a dash for the makeup so that she could hide behind her mask, but it was too late. Lance was watching her, and his intense scrutiny held her riveted, as though she were powerless to move.

Seeing her for the first time without a heavy layer of powder and rouge took Lance unawares. He had always known that a natural beauty lay beneath the face paint; therefore, he was not surprised to find that she was so lovely. It wasn't her beauty that held him mesmerized, it was something else—something he couldn't quite put his finger on. Then, it quickly dawned on him. She looked familiar! He felt as though he had seen her before, although, that didn't seem possible. He mulled it over in his mind as he tried to place her. Suddenly, he remembered where he had seen her face.

Sharla didn't see the tiny smile hidden beneath his mustache, nor did she detect a humorous glint in his eyes as he motioned for her to join him. "Supper's about ready," he said, as though nothing had changed.

She was hesitant. Sitting close to him might prove to be a mistake. He probably didn't recognize her now because he hadn't seen her up close. She made a move toward her saddlebags.

Lance read her intent. He bounded to his feet, moved quickly and caught her arm. "Come on," he coaxed. "It's time to eat. I don't know about you, but I'm as hungry as a bear." Keeping a firm grip on her arm, he led her to the fire.

Sharla sat down, tucked the blanket tightly about her and watched as he dished up a plate of stew. "Your dinner, Miss Lawrence," he said, handing her a filled bowl.

She accepted the food, and with a sigh of relief, she began to eat. Thank goodness he failed to recognize her face as the one on the wanted poster! She supposed she shouldn't be too amazed, since the artist hadn't done that good of a job. It bore a likeness to her, but that was about it. She suddenly felt hopeful, if Lance didn't recognize her, then chances were good that no one else would. Maybe she could forego the powder and rouge. She hated wearing the heavy makeup; it made her look ridiculous. Furthermore, they were now a long way from St. Louis, and she doubted if Dexter's wanted posters had traveled this far. Even if he decided to send them westward, she would be one step ahead. By the time the posters reached San Antonio, Jenny would have her safely hidden. She decided there was no reason to continue wearing makeup. Lance didn't recognize her, and she had no one else to fear.

Lance ate his dinner in silence. He was anxious to get his hands on that wanted poster and look closely at the drawing. He strongly suspected that his traveling companion was Sharla Matthews, but he needed to double check. Finished, he put down his plate, and announced that he was going to take a bath.

Going through his belongings, he got a change of clothes, plus a blanket and the soap. Stealthily, he retrieved the wanted poster and hid it in his pocket.

He hurried downstream, removed the poster and struck a match. Holding the flame over the paper, he studied the sketch carefully. He grinned wryly and blew out the match. "Well, I'll be damned," he murmured aloud. "That little vixen had me completely buffaloed."

He started to go back and confront her with his discovery, but he suddenly changed his mind. Apparently, Miss

Matthews liked to play games. Well, he was also good at games, only now they would play by his rules. He didn't intend to continue the ruse indefinitely, only long enough to even the score.

He undressed, waded into the river, and began to wash. His lovely traveling companion had puzzled him, but the pieces were now starting to fall into place. He chuckled lightly as he recalled the way she had looked at him when he told her to undress in front of their uninvited guests. It was no wonder that she had been appalled. Admiration for Sharla swept through him; despite such humiliation, she had cooperated. But he now realized how difficult it must have been.

His thoughts turned to the real Trish Lawrence. He wondered what had become of her. He intended to question Sharla about her, but not just yet. He still had a game to play. A devilish grin appeared; he was looking forward to evening the score. He wasn't planning to be mean or vindictive; he simply wanted to turn things around in his favor.

Finished washing, he returned to the bank and dried off with the blanket. Full night had descended, and the moon, surrounded by a myriad of stars, cast its golden beam upon Lance's sinewy frame. Strong muscles rippled through his shoulders as he reached for his clothes. His physique, tall, lithe, and supple, was flawlessly proportioned.

He began to dress, his thoughts still on Sharla. He no longer harbored hard feelings toward her, or believed that she was self-centered. He now understood why she didn't respond to his family's murder; she didn't know anything about it. He surmised she had decided her wisest recourse was to say nothing at all. He also understood why she had worn so much makeup. The powder and rouge had been her disguise.

Lance didn't believe for a moment that Sharla might be

guilty of killing James Rayfield, for he didn't think her capable of such a brutal act.

As he headed back toward camp, Maxine Reynolds came to mind. That she was somehow connected to a well-bred lady like Sharla was indeed a mystery. It was one he planned to solve, but not now. First he had a game to play—a game started by Sharla, but one he intended to finish, though not until he had tired of it.

Sharla had cleaned the supper dishes and was sitting at the fire when Lance returned. He put away his things, joined her, and poured himself a cup of coffee.

His nearness unsettled her, for she was acutely aware of his masculinity. Still, her eyes were drawn to him. His dark hair, damp from the river, glistened with black highlights, and a wayward ringlet, falling across his brow, was starkly sensual. He had changed into buckskins, and the suede shirt and pants adhered to his strong frame like a second skin. The top laces on his fringed shirt were untied, baring an apex of dark, curly hair.

Feeling her silent scrutiny, he turned his head and looked at her. She quickly lowered her gaze and stared down at her lap, as though there was something there of interest. Lance smiled inwardly. He knew she had been studying him as a woman studies a man, and he found her shyness delightful. Ladies like Sharla were schooled in many things, but he knew sexual awareness was not one of them. As she continued gazing down at her lap, his eyes traveled over her leisurely. In his absence, she had brushed her hair, and the shiny tresses fell past her shoulders. In the firelight, the radiant curls reminded Lance of spun gold. Her profile was delicate, exquisitely feminine, and her lashes, lowered, for her eyes were still downcast, were beautifully long and thick. The tightly wrapped blanket hugged her womanly curves, and as Lance's eyes roamed over the slender, curvaceous form beneath the blanket's folds, passion stirred in his loins. He quickly turned away from such tempting beauty; otherwise, seduction might become uppermost in his mind. Seducing Sharla was a pleasant thought, but he wasn't about to take advantage of her. Considering her circumstances, she was probably vulnerable, a little frightened, and would welcome a comforting shoulder and a pair of strong arms. That, of course, would lead to desire, which in turn would lead to making love, and would ultimately end in a commitment, one he wasn't ready to make. Settling down with a wife and raising a family was not on the horizon. His life was dedicated to finding the men who had murdered his family. Until that was taken care of, he had no intentions of building a future for himself, and he was perfectly aware that Sharla Matthews was not the kind of woman he could love and then forget.

The silence between them became uncomfortable to Sharla. She had sensed his scrutiny. The power behind his gaze had seemed almost tangible. Her flesh was warm and tingly, as though his perusal had been a caress that touched every part of her body. She was somewhat in awe of these feelings, for she had never before felt such a sexual response. Nevertheless, the silence between them was more unnerving than Lance's scrutiny, or the way it made her feel.

She cleared her throat uneasily, turned and met his eyes, which were again watching her. "It's late. I guess we should turn in."

"It's not that late," he was quick to point out. "Let's spend time getting better acquainted, shall we?"

"I don't think that's a good idea" she responded, hoping to avoid personal chitchat. She didn't know enough about Trish, Bill, or Bill's family to carry on a detailed conversation.

"But I think we *should* become better acquainted," Lance egged her on. "When you and Bill marry, we'll be family. Family members should know each other well. Don't you agree?"

"That depends," she mumbled, wishing he hadn't all of a sudden decided to be so dadblasted friendly.

"Depends on what?" he asked, his eyes watching her like a hawk measuring an unsuspecting prey.

"It would depend on whether or not we were going to spend much time together. Considering you're a bounty hunter, I don't imagine you spend a lot of time at Bill's ranch." She hoped that answer would satisfy him.

He smiled inwardly. She was clever and could come back with a quick answer. He admired her talent for improvisation. She was exceptionally sharp, taking into consideration that she didn't have much to go on. Still, he was not about to let her off the hook—not just yet! The game was just getting interesting.

"I visit Bill often. When he told you about me, didn't he tell you that?"

She shrugged her shoulders. "I suppose; I can't really remember. I didn't pay that much attention."

"I should think you would've paid close attention to things Bill told you."

Her nerves were on edge, and she turned to anger as a means to defend herself. "I always listened closely to Bill, except when he talked about you. I didn't find you an interesting topic of conversation." She rose quickly to her feet, intending to retreat to her bedroll.

Lance reached up a hand and captured her wrist. "Why didn't you find me interesting?"

"I didn't approve of your profession, and now that I've met you, I don't especially approve of you." She drew her wrist free, whirled about, and went to her bed. She lay down, drew up the top blanket and turned her back to the fire. She wondered if she had been too harsh. She thought about it for a while, then decided it didn't matter. It was imperative that she keep an impersonal gap between her and Lance. A friendly relationship might spawn questions she couldn't answer, which would arouse Lance's suspicions. It wouldn't take him long to figure out she was a fraud. After that, he would probably put it all together and realize she was the fugitive Dexter was bent on finding. Would he turn her in for the reward? She wasn't sure. At times Lance seemed likable enough and even considerate, but there were other times when she got the impression that he was cold and unrelenting. She decided to play it safe. She would continue to impersonate Trish for as long as it was necessary.

She closed her eyes, willfully cleared her mind, and waited impatiently for sleep to overtake her.

In the meantime, Lance had poured another cup of coffee and was smoking a cheroot. His conscience gnawed at him, and he considered telling Sharla that he was on to her disguise. But he couldn't quite bring himself to give in; she had tricked him and he deserved a little harmless revenge. He wondered how she planned to deal with Bill. He thought it over. There was no conceivable way. Apparently, she didn't plan to come face-to-face with him, which meant she had no intentions of ever reaching his ranch. Somewhere along the trail, she planned to go her own way.

He drained his cup, put out his cheroot, and retired to his bedroll. Before tonight, he had viewed this trip as tedious and not to his liking, but now that view had undergone a drastic change. Sharla Matthews was a remarkable young lady, and now that he was wise to her masquerade, having her as a traveling companion might prove to be very entertaining.

The next morning, Sharla didn't bother to put on powder and rouge, nor did she bother to fetch her earrings from the riverbank. At first, she was a little leery, worried that in daylight Lance might recognize her. But her worries were quickly dispelled, for Lance showed no signs of recognition. He knew, of course, why she had decided to discard her disguise. Her decision pleased him, for her face was much lovelier without the powder and rouge.

They ate a quick breakfast, broke camp, and were soon back on the road. The morning air was cool, for the sun hadn't yet warmed the landscape. Sharla wore her jacket, but she knew she would shed it by the noon hour. The mornings and nights were a little chilly, but by midday the temperatures were quite warm.

"There's a traders' store about two hours' ride from here," Lance told Sharla. "It's also a waystation for stages, where the proprietor and his wife feed the driver and his passengers. We'll stop there. We need to replenish our supplies, and the horses could use some oats."

Sharla wasn't looking forward to stopping. She remembered too well what had happened at the last waystation.

Lance sensed her thoughts. "It'll be different this time. Without all that face paint . . . ? Well, you look very lovely and very—"

"Respectable?" Sharla cut in.

Actually, he had been about to say "innocent," but he decided to agree with her. "Yes, you look quite respectable."

Her sudden smile was warm and enticing. "I suppose you are wondering why I'm no longer wearing powder and rouge."

He raised a brow, as though totally mystified. "Well, it did cross my mind."

"I've decided to be more cooperative." She felt she owed him some kind of explanation. After all, for days she had stubbornly refused to stop layering her face.

"Your cooperation is appreciated," Lance said. "Flaunting your profession was going to get me, or some unlucky devil, killed."

"Fighting for my honor?"

"It's a little late for that, isn't it?" He watched her closely, amused to find that she had backed herself into a corner. He waited for her retort.

She resorted to a defiant tilt of her chin, met his eyes, and replied crisply, "I have turned over a new leaf. Falling in love with Bill has changed everything."

"I'm glad to hear that," he said. "Bill's crazy about you, but I don't guess I have to tell you how he feels. Maybe we should stop at the next town, wire him, and ask him to meet us halfway."

"No!" Sharla blurted out.

Lance pretended surprise. "Why not? Aren't you anxious to see him?"

"Of course I am. But . . . but I prefer to wait and see him at his ranch."

"Whatever you say," he replied, as though willing to please. He chuckled inwardly. He also berated himself good-naturedly for being such a skunk.

Their conversation became impersonal and sporadic, and stayed that way as they covered the miles to the traders' store. The building, constructed of logs, sat a short distance from the road. A corral and a barn were located at the rear. Behind them the clearing extended to include a vegetable garden.

Four hounds leapt from the porch, and greeted them with friendly barks as they reined in.

"I've known the owner and his wife a long time," Lance told Sharla, dismounting and petting the hounds, who were competing for his attention. "Merle and his wife, Wanda, have lived here as long as I've known them. I always stop by on my way back and forth from St. Louis."

Sharla got down from her horse, and looped the reins about the hitching rail. The friendly hounds now turned to her for attention, and she laughed at their playfulness as she gave each one a gentle pat on the head.

The door suddenly swung open, and a burly, middle-aged man hurried outside. "Lance!" he said excitedly. "I saw you ride up. I've got news for you!"

"Can't it wait until we get inside? I'd like a cup of coffee, and I sure hope Wanda has baked one of her delicious apple pies." He took Sharla's arm, and drew her to his side. "Merle, this is Miss Lawrence."

Despite Merle's excitement, he responded politely. "How do you do, ma'am?" he said, then quickly turned back to Lance. "There was a stranger here about three hours ago. He was riding your palomino."

Lance tensed. "Are you sure it was my palomino?"

"I'd know that horse anywhere. And even if I didn't, I'd recognize that scar on its rump." Merle and his wife had known Slade before his family was murdered. Back then, he had ridden a magnificent palomino a gift from his father.

"The stranger left about three hours ago?" Lance asked.

"Yes, and he was headed west."

"Merle, do you mind if I leave Miss Lawrence with you and Wanda? I'll be back for her as soon as I can."

"Leave me?" Sharla exclaimed.

"I shouldn't be gone long."

"No!" she said firmly. "I can't stay!" Waiting here for Lance was too risky. Too many travelers frequented this place, and if one or more of them was from St. Louis, they might have seen the wanted poster! What if they recognized her?

But the wanted poster on Sharla was not on Lance's mind. The rider of the palomino could very well be one of the men who had killed his family. There was no force strong enough to keep him from his pursuit. He was a man obsessed with revenge, and as a vision of his murdered family flashed across his mind, he turned granite-hard eyes in Sharla's direction.

"I don't have time to argue with you!" he told her testily.

Then, without warning, his demeanor softened. He squeezed her hand gently, and said with a halfway smile, "Merle and Wanda will take care of you. You'll be all right." With that, he went to his horse, mounted, and galloped away without a backward glance.

Sharla was dumbfounded. Knowing nothing about his family, she couldn't imagine why he had left her behind. Alone, vulnerable, and without her disguise, she was suddenly very afraid.

Twelve

Merle opened the front door and waited for Sharla to precede him. She went inside; her emotions somewhat numb. She could hardly believe that Lance had left her behind.

Merle introduced her to his wife, a middle-aged, plump woman with a friendly face. She invited Sharla to sit at the table, then went into the kitchen to get her guest a cup of coffee. Merle followed, and told her that Miss Lawrence would be staying with them until Lance came back.

Wanda returned to Sharla with the coffee, sat at the table, and said, "Merle mentioned that you'll be staying. I want you to know that you're more than welcome. Lance shouldn't be gone long."

"Why did he leave?" Sharla asked. "I can't believe he left me like this!"

Wanda glanced up at her husband. Married over thirty years, they understood the other's thoughts simply by looking at each other. They knew Lance as a very private person, and it would seem that he hadn't told his traveling companion about his family. They didn't feel it was their place to tell her, for Lance might not approve.

"Miss Lawrence," Merle said, pulling out a chair and sitting. "How well do you know Lance?"

"We only met a few days ago. He's taking me to . . ." She paused. It was time to lie again, and she hated lying to these people. "He's taking me to Texas to marry his cousin."

"Bill?" Wanda asked.

"Yes. Do you know him?"

"He always stops here on his way to St. Louis. He visits his parents twice a year." She reached over and patted Sharla's hand. "I'm happy for Bill. It's about time he found a wife. If only Lance would do the same. But I have a feeling that man's determined to spend his days wanderin'."

At that moment, the front door opened. They turned and watched as an elderly woman stepped inside. She was accompanied by a man whose frame was as big as a lumberjack's.

Merle and Wanda got up to greet their guests. They said they needed breakfast and supplies. Merle led them to the table, as Wanda went to the kitchen. The woman handed Merle a list of supplies, and he left to fill the order.

"Good morning," the woman said to Sharla. "My name's Mary Simmons." She indicated the man with her, who was seated across the table. "This is Hiram Jones."

"How do you do?" Sharla replied. She swallowed heavily. Time to lie again. "My name's Trish Lawrence."

Mary now studied her intently, as though she found her very interesting. Such intent scrutiny made Sharla uneasy. Was the woman from St. Louis, and had she seen the wanted poster? Had she suddenly recognized her? Or was she staring at her because she was wearing trousers? Did she think such attire unbecoming on a woman?

A warm smile appeared on Mary's face, and her gaze became less intense. "Excuse me for staring, dear. But you seem troubled. Are you?"

"A little," she murmured. She breathed somewhat easier. Maybe the woman hadn't seen the poster. "Where are you from?" Sharla asked, hoping she hadn't arrived here from St. Louis.

"I'm from a small town about twenty-five miles from here. You've probably never heard of it. It's so small that it isn't even on the map. I'm on my way to San Antonio. I have a brother there; he's the blacksmith. I was living on the farm with my son and his family, but I decided I needed a change. My brother was widowed a few months back, and I reckon he could use my help. My son and his family sure don't need me for anything."

Sharla guessed the woman to be in her mid-seventies; she hoped the trip wouldn't be too hard on her. "Are you traveling by wagon?" she asked.

"I have a covered wagon, four strong horses, and Hiram to drive the team."

"I'm going to San Antonio, too."

"You don't say!" she exclaimed. She glanced about the room, as though looking for someone. "Who are you traveling with?"

"A friend, but he left. He asked me to stay here until he got back." She suspected Lance was hunting a bounty; she could think of no other reason why he was so determined to leave. Collecting a reward meant more to him than staying with her. He had apparently crossed paths with this man before, for he had stolen Lance's palomino. Or maybe there was no bounty, and Lance's only motive was to reclaim his horse. Either possibility flamed Sharla's anger. He shouldn't have left her like this! An idea suddenly occurred to her. She thought it over for a minute or so, then decided to go through with it.

"Mrs. Simmons—" she began.

"Mary," the woman cut in.

Sharla smiled congenially. "Mary, I don't want to wait here for my friend. May I travel with you? I'll pay my part of the expenses."

"Of course you can come along. But what about your friend? How can you leave him?"

A testy frown furrowed Sharla's brow. "He had no

qualms about leaving me! Besides, we aren't really friends." Her scowl deepened. Another fib was about to emerge, "My fiancé asked Mr. Slade to escort me to Texas. When Slade returns to find me gone, he'll probably be relieved that he's no longer responsible for me. You see, he doesn't like me very much and . . . and I can barely tolerate him."

Sharla looked across the table at Mary's companion. "Mr. Jones, do you care if I travel with you and Mary? I don't want to impose."

The man shrugged his powerful shoulders. "It don't matter none to me. I'm just a hired driver."

"Hiram was doing some work for my son," Mary explained. "When I knew I was going to make this trip, I hired him as a driver."

Hiram eyed Mary dubiously. The woman's decision to move to San Antonio had been made quite unexpectedly. Her son and his wife had been dumbfounded; he, himself had been amazed. He knew the old woman had lived on that farm for over fifty years, then, out of the clear, she made up her mind to leave. Although her son had tried, there was no talking her out of it. But her reason for leaving didn't really matter to Hiram; he was simply a little curious. He was, however, glad that she had hired him as a driver, for he intended to make the most of a fortunate situation.

Sharla turned back to Mary. "Are you sure you don't mind if I travel with you?"

"Heavens no, I don't mind! I'll enjoy your company."

Merle, having filled Mary's order, brought a fresh pot of coffee and cups to the table. "Your breakfast will be ready in a few minutes," he told his guests.

"I've decided to leave with these people," Sharla said to Merle. "They are going in my direction. Tell Lance that I didn't feel like sitting around and waiting for him to return. If you don't mind, I'll leave the mule and our supplies. They belong to Lance; he paid for them."

"Miss Lawrence, are you sure you want to do this? Lance won't be gone all that long. I'm sure he expects you to be here when he gets back."

"Lance Slade is not my keeper. I am free to do as I please, and I please to leave with these kind people. You can quote that to Mr. Slade."

"Yes, ma'am," Merle replied. He had a feeling that Lance was not going to like this, but there was nothing he could do. He couldn't very well force the young lady to stay.

"As soon as we have breakfast," Mary began, "we'll be on our way." Again, she looked very closely at Sharla, and her hand, wrinkled with age, squeezed Sharla's gently. "By the time we reach San Antonio, we'll be good friends."

Sharla had taken an instant liking to Mary, and she found herself looking forward to spending time with her. As her hand returned Mary's gentle squeeze, she suddenly experienced a strange sensation. She couldn't quite define the feeling, but it was as though she and this woman had already bonded.

Sharla tied her mare to the back of the wagon, and joined Mary beneath the canvas top, where they were sheltered from the sun as Hiram drove the team. Sharla knew going by wagon was a lot slower than traveling horseback; therefore, there was a good possibility that eventually Lance would catch up to them. But she wasn't sure if he would even try. He would probably be relieved to be rid of her. After all, he had made it clear from the very beginning that he was opposed to taking her to Texas. She cleared her mind of Lance. Thinking about him always sent her emotions into turmoil.

A pine rocker was inside the wagon, and that's where

Mary sat. Sharla had chosen to sit on a stack of blankets at Mary's feet.

The woman caressed the arms of the rocker, and her expression turned dreamy as she murmured, "My husband made this chair for me. He presented it to me on our wedding night. I wasn't about to leave it behind."

"Is your husband dead?"

"He's been gone now over twenty years. He died in the war. He was too dadgum old to join the Army, but my Ezra never could turn down a fight. 'Sides, he was originally from Tennessee, and he believed his homeland needed him. He was already in his fifties, but he wasn't about to let that stop him. He was still as spry as a man in his thirties. Age didn't stop him; it was a Yankee cannon."

"Were you living in Missouri?"

"Yes, I was. Ezra and I bought our farm years before the war. My son was also in the Army. Thank God I didn't lose him, too."

"Did you have only one child?"

"Had four altogether. I buried two sons before their first birthdays. My youngest was a daughter."

"Where is she?"

"She lives in St. Louis. But enough about me. Tell me about yourself."

Sharla didn't want to talk about her life, for it would all be lies. She liked this woman too much to deceive her. She was nearly tempted to tell her the truth—that she was a fugitive. But caution held her back. It was too soon; she didn't really know Mary Simmons.

"If you don't mind, I'd rather not talk about myself. Maybe later . . . ?"

"I didn't mean to pry. Honey, if you don't feel free to talk about yourself, then that's fine with me."

"Thank you," Sharla murmured. She felt at ease in Mary's presence, for she exuded a grandmotherly aura that wrapped itself about Sharla like a warm cocoon.

As the wagon steadily rolled away the miles, the women talked about the war, San Antonio, and trivial matters. Sharla said nothing about her personal life, and Mary, true to her word, didn't press her.

The sun had passed its meridian when Hiram drew back on the reins and brought the horses to a halt. He announced that it was time for lunch, then he jumped to the ground and helped the ladies down from the wagon.

They had cold biscuits and honey, for they preferred not to waste time building a fire. Sharla had spread a blanket, and she and Mary sat there as they ate lunch. Hiram sat alone in the shade of a tree.

"Mr. Jones isn't very friendly, is he?" Sharla asked Mary, her voice lowered so Hiram couldn't overhear.

"I've only known him about two months. Like I said earlier, he worked for my son. He's always been quiet and keeps to himself. He's kind of strange, but he's a good worker. When I offered to pay him to drive me to San Antonio, he was real polite about accepting. My son had reservations about me leaving with him because Hiram's so . . . so different. But I've met other men like Hiram. Just because he's quiet and standoffish doesn't mean he isn't trustworthy."

Sharla, finished eating, opened a canteen and poured two cups of water. She handed one to Mary, then glanced up at the sky. Clouds were gathering in the west, and they appeared a little ominous. "It looks as though we're in for rain," she observed.

The sun directly overhead was bright, and Mary shaded her eyes with her hand as she peered toward the horizon. "It's that time of year when we get a lot of rain." She turned her gaze back to Sharla. "You aren't scared of storms, are you?"

"Of course not. I was just thinking about Mr. Slade. We can find shelter inside the wagon, but he'll be in the open."

"Why are you so concerned? I thought you said that you can barely tolerate the man."

"He's a rude skunk, a bounty hunter, and can be totally insufferable. However, there's also a gentle side to him. I certainly wish him no harm." She shrugged her shoulders, as though she were shrugging Lance aside. "I don't even know why I thought about him. He's nothing to me."

Mary suspected otherwise, but she didn't say anything. However, she felt if her companion was falling in love with this man, then she should stand firm and face her feelings instead of running away from them.

As Hiram stood, ambled to the wagon and got his rifle, neither woman paid him any mind. They didn't really notice him until he approached their blanket, his weapon in hand. He didn't aim the rifle, but cradled it in his arms and said to Mary, "I'm takin' that money you got stashed in the wagon. I know you got it hid in a tobacco can."

Sharla bounded to her feet, and gave Mary a hand up. The elderly woman leaned against her young companion as though she were too weak in the knees to stand alone.

"You lowdown, lying sneak!" Mary exclaimed, shocked. "I can't believe you are doing this!"

His grin resembled a sneer. "Believe it, old woman. Now get me that tobacco can."

"That's all the money I have. It's my life's savings!"

"I don't give a damn how many years it took you to get it. I just care how long it's gonna take me to get it away from you. And you're wastin' my time standin' here talkin'. Do you want me to tear that wagon apart lookin' for that tobacco can, or do you intend to hand it over?" He turned an angry gaze to Sharla. "Or better yet, maybe I'll just knock her around until you do as I say."

"No!" Mary cried. "Don't touch her! I'll give you the money."

"I thought you'd cooperate." He waved a hand toward the wagon. "Let's go."

He followed the women to the lowered backboard, then ordered Sharla to help Mary inside. She returned momentarily, and she had the tobacco can with her. Sharla offered Mary her arm and assisted her to the ground.

Grabbing the can, Hiram opened it and checked the contents. He then turned to Sharla and asked, "Where's your money? And don't tell me you ain't got none 'cause I know better. You done offered to help with expenses. Hand over what you got or I'll knock this old woman to the ground so hard that she might never get up."

Part of the money Maxine had insisted that she accept was in Sharla's pocket. She reached inside, withdrew the bills, and gave them to Hiram. "Take it!" she spat. "I swear to God if my path ever crosses with yours again, you're going to regret doing this!"

He laughed harshly. "Little lady, you got me quaking in my boots. I ain't never been so scared." He was still laughing as he untied Sharla's mare. He swung into the saddle, his leg grazing her new Winchester, then headed west at a fast gallop. That he stole her horse and rifle enraged Sharla even more. However, she knew that she and Mary weren't totally without protection, for she had seen a shotgun inside the wagon.

"My son was right," Mary groaned. Her eyes were still on the fleeing thief whose image would soon be a mote on the horizon. "I didn't know Hiram well enough to trust him. I should have used better judgment. If only I hadn't been so overly eager to leave."

"Why were you so anxious?"

"Once I made up my mind to leave the farm, I didn't see any reason to dally." There was more to it than that, but she wasn't about to tell Sharla. She purposely changed the subject. "Well, what are we going to do now? We're alone without a penny to our names."

"We aren't exactly penniless," Sharla replied. "Hiram

didn't get all my money." She had more stashed in her carpetbag, along with her hidden jewelry.

"I don't feel right about this," Mary said miserably. "You shouldn't have to pay for this trip. I feel as though I'm taking charity."

"Nonsense," Sharla was quick to say. "The wagon and the horses are yours. You've already paid your part." She laid a consoling hand on the woman's arm, and asked gently, "How much money did you have?"

"A little over four hundred dollars. That money and my belongings inside the wagon are all I have to show for a lifetime of labor."

Sharla's anger stirred again. She despised Hiram Jones. Anyone who could steal an old woman's savings was the scum of the earth. She seriously hoped she would see him again; next time she wouldn't be taken unawares. Quite the contrary, she'd be armed and ready to deal with him.

"We might as well move on," Sharla said. "I'll drive the team."

"Have you ever driven a team?"

"No, but it can't be that difficult." She smiled encouragingly. "I'll consider it learning firsthand."

"I know how to drive a team. It's been years, but I can still teach you. I'd handle the horses myself if I was younger and stronger.

"Was Hiram using a map?"

"Yes, he was. Our route is marked; all we have to do is follow it."

"Then let's get started. We don't want to waste time."

They broke camp, then climbed up onto the wagon's seat. Mary sat beside Sharla and instructed her on handling the four-horse team.

The approaching storm grew closer, and menacing thunder could now be heard. Rain clouds, propelled by a brisk wind, traveled quickly across the darkening sky.

Sharla's nerves tightened. She hoped the horses didn't

fear lightning and thunder. If they were to panic, how could she, a novice driver, control a frightened team?

As Sharla was worrying about controlling the horses, Maxine, enclosed in her office with Jerome Bailey, was waiting for the man to deliver his report. She wasn't expecting an informative statement from the private detective, for she hadn't given him much information on Claudia's parents.

"I checked the courthouse records," Bailey began. "The marriage between Jacob Wilkens and Alice Donaldson was on file. The application for the marriage license was also on file. I got what information I could use, then started making inquiries. Alice and Jacob had one child: Claudia. They hadn't been married very long when Alice was left on her own. She became a domestic servant. She and her daughter lived in more than one estate. Claudia attended public school until she was sixteen. Then she also became a servant . . ."

"I know all this," Maxine cut in. "Tell me about Jacob. Did you learn anything about him?"

"Yes, I did," he replied with a pleased smile. He took pride in his work and the fact that he was always successful. "What I'm about to tell you is somewhat shocking. Jacob Wilkens died in the insane asylum. He was locked in a ward for the violently insane. He didn't exactly desert his wife and daughter. He went berserk and the law had him put away. I imagine Alice told Claudia that he deserted them because she didn't want her to know the truth."

Maxine was astounded. "What caused him to go insane?"

"I have several important connections, and through them I was able to obtain Jacob's medical papers. The doctors affiliated with his case believed his insanity was hereditary. Maybe they were right; who knows for sure?

Doctors don't know much about the human mind and how it works. They questioned Jacob, experimented on him, then locked him away for good. He died five years ago, his mind completely gone."

"My God!" Maxine cried softly. "What if Claudia has inherited her father's insanity?"

"What makes you think that? Does the girl act strangely or violently?"

"I think she committed a very violent act," Maxine replied. "However, I must ask you to keep this conversation confidential."

"You have my professional word," he assured her. A folder was in his lap, and he placed it on Maxine's desk. "This is my written report"—he smiled charmingly— "along with my bill."

As she opened the file, a knock sounded at the door. She left her chair to answer it. It was one of her bartenders reporting that trouble was brewing in the poker room. One player had accused another of cheating. Maxine knew it was vital that she quickly restore peace, for an argument over a card game could very well end in a duel. Bailey offered to go with her, and they followed the bartender back to the poker room.

Maxine didn't usually make mistakes, but because of this unexpected crisis the detective's written report, now exposed on her desk, completely slipped her mind.

Thirteen

Claudia, looking for Maxine, left her bedroom and started down the stairs. She didn't rush, for she was in no hurry. She intended to talk to Maxine about a new wardrobe. Trish's clothes were fine, but she wanted her own things. Claudia was well pleased with her new employment. This morning she had slept late, had breakfast in bed, then soaked leisurely in a bathtub filled with perfumed bubbles. Thus far, Dexter had requested every evening and had been her only customer. He hadn't said that he would see her tonight, and she supposed she would entertain someone else, maybe even two or three men before the evening was over. She wasn't apprehensive, for she now had confidence in her ability to please. After all, Dexter had returned every night, and he never left until well after dawn.

A smile curved her lips as she left the stairs and moved toward Maxine's office. She had a strong feeling that prostitution was her forte. That she had worked as a maid drawing small wages now inflamed her. She had been a fool to waste her talents and her body on domestic work and ungrateful lovers—especially James Rayfield. Well, she was a lot smarter now and no man would ever take advantage of her again.

The door to Maxine's office was slightly ajar. Claudia rapped softly and opened it wider. There was no one inside. Deciding to wait for her employer, she went into the room and sat in the chair facing the desk. She saw the open folder, and it caught her attention. Curious, she moved it at an angle that made it easier for her to scan it. She never dreamed that it concerned her; she was simply being nosy. Soon, however, she became very interested in the document. She leapt to her feet, picked up the written statement and read every word, her eyes glazed with shock and her heart pounding rapidly. She read it a second time, as though an added scan would somehow change its contents.

She carefully placed the folder in the exact position that she had found it, turned around, walked out of the office and up the stairs to her room. She moved stiffly, her mind in shock and her emotions in turmoil.

She closed her door, locked it, then stood in front of her dresser, staring at her reflection as though she were viewing a stranger. She leaned in closer, peered deeply into her own eyes and searched for a sign of madness. She saw nothing except a look of shock.

She started pacing back and forth. Her father had died in an insane asylum. She could hardly believe that she had read such a startling statement. It couldn't be true! It just couldn't!

Her pacing stopped abruptly. Tears smarted her eyes, and her body suddenly went limp, as though she had given in to defeat. In a way she had, for somewhere deep inside, she knew every word in the report was probably true. She had memories of her father. They were few and had dimmed with time, but she did clearly remember his violent temper. She had been afraid of him, and so had her mother.

She returned to the mirror, and spoke firmly to her reflection. "Just because my father was crazy doesn't mean I am! I'm not like him. I'm not!" An image of James, his body covered with blood, flashed across her mind. She had killed like a raving maniac! She didn't really remember stabbing him over and over. The actual killing she had managed to block from memory. It had been too brutal, too bloody, to remember without . . . ?

"Without losing my mind," she murmured aloud. Her fear turned to anger, and her arm swung out viciously, knocking perfume bottles, a box of powder, a jar of rouge, and other small articles from the dresser top onto the floor. The plush carpet cushioned their falls; nothing was broken.

Her tantrum now in full swing, she stormed to her bed and ripped off the spread and sheets, throwing them to the floor, then stamping on them as though they were living matter. Rage burned in her eyes, and her face was so distorted with anger that she looked very much like a woman violently insane.

She stopped mauling the covers, fell across the bed and pounded the pillows with her fists. She continued her assault until, finally, her fury began to wane. Her emotions settled and rationality returned. That she had thrown such a violent tantrum didn't really concern her; she had experienced them for years. Despite what she had just learned about her father, she refused to connect her uncontrolled temper to his insanity. She wasn't crazy. Of that, she was certain!

She remade her bed, then put everything back on the dresser. She returned to pacing, her mind on Maxine instead of her father. Why had the woman delved so deeply into her life? She could understand an employer's interest in a new employee, but this was going entirely too far. Maxine was up to something, but she hadn't a clue what it might be. She supposed she should have been suspicious of Maxine from the very beginning. She now doubted that the woman had spotted her in town and was so impressed with her beauty that she had gone to the trouble of learning her identity, sending for her, then offering her a job so unrelated to that of a maid's.

She concentrated intently. Maxine had a motive, but what could it possibly be? She had never done anything to the woman. She didn't even know her until lately. Why had she gone to such lengths to hire her, and why was she probing into her past? Could this possibly have anything to do with James Rayfield? The questions, unanswered, swirled through Claudia's mind.

She cast the questions aside. There was no solution to the puzzle. Rather, there was no solution at the moment. She certainly intended to find the answers—one way or another! She would stay on guard, keep her ears open, and take advantage of any opportunity that might arise.

She turned back to the mirror and spoke again to her reflection. "I'll find out what's going on." Again, her murdered victim came to mind, and her eyes glazed over with an expression that was frightening. Such craze escaped Claudia, for she was blind to her own madness.

"If James's murder has anything to do with Maxine hiring me," Claudia swore, "then she'll be sorry she tried to trick me. I'll make her good and sorry!"

Sharla's arms ached, for controlling the four-horse team was not only tiring, but getting more difficult by the moment. The storm was now very close, and the intermittent lightning, followed by loud claps of thunder, was making the horses very skittish and extremely hard to handle.

"We'd better stop and tether the horses," Mary suggested.

Suddenly another streak of lightning flashed overhead, and thunder proceeded almost immediately. The team nearly bolted. It took all of Sharla's strength to hold them in check, then guide them off the road and bring the wagon to a halt.

"There's rope in back," Mary said as she climbed over the seat to get it. Returning quickly, she stepped back over the seat with the agility of a woman several years younger.

Sharla secured the brake, then she and Mary got down from the wagon, and as they worked together, Mary told Sharla how to properly tether the horses. The experience was a little frightening for Sharla, for the horses were terribly nervous, and that she might be kicked was a distinct possibility. Bright lightning ripped across the sky, accompanied by a bass rumble of thunder.

The wind picked up, and rain began to fall. It fell in heavy sheets, soaking both women before they could complete their tasks and seek shelter inside the wagon. Drenched, they discarded their wet apparel and wrapped themselves in blankets.

"You did real good," Mary told Sharla, huddled inside her blanket, for the rain had left her chilled.

"Pardon?" Sharla questioned.

"Tethering the horses," Mary explained. "It's a dangerous job. A lot of young women couldn't have done it. They would have been too afraid."

"I was afraid," Sharla admitted.

"Yes, but that didn't stop you. You're very brave, probably a lot braver than you realize."

"I never really thought of myself as being brave."

"Did you ever consider that you come from brave stock?"

"I wouldn't know. You see, I was an orphan. I never knew my family."

"Did you grow up in an orphanage, or were you adopted?" Mary already knew the answer; she only asked because it was the polite thing to do. She knew a lot about Sharla's life, but she couldn't tell her this. Like Sharla, she was held captive by deceit.

"I was never adopted," Sharla replied. She didn't say

any more, for she couldn't tell Mary about Olivia, since she was supposed to be Trish Lawrence.

Mary could see that she was uncomfortable with the subject, so she decided to change it. "Do you now wish you had stayed at the waystation and waited for Mr. Slade?"

"No," she replied honestly. "I'm glad I came with you. If I hadn't come along, I think Hiram would still have stolen your money. You'd be alone."

Mary turned her face away. She didn't want Sharla to see the tears in her eyes. She was deeply touched by Sharla's compassion and generosity. She fought the compulsion to take her into her arms and explain why their encounter had been somewhat unexpected, but certainly not all that surprising.

As the storm unleashed its fury, cracking the sky with lightning and resonating the earth with deafening thunder, Mary lay back on her pallet and closed her eyes. Although her body was tired, her thoughts were as turbulent as the raging weather. She longed desperately to tell Sharla who she really was, but she couldn't do that without betraying Hattie. She supposed it would also be a betrayal against Maxine. But it wasn't Maxine whom she was trying to protect. Hattie had her loyalty and her concern lay with Sharla.

She was entangled in a web that she had never weaved, a web that had imprisoned her for several years. However, she knew she wasn't without blame, for she had allowed it to happen. She suddenly felt very ashamed, and she didn't like herself very much. She wondered if she should make amends and set everything right. She had to do so soon, for she didn't want to carry such guilt to her grave.

Gradually, fatigue became stronger than Mary's troubled mind, and she drifted into sleep.

The wagon was now rocking beneath the wind's force as though it was a ship adrift on a raging sea. Sharla was somewhat frightened and wondered if the storm was really a tornado about to suck them into its deadly funnel. She looked at Mary, who didn't seem in the least afraid. In fact, she appeared to be asleep.

Sharla, deciding to think about something besides the storm, delved into her carpetbag and withdrew a blouse and a riding skirt. Her trousers and shirt were soaking wet. She hated returning to such flashy apparel, but she was left with no other choice.

She dressed quickly, then brushed her damp hair and drew the long tresses away from her face, securing them in place with a silk ribbon.

The pouring rain let up quite suddenly, turning into a fine drizzle. At the same time, the wind died down considerably. The lightning and thunder eventually passed, and birds left their shelters to twerp musically at the sun's return.

Sharla checked on Mary, and found that she was still asleep. Not wanting to disturb her, she left the wagon and managed to untether the horses. By now the rain had stopped, and she climbed up on the seat, released the brake, and guided the team back onto the road.

The wagon's movement roused Mary, and she was soon dressed and sitting beside Sharla.

"You should have awakened me. I could have helped."

"As you can see, I managed just fine. Besides, you need your rest."

Mary's eyes swept over Sharla's attire. The skirt was bright purple and the violet-colored blouse was so thin that her lace chemise was clearly visible.

Sharla attempted to excuse her apparel: "I realize this blouse is inappropriate. That's why I was wearing trousers and a shirt. As soon as they are dry, I'll change back into them. I suppose you are wondering why I even own such a . . . a revealing blouse. I wish I could explain, but I can't."

Mary patted her hand. "You owe me no explanations, my dear."

They had come to a fork in the road, and Sharla suddenly sat up straighter, arching her neck to look over the horses' heads. "Look!" she pointed out. "Aren't those hoof prints?"

Mary could see them also, for the prints were clearly defined in the muddy terrain.

Sharla stopped the team, and leapt to the ground. Dense shrubbery bordered the road, and several of the bushes were bent and twisted, as though someone had crawled into them for shelter. Boot tracks and horse prints were located next to the foliage.

Sharla turned and looked back at Mary. "I bet Hiram stopped here to wait out the storm." She indicated the road heading north. "It appears as though he went that way."

She hurried back to the wagon, climbed up onto the seat and took out the map. She studied it carefully. "That road leads to a small town. It's only a few miles from here and that's probably where he's headed."

"What do you have in mind?" Mary asked.

"We're going after him."

"That could be dangerous."

"Dangerous or not, I intend to get our money back. He also has my horse and rifle."

Mary was very proud of her companion, for she admired courage and grit. "Let's get him!" she said, waving an enthusiastic fist.

Sharla guided the team onto the road Hiram had taken. She, in turn, was impressed with her partner. Despite Mary's age, she was mighty feisty.

"Taking this detour is going to put us a day or more behind," Sharla said.

"We have plenty of time," Mary replied.

But Sharla knew she didn't really have time to spare.

There might be wanted posters traveling behind her, and she needed to stay ahead of them. Pursuing Hiram was risky, and in the long run, it could cost her her freedom. However, she didn't veer their course; that Hiram had stolen Mary's life's savings was the deciding factor that drove her. She wasn't sure how she'd deal with the man when she confronted him, but she did intend to be armed.

"Is that shotgun in the wagon loaded?" she asked Mary.

"Both barrels," she replied.

"I'm experienced with a rifle, but I've never fired a shotgun."

"There's nothing to it. You just aim it in the general direction and fire. You can't miss with a shotgun, that's why it's a good weapon. But you gotta be fairly close to your target."

"I don't want to kill Hiram, I only want back what he stole from us."

"My Ezra used to say that you never aim a gun at someone unless you're willing to use it."

"I don't think I'm capable of shooting Hiram or anyone else."

"Not even in self-defense?"

"I don't know," she murmured. "I guess that's something I will never know unless I'm faced with it."

"Maybe we should forget Hiram, and turn back around. We might be biting off more than we can chew."

"No!" Sharla remarked. "We can do this! He stole from us because we're women, and he figured we'd be too scared to do anything about it. Well, we're going to prove him wrong! Are you with me or not?"

She clasped Sharla's hand and shook it firmly. "I'm with you!"

Two hours later, Lance arrived at the fork in the road. As he studied the wheel tracks left behind, a puzzled frown furrowed his brow. Why had Sharla and the others changed their course? He had no way of knowing that the women were now alone, for the rain had washed away the tracks Hiram had left when he stole their money and fled.

Looking about the area, Lance found two different boot prints, along with signs of a horse's hooves. His gaze followed the horse tracks. They led north, which was the same direction the wagon had taken. He observed the area more and noted the twisted and bent shrubbery. Concern suddenly gnawed at him, for he had a feeling that something was wrong.

Leading the pack mule, he started down the track-laden road. Wanting to catch up to the wagon before dark, he urged his stallion into a brisk gallop. The mule brayed a complaint, then matched its strides to those of the horse's.

Lance could hardly believe that Sharla had taken off with two strangers. However, he blamed himself. He shouldn't have left her without explaining why. But he had considered time of the essence, and wanted to hunt down the man on the palomino without a moment's delay. Traveling speedily, it had taken him only a couple of hours to spot his prey, for along the way the man had stopped for a long nap.

The man spotted him at the same time, reined in, and as he kept a cautious hand close to his holstered pistol, he waited for the stranger to ride in closer.

When Lance was within range, he halted and asked the man where he had gotten the palomino. He told Lance that he had bought the horse at a public auction. Carefully delving into his shirt pocket, the man removed a badge identifying himself as a U.S. marshal.

Lance rode to the lawman's side and explained why he had followed him. A close examination of the palomino proved that Merle had been mistaken. The horse had never belonged to Lance. However, the scar on its rump was similar to the one on Lance's palomino. Merle's error was understandable.

Lance thanked the marshal for his cooperation, then returned to the waystation to find that Sharla had left with a man and a woman in a covered wagon. He remained long enough to eat lunch and buy more supplies.

He wasn't on the trail very long when the storm hit. Seeking shelter on the side of the road, he covered himself with a blanket and waited for the tempest to pass.

Now, as he followed the wagon tracks at a steady gallop, concern for Sharla still gnawed at him. The feeling wouldn't go away. He grew more uneasy by the minute and was tempted to leave the mule behind and race his stallion down the road. That, of course, was not logical. The horse would merely tire, then he'd be forced to hole up and rest the exhausted steed. A steady but untiring pace was his only choice.

The wheel tracks were fresh, and he figured he'd come upon the wagon within a couple of hours. That did little to soothe his concern. A lot could happen in two hours.

Fourteen

Dusk was settling over the small town as Sharla and Mary traveled down its main street. Two stores, a barbershop, and a post office, which also served as a stage depot, were located on the east and west sides of the road. There was also a sheriff's office, and directly across the street was a saloon. Not very many people were mingling about, for it was the time when most families were having dinner.

Sharla's horse was tied at the hitching rail in front of the saloon. She recognized it immediately, for her Winchester was encased inside the leather sheath. She steered the team to the side of the road, pulled up close to the saloon, and secured the brake.

"That's my mare," she said to Mary. "Hiram must be inside. You stay here; I'll be back as soon as I can."

She started to leave, but Mary placed a halting hand on her arm. "What do you think you're doing?" she exclaimed. "You can't confront a man like Hiram alone. Let's get the sheriff."

Sharla preferred not to involve the sheriff. She was a fugitive and he might ask too many questions. Also, a description of her could very well have traveled by wire to every law officer in the region. Bringing in the sheriff might inevitably lead to her own arrest.

"We don't need the sheriff," Sharla said firmly. "It won't take but a minute to reclaim our stolen property, then we'll be on our way. If we involve the sheriff, he'll expect us to stay here and press charges. We could be delayed for days."

Mary nodded. She agreed with Sharla's reason for not wanting to involve the sheriff, but, more importantly, she suddenly remembered that Sharla must avoid all lawmen. That she could have forgotten even for a moment made her feel very foolish.

"All right," she told Sharla. "We'll forget the sheriff. But you aren't going in there alone; I'm coming with you." The loaded shotgun lay at her feet. She reached down and picked it up.

"I won't need that," Sharla said. "Hiram left my rifle on the mare."

"It's not for you, it's for me. Two guns are better than one. Besides, if Hiram tries anything, I'm not sure if you have what it takes to shoot him."

"And I suppose you do?"

"It won't be the first time I filled a varmint with buckshot." With that, Mary left the wagon with her shotgun.

Sharla wrapped the multiple reins about the brake handle, then climbed down to the ground and went to her mare. She slipped her Winchester from its sheath and checked to see if it was still loaded. It was, and cradling the rifle in her arms, she turned and looked at Mary. The elderly woman stood ramrod straight, her face devoid of fear, her demeanor stalwart.

"Are you ready?" Sharla asked.

"As ready as I'll ever be."

Despite Mary's determination, she suddenly seemed very frail to Sharla, and she considered calling the whole thing off. Mary's life's savings and her own money weren't worth risking the elderly woman's health.

As though Mary had read her mind, she moved to the saloon's swinging doors and barged inside with the gusto of a person much younger. A surprised Sharla quickly followed.

The establishment wasn't very crowded. Two tables were occupied, and three patrons stood at the bar. A piano that no one was playing filled a corner of the room. The bartender, who was also the proprietor, was pouring drinks when the two women entered his saloon. The sight of two armed ladies almost caused him to drop the bottle he was holding, and only a quick reflex staved off spilled whiskey. The customers, who were all men, were as startled as the bartender.

Sharla knew that she and Mary were a strange sight. A blush touched her cheeks, for she suddenly realized that she was still wearing the bright-colored skirt and thin fabric blouse. Her apparel, however, was a fleeting thought, for she had spotted Hiram. He was seated at a table with another gentleman. A deck of cards was between them, and bills were neatly stacked in front of each man.

Hiram could hardly believe that the women had hunted him down. Never in his wildest dreams did he imagine that these two would arm themselves and come after him. He figured they had turned the wagon around and were headed back home. Their presence was so amazing that he sat numbly—too incredulous to rise from his chair.

Sharla, with Mary right behind her, moved to Hiram's table, glanced at the cards and said evenly, as though their meeting was casual, "I hope you aren't losing, considering the money isn't yours." She shifted the Winchester so that its barrel was facing Hiram. "Hand it over; all of it!"

Mary and Sharla, their attention riveted on Hiram, didn't notice as one of the customers slipped outside to fetch the sheriff. He almost collided with Lance, who was entering as he was leaving. Standing back, Lance watched the proceedings. A wry grin was on his lips; nevertheless, he was very impressed with Sharla and the woman with her.

Unaware of Lance's arrival, Sharla said again to Hiram, "Give us back our money."

"I don't know what the hell you're talking about," he replied. "You two women are crazy! I ain't never seen either one of you in my life. You got me confused with someone else."

Sharla noticed a carpetbag at his feet. "Is Mary's money still in the tobacco can?"

"What kind of crazy talk is that?"

The man at Hiram's table had remained silent, finding the scene entertaining and the young woman quite extraordinary. A professional gambler, he'd found it easy to take Hiram's money. It hadn't crossed his mind that his winnings might be stolen. He pushed back his chair and got to his feet.

Sharla looked at him for the first time. A Colt .45 was strapped to his hip, and she hoped he wasn't planning to draw it.

The man's sudden movement caused Lance to tense, and his hand hovered above his own holstered weapon.

Holding his hands palms up, the gambler smiled at Sharla and said, "Don't shoot, ma'am." He indicated the carpetbag. "May I look inside?"

"Please do," she replied.

"Why are you askin' her?" Hiram complained. "It's my bag!"

"But it's her tobacco can, and if it's in your bag, then that makes you a thief." He moved around Hiram's chair, knelt, and opened the bag. The tobacco can, still filled with Mary's money, was inside. He stood and held it up for everyone to see. "It seems the lady is telling the truth." He gave the can to Sharla, then scooped up the money on Hiram's side of the table and handed her the bills. Returning to his own cash, he carefully counted out the amount he had won, moved to Sharla, and placed the money in her hand. He smiled charmingly. "Madam, I could not sleep at night knowing I won money stolen from two such gracious ladies."

Sharla pegged him as a man who made his living with a deck of cards. He was no doubt a rogue, but a very likable one. He was also blatantly handsome. He was wearing a tan dress jacket with matching trousers, a white shirt, and well-polished boots. Such fine apparel looked out of place with his drab surroundings. He sported a well-trimmed beard, its shade as sandy-blond as his hair. Brown, twinkling eyes were deeply set under prominent brows, and his features were arresting and almost too delicate for a man's. His tall frame was languid, and he moved with a muscled grace. The stranger was perfect. Sharla could think of no better word to describe him.

The man was waiting eagerly for Sharla to acknowledge him, for she was more intriguing than any lady he had ever encountered. Her bearing was in complete contrast with her flashy clothes, and he found her as mystifying as she was beautiful.

At that moment, the sheriff came inside, accompanied by the gent who had fetched him. "What's going on?" he asked, moving toward Sharla and Mary. Sharla regarded the sheriff warily, wondering if he had seen the wanted poster or read a wire with her description. He showed no signs of having done either one.

The gambler took it upon himself to explain, and waving a hand at Hiram, he said, "This man stole money that belongs to these ladies." He told the sheriff about finding the tobacco can.

"He also stole my horse and rifle," Sharla added. She put her money in her pocket, then handed the can to Mary.

The law officer seemed a little confused, and Mary gave him a detailed account. Lance, still unnoticed by Sharla, listened very closely to Mary's story. He was impressed with the women's courage and determination.

The sheriff turned angry eyes to Hiram, who had said nothing during Mary's lengthy explanation. "Jail's too good for a thieving skunk like you! Robbing an old woman's life's savings! Why, you oughta be strung up and lashed with a whip!" He looked away from Hiram, for he was on the verge of losing his temper. He had been a sheriff for fifteen years, and was too professional to let his personal feelings interfere with his job. He spoke to Sharla and Mary. "If you ladies will come to my office, I'll fill out the necessary papers. The circuit judge will be here next week, and you two will have to testify in court. The judge is strict and has no mercy for thieves like this one. Don't worry, he'll give him the maximum sentence."

"We can't stay," Sharla replied.

The sheriff was surprised. "But if you don't press charges, I can't make an arrest."

"We have our stolen property back, and that's all we wanted."

"If you let this weasel go free, he'll steal from someone else."

"I'm sorry," Sharla murmured. "Staying here is out of the question. It's important that we get back on the road."

The lawman waved his hands testily. "Have it your way, ma'am!"

Sharla looked over to Mary. "Let's go," she urged. Remembering the man who had helped her, she turned back and said, "Thanks for your help."

He bowed obsequiously. "It was an honor to assist such a beautiful lady." He offered Mary a warm smile. "Goodbye, ma'am. And, this time, hold on to that tobacco can."

"Don't worry, I will."

The women started toward the door. Suddenly, however, Sharla stopped dead in her tracks, her attention riveted on the man poised by the entrance. He was simply standing there, watching her.

"Lance!" she gasped. "How long have you been here?"

"Long enough," he replied, his expression indiscernible. He indicated the swinging doors. "Shall we?"

Sharla moved past him briskly, as though his presence didn't faze her. But inwardly she was a little shaken. Mary and Lance followed her outside. Taking the mare, Sharla led her to the wagon, tied her to the backboard, and slipped her rifle back into the leather sheath. In the meantime, Lance helped Mary up onto the wagon seat.

Sharla had just finished sheathing her rifle when Lance came around the corner of the wagon. His gray eyes pinned her with a long, silent scrutiny.

Her patience snapped. "Well, do you have something to say, or do you intend to just leer at me as though I'm a naughty child?"

"A child you certainly aren't," he replied, his eyes now raking her with a fiercely possessive look. Taking her totally unawares, he drew her into his arms and kissed her with an aggressive passion.

For a moment, no longer than a heartbeat, Sharla offered no response, but the breathless wonder of his kiss was soon overpowering. He crushed her body to his, and she trembled in his arms as a small moan of desire came from deep in her throat. She was conscious only of his virile nearness, and the touch of his lips on hers.

Lance released her as suddenly as he had embraced her. He took a hasty step backward, as though he now found it imperative that he not stand too close. Her kiss, so sweet and vulnerable, had stirred feelings in him that he wished to avoid. There was no place in his life for Sharla Matthews; his life was filled to the brim with revenge.

Sharla, her emotions in an upheaval, took a deep, calming breath. Lance's sudden kiss, followed by such an abrupt ending, left her so confused that she didn't know what to say or do.

Lance settled her dilemma. He spanned her waist with his hands and lifted her over the backboard and into the wagon. He went to his horse and mule; they were at the hitching rail. He swung into the saddle, grabbed the reins to the mule, looked back at Sharla and remarked, "I said I'd make this trip with you, and that's what I intend to do. The next time I ask you to stay put—if there is a next time—I hope you'll be more cooperative." He turned his horse away from the hitching rail. "I'll take the lead; you follow in the wagon."

It was on the tip of her tongue not to let him off so easily. She deserved an explanation. How dare he kiss her, then act as though nothing had happened! But Sharla's pride was stronger than her hurt feelings, and she turned away as though she couldn't have cared less. She moved to the front of the wagon, climbed over the seat, and took her place beside Mary. She freed the brake, lifted the reins and slapped them against the team.

With Lance leading the way, they rode down the main street and out of town. Sharla was anxious to put distance between herself and the town's sheriff. Even though he didn't react to her presence, she still felt it was important to avoid the law whenever possible. She didn't doubt that wanted posters were being widely distributed. She knew Dexter Rayfield very well. He was not the type to give up. He'd hunt her down if it took him a lifetime. Her only hope was Maxine. But how, she wondered, could Maxine possibly extract a confession from Claudia? It didn't seem plausible, and Sharla had a sinking feeling that running away would serve no real purpose. She was doomed. It was only a matter of time!

Claudia moved furtively down the hall and to the servants' stairway, which led to the side door that opened into the kitchen. She planned to stand on the bottom step, crack the door an inch, then eavesdrop on anyone who might be inside. Working as a maid, she knew that servants loved to gossip about their employers. She wasn't too hopeful that she'd learn anything of value, for she doubted that, with the exception of Hattie, Maxine's employees would know why their boss had hired a private detective. Claudia suspected that the Negro woman knew just about everything that concerned Maxine.

She reached the bottom step, and eyed the closed door. Her expectations were about as low as they could be, for she seriously doubted that she'd overhear anything regarding her situation. However, she was desperate, and was willing to take her chances, regardless of how remote they might be. She put her hand on the knob, turned it carefully, and opened the door a mere slit. Her eyes immediately lit up with interest, for Maxine's voice was the first to reach her ears. She was talking to Hattie.

"I'll be in my office if you need me."

Hattie was standing at the stove, preparing dinner. "Do you want me to bring you in a tray, or would you rather eat in the dining room?"

Before Maxine could reply, a firm knocking sounded at the back door. She moved to answer it, thinking she was about to admit a customer who wished to avoid detection.

She was startled to find Agnes instead. She quickly waved her inside. "Why are you here? Did anyone see you?"

"Nobody saw me. I made sure of that."

Claudia, listening, recognized Agnes's voice. Her interest deepened, and her pulse began to race with excitement.

"You shouldn't be here," Maxine fretted. "It's too risky. If Dexter or the constable were to see you, it wouldn't take them long to connect me to Sharla."

"I'm sorry," Agnes murmured. "But I'm just so worried about Miss Sharla. It's so hard not knowing anything about her. Is she still here?"

"No, she isn't. I was able to get her safely out of town."

"Have you heard from her?"

"No, that's not possible right now. Later, I expect to hear about her." Maxine, touched by Agnes's grave concern, smiled tenderly and said, "I promise I'll let you know how she's doing."

"Thank you, ma'am. I'll go now. I know I shouldn't be here." She opened the back door and darted outside. Albert, who had driven her in James Rayfield's carriage, was waiting in the shadows.

Maxine turned worried eyes to Hattie. "I certainly hope nobody saw her." Her nerves were tightly strung, and she suddenly felt very tired. "Instead of going to my office, I think I'll go to my room and rest for an hour. Worrying about Sharla keeps me awake at night."

"You do look mighty tired," Hattie observed. She then began to chastise Maxine for not taking better care of herself.

Hattie's chatter drowned out a faint clicking sound as Claudia drew the cracked door to a close, then sped up the steps on feet that moved silently. Reaching her room, she hurried inside and closed the door. She stood perfectly still, as though her body was suddenly gripped with paralysis. Not even her eyes moved. They glared into space, their expression cold, empty—like a dead person's sightless stare.

Her mind, however, was active, and it screamed at her to do something. Maxine had trapped her like a rabbit in a snare. She wondered when the woman intended to move in for the kill.

Slowly, movement returned to her body, and she limped across the room like a wounded animal, sat on the bed, and covered her face with her hands. Surrendering to fear, she cried brokenly until her throat actually ached from such heaving sobs.

Minutes passed, spent in stone silence as Claudia regained control. That Maxine was somehow connected to Sharla was mind-boggling, and made no sense whatsoever.

What, she wondered, did a well-brought-up lady and a prostitute have in common? She could think of nothing.

She was, however, certain that Maxine hired her for only one reason. She must suspect her of killing James and somehow she hoped to prove it.

"Never!" Claudia whispered with quiet rage. "She'll never prove I did it." She left the bed and began to pace nervously. She knew she couldn't stay here much longer; this place was a trap! But where could she go? The thought of returning to domestic work was depressing. She wanted more out of life—money and the self-confidence that came with it.

Her pacing stopped, and renewed tears filled her eyes. Where could she possibly find money and self-confidence except in a house of ill repute? After all, she was just a nobody with a pretty face. That wasn't much to go on, not in a populated place like St. Louis. The city was overflowing with women who had nothing to offer except their good looks. She would only be one in hundreds.

Returning to the bed, she fell across it and once again surrendered to tears. She was not only terribly worried, but she also felt very sorry for herself.

Lance, leaving the road, found a small area surrounded by trees and dense shrubbery. It was the ideal place to camp for the night. He rode back to the wagon and led the way to the clearing.

As the women started supper, Lance tended to the horses and the mule. It didn't take long to prepare a meal. Sharla merely opened a can of stew as Mary brewed the coffee. Little was said over the campfire. Mary made a few failed attempts to start a group conversation, but it soon became obvious that Sharla and Lance were not going to cooperate. The tension between them was so thick, it was almost tangible.

Sharla, wishing to avoid Lance, excused herself directly after supper and sought solitude inside the wagon.

Lance was sitting beside Mary, and she picked up the coffeepot and refilled his cup. Now that Sharla was gone, she intended to draw him into a lengthy conversation, for he piqued her curiosity.

"I understand you're a bounty hunter. Is that true?"

He smiled disarmingly. "It seems you know more about me than I know about you. I suppose Sharla . . ." He paused abruptly, silently cursing himself for such a slip of the tongue. However, he wasn't too concerned, for he didn't think Mary had a reason to pick up on its importance. He was about to continue, this time using the name Trish, but the startled look on Mary's face stopped him.

"You know who she really is!" Mary exclaimed, the words bursting forth before she could stop them. Her deception was now as exposed as Lance's. She decided it didn't really matter; she was tired of pretending. "Considering you're a bounty hunter," she continued, "why haven't you taken Sharla back to St. Louis?"

Lance was quite amazed. "I'm surprised she told you who she really is. She only met you this morning."

There was something about Slade that Mary instinctively liked and trusted. Acting on these instincts, she chose to be perfectly candid. Besides, she needed someone to confide in. Maybe a full confession would help lighten her burden.

"She didn't tell me who she is," Mary replied. "As far as she knows, I think her name is Trish Lawrence."

"You have me completely confused."

"I made this trip with only one purpose in mind—to find Sharla."

"Are you saying you know her, but she doesn't know you?"

"Yes, something like that."

"Now, I'm even more confused."

Mary poured herself a second cup of coffee, collected her thoughts, then said, "Before I go any further, I have a question."

"What's that?"

"Do you intend to turn Sharla over to the law? Please be honest."

"If I had that in mind, she'd already be behind bars. Ma'am, I don't believe for one minute that Sharla murdered James Rayfield."

Mary gasped. "Is that why she's running from the law? Murder?"

"You didn't know?"

"I only knew she was in trouble. I didn't know the reason why."

Lance was impatient for an explanation. "You're a stranger to Sharla, so why would you know anything about her?"

"I'm not really a stranger. She only thinks I am." A trace of tears were in Mary's eyes as she turned to Lance and murmured, "I'm Sharla's grandmother."

Fifteen

Lance was more confused than ever. "You're Sharla's grandmother?" he asked, as though he needed a second admission in order to believe her.

"Yes, I am," Mary murmured. "Sharla's mother is my daughter—my estranged daughter. I haven't talked to her in nearly thirty years." She drew a deep breath. "I'd like to explain everything if you don't mind listening."

"I don't mind, but shouldn't you be telling this to Sharla?"

"I'm not sure. Maybe she's better off not learning the truth. How much do you know about Sharla's life?"

"Not much. I know she's James Rayfield's ward, and that she's accused of killing him. I also know that she's somehow connected to Maxine Reynolds, who runs a house of prostitution. She's pretending to be Trish Lawrence. Trish works for Maxine. My cousin met Trish when he visited St. Louis. They fell in love, but when he learned that she was a prostitute, he broke off their relationship. He returned to his ranch in Texas, but he couldn't forget her. When he heard that I was going to St. Louis, he asked me to bring Trish back with me. Considering I had never seen Trish, I had no reason to suspect that Sharla was impersonating her."

"Poor Sharla," Mary said sadly. "Not only was she accused of murder, but she was forced to pretend she was a prostitute. How difficult all this must be for her."

"Yes, but she's holding up remarkably well."

Mary smiled with pride. "That's because she comes from strong stock. She reminds me a lot of myself when I was her age."

Lance looked closely at Mary. "I can see a resemblance between you two. I never noticed it before, but then I wasn't looking for it." Finished with his coffee, he lit a cheroot and made himself as comfortable as possible. He figured it would take some time for Mary to explain everything.

That he was waiting for her to begin was apparent to Mary; small talk was over. She wasn't sure exactly where to begin. She thought about it and decided to start with Maxine. "I had four children," she began. "Three sons and a daughter. My two oldest sons died in infancy. My daughter was my youngest child. She looked a lot like me—fair complexion and blond hair. But she had her father's temperament. She was stubborn, rebellious, and had a mind of her own."

As Mary's story unfolded, Lance listened closely, interrupting now and then to ask a question. But, for the most part, he simply listened. He found it quite amazing that this woman, who was obviously intelligent and caring, had allowed pride, principles, and her husband's dominance to come between her and her daughter.

Mary talked steadily, for she had a lot to say. By the time she was finished, the fire had died down to glowing embers.

Lance sat quietly for a minute or so. He then turned to Mary and said firmly, "You have to tell Sharla who you are."

"If only I could be sure it's the right thing to do."

"She has a right to know."

"But what will the truth do to her?"

"She's strong, and she'll come through this. She'll be shocked, and she'll probably be bitter and resentful. But in time those feelings will pass. The important thing here is the truth."

Mary eyed him skeptically. "What about you, Mr. Slade? Why haven't you been truthful with Sharla?"

His sudden smile was somewhat contrite. "I decided to play a game of getting even—a little harmless revenge. I didn't intend to keep it up much longer. I thought Sharla deserved a taste of her own medicine. It was days before I caught on to her disguise, and turning the tables is how I decided to deal with it."

"When do you plan to be honest with her?"

"Later. Right now what you have to tell her is much more important."

"Do you really think I should tell her everything?" she asked, her tone desperate.

"If it was me, I'd want to know. Wouldn't you?"

She nodded, as though she was resigned. She got up slowly, and looked at the covered wagon. A lantern was burning, casting Sharla's silhouette onto the white canvas. She was brushing her hair. Mary turned back to Lance, who was watching her.

"Sharla doesn't deserve this," she murmured. "She never deserved any of it—abandoned by her mother and family, and put into an orphanage. I just thank God that a woman like Olivia Matthews took pity on her."

"Wasn't Olivia's name Rayfield?"

"It was Matthews before she married James Rayfield. Although she couldn't adopt Sharla, she was able to legally arrange for her ward to become a Matthews. Before then, Sharla didn't even have a last name." She squared her shoulders, mentally prepared herself for what lay ahead, and started toward the wagon.

Lance watched as she went to the lowered backboard. A stepstool was placed so that she could use it to enter the wagon. He turned back to the dying fire. Extra kindling was within reach, and he pitched a few branches onto the hot embers. He sat very still, staring thoughtfully at the fire that was now burning brightly. He tried to put himself in Sharla's place, but such a scenario was impossible, for he had known his family. His parents had loved him, raised him, and had always been there for him. He couldn't personally relate to the shock Sharla was about to receive, but if she needed his support, he certainly intended to give it to her.

He thought about the kiss they had shared. A frown wrinkled his brow. He shouldn't have let that happen. Let? he silently questioned. Hell, he had instigated it! He knew it was important that he not become too involved with Sharla, for he wasn't free to make a binding commitment. Not now, maybe not ever! He was bent on finding his family's killers if it took him a lifetime. He did, however, intend to help Sharla. He wasn't about to leave her a fugitive forced into hiding. He wasn't sure what he could do, but he did know that he wasn't going to run out on her.

Despite his resolve, his mind returned to their kiss. The memory of Sharla's passionate yet vulnerable response roused feelings in him that he had put to sleep years ago. Fighting back these awakening emotions, he got up, went to his carpetbag and removed a bottle of whiskey. Wrenching it open, he tilted it to his mouth, took a big swig, and reminded himself that his future was set. Not Sharla or anyone else was going to alter its course!

Claudia was in her room, frightened, her thoughts in turmoil, when a knock sounded at her door. She was almost afraid to answer it, for in her mind she pictured the constable on the other side, waiting to arrest her. She quickly erased such a possibility. It was obvious that Maxine suspected her of murder, but she had no evidence to support such a theory; therefore, she wouldn't send for the constable. Claudia knew she was letting her imagination run away with her.

She answered the knock, and was surprised to find Dexter. She wasn't expecting him, for he hadn't said that he'd see her tonight. She waved him inside and closed the door.

"Do you intend to pay for my services every night of the week?" she asked, his presence lifting her spirits. "Do you realize you have been my only customer?"

His eyes raked her intently. She was wearing a gossamer dressing gown that barely concealed her voluptuous curves. He knew every inch of her body, and the thought of another man touching her naked flesh was infuriating. He didn't understand why he was obsessed with Claudia; she held a power over him that went beyond his comprehension.

His scrutiny was making her uncomfortable. Did he suspect her of killing James? Was he about to threaten her, maybe even try and force her into confessing? "Dexter, is something wrong?" she asked warily. "Why are you staring at me?"

His hands suddenly gripped her shoulders, and his fingers dug into her flesh as he jerked her body flush to his. "I don't want to share you with other men!" he uttered harshly.

Claudia's fear of detection dissipated, and she sighed inwardly with relief. Thank goodness her apprehensions were unfounded! Dexter didn't suspect her of murder; he was simply jealous! His grip was painful, and she pried herself loose.

"I'm sorry," Dexter apologized. "I guess I came on a little too strong."

"That's all right," she replied. "But, Dexter, what do you want from me? It's my job to sleep with other men."

"That doesn't have to be your job," he argued.

"Do you have something better in mind?"

"Yes, I do. I want you to become my mistress."

"Do you really expect me to give up such lucrative employment simply to appease your jealousy?" She had every intention of doing just that, for she knew she couldn't stay here. However, if she feigned resistance, Dexter would be more generous with his money.

"You'll receive a monthly income, and it'll be more than you make here. I'll even rent you a house."

"No, you'll buy me a house. And I want the title in my name."

He thought it over. This strange obsession with Claudia was going to cost him a great deal. He strove for the strength to walk out of this room and out of her life. But he couldn't find it in himself to do so. He had to possess this woman—at any cost!

"You'll get your house," he agreed. "Until that can be taken care of, you'll live in my home. I'm not about to leave you here." The expression in his eyes turned threatening, and he again gripped her shoulders. "I hope I never catch you cheating on me!"

"You don't have to worry about that. I won't see anyone else."

"Just make sure you don't!" he warned, releasing her abruptly.

At that moment, someone knocked on the door.

"Get rid of whoever it is," Dexter ordered. "I want to take you to bed right now. I can't wait." His loins were on fire; his desire for Claudia was never completely doused; it merely smoldered like warm embers. The sight of her never failed to ignite the embers into leaping flames.

The intruder was Maxine's doorman. He said that Mr. Rayfield had a visitor downstairs who wished to talk to him about Miss Matthews.

Dexter went to the doorway. "Who is this visitor?" he asked.

"Arnold Shelby—he works at the telegraph office. I'm

sorry to disturb you, Mr. Rayfield, but Shelby said that his information is very important. I figured you'd want to talk to him."

"I certainly do," he replied, his desire for Claudia temporarily forgotten. He told her he'd be back in a few minutes, then followed the doorman downstairs and to the bar area. Shelby was sitting alone at a table.

He got to his feet at Rayfield's approach. "Good evening, sir," he said politely.

Dexter's response was a terse nod. He pulled out a chair, sat down, and waited for Shelby to return to his own chair. "I understand you have information that concerns Miss Matthews."

Arnold Shelby was not the kind of man who would stand out in a crowd. Small, wiry, and balding, he seemed to blend in with his surroundings, regardless of where he might be. Timid, and lacking self-confidence, he was somewhat in awe of Dexter Rayfield, for the man was everything he wasn't: handsome, successful, and sure of himself. He cleared his throat, adjusted his wire-rimmed glasses, and said in a meek tone, "I hope my information is helpful, but I can't be sure."

Dexter scowled impatiently. "What do you mean, you can't be sure? Do you or do you not know something about Miss Matthews?"

The man seemed to physically shrink under Rayfield's dominance. "A few days ago," he began tentatively, "Maxine Reynolds' servant came to the telegraph office."

"Which servant?"

"The Negro woman—Hattie."

"Go on."

"She had me send a wire to a woman named Mary Simmons. She lives in a small town in southern Missouri."

Dexter couldn't understand what any of this had to do with Sharla. A constant and distracting tapping of his foot displayed his impatience.

Shelby continued, his voice even weaker than before, "The telegram said: Our girl in serious trouble with the law and must leave city—She's traveling to San Antonio with male escort—The time has come to face your past—Please help her—She needs you." Shelby wiped a hand across his perspiring brow. "I might be off a word or so, but that's as close as I can remember."

Dexter's foot was no longer tapping; the timid man had gained his full attention. "You said that Hattie sent the wire days ago, so why did you wait so long to tell me?"

He swallowed nervously. "I'm not very observant, Mr. Rayfield. I never really looked at the wanted posters on Miss Matthews. Nor did I connect her disappearance to Hattie's telegram. Then earlier today, I went shopping with my wife. We saw one of the posters, and my wife commented on the huge reward. For some reason, I suddenly wondered if Hattie's telegram had anything to do with Miss Matthews's whereabouts. I mentioned it to my wife, and she convinced me that I should contact you. This evening I went to your home, and when I stated my business, your butler sent me here."

"That wire may have nothing to do with Miss Matthews."

"I realize that. But if my information leads to her arrest, will I receive the reward?"

Dexter got to his feet. "Yes, you will. I'll be in touch." With that, he left Shelby sitting at the table staring at his departing back.

As Dexter started up the stairs to Claudia's room, his thoughts were jumbled. He couldn't imagine Hattie having anything to do with Sharla. Furthermore, who was Mary Simmons? If this woman was somehow associated with Sharla, wouldn't he know about it? He had known Sharla since she was fourteen, and in that time she had never made a trip to southern Missouri. He couldn't recall anyone named Mary Simmons visiting Sharla, and he would certainly have known about that, for he stopped by his brother's home on a regular basis.

He shook his head, as though trying to shake off Shelby's information. That Hattie was involved with Sharla's disappearance seemed too farfetched to even consider.

He went inside Claudia's bedroom without knocking. She was in bed, waiting for him. He locked the door, then moved over and sat beside her. She appeared very seductive. Her long tresses were splayed across the pillow, the sheet barely covered her naked breasts, and her dark eyes were bewitching, yet such a vision failed to rekindle his passion. He couldn't get that damned telegram out of his mind!

"You seem troubled," Claudia murmured, placing a hand on his arm, her fingers a gentle caress. She was desperate to learn what was said between him and Arnold Shelby. But she knew she couldn't appear too anxious, for he might question such intense interest.

He gave her a full account. "The whole thing is outrageous," he continued. "Hattie helping Sharla is absurd!"

"Maybe it's not as absurd as you think," Claudia replied. She wanted Sharla dead. The case would then be permanently closed. That it could be reopened didn't occur to Claudia; her sick mind was only capable of considering one thing at a time.

Dexter eyed her questioningly. "What do you mean it's not absurd?"

She intended to tell Dexter about Agnes's visit, but she wasn't about to tell him that she had been eavesdropping; he would certainly ask her why she had done such a thing. He might even grow suspicious. Her calculating mind worked quickly.

Her bedroom faced the back of the house, which made her lie more plausible. "Earlier, I happened to look out my window. I saw Agnes leave by the kitchen door. Albert was waiting for her in your brother's carriage."

"Agnes was here!" he exclaimed. "My God, why didn't you tell me? You must know that she and Sharla are close-knit."

"I just figured she was friends with one of the servants who works for Maxine. I never dreamed that her presence here could have anything to do with Sharla; not until now. I mean, Agnes and I never liked each other, so I certainly don't know who her friends are. That she could know someone who works here seemed logical to me. Why would I even suspect that her visit was somehow connected to Sharla? What does Sharla have in common with a house of ill repute?"

"That's what I'd like to know!" Dexter grumbled. "But it sure looks as if there is a connection. Hattie's wire? Agnes's visit? That's too much to be coincidental. I think it's time I had a long talk with Hattie, as well as Maxine. This whole matter is so incredulous that I wouldn't be surprised to learn that Maxine's also involved."

Claudia didn't want him talking to Maxine, for she would certainly relay her own suspicions to Dexter. Claudia didn't doubt that Maxine suspected her of James's murder.

She sat up in bed, grasped his arm, and said strongly, "You shouldn't confront Hattie or Maxine! If you do, they'll contact Sharla. Then you may never find her. If that telegram is about Sharla, you already know she's on her way to San Antonio."

"You're right. I'll wire the sheriff and have her arrested the moment she arrives."

"No, don't do that," Claudia replied. The opportunity to ensure Sharla's death was now within her grasp. "A Texas sheriff's liable to disregard your wire. Who you are won't carry much weight down there. Sharla will turn on the tears, act helpless, and convince him that she's innocent. There's only one way you can guarantee that she pays for your brother's murder."

"How's that?" he asked, his attention riveted.

"Buy a hired gun."

"You mean, have her killed?"

"Why not?"

Dexter actually considered it, but he quickly discarded the possibility; his revenge didn't stretch quite that far. He wasn't about to be an accomplice to murder. However, much of Claudia's advice was taken seriously. He rose to his feet, and began pacing in front of the bed.

"You could be right about the sheriff," he said. "I can't depend on someone I don't know to arrest Sharla. Therefore, I'll depend on myself. Tomorrow, I'll advertise for a couple of men who are good with guns, and hire them to accompany me to San Antonio. I'm not about to travel to Texas without the right kind of protection. That place is too uncivilized. Once I get to San Antonio, I'll find Sharla if I have to bribe everyone in town. Then I'll personally escort her back here to stand trial."

Claudia wasn't too discouraged; she might still find a way to get rid of Sharla. But for that to happen, she had to travel with Dexter.

She got out of bed, stood naked before him, and gazed into his eyes with seduction. "Let me go with you," she said, provocatively moistening her lips with the tip of her tongue. "Having me along will make the trip much more pleasant for you."

That was a possibility he didn't need to consider; he was too possessively jealous to leave her behind. He drew her into his arms and kissed her with passion. "You're damned right you're coming with me. That way, I'll know where you are and what you're doing."

"You aren't going to say anything about this trip to Maxine or Hattie, are you?"

"Of course not. They'd merely warn Sharla." He released her, stepped back, and brushed a distracted hand through his hair. "God, I hope this doesn't turn out to be a wild-goose chase. You know, it is possible that Hattie's wire and Agnes's visit have nothing to do with Sharla."

"Yes, it's possible. But certainly not probable." She moved back into his arms, locked her hands about his neck, and pressed her naked body tightly to his. "Nothing can be solved tonight. Don't you think it's about time you started getting your money's worth? After all, you're paying Maxine for my company."

"Yes, but this is the last time. After tonight, you'll belong to me! And don't you ever forget it!" He swept her roughly off her feet and carried her to bed.

Sixteen

Sharla put her brush away; the brisk strokes left her blond tresses shining with highlights, and as Mary entered the wagon, Sharla, her hair the color of gold, reminded Mary very much of herself when she was Sharla's age.

Her young companion greeted her with a concerned expression. "You look tired. Are you feeling all right?"

"I'm fine," Mary replied. She moved her rocker close to Sharla, who was using a cedar chest as a chair. Sitting, Mary continued, "I probably do look haggard, but it's because I'm worried."

"Why are you worried?"

Mary sighed heavily. *Lord,* she wondered, *where do I begin?* She searched for the right words, but nothing came to her. She wanted to soften the blow, to make this easier for Sharla; however, there was no easy solution. She folded her hands in her lap, gently rocked her chair, and drew a bolstering breath. She spoke softly, her eyes meeting Sharla's. "I need to talk to you about my daughter. She lives in St. Louis."

"Yes, I know. You mentioned that the day we met."

"My daughter and I have been estranged for nearly thirty years."

Sharla, having never known her mother, couldn't imagine such a thing. "I've spent my whole life wishing for my mother. Your daughter has a mother and doesn't even care. Somehow, it doesn't seem fair."

"Don't put all the blame on my daughter. Our estrangement was just as much my fault as hers. I let it happen."

"Why?" Sharla asked, bewildered. "Why would you do something like that?"

"It's a long story. I need to start at the beginning. Ezra and I raised our children by the Bible. We took them to church every Sunday, and taught them right from wrong. Ezra was a strict father, and he laid down the law to our children. When it came to morality, he was unbending. But there was another side to Ezra. He had a wonderful sense of humor—he made time for his children and took a lot of interest in them. He loved our son and daughter very much. The two babies we lost nearly destroyed him. Only his strong religion carried him through both tragedies. Like Ezra, I also turned to God. Otherwise, I couldn't have made it without dying inside. Losing our first two babies made us cling all the more to the two who survived.

"We never had any problems with our son, but our daughter was headstrong, rebellious, and hated living on a farm. She felt as though life was passing her by. She longed for pretty clothes, parties, and excitement. She was also very beautiful. I think her beauty scared Ezra, for he knew men would be drawn to her like moths to a flame. He was afraid that some passing rogue might whisk her away. It wouldn't take much persuasion, for my daughter wanted to leave the farm so much, it was all she could think about.

"Well, Ezra's fear came true. A charming, handsome stranger came to the farm. He was on his way to St. Louis when his horse pulled up lame. He was so likable that he even charmed Ezra, and he invited him to stay at the farm until his horse was healed.

"Two weeks later, he left in the middle of the night,

taking our daughter with him. Ezra and I went to St. Louis, but we couldn't find them.

"We finally received a letter from our daughter. It came from New Orleans, but had no return address. She was determined to avoid us. In the letter, she didn't say whether or not they had married. I took for granted they hadn't. We never received a letter after the first one. I wanted us to go to New Orleans and find our daughter, but Ezra refused. She was living in sin, and he had washed his hands of her.

"A year later, Ezra and I took a shopping trip to St. Louis. We happened to catch a glimpse of our daughter on the street. I couldn't believe it. She was in St. Louis! I called out to her, but she didn't hear me. Seeing her again, even though it was fleeting, changed Ezra. His heart softened. He still loved her, and he longed to forgive and forget. For three days, we combed the streets, hoping to see her again. Then it happened—we saw her coming out of a dress shop. She was a distance ahead, and we followed her. Before we could catch up to her, a passing buggy stopped and offered her a ride. Ezra asked a man who was walking past us if he knew who owned the buggy. It was a grand carriage, drawn by a pair of magnificent white horses. The owner had to be quite wealthy. The man told us that the carriage belonged to Marcia Monroe, who operated a house of ill repute. Ezra and I were shocked. Why would our daughter accept a ride from someone like that? Ezra got directions to the woman's place of business; he intended to find out if our daughter was actually at that terrible place. He told me to return to the hotel, but I stood firm, and for the first time in our marriage, I defied my vow to obey my husband. He wasn't going there without me!

"The house was located at the edge of town, the rear grounds overlooking the Mississippi River."

Sharla didn't say anything, but she was familiar with this house, and knew it was now owned by Maxine Reynolds.

"We walked right up to the front door and knocked," Mary continued. "A Negro woman answered. We stated our business, she showed us inside, and took us to a room that was actually an office. Moments later, a woman identifying herself as Marcia Monroe, joined us there. We asked her about our daughter. She denied knowing her. We told her that we had seen her give our daughter a ride. Caught in a lie, she decided there was no reason to keep up a pretense. She left, saying she would send our daughter to us.

"We were kept waiting quite a long time, but finally our daughter got up the courage to face us. Ezra confronted her the moment she stepped into the room. Was she a prostitute? She said that she was; she admitted it softly. She was on the verge of tears. Ezra's temper exploded. He could forgive her for living with a man who wasn't her husband, but he couldn't forgive her for turning to prostitution. He drew upon anger to heal his pain. Disowning her, he said that he never wanted to lay eyes on her again. He grabbed my arm and dragged me out of there. I never had a chance to say one word to my daughter.

"I couldn't leave St. Louis without talking to her. That night, after Ezra was asleep, I sneaked out of our hotel room and returned. Again, the Negro woman let me in and showed me to the office. A few minutes later, my daughter arrived. To this day, I'm not sure what I intended to say to her. Was I going to ask her to come back with me and beg her father's forgiveness? Or did I go there to punish her, as well as myself? I don't know, for I never got the chance to search my heart for answers. My daughter had changed since our earlier meeting, and she met me with cold defiance. She told me to stay out of her life. She never wanted to see me again. I felt as though I were looking into the eyes of a complete stranger. She was inflexible, frigid, and terribly angry. She stormed out of the office, leaving me in tears. The Negro woman returned to show me to the door. I must have been a pathetic sight, for she took pity on me and offered me the comfort of her arms. I cried on her shoulder as though she were an old friend and not a stranger."

Sharla had a feeling she was talking about Hattie.

"She took me to the kitchen," Mary proceeded. "We sat at the table, drank coffee, and talked for a long time. It was obvious that she cared a great deal about my daughter. She didn't try to reconcile our differences. I'm sure she believed they were beyond repair. But she did offer to correspond with me without my daughter knowing about it. That way, I wouldn't completely lose touch with her. I knew Ezra would firmly object, but I didn't care. I was determined to go through with it.

"When he learned about it, he was even angrier than I had imagined. Nevertheless, I stuck to my guns. He never read any of the letters I received, nor did he ask about them. True to his word, he had disowned our daughter. He even erased her name from the family Bible."

Sharla gently touched Mary's arm. "Through this whole story, you have never mentioned your daughter's name. It's Maxine, isn't it?"

"Yes," she murmured.

"And the woman who helped you is Hattie?"

She nodded.

"Why did you avoid their names? What is it that you aren't telling me?"

"I'm leading up to it."

"You know who I am, don't you?"

"Yes, you're Sharla Matthews."

"I don't understand. Did Hattie send you to me, and if so, why? Why would she involve you?"

"I'll explain," she replied. "It'll be easier for me if you save your questions until I'm finished."

She agreed to try.

"Through Hattie's letters, I knew that Maxine remained working for Marcia Monroe. It was a depressing, heartbreaking burden for me to carry. I wondered where I had gone wrong. Sometimes I blamed myself, other times I blamed Ezra. Maybe neither of us were to blame. I don't know. I've never known why Maxine chose such a life.

"The years went by, then the war broke out. Ezra went to Tennessee and joined the Confederate Army. My son soon followed. I took care of the farm with the help of a hired hand. During this time, Hattie wrote that Maxine had left Marcia's and was now the mistress of a very wealthy man. She said that he was a gentleman, and that he sincerely cared about Maxine. The man bought Maxine a lovely home on the outskirts of the city. He was married, but managed to keep this affair hidden from his wife." Mary stopped to shrug her shoulders. "Or at least he thought he was getting away with it; wives are usually more perceptive than their husbands think. Sometimes, the wives, for whatever reasons, decide to look the other way.

"Another year went by, then Hattie wrote that Maxine was pregnant and was leaving town. Her lover had arranged for her to have her child at a convent in St. Joseph. To arrange that, he must have made a very lucrative contribution. Hattie went with her, and several months passed before I received another letter. By this time, Ezra had died in battle, and I had no idea where my son was, or if he was even alive. Hattie wrote that she and Maxine had returned to St. Louis."

"What happened to the child?" Sharla asked. A creeping uneasiness began to gnaw at her.

"The convent arranged for the child to be placed in the orphanage in St. Louis. It was carried out very secretively. The child's father had no children, and he planned to talk his wife into adopting a baby. He intended, of course, to choose the child that was his without his wife being the wiser. But before he could carry out his plan, he fell seriously ill. He was sick a very long time. When he knew he wasn't going to recover, he sent his lawyer to Maxine. He gave her a generous amount of money, and she used it to buy out Marcia Monroe.''

Mary paused for a long moment, dreading her next words.

Sharla didn't say anything, but she was as apprehensive as a child who had stumbled on to something she couldn't quite understand, and must wait obediently for an explanation.

"Before he died, he confessed everything to his wife," Mary continued. "He told her about his child and that his lawyer had made arrangements behind closed doors that the child was not to be adopted by anyone but his client. On his death bed, he begged his wife to give his child a home. But it was a long time before she could do that. She was too hurt and too bitter. As time passed, her heart began to mend. She had loved her husband very much, and knowing that a part of him still lived on in his child began to prick at her heart. She finally contacted her husband's lawyer, and had him take her to the orphanage. She fell in love with the child at first sight."

Every nerve leapt and shuddered in Sharla, yet she sat unmoving as though she were riveted to her seat. Her throat was parched, her voice thin as she whispered, "My God! This can't be real!"

Mary reached out a hand and placed it on Sharla's arm; she could feel the tightness in her muscles. "You were that child, Sharla. Olivia's husband, John Matthews, was your father. Maxine is your mother."

She threw off her hand. Mobility returned, and she bounded to her feet. "No!" she cried, denying the inevitable. Every word Mary said was true, and deep inside she knew it was true—but she wasn't ready to deal with it. She wanted to deny it—to wish this night would miraculously disappear. The truth was more than she could bear.

Mary rose to her feet, and again grasped Sharla's arm. "I'm not finished. You must hear the rest."

"What's left to say?" Sharla spat angrily. "My whole life has been nothing but lies! I'm sorry, but right now I feel as though I hate Maxine, Olivia, and the man who was my father! Lies! How dare they decide my future on lies!"

"You're upset, and that's understandable. But please let me tell you the rest."

"No! I can't stand any more. I need to be alone!" She brushed past Mary, leaving the wagon quickly, as though all the lies were in heavy pursuit.

Running blindly, she hastened past the campfire, where Lance was sitting. He watched as she headed into the surrounding shrubbery. He jumped to his feet, wondering if he should follow her. His hesitancy lasted only a moment, and pitching his cheroot into the fire, he went after her.

Dexter's desire for Claudia was insatiable, and although they had already made passionate love, he needed her again. He took her roughly, hunger rising and flaring in him like a savage animal. Claudia responded wildly to each powerful thrust, her arching hips matching his aggressive rhythm. The final explosion of physical sensation rocked them at the same time, and they clung tightly as their bodies trembled with breathless satisfaction.

Dexter withdrew, and lay at her side, winded, his chest rising rapidly.

Claudia snuggled against him. Her fingers absently toyed with the curly hair that grew about his nipples.

When Rayfield's breathing had slowed to normal, he sat up and swung his legs over the bed. "Pack your clothes," he ordered brusquely.

His demand took Claudia by surprise. "Am I going somewhere?"

"I'm taking you home with me. I've already paid for the entire night, so we might as well leave together. I'll get dressed, go downstairs and tell Maxine that you no longer work here. While I do that, pack your things. Don't bother with the clothes Maxine gave you. I'll buy you a new wardrobe and one that is more to my liking."

Claudia was still against Dexter talking alone with Maxine. She would undoubtedly tell him of her suspicions. She didn't think Dexter would believe her, but she couldn't be sure. "I'll talk to Maxine," she said, getting out of bed. "It's my place to tell her I'm leaving. I'll pack, then on our way out, I'll stop at her office."

Dexter was agreeable; it didn't really matter who told Maxine. He just wanted Claudia out of there as fast as possible. He wanted her where he could keep an eye on her, for he wasn't sure if he could trust her. He had no control over his jealousy; he was totally consumed by it.

It didn't take Claudia long to pack, for she didn't own very many clothes. Leaving all of Trish's things behind, she wore a simple cotton dress that she had brought with her.

They left the room, Dexter carrying her small suitcase. As they were descending the stairs, Maxine was on her way up. They met halfway.

Eying the bag in Dexter's hand, Maxine asked, "What's going on?"

"I'm leaving," Claudia remarked.

"Leaving? But why?"

"I've had a better offer. Tally up what you owe me, and I'll be back in a couple of days to collect it." She slipped her hand in the crook of Dexter's arm, and drew him down the stairs with her.

The doorman was on duty, and he opened the door for them. They walked outside without a backward glance.

Maxine was stunned; she was also very worried. Proving Sharla's innocence would now be even more difficult. Difficult? she asked herself. *Impossible* was a better word! She changed her course and moved back down the stairs. She gave in to defeat; she felt she should have surrendered from the beginning. She never really had a chance to save Sharla; she had just wanted it so badly that she had grasped at straws.

She went into the kitchen, hoping to find Hattie. She was putting away supper dishes.

"Claudia left!" Maxine blurted out.

"Left?" Hattie gasped. "But why?"

"Dexter Rayfield, that's why. The fool's obviously obsessed with her. He's paid for her every night she's been here. Evidently, he asked her to be his mistress. He had to promise her a lot, for she was making good money."

Maxine sat in a kitchen chair, propped her elbows on the table, and leaned her face into her hands. "Oh, Hattie!" she moaned tearfully. "What can I do? How can I help Sharla?"

Hattie hurried over and placed a caring hand on Maxine's shoulder. "I wish I knew what to tell you."

"Please, just tell me anything! I'm desperate!"

"Well, you could go to the constable. Show him the report Mr. Bailey brought you. Maybe that will convince him to consider Claudia a suspect."

"He'll want to know why I am involved in this case. What should I tell him?"

"Why don't you tell him the truth?"

"No! I can't do that! I can't trust him not to tell anyone. Eventually, half the city might know. If Sharla is proven innocent, I don't want her to return home, only to learn the truth about her mother!"

"You have to ask yourself which is more important—asking for the constable's help, or protecting your own shame."

Maxine looked at her with surprise. "I'm not protecting myself. Everything I've done has been to protect Sharla."

"What that child really needed was her mother's arms."

"I never knew you felt this way."

"That's because you never heard what you didn't want to hear. From the moment Sharla was born, I tried to tell you not to let her go."

"I don't care what you say!" she replied angrily. "It was the right thing to do!"

"Yes, the right thing for you and John Matthews."

She leapt to her feet, screeching, "Stop it! My God, why must you punish me like this?"

Hattie met her anger without a flinch. "I don't mean to punish you, but I'm mighty afraid you're going to desert your daughter a second time. You get to the constable, give him that report, and tell him the truth! He's Sharla's only hope!"

Maxine's rage drained from her as though a dam had opened, releasing all her pent-up emotions. She dropped back into the chair, her body as limp as a ragdoll's. "I won't desert my daughter a second time. I'll talk to the constable in the morning."

Seventeen

Lance found Sharla leaning back against the wide trunk of a towering oak. She seemed too fatigued to stand without support. Her arms were folded across her chest, and she was staring straight ahead. Moonlight lancing through the oak's branches fell across her face. As Slade drew closer, he was touched to see tears in her eyes. She was on the brink of giving in to despair. Her chin trembled and she had an ache in her throat, but she was afraid if she really started crying, she might not stop for a very long time. Determined to remain in control, she wiped away the tears, lifted her chin, and swallowed back the constricting ache.

She stood straight, unfolded her arms, and asked Lance, "Why did you follow me?" That Mary had taken him into her confidence was a possibility Sharla didn't consider.

"I thought you might need a friend."

She regarded him uncertainly. "Why would you think that?"

"Before Mary talked to you, she told me everything."

Sharla was astounded. "Why did she confide in you?" Not waiting for a reply, she went on, "This means . . . it means . . . you know I'm not Trish!"

Lance smiled disarmingly. "I've known that since the night you bathed in the river and forgot your face powder and rouge."

"Why didn't you say something?"

"I figured two could play your game. I yearned for a little harmless revenge. I wasn't planning to keep up the pretense very long, only long enough to even the score. But then you left the waystation without me, and due to everything that has happened since, the game lost its appeal."

"Game!" she said angrily. "My life is in jeopardy, and you call it a game!"

"This . . . misunderstanding . . . could have been avoided if you had been honest with me."

"You can't mean that! Why would I tell a bounty hunter that I'm a fugitive with a reward on my head?"

"Do you think I'm the kind of a man who would turn you over to the law? If you think that, then you don't know me at all."

"I don't know you," she replied. "My God, I don't even know myself!" The ache returned to her throat, and tears again threatened. However, her resolve held firm, and her anger turned away the tears. "No wonder Maxine was so willing to help!" she spat harshly, as though they had been discussing the woman. "She figured that was the least she could do for her daughter!"

Lance detected bitterness in her voice; he supposed that was to be expected.

"Olivia, Maxine, and John Matthews!" she continued sharply. "How cleverly they guarded their sordid conspiracy! I feel as though I hate them!"

"How do you feel about Mary?"

"Anger, I think."

"And Hattie?"

"I don't blame her."

"What about Agnes?"

"Agnes? What does she have to do with this?"

"Didn't Mary tell you everything?"

"No. I heard all I could stand, and left the wagon."

"Olivia took Agnes into her confidence."

"Then that explains why she sent me to Maxine." She continued fiercely, her eyes shining, "I grew up believing in Agnes and Olivia. I trusted them. They were my security, my haven, and I loved them as though they were truly my family. Everything I believed in was lies! Nothing but lies!"

"Not entirely," Lance replied softly. "Agnes and Olivia did keep you secure, offered you a haven, and I'm sure they loved you as much as you loved them."

"But it was all built on lies!"

"I should think the lie you've been forced into would grant you a little empathy for others. Sometimes circumstances force people into sensitive situations. I'm not saying what they did was right, but I think they believed they made the best decision for everyone concerned. Hating them isn't going to change anything, or make this any easier for you to accept."

"I don't know if I'll ever learn to accept it." She now sounded more disillusioned than angry.

Lance placed gentle hands on her shoulders, and when she showed no resistance, he urged her into his embrace. He held her close, and she rested her head on his shoulder. She welcomed the strength and comfort of his arms. She felt terribly alone, but in Lance's embrace that feeling of loneliness left her, as though the night's breeze had magically swept it over the treetops and into the vast heavens. She wrapped her arms about him tightly, for she needed his warmth and understanding. Soon, however, she became acutely aware of his body pressed intimately against hers. Her troubled emotions were suddenly supplanted by desire, and she was conscious only of Lance's nearness and the excitement mounting within her.

Her hand moved to the back of his neck, and taking the initiative, she reached up and placed her lips to his. At first, the contact was feather-light, but Lance's passion was quickly ignited. His mouth claimed hers aggressively, needing and demanding her total response. Surrendering completely, she welcomed his questing kiss, parting her lips in mute invitation.

His hand moved upward to cup a breast, caressing its fullness. No man had ever touched her this way before, and she drew back, but only for a moment—the pressure of his hand, the firmness of his body, and the hunger in his kiss were too overpowering. She longed to stay in his arms forever, and to never lose this feeling of love, desire, and physical surrender.

Sharla's dream of forever didn't last very long, for Lance's better judgment unexpectedly intruded, causing him to release her quite abruptly. He silently berated himself for taking advantage of her vulnerability and innocence. She needed and deserved a man who could make a total commitment. Someday, he might be free to be that man, but not now. In his avenging mind, retribution came first. For the past five years, he had lived for revenge, doted on it, and it had been the driving factor behind his every move. His life was irrevocably dedicated to finding his family's murderers.

"I'm sorry," he murmured gently. "That kiss shouldn't have happened."

"Why not?" she asked, desperation creeping into her voice. Twice now, he had kissed her, only to release her as though he were fighting against his own feelings.

Lance answered carefully; "Sharla, you deserve more than I can give you. If things were different . . . but there's no place in my life for you—not now. I wish I could make you understand. There's so much I should tell you, but this doesn't seem to be the time. Right now, you're trying to cope with your own problems; you certainly don't need to hear mine."

Sharla felt this was a rejection, a gentle one perhaps, but a rejection nonetheless. Evidently, he didn't share her feelings; her passion maybe, but he certainly wasn't falling in love. She, on the other hand, was falling very much in love. That revelation hit unexpectedly, taking her unawares. She didn't try to deny it; she simply accepted it. Nevertheless, she wasn't going to throw herself at his feet, nor was she about to let him break her heart.

"There's no reason for you to feel apologetic," she remarked with as much poise as she could muster. "Besides, I instigated the kiss."

She was very lovely in the golden moonlight, her beauty beyond description. He detected a wounded look in her sapphire eyes that she was unable to disguise. He cared too deeply not to respond, and he was dangerously close to taking her back into his arms when the sound of a horse grabbed his attention.

He took Sharla's hand, and they hastened back to camp, arriving just as a rider drew in and dismounted. They recognized him as the gambler who had played cards with Hiram.

"Evening," he said, tipping his Stetson. "Do you mind if I camp here tonight? I don't mean to intrude, and if it's not convenient, I'll move on."

Lance felt obligated to the man, for he had helped Sharla. "You're more than welcome," he replied, walking over and shaking the visitor's hand. "My name's Lance Slade."

"Well, I'll be damned. So you're Lance Slade. I've heard of you. Your reputation's widely known. Excuse my manners. My name's Steve Jordan."

"Are you from around here?" Lance asked.

"Not anymore. I used to live in St. Charles, and like the prodigal son, I return home every so often to visit my family. Now, I'm headed back West."

Sharla moved over and stood beside Lance. Jordan's eyes raked her furtively; he found her exceptionally beautiful.

"The lady's name is Trish Lawrence," Lance remarked.

He wasn't about to divulge her true identity, for Jordan might have seen one of Rayfield's wanted posters.

"It's a pleasure to meet you, ma'am," he said with a winsome smile.

"I want to thank you again for your help."

"I'm just glad I was able to assist two such courageous ladies."

Sharla couldn't help but smile, for Steve Jordan was undoubtedly a smooth talker. She suspected he was also somewhat of a scoundrel, but a very charming one. She instinctively liked him.

Lance offered Jordan supper and said he'd brew more coffee. He accepted gratefully, saying he'd pay for his food. His money was firmly refused. Before building up the campfire, Lance took Sharla aside and suggested that she return to Mary, for the woman still had a lot to tell her.

Sharla relented, albeit reluctantly. She didn't really want to hear the rest, for she knew it would only upset her. But avoiding the truth was pointless and cowardly. She went to the back of the wagon and climbed inside. Mary was still sitting in the rocker. Her eyes were red and swollen, and it was obvious that she had been crying.

Sharla moved over and sat on the cedar chest. Mary's hands were folded in her lap, and Sharla placed her hand on top of Mary's. She smiled kindly, and whispered, "You're my grandmother. I didn't really think about that until this moment."

"That's understandable. You've had so many other things to think about. Maybe I shouldn't have told you so much so soon."

"It's not exactly something you could break to me gradually."

Mary's eyes shone with admiration as she gazed into her granddaughter's face. "You're a remarkable young lady. Olivia did a wonderful job raising you."

Sharla stiffened at the mention of Olivia. Why didn't

the woman tell her the truth? Why did she have to lie to her, time and time again! She pushed Olivia's deceit to the back of her mind and said to Mary, "I'm ready to hear the rest."

Mary obliged and continued the story. "Through the years, Hattie and I stayed in touch. She wrote me that Maxine saw you often, always from a distance, of course. You never knew she was watching you."

"Did Olivia and Maxine ever talk to each other?" Sharla asked.

"Yes, a few times. They certainly didn't become friends, but they had a common bond—you, and their love for John Matthews. Maxine was very grateful to Olivia for giving you a loving home. Olivia never told anyone that you were her husband's child, except for her servant, Agnes. And Maxine, of course, never breathed a word of it. Protecting you meant everything to her."

"How did you learn so quickly that I was in trouble?"

"Hattie sent me a wire. She said that our girl was in trouble and had to flee from the law and that she was traveling to San Antonio with a male escort. I wasn't sure if Hattie was referring to you or Maxine. But I had a feeling it was you. When I met you at the waystation and you said that your name was Trish Lawrence, I became very suspicious. You see, in her letters Hattie had mentioned Trish a couple of times. Then when I took a good look at you, I knew you were my granddaughter. You resemble your mother, and you look a lot like I did when I was your age."

"Does your son know about the telegram?"

"No, I didn't tell him. The morning I got the wire he was working in the fields, and my daughter-in-law wasn't home. I immediately made arrangements to leave, telling my son that I had decided to move in with my brother in San Antonio."

"So you really do have a brother there?"

"Yes, I do. Ironic, I know, but true. He moved to San

Antonio a long time ago. Maxine doesn't know he lives there. But Hattie knows, and I'm sure that was her main reason for sending me the wire. She knew I could go to San Antonio and find you. When Hiram and I left, I hoped and prayed that I'd come across you on the trail. I wanted to be with you, and to help you if I could. I didn't know what kind of trouble you were in since Hattie's wire only said that you were fleeing from the law. Mr. Slade told me that you were accused of killing James Rayfield."

"I didn't do it."

Mary smiled tenderly. "I never thought for one moment that you did. Do you mind telling me exactly what happened?"

Sharla gave her a full explanation.

"I can well imagine your shock when Agnes sent you to Maxine."

Sharla nodded, then asked, "When you left the farm hoping to find me, were you planning on telling me the truth?"

"I didn't know if I would or not."

"What convinced you?"

"Mr. Slade's encouragement played a part, but mostly I was compelled by love—my love for you."

Sharla got to her feet. Love! She almost spat the word harshly. This family of hers had a strange definition of love: Mary and Maxine estranged for nearly thirty years, a mother giving up her own child in favor of prostitution, and a grandmother who looked the other way like an ostrich burying its head in the sand. She wanted no part of this family. She wasn't like them. She had survived almost twenty-one years without knowing of their existence, and she didn't need them now. It was too little, too late!

She spoke gently to Mary, for she had no wish to hurt her. "What's done is done. The past can't be changed. I hope in time my anger will mellow, and I'll be able to forgive Maxine, Olivia, and the man who was my father.

But I do believe that I'm hurt beyond repair, and a certain amount of bitterness will always remain."

"What about us?" Mary asked cautiously. "Do I dare hope that someday you'll love me as your grandmother?"

"When I was a child, I longed for a grandmother who would dote on me as my friends' grandmothers doted on them. But I'm no longer a child."

"You must hate me," Mary murmured.

"No," Sharla replied at once. "I don't hate you. Please don't think that. Truthfully, I'm not sure how I feel, but I do know that my heart holds no hate for you."

"Thank God!" Mary sighed, her head bowed as though she could no longer face the granddaughter she had rejected so many years ago.

Sharla was ready to change the subject. Bearing up was becoming too difficult. "The man who played cards with Hiram is here. His name is Steve Jordan. He's going to camp here for the night. I think I'll talk to him and Lance for a while before I go to bed." She went to the backboard, glanced over her shoulder, and asked, "Are you coming?"

Mary's head was still bowed, but when she raised her face, her expression was calm, her emotions under control. She got up slowly from her rocking chair and followed Sharla to the campfire.

Jordan was eating warmed-up stew. Lance, seated across the fire, was nursing a cup of coffee. Sharla chose to sit next to their guest, preferring to avoid Slade's proximity. Such closeness would only disrupt her emotions, which were hanging by a mere thread.

Lance offered to get Mary her rocker. She declined, and, contradicting her advanced years, she sat beside him with the ease of a woman much younger. "Mr. Jordan," she began, "it's nice to see you again."

"Please call me Steve," he said. "That goes for all of you."

"Exactly where are you headed?" Mary asked.

He shrugged. "Texas—Nevada—it doesn't really matter. I stay wherever I happen to hang my hat. But I do have a definite stop to make. There's a town about twenty miles after you cross into Texas from Arkansas. It's called Madison Creek; it's not much of a town. I don't think it'll be around much longer. That area isn't good grazing land. It's suitable for farming, but for some reason very few farmers have settled there. I have a brother in Madison Creek; he owns the town's only saloon. A few weeks back I stopped in town to visit him and his family. Three strangers rode in and robbed the bank. That they chose to rob the bank in Madison Creek doesn't say much for their intelligence, since there's not much money there. When they left the bank, there was a shootout. My brother's ten-year-old daughter was on her way home and was caught in the crossfire. One of the robbers shot her, and she died a few minutes later. The sheriff got up a posse. My brother was too grief-stricken to ride with them, so I went along. One of the robbers was wounded, and his two comrades left him behind. We never found them, but the wounded man was taken back to town, and the doctor managed to save his life. The sheriff held off a lynching, locked the man up, and said he'd stay there until the circuit judge was notified. I went on to St. Charles, but I told my brother I'd be back. I imagine by now the judge has come and gone and the trial is over. I just hope I get there in time to see that murdering bastard hang."

"Do you know who the bank robbers were?" Lance asked.

"I know the name of the one who's gonna swing from a rope: Randy Severs."

"Severs!" Lance repeated, sitting up straight, his muscles taut.

"Do you know him?" Steve asked.

"Yeah, I know him, but I haven't seen him in years."

He looked to Mary, and then to Sharla. "We're going to take a small detour to Madison Creek."

"Do you mind telling us why?" Sharla asked.

"I'd rather not say," he replied. His eyes had turned cold and unyielding.

"Since we're all going to Madison Creek," Jordan began, "I don't suppose you mind if I travel with you."

"You're welcome to come along," Lance said, getting to his feet. He walked away without saying anything more.

Sharla watched as he went to his bedroll and lay down. Folding his arms beneath his head, he stared up at the night sky that was dotted with a multitude of twinkling stars. Sharla longed to question him, to learn his reason for detouring to Madison Creek. She sighed deeply. She didn't really know Lance, but she did know him well enough to sense that he wouldn't tell her or the others until he was ready.

Mary and Sharla talked a little longer with Jordan, then they returned to the wagon and went to bed. Although Mary yearned to reopen the past and discuss it further, there was an aloofness about Sharla that warded off any such attempt. Therefore, she said nothing, but she knew the past was not a topic Sharla could continue to avoid. Sooner or later, she had to stand and face it. When that happened, Mary intended to be there for her.

Hattie found Maxine in her office, sitting at her desk with an open bottle of brandy facing her. The servant closed the door, then sat in the chair across from her employer's. "I need to talk to you," Hattie said.

"What is it?" Maxine asked, filling her glass for the third time.

Sidetracked by Maxine's drinking, Hattie remarked, "You've been doing a lot of that lately. Even the customers have noticed it."

Maxine raised a brow. "I take it you're referring to my drinking. Well, I'm sorry if it bothers you and the customers, but it isn't your concern, or theirs."

"I know how troubled you are, but that doesn't give you the right to talk to me like this."

Maxine was instantly contrite. "I'm sorry, Hattie. Please forgive me. I know I'm drinking too much, but it's the only thing that helps. The past keeps haunting me, and I wonder if I did the right thing. When I gave up my daughter, I thought I was doing it for her. But what you said to me keeps running through my mind. Did I really do it for Sharla, or did I do it for myself and John?" She leaned back in her chair and sighed dismally, "Oh, Hattie, you're so much wiser than I am. Please tell me what to do. Where do I go from here?"

"I'm not as wise as you think I am. I did something very foolish."

Maxine tensed. "What did you do?"

"Before I tell you that, I've got a confession to make."

"A confession?" she questioned, totally perplexed.

Hattie drew a deep breath, then, speaking steadily, robbing Maxine of the opportunity to interrupt, she told her that she and Mary had corresponded all these years. Finished, she waited uneasily for Maxine's outburst.

However, no outburst was forthcoming. Instead, Maxine simply smiled. "Hattie, I've always known about those letters. You made the mistake of leaving one in your room. I went there to look for you, and the letter was in the open. From what I read, it was evident that you and Mama had corresponded regularly."

"Why didn't you ever say anything?"

"What was there to say? Any relationship I could possibly have with Mama was destroyed that day she and Papa came to St. Louis. I put that part of my life permanently behind me." She frowned with self-reproach, "I do that a lot, don't

I? Put things behind me, instead of facing them?" It was a question that didn't require an answer.

"When I learned that Sharla was going to San Antonio," Hattie began, dreading what she had to say, "I slipped away from the house and went to the telegraph office. I sent a wire to Mary, asking her to find Sharla and help her. I never mentioned Sharla by name, but I did say that she was fleeing from the law."

Hattie, now too upset to remain seated, rose from her chair. "A few minutes ago, the doorman told me that Arnold Shelby, who sent the wire, was here looking for Dexter Rayfield. He said they talked in the bar."

"Good Lord!" Maxine cried. "Hattie, how could you have done something so . . . so . . ."

"Stupid?" Hattie finished for her. "I don't have an excuse. I was just so worried about Sharla!"

"Apparently, Mr. Shelby connected your wire to Sharla's disappearance. I wonder why Dexter hasn't questioned you."

Hattie returned to her chair. "I don't know," she murmured gravely. "But I'm afraid that man's up to something."

"Whatever he's up to, I bet Claudia's right in the middle of it. I still intend to take Bailey's report to the constable. I'll do that first thing in the morning. Surely, that report will convince him to consider Claudia a suspect."

"I'm sorry about sending that wire," Hattie said tearfully. "Please don't hate me!"

Maxine left her chair, went to her good friend, and placed an arm about her shoulders. "Hate you?" she murmured. "I love you, Hattie. For thirty years, you've been my only family."

Eighteen

Claudia slept late, and the sun was approaching the noon hour when she climbed out of bed. She had spent the night in Dexter's room. They had made love before falling asleep, and Dexter had wanted her again this morning before leaving for work. He was involved in three different businesses. They had belonged to Olivia, then to James. Now that they were both deceased, Dexter was sure he would inherit full control.

Claudia looked through her suitcase and took out a cotton gown. She eyed it scornfully; it was drab and unflattering. The moment Dexter returned home, she intended to talk to him about purchasing a new wardrobe for her.

She took her time dressing, stopping every so often to admire her surroundings. The master bedroom was elaborate, decorated with only the finest and most expensive furnishings. She hadn't seen the entire house, but she had seen enough to know that it blatantly reflected its owner's wealth. However, she preferred Olivia's house over this one. There was a certain artistic touch to Olivia's home that was lacking here. Her former employer's refinement was elegantly displayed in every room, and if Claudia could choose a home of her own, she'd choose Olivia's.

She shrugged aside the dream. Dexter would buy her a home, but it certainly would not compare to Olivia's. Only grand ladies lived in such luxury, and that was an honor bestowed by birth. Nevertheless, she intended to achieve riches, for she had beauty and a keen mind. Someday she planned to be as successful as Maxine Reynolds.

She left the bedroom and started downstairs. The marble stairway faced the front entrance, and she had descended halfway when Dexter opened the door. He stepped inside, followed by two men Claudia had never seen.

He waited for her to join him, then giving her a peck on the cheek, he ushered her into the parlor. His companions came in behind them.

"Claudia," Dexter began, indicating each guest, "I'd like you to meet Lou Jackson and Jeff Chambers."

Nodding a hello, she regarded the pair closely. They were dressed in western attire and both sported holstered pistols. Lou Jackson had a dark, hawkish face. His friend's features were craggy. A cigarette hung in one side of his mouth, sending smoke sneering across his whiskers.

"I stopped this morning," Dexter explained, "to put an ad in the paper. A friend of mine happened to be there and he told me about Jackson and Chambers. He played cards with them last night at Maxine's. He said that those two are the kind of men I'm looking for. I located them, and they agreed to travel to San Antonio with us. We'll be leaving in the morning."

"So soon?" Claudia questioned. "But I was hoping you'd take me shopping. I need new clothes."

"I don't have time to worry about something like that," he replied impatiently. "I have a lot to do before I can leave. I'll be gone until late tonight." She received another kiss on the cheek, then Dexter and his bodyguards were gone.

Claudia was riled. Shopping meant more to her than leaving so quickly for San Antonio. What was she supposed to do all day? Wandering through this big house held no appeal and visiting with the servants was out of the question. Although they showed her respect, Claudia knew they didn't really mean it. In their eyes she was a harlot.

Claudia managed to pass the day. She ate lunch alone, and walked the grounds out back. Then she checked Dexter's library for a book, but the literature was not to her liking. She spent hours pacing the parlor, the bedroom, and then finally went downstairs for dinner.

She was halfway through the meal when she suddenly remembered that Maxine had money belonging to her. She had planned to go back and collect it in a couple of days, but that was now impossible, for she and Dexter were leaving in the morning.

Claudia hurried upstairs, grabbed her purse, then left the house without saying anything to the servants. She intended to visit Maxine's, but she couldn't use the coachman, for he was with Dexter. She didn't have to walk very far before hailing a public conveyance. The driver stopped, and she told him where to take her, then got inside the enclosed carriage.

She leaned back against the soft upholstery and closed her eyes. Her thoughts drifted to James. She still loved him and thinking about him was painful. Why, she wondered, did he still have the power to put this ache in her heart? She should be thinking about Dexter, not James. After all, Dexter was more considerate, kinder, and a much better lover.

She pushed such puzzling thoughts aside. James was dead, and that was that! Anger built up inside her. He deserved to die, for he was a cold, insensitive devil!

Claudia grew impatient to get this over with, and the ride to Maxine's seemed as slow as a snail's pace. By the time the driver turned onto the winding lane leading to the front door, Claudia's nerves were tightly strung.

She left the carriage, and asked the driver to wait. When the doorman admitted her, she told him she wanted to see Maxine. He led her to his employer's office and knocked on the door.

"Come in!" Maxine called.

He opened the door, gestured for Claudia to enter, then returned to his post.

Maxine was at her desk, but the sight of Claudia sent her bolting to her feet. She hadn't expected to see her so soon.

Claudia moved across the room with an air of self-assurance, sat in the chair facing Maxine, and said calmly, "I'm here to collect my wages."

"Very well," she replied, taking a key from her desk and opening the top drawer. She counted out the correct amount and handed it to Claudia, who put the bills in her purse.

"Aren't you going to count it?" Maxine asked.

"Why? I trust you."

"Do you? Well, I can't say the same about you."

Claudia rose to her feet. "I didn't come here to listen to your innuendos. Now, if you'll excuse me . . . ?" She started to turn away.

"I'm not going to let you off that easily!" Maxine retorted.

"What does that mean?" Claudia asked.

"You killed James Rayfield, didn't you?"

She pretended amazement. "How dare you!"

"You can fool the constable and Dexter, but you can't fool me! I've known all along that you killed James. And I'm not going to let you get by with murder!"

Claudia dropped the pretense. "There's nothing you can do! You have no evidence."

"Maybe not, but I do have a report on your family. Did you know your father was violently insane? He never deserted you and your mother, he was put into an insane asylum. He remained there until he died. I think you are as dangerous as your father, and I intend to prove it."

"I read that report. You were stupid enough to leave it on your desk. But it doesn't prove anything."

"No, but it is valuable information." She fixed Claudia with a threatening glare. "Information that Dexter will find very interesting."

Rage, like that of a cornered animal's, flared savagely in Claudia. "If you show that report to Dexter, I'll . . . I'll . . ."

"You'll what? Kill me? Do you think you can get by with murder twice?" She started to tell her that she had already shown the report to the constable, but decided it might be wiser not to say too much.

Claudia remained calm. "Show Dexter that report; I don't care. It won't change his feelings toward me."

"If you believe that, then you are a bigger fool than I thought. You might control Dexter's passion, but I doubt that you control his reasoning. I'm taking that report to him tonight, and you'll see that I'm right about him."

Claudia battled for self-control. She wanted desperately to kill this woman, but there was no escape. She surely would be caught and arrested. She stood stiffly, every muscle in her body strained, her heart pounding erratically. Perspiration broke out on her brow, as though the temperature inside the room had suddenly risen to an unbearable degree. A window was open, and as a brisk breeze drifted inside, Claudia turned her face toward the refreshing draft. It not only cooled her brow, but it also soothed her inner turmoil. She knew what she had to do, and the open window was like an invitation to murder.

Claudia was smiling as she faced her former employer, her smile so chilling that it sent a shiver up Maxine's spine. "I'm not afraid of you, nor am I afraid of your threats." With that, she whirled about and left the office.

The doorman showed her outside. The driver was waiting and she gave him Dexter's address and climbed into the carriage. The moment they turned off the winding lane and Maxine's house was out of sight, she ordered the driver to stop. Alighting, she said that she had decided to walk. She paid the fare, plus a generous tip, then sent him on his way.

Keeping to the shadows, she hurried back up the lane and to the side of the house. There, the open window awaited her return. She crept closer and peeked into the office. Maxine was still at her desk, a glass of brandy in her hand. Claudia watched as she drank the liquor as though it were water and she was dying of thirst.

Now that Claudia was at the open window with murder on her mind, she wondered exactly how to go about it. If she were to climb inside, Maxine would surely hear her. Violent frustration swept through her. She had to silence this woman, for she couldn't let her show that report to Dexter.

At that moment, a knock sounded at the office door. Maxine put down her glass, went to the door and opened it. One of her bartenders needed her assistance with inventory. She left with him, closing the door behind her.

Claudia quickly climbed through the window, moved to the fireplace and picked up an iron poker. Her eyes darted about the room, searching for a place to hide. The window was adorned with floor-length drapes. Drawn aside they afforded the ideal cover. Carrying the iron poker, she scooted in between the wall and the heavy drapes, and waited for Maxine's return. She hoped desperately that the woman would indeed come back before leaving to visit Dexter. That worry sent her heart beating rapidly. Her stomach began to roil and her head started throbbing. For a moment she thought she might faint, but anger quickly took precedence over her fear. Her heart slowed, her stomach settled, and her head stopped aching.

Like a wild predator, now eager for the kill, she waited anxiously for her prey's return.

* * *

Agnes was in her quarters when she heard a loud knocking at the back door. Her room was adjacent to the kitchen. No lights were burning in there, so taking a lamp with her, she walked past the huge stove, around the kitchen table, went to the locked door and asked who was calling.

"Tom Woodson," a man voice's replied.

Agnes recognized the constable's voice, and she admitted him without hesitation.

"Excuse me for calling at this hour, but I was on my way home when I got this notion to stop here. I came to the kitchen door because I figured at this time of night you'd be in the back of the house."

"What can I do for you, Constable?"

"I'd like to search Claudia's room."

Agnes was totally surprised. "Why do you want to do that?"

"I have my reasons," he replied, keeping his suspicions to himself. Maxine had visited him early this morning and had shown him the report on Claudia's father. At the time, he hadn't given it much credence; in his mind, Sharla Matthews was undoubtedly guilty. However, as the day wore on, that report kept gnawing at him.

Agnes waved a hand toward the rear stairway. "If you'll come with me, I'll take you to her room." She kept the lamp with her, for the upstairs was dark.

He followed her up to the third floor, where the servants' quarters were located. She took him to a room at the end of the hall and opened the door.

The constable went inside, lit a lamp, then began looking about the small room. "Has anybody cleaned in here since Claudia left?" he asked.

"No," Agnes replied. She stood in the open doorway, watching curiously as the officer pulled out drawers, looked under the bed, and behind the curtain where Claudia used to hang her clothes. She had left behind two uniforms. There was no standing wardrobe or closet for him to search. The room simply consisted of a chest of drawers and a narrow bed. A small fireplace provided heat for cold winter days and nights.

The constable came up empty-handed. Claudia had left nothing behind that could be construed as evidence. He extinguished the bedroom lamp, and followed Agnes back to the kitchen.

"Thanks for your help," he told her, heading for the door.

"Wait," Agnes said. "What were you looking for?"

"I'd rather not say," he replied, opening the door and leaving. Actually, he had been looking for bloody clothes, or anything that might connect Claudia to James's murder. He hurried around the house and to his carriage, which was parked out front. He climbed inside, freed the reins, and slapped them against the horse. He was anxious to get home and was impatient with himself for stopping here first. The report Maxine showed him on Claudia's father had nothing to do with James's murder, and he shouldn't have given it a moment's importance. Sharla Matthews was guilty. Twice, she had threatened Rayfield's life, his blood was on her clothes, and she certainly had the opportunity to kill him. The constable wasn't sure about her motive. Maybe she wanted Olivia's full estate, or she might have killed out of a jealous rage. That she and James were lovers was certainly a possibility.

He shrugged the case aside. His wife was home waiting dinner and he was ready to put the day behind him and enjoy a restful evening.

As the constable was heading home, Sharla and her companions were sitting about the campfire. Dinner was over, and Steve Jordan was entertaining everyone with exciting and humorous accounts of his adventures as a roving gambler. He was quite a talker, and definitely had a talent for capturing and holding his listeners' interest.

Sharla was very impressed with Steve, and she wished Lance was more like him instead of so close-mouthed and secretive. She had known Steve less than a day, yet she felt as though he were an old friend. Lance, on the other hand, she didn't really know at all.

Sharla was sitting beside Steve, and as he talked, he often touched her arm or her hand, but he wasn't making subtle advances; touching was his way of generating warmth and friendliness. Not that he didn't find Sharla attractive, but he wasn't sure about her relationship with Lance, and he wasn't about to tread where he didn't belong.

Lance, sitting across the fire, watched Steve's every move. He considered himself a keen judge of character, and he didn't think Jordan was going too far with Sharla. He had taken an instant liking to the gambler; nevertheless, he couldn't help but experience a pang of jealousy as Jordan held Sharla riveted with his wit and charm.

By now the campfire had burned down to red embers, and everyone decided it was time to retire. The women went to the wagon, undressed, and slipped into nightgowns. Sharla spread out their pallets as Mary released her thick tresses; from their confining bun. She brushed her hair, then neatly plaited the gray strands into one long braid. She looked at Sharla, who was watching her. "My hair used to be the same color as yours," she said wistfully. "When Ezra and I married, my hair was so long I could sit on it. Ezra brushed it for me every night before we went to bed."

"You loved him very much, didn't you?"

"Yes, of course I did. He was my husband."

Sharla started to respond, but thought better of it.

"What were you about to say?" Mary asked. "Do you find it surprising I could love a man who disowned his daughter?"

"Yes, something like that," she admitted.

"It wasn't entirely Ezra's fault. Maxine knew what her profession would do to her father, but that didn't stop her. She broke Ezra's heart; he was never the same after he saw her in St. Louis. I think that was his main reason for going off to war. He needed a release for all that anger and hurt inside him."

"How do you feel about Maxine?"

"She's my daughter—I've never stopped loving her."

"I don't understand that kind of love."

"What do you mean?"

"If you love her, how can you go thirty years without seeing her? For that matter, if Maxine loved me, how could she have given me away? Her love is as strange as yours."

"I hear bitterness in your voice."

"There *is* bitterness, a lot of bitterness. I think your side of the family is cold and unforgiving. I'll never understand your kind of love." She went to her pallet, lay down, and turned her back.

Mary extinguished the lantern and moved to her own pallet, which was beside Sharla's. "You may never understand my kind of love or Maxine's," she murmured softly. "But I do believe with all my heart that giving you away was the hardest thing Maxine ever did in her life. She wanted your father to raise you; he had so much more to offer."

"Yes, raise me as his adopted child," Sharla muttered, keeping her back turned. "My parents were liars, cheats, and cowards. I have no respect for either of them."

"Your feelings are understandable, but in time these feelings will soften."

"I don't think so," Sharla replied.

"When James Rayfield's murderer is apprehended, there's no reason why you can't have a relationship with Maxine. Don't let the same mistake happen twice."

"What do you mean by that?"

"I pray you and Maxine don't make the same mistake she and I made. The relationship between a mother and a daughter is too precious to throw away."

Sharla didn't say anything, but she questioned how she could throw away what she never had.

Nearly an hour passed before Maxine returned to her office. The inventory had taken much longer than she thought it would. Considering the late hour, she decided not to visit Dexter until morning. She sat at her desk and poured a glass of brandy. She knew she should stop drinking so heavily, but without the numbing power of liquor, the past was too painful to face. Sharla's sudden intrusion into her well-ordered life had reopened memories that she had locked away years ago. Forced to confront her past, her only comfort came in a brandy bottle. She had made so many mistakes, and if she had it all to do over again, everything would be different.

She thought about her father. After finding that first letter in Hattie's room, she had often slipped back to read more letters. That was how she learned of her father's death. After that, she never returned to read more of her mother's letters; she permanently closed the door on that part of her life. Remembering was too painful. But she couldn't completely separate herself from her daughter. She had to continue to see her, if only from a distance. She had secretly watched Sharla grow from a child into a woman.

As Maxine was dealing with her feelings, Claudia was sneaking out from behind the drapes. The window was behind Maxine's desk, which put her back facing her intended attacker.

The thick carpet cushioned Claudia's steps as she advanced slowly and cautiously. She raised the iron poker over her head, and when she was close enough, she sent the deadly weapon crashing against Maxine's skull. The fatal blow knocked her victim out of her chair and onto the floor.

A water pitcher and basin were on a nearby table. Claudia hurried over, wet the bottom of her petticoat, washed the blood from the poker and returned it to its rightful place. She then dragged her victim to the fireplace and positioned her so that her head was resting on the brick hearth. She checked for blood spots on the carpet, where Maxine had fallen but there were none. The gash was at the back of Maxine's head, and she had hit the carpet on her side. Grabbing the brandy glass, which was more than halfway full, she placed it close to Maxine's hand, then gently pushed it over so that the contents would spill. The smell of brandy was now overwhelming.

She stood, glared down at her dead victim, and muttered harshly, "You were drunk, fell, and hit your head. You fool! Did you really think I'd stand by and let you ruin my life?"

A chilling giggle spewed forth, gone as fast as it had arrived. She had to get out of here now! She crawled back through the window, and, staying in the shadows, she made her way past the meandering lane and to the street. Running, she put a good distance between herself and the house before hailing a public conveyance.

Nineteen

Claudia was dressed for bed when Dexter returned home. He entered the room carrying a packed valise. He placed it at Claudia's feet and said, "I'm sorry I didn't have time to take you shopping, but these clothes will do fine for the trip."

She looked at the valise as though she wasn't sure what to make of it. "Where did you find clothes this time of night?"

He removed his jacket, slung it across a chair, and went to a well-stocked liquor cart located beside a huge wardrobe. "I stopped by my brother's home," he said, pouring a glass of port. "I packed some of Sharla's things."

Anger flared inside Claudia, and she was tempted to kick the valise across the room. How dare Dexter bring her secondhand clothes! She wanted a new, expensive wardrobe, not clothes belonging to someone else! She was suddenly struck with a bitter memory. When she was a child, used clothing always hung in her closets. Rich employers considered their discarded clothes a servants' bonus. Her mother had taken their charity, dressing her daughter in clothes that were somewhat worn but still serviceable. Later, when Claudia matured, she refused such charity; she would rather wear rags than wear handouts!

Now, as she stared resentfully at the packed valise, she controlled the urge to kick it as far as she could. Although it seemed to represent everything that was downtrodden in her life, she suppressed her anger, swallowed her pride, and said to Dexter, "I suppose Sharla's clothes will fit, but I am more full-figured than she."

Taking his glass, Dexter moved to the bed and sat on the edge. "I plan to leave at dawn," he began. "Jackson and Chambers will meet us here. We're traveling horseback; that's why I chose riding apparel for you."

Claudia stepped around the valise, pulling aside the hem of her nightgown as though she found the bag so offensive that she dared not even allow her hem to brush against it.

Dexter's bedchamber was decorated to please a man, so there was no vanity and Claudia had to stand in front of a bureau to brush her hair. The costly piece, sporting an elongated mirror, matched the large, dark ebonized cherry bed. The bureau and bed were blatantly expensive and totally masculine.

Claudia couldn't help but feel somewhat disillusioned. She longed for her own bedroom, one decorated with as much elegance and femininity as Sharla's. She wanted to wear beautiful clothes, live in a grand house, and enjoy all the benefits of wealth. Instead, she was forced to sleep in a man's bedroom, wear used clothes, and ride horseback to Texas. She dreaded the journey, for she was not accustomed to sitting in a saddle all day.

As she continued brushing her hair, she began to feel more and more sorry for herself. That she had committed murder less than an hour ago barely fazed her. She had pushed Maxine's murder to the far recesses of her mind with the same ease that she had discarded James Rayfield's. She would not think about it unless a chance of detection should arise. Otherwise, she would simply block it from her thoughts as one would block out a bad dream.

She put down the brush, moved to Dexter and sat on the bed beside him. "When do I get my own home and a generous allowance?" she asked bluntly, for luxury meant everything to her.

"As soon as we get back from San Antonio," he replied.

She pouted childishly. "How long will that take?"

"I don't know," he answered. He finished his port, and placed the glass on the bedside table. Claudia was wearing a modest nightgown that she had owned for years, but the plain garment didn't make her any less desirable in Rayfield's eyes. He was too enamored of the beauty concealed beneath the gown's cotton folds.

Taking her into his arms, he eased her back onto the bed. He kissed her passionately, then gazing into her eyes, he murmured huskily, "I think it will take a long time before I tire of you."

His words took her unawares, and, for a moment, she was actually stunned. But she recovered quickly. Naturally he would someday grow weary of her and move on to someone else. She was his mistress, not his future bride! In this regard, Dexter was just like his brother. He used women. Well, this time she would not be taken advantage of; she would come out ahead. While she still had Dexter under her sexual power, she would use her power to reap bountiful rewards. First, however, the trip to San Antonio had to be taken care of. Once that was over—with Sharla dead or behind bars—she would demand that Dexter buy her a home, give her expensive gems, and provide her with ample funds.

A smile, as calculating as it was enticing, curled Claudia's lips as she returned Dexter's probing gaze. "Maybe I will tire of you before you tire of me," she murmured.

He found her response irritating. She seemed determined to hold the upper hand in their relationship. If she wasn't so passionate, and if she didn't have this sexual control over him, he'd send the insolent wench back to Maxine's. But Claudia was like a thirst he couldn't quench—a hunger he couldn't appease. He couldn't get enough of her—not yet!

His mouth swooped down on hers with a savage force, and he slipped his hand beneath her gown, fondling her roughly as though his brutality put him in charge of her body, as well as her emotions.

However, Claudia relished his sexual assault, and she responded so fervently that she, and not Dexter, soon dominated their aggressive foreplay, and the unbridled coupling that followed.

Constable Woodson grumbled under his breath as he stopped his carriage in front of Maxine's establishment. Alighting, his grumbling grew more pronounced. His disposition was cranky, for he had been awakened from a sound sleep. Following dinner, he had left his wife with her mending and had gone directly to bed. Shortly thereafter, his wife had roused him from slumber, telling him that a uniformed policeman was downstairs.

He threw on his clothes, then hurried to the parlor, where the policeman had informed him that Maxine Reynolds was dead. The young officer was apologetic for disturbing his superior, but he thought he would want to know right away.

Woodson hitched up his buggy, and with his comrade accompanying him on horseback, he drove across town to Maxine's house.

Now, as he lumbered to the front door, he suppressed his cranky temperament and became totally professional. A suspicious death had occurred, and he intended to thoroughly investigate. He had questioned the young policeman, but his information was limited. He didn't know if Maxine Reynolds's death was murder or an accident.

The doorman admitted Woodson. Patrons and employees were standing about, talking in hushed tones. Several of them appeared shocked, and some of the women were crying softly. The doorman showed the constable into the office, where he found two more uniformed policemen and Dr. Eastman.

The physician was kneeling beside Maxine's body, but he stood at the constable's arrival, gestured toward the body, and announced with certainty, "She apparently fell, and hit her head on the hearth."

Woodson moved to the fireplace, his experienced eyes taking in the entire scene. The smell of spilled brandy was still strong, and he told one of the officers to open the windows wider.

"Maxine was drinking a lot lately," Eastman said, as though Woodson had broached the subject. "I come here often, and the last few times I talked to Maxine, it was obvious that she was tipsy."

That the doctor was a frequent visitor came as no surprise to Woodson. The man was a widower and could spend his free time as he pleased. As Woodson's gaze centered on the deceased, he experienced a pang of sympathy. He knew why Maxine had been drinking heavily. When she showed him the report on Claudia's father, she had been totally open with him and had confessed that Sharla was her child. She didn't divulge the father's identity, and Woodson didn't ask. He strongly suspected that Maxine knew Sharla's whereabouts, but again he didn't ask; it would have been a waste of breath and time. She would have died before revealing Sharla's location. Woodson now wondered if perhaps she had indeed died for that purpose.

He told one of the officers to find the doorman, for he wanted to question him. He returned momentarily with his charge, and Woodson said he needed to talk to the man alone. The two policemen and the doctor left the room.

The doorman, whose job it was to enforce order also, was young and powerfully built. He kept his eyes averted from Maxine's body, for he had been very fond of his employer and he didn't want to see her this way.

"Did Miss Reynolds have any visitors this evening?" Woodson asked him.

"Claudia came by. She worked here for a short time, but she left with Dexter Rayfield. I guess she's living with him."

"Was Claudia alone in here with Miss Reynolds?"

"Yes, but she only stayed a few minutes. I showed her out."

"Did you see Miss Reynolds after Claudia left?"

"Yes, I did. She and the bartender were taking care of inventory."

The man's words dashed Woodson's prime suspect. Claudia had left Maxine very much alive! He suddenly felt somewhat foolish. He was treating this as a murder case when in all probability it was an unfortunate accident. There was nothing at the scene that pointed to foul play. Nevertheless, he left the room and questioned more employees and some of the patrons. No one had seen Maxine after she finished with inventory and closed herself in her office. However, many of them said that she appeared to be under the influence of liquor. He was about to leave, go to the station and fill out an accidental death report, when he suddenly missed Hattie. He knew that the woman had been with Maxine for years, and therefore, the two women had to be very close. He sought the doorman, and asked him where he could find Hattie. He said that she was in her room, and was very upset, for she was the one who had found Maxine's body. The man showed Woodson to Hattie's quarters, which adjoined Maxine's.

Woodson dismissed him, then knocked softly on the closed door. He waited, but there was no reply. He was about to rap again when the door opened slowly. Hattie stood in the dark. The only light came from the hall lamps. The saffron glow illuminated her grief-stricken face.

"May I come in?" Woodson asked. He wished he didn't have to infringe on her sorrow, but he felt it was important that he question her.

Inviting him in, she lit a couple of lamps and the room was immediately transformed from gloomy darkness to cheery warmth. Despite Hattie's domestic station, her quarters reflected wealth and impeccable taste.

"Maxine was murdered," she told Woodson, the statement spoken without any provocation on his part.

"Why do you say that?" he asked.

"Maxine was drinking too much, I don't deny that. But she never got fallin' down drunk. She had too much class."

"Who do you think killed her?"

"Claudia!" she replied harshly. "The same as she killed James Rayfield. She got by with that murder, and she'll probably get by with this one too."

"Maxine was alive when Claudia left."

"I don't care. I tell you, somehow she came back and killed Maxine!"

"I realize you're upset, but is it really so improbable that Maxine tripped, fell, and hit her head?"

It was on the tip of Hattie's tongue to firmly reject the possibility, but accidents did indeed happen. She relented, barely, "Something like that could happen, I suppose. But I don't much believe it."

"I'll talk to Claudia first thing in the morning. And if it'll make you feel any better, I'll leave this case open until I'm fully convinced that Maxine's death was an accident."

She didn't feel any better; there was nothing that could even begin to ease her pain. However, she thanked the constable for his kindness, showed him out, and locked the door behind him. She extinguished the lamps, fell across her bed and waited for tears that failed to materialize. They were there, barely beneath the surface, but since the moment she had discovered Maxine's body, they had refused to flow. She wanted to cry, for surely a stream of tears would help wash away this terrible grief squeezing her heart as tenaciously as a boa constrictor squeezing its prey.

Hattie couldn't imagine life without Maxine. They had been together for so many years. She had watched over Maxine, tended to her, shared the good times with her as well as the bad. Now, that part of her life was over. Maxine was dead.

At last, Hattie's bottled-up tears forced their way free, filling her eyes, burning them, and then overflowing.

Mary, moaning in her sleep, tossed and turned on her pallet. Her groans grew louder, her tossing more violent. She kicked off her blanket, and it lay crumpled at her feet. As her nightmare turned from fear to terror, her body broke out in a cold sweat and the sheet, now damp, twisted about her legs as she rolled back and forth, her frail arms lashing out as though she were fighting an invisible demon.

Her moans awakened Sharla, and she hurried from her pallet to Mary's. She sat beside the woman, gripped her shoulder and shook it firmly. "Mary, wake up. Wake up! You're having a bad dream."

Her eyes flew open and she sat up with a start. She stared about the moonlit wagon, her expression oddly vacant. For a moment she didn't seem to realize where she was. She looked at Sharla, who was watching her closely. Suddenly, Mary's sleep-laced thoughts cleared, and she managed to summon a shaky smile.

"You must have had a terrible dream," Sharla murmured. "You were moaning and thrashing."

Mary sighed gravely and grasped Sharla's hand, her fingers gripping tightly. "It was worse than terrible, it was horrifying."

"Do you want to tell me about it?"

"I dreamt about Maxine," she began, her voice strained, for reliving the nightmare made it too real. She started with a factual event, "When Maxine was four years old, she fell into the river. She got caught in a swift current and almost drowned. Ezra was a good swimmer, and he managed to reach her. Somehow, he found the strength to keep Maxine's head above water, fight the current, and swim safely to the bank. Maxine would have died if not for Ezra."

She paused, and asked for a drink of water. Sharla found a canteen, filled a cup, and brought it to her.

Mary's throat was parched and she drank thirstily. "I was dreaming about that day," she continued. "Maxine was again four years old, and again she fell into the river. Only this time, Ezra wasn't there to save her. I swam in after her, but the current kept sweeping her farther and farther away from me. I couldn't reach her. She went under, came back up and screamed for her mother. A wave, one as high as you would see in the ocean, came crashing down over her head. The wave suddenly disappeared, and the river grew strangely calm. Maxine was gone. I swam to the spot where she disappeared, dove under the water time and time again, but she wasn't there." Mary took another drink, for her throat still seemed terribly parched. "I was searching for her when you woke me up."

Sharla pried her hand loose, for Mary's tight grip had become uncomfortable. She patted the woman's hand soothingly as she placed it in its owner's lap. "It was only a bad dream," she said gently, as one would calm a small child. "You mustn't let it bother you."

"No," Mary replied. "It was more than a dream. Something's wrong."

"What do you mean?"

"Something has happened to Maxine."

"That's absurd," Sharla chided. "Dreams aren't omens. They are dreams and nothing more."

Mary shook her head. "I'm not so sure. A strong bond exists between mother and child. A woman can't carry a baby in her womb for nine months and not be a permanent part of that child's life. You probably think I'm a senile old woman talking a lot of nonsense. But someday when you're a mother, you'll understand what I'm saying."

Sharla's bitterness loomed, and she responded sharply, "How can you share a bond with a daughter you haven't seen in thirty years? You are talking a lot of nonsense. You should go back to sleep and forget that dream." She rose to her feet. "I'm going outside to get a breath of fresh air."

She quickly put on a robe and a pair of slippers. She didn't bother to lower the backboard, but climbed over it and leapt lightly to the ground.

She paused, surprised to find that her heart was hammering as though she were exhausted. She supposed she was exhausted, but her exhaustion was mental fatigue. This new family of hers tried her emotions; she didn't understand them. She liked Mary, but there was a part of her that strongly resented the woman. Her resentment didn't end with Mary, but included Ezra, Maxine, and John Matthews. It even encompassed Olivia, the woman she had loved as a mother.

She moved away from the wagon and headed toward the campfire that had now burned down to glowing embers. She stepped quietly past Steve Jordan's bedroll. He didn't stir, and she figured he was sound asleep. She glanced toward Lance's bedroll and saw that it was empty. She decided to look for him. She wasn't sure why, for their encounters were usually upsetting. The man's reticence piqued her patience, and his swings in mood normally aroused her anger. Nevertheless, she went into the dense shrubbery, finding her way through prickly bushes and past flowering trees that were mingled with oaks and tall pines. Thick branches blocked most of the moon's rays, and the terrain became shadowy and somewhat frightening. Sharla was about to turn around and head back to camp when, all at once, Lance stepped in front of her. He seemed to come out of nowhere, his steps silent, as though no fallen leaves or cones covered the forest floor. Sharla was astounded that he could move through the woods without the leaves and cones snapping beneath his feet.

"What are you doing here?" he asked. His tone was flat, emotionless, and she smelled whiskey on his breath. She glanced down at his hand and was not surprised to see that he carried a bottle.

"I was looking for you," she replied.

"You should be in bed."

"I was, but Mary woke me up having a bad dream."

He took a swig of whiskey. "Was there any special reason why you wanted to find me?"

"Not really," she murmured, now wishing she hadn't come looking for him. His mood wasn't very friendly.

Suddenly, taking her by surprise, he grabbed her hand and urged her to walk beside him; however, they headed in the opposite direction of camp.

"Where are we going?" she asked.

"There's a clearing up ahead. These woods are full of ticks and chiggers."

His pace was brisk, but she had no problem staying abreast of him. "Why were you out here instead of in bed?" she asked.

"I couldn't sleep," he replied. They reached the clearing; here, moonlight reigned supreme, for there were no trees to shade its golden beams. Lance stopped, turned to Sharla and raked her with an expression she couldn't define.

She attempted to reach out to him, as one friend to another. "Lance, I know something is bothering you. It might help to talk about it, you know."

"The only thing bothering me at this moment is you," he said, his tone heavy with passion.

She tensed, and her pulse began to race. Her better judgment warned her to flee back to camp, but her heart, which was beating with anticipation, wanted her to remain.

Sharla was breathtaking in the saffron moonlight, her visage pure and lovely—almost angelic. Beneath her plain robe, which she had borrowed from Mary, was a nightgown so sheer that it was almost transparent. Maxine had packed it in Sharla's carpetbag, along with the other garments belonging to Trish. Sharla was not aware that the robe's sash was no longer securely tied but had loosened to such a degree that the sheer gown was exposed to Lance's intense gaze.

Slade was mesmerized by such perfect beauty, and desire thundered through him with the force of gigantic waves slamming against the seashore. His heart beat strongly, passion stirred in his loins, and the need to fully possess Sharla was overwhelming. He let the whiskey bottle slip from his fingers, no longer interested in drinking. A bed of grass cushioned the bottle, and it lay there, unbroken. His hands were suddenly on her shoulders, their grip firm, as though he intended to pull her into his arms, with or without her permission.

Sharla was held riveted by the desire burning in his dark, penetrating eyes. No man had ever wielded such sexual dominance over her, and she found it exciting, as well as a little unnerving. She had always prided herself on staying in control of any situation, but she knew she had no control over this moment, this man, or the desire to be in his arms. His hands on her shoulders were like hot irons, igniting a fire deep within her—a fire so passionate and primitive that she feared it as much as she welcomed it. Her emotions were as erratic and uncontrollable as a mighty whirlwind.

Lance's emotions were also out of control, maybe more

so than Sharla's, for whiskey had numbed his better judgment—his sense of right and wrong. Nothing mattered to him at this moment except taking Sharla into his arms and kissing her. He suddenly drew her against him, forcefully, as though he were afraid that she might turn and run. When he bent his head, she met his lips halfway, for she wanted his kiss as badly as he wanted hers. He explored her mouth sensually—demandingly. A need more powerful than he had ever experienced aroused his passion to a dangerous height, yet, as a gentle warmth filled his heart, he took his lips from hers and whispered in her ear, "You're so sweet, so innocent. Go back to the wagon, Sharla, before it's too late."

"It's already too late," she murmured, her voice hoarse with passion. "It was too late the moment you took me into your arms." She trembled in spite of the warm night.

"Are you cold?" he asked.

She smiled as she gazed up into his face, admiring his dark eyes, the shape of his lips, his strong jawline—his masculine countenance. "It's not the night air than makes me tremble," she said softly. "It's you, and what you do to me. I've never known such . . . such . . ."

"Desire?" he asked.

"It's more than that," she admitted. "I'm falling in love with you, Lance." She wrapped her arms about his neck, stood on tiptoe, and kissed him.

Lance's tentative control crumbled, and he drew her ever closer, holding her body intimately to his, his passion so aroused that she could feel his hardness pressed against her thighs.

At that moment, the sound of Mary's voice interrupted their embrace, separating the lovers as though it were an invisible force wedging its way between them.

Her voice was at a distance, but was drawing closer. "I'm over here," Sharla called in Mary's general direction.

A moment later, the woman appeared. She was surprised

to find Sharla with Lance, for she hadn't noticed that his bedroll was unoccupied. "I'm sorry to interrupt," she apologized, speaking mostly to Sharla. "But when you didn't come back to the wagon, I grew worried." She turned to leave, somewhat embarrassed that she had intruded.

"Wait," Lance said to her. "Sharla's going back with you." Mary's presence had bridled his passion and sobered his thoughts.

Sharla was stunned that he could let her go so abruptly. Her body still longed for fulfillment, and her heart was so overflowing with love that it actually ached.

He touched her arm firmly and urged her toward Mary. "Go on," he said, his tone brooking no argument. "You need your sleep."

Sleep? She needed him! However, Sharla had her pride, and she was not about to relinquish it. With a proud lift to her chin, she met his eyes, which gave away nothing. But Sharla's eyes perfectly mirrored her thoughts, and they flashed defiantly as she said with forced indifference, "Good night, Lance."

He watched as she and Mary left the clearing and disappeared into the dense vegetation. Then, picking up the whiskey bottle that lay at his feet, he opened it and took a gulping swig. He wiped a hand across his brow, for it had suddenly broken out in perspiration. He had come very close to making an enormous mistake. He wasn't free to fall in love—he was too committed to revenge.

Twenty

The journey through Arkansas passed without incident. The days were so tiring that dusk was always welcomed, for it meant a hot supper and a full night's rest.

They crossed into Texas and detoured northward toward Madison Creek. It was a short trek, for the town wasn't very far from the border. Madison Creek was small and mostly nondescript. Most of the buildings were in need of repair; a recent rain had turned the main street into a muddy thoroughfare. Slate clouds skimmed the sky, and they seemed as gray as the town beneath them. The town's buildings and homes were constructed of lumber, the majority badly in need of paint. Madison Creek's imminent demise was apparent, and its few remaining residents were losing the will to hold on to a town that was doomed.

Steve Jordan's brother had a small house at the edge of town. It was better kept than most of the homes in and around Madison Creek. A colorful flower garden helped camouflage the house's decline, and two tall oaks, their limbs heavy with foliage, shaded the front porch. At first glance, the house seemed like a perfect, cozy cottage, but a closer perusal revealed chipped paint, cracked window-panes, and an aging roof.

Steve and Lance stopped in front of the Jordans' home. Sharla, following in the wagon, pulled back on the reins and brought the team to a halt. The men dismounted, then helped the ladies down from the wagon.

"It's the noon hour, so my brother should be here," Steve said, leading the way to the front door. "Wyatt always eats lunch at home."

Jordan opened the door, stepped inside and called, "Anybody home?"

"Steve!" a woman's voice responded. She and her husband were in the kitchen, but they hurried away from the table and into the parlor to greet their relative.

Steve received a big bear hug from his brother and a kiss from his sister-in-law. He then introduced his traveling companions. The Jordans welcomed them to their home.

Wyatt was much larger than his younger brother, but there was a noticeable resemblance, for they shared the same color hair and eyes. Wyatt's wife, Emma, was a big woman. Her hair, the color of warm honey, was pulled back from her face and pinned into a neat bun.

Once everyone was seated, Steve asked Wyatt about Randy Severs.

"He's gonna hang in the morning," Wyatt replied. "And I'm gonna have a ringside seat. Watching that murdering scum die will give me pleasure. I just wish they could hang him more than once."

Emma wrung her hands apprehensively. "Lord, Wyatt! They could hang him a hundred times, and it still wouldn't bring back our daughter. When you talk so . . . so cold and violent, it worries me."

He was sitting beside her, and he patted her hands gently. "Now, Emma, don't you fret. Why don't you show these ladies to the spare bedroom? They would probably like to freshen up and rest."

"We don't want to impose," Sharla said. "We'll go to a hotel."

"This town doesn't have a hotel," Wyatt replied.

"Surely there are rooms to rent," Sharla insisted.

"I have a few rooms above the saloon that I rent. But they aren't for ladies."

"They certainly aren't," Emma agreed with Wyatt. "You and Mary must stay here. And you aren't imposing. Quite the contrary, I'm looking forward to your company."

"You're very kind," Sharla replied, her sentiments reiterated by Mary.

Rising from the sofa, Emma said, "If you'll come with me, I'll take you to the spare room."

The moment the ladies left the parlor, Lance mumbled an excuse and hurried out of the house.

"Where's he goin' in such a rush?" Wyatt asked Steve.

"I think he's going to see Severs."

"What business does he have with him?"

"I don't know," he replied.

That Steve's friend would visit his daughter's murderer bothered Wyatt, but he kept his feelings to himself.

Lance found the sheriff at his desk, slumped in his chair, dozing. He closed the front door loudly, bringing the lawman awake with a start.

Bolting from his chair, the sheriff's hand went to his holstered pistol as though he expected to use it. With a cautious eye fixed on the stranger, he asked, "What can I do for you?"

Sheriff Langley was past his prime. He was balding, overweight, and his reflexes weren't as quick as they used to be. His years of experience told him that this stranger was a gunman. There was a certain aura about these renegades that Langley never failed to sense.

"How do you do, Sheriff," Lance said amicably. "My name's Lance Slade."

The law officer's mouth dropped open, and he stared at Slade with wonder. "Well, I'll be dipped in lard! So you're Lance Slade! Your reputation's so widely known that it even reached this one-horse town. What the hell is a bounty hunter doin' here?"

"I'm just passing through. I'm traveling with two ladies and Steve Jordan."

"Wyatt's brother?"

Lance nodded.

"I reckon Steve's anxious to see the hangin'."

"That's why he's here."

"You'll be there in the mornin', won't you?"

Lance didn't answer the sheriff's question; instead, he asked one of his own. "Can Severs have visitors?"

"Yeah, I reckon. But I've had that murderer locked up for weeks, and so far no one's wanted to see him."

"I'd like to see him if you don't mind."

"What the hell for?"

"It's personal."

Langley seemed hesitant.

"He might have information I can use," Lance continued, hoping to persuade the sheriff.

"What kind of information?" Langley was not about to let a notorious gunman visit his prisoner without questioning his motive.

"Five years ago my family was murdered. Severs might know where I can find the men who killed them."

"Sorry to hear about your family," Langley replied. "Sure, you can see Severs, but you'll have to leave your gun with me."

Lance unholstered his pistol and placed it on the desk. He half expected Langley to frisk him, but he didn't.

"Come with me," the sheriff said, leading the way to a rear door. A wall peg held a set of keys, and Langley used one of them to unlock the door. Inside were two cells. Severs occupied one; the second one was empty.

The prisoner recognized Slade; he was the last person he expected to see.

"Can't let you inside the cell," Langley told Slade. "I

ain't pickin' on you; it's always been a rule of mine. You can stand here and talk to this horse's butt as long as you want."

He left, closing and locking the door behind him. That door was the only way out.

Severs stood beside his cot, keeping a safe distance between himself and his visitor. If he got too close, Slade's arms were liable to reach through the bars and grab him.

Randy Severs was twenty-six years old; he first killed when he was twenty. Since then, he had six murders to his credit. His hair looked as though it had never known a comb. Unwashed strands hung listlessly to his shoulders. A scraggly beard added to his overall disheveled appearance. He was average height, and was so scrawny that his clothes always looked a size too big.

"I have a couple of questions for you, Randy," Lance said.

"I ain't answerin' none of your questions," Severs replied in a nasal whine.

"Where are they?" Lance demanded.

"Where's who?" he asked, playing dumb.

"Answer me, or I'll find a way to get in that cell and choke your scrawny neck!"

"I don't know where they are. I ain't seen any of 'em in years."

"You're lying."

"What if I am? There ain't nothin' you can do about it."

"Sure there is. I can break you out of here."

Lance's remark was made so calmly that Randy was afraid he hadn't heard correctly. "What'd you say?"

"You heard me."

Randy, riveted, stared at Lance with disbelief, but with a shred of hope building. The thought of tomorrow's hanging was terrifying. He wasn't brave—most of his victims had died shot in the back. Every night for the past week, he had dreamt of the hanging. In his dreams he was dragged to the gallows screaming and kicking, as the spectators laughed and taunted him.

"What do you mean, you can break me out?" Randy asked, eyeing Lance intently, his heart thumping.

"Tell me where I can find Chambers, Jackson, and Walker."

"You think I'm loco?" Randy exclaimed. "I ain't gonna say nothin'. Not as long as I'm behind these bars."

Lance had no qualms about breaking Randy out of jail. Finding his family's murderers was his only priority. Besides, he didn't intend to set Severs free indefinitely, but hoped to bring him back to keep his date with a hangman's noose. He'd just be a little late.

"I'm not breaking you out of here," Lance began, "unless you give me a reason to."

"All right! All right!" Randy said excitedly. "I know where Walker is. Well, I can't be a hundred percent sure, but I'm pretty damned sure I can find 'im."

"Sure enough to bet your life on it? If you're lyin' to me, Randy, I'll kill you and spare the hangman the pleasure."

"I ain't lyin'," he replied, an irritating whine returning to his voice.

"How far away is Walker?"

" 'Bout six hours' ride from here."

"Was he with you when you robbed the Madison Creek bank?"

"Yeah. Him and a man called Shark."

"Shark?"

"That's what he calls himself. He says he's as mean as a shark and twice as fast."

"If Walker and Shark are only six hours away, why haven't they tried to break you out of here?"

"They're sons-of-bitches!" Randy spat angrily. "Yellow, no good, dog-eatin' sons-of-bitches! That's why they ain't tried to help me. Considerin' they ain't done nothin' for me, I don't owe them no loyalty. No, sir, Mr. Slade, I'll take you right to 'em.''

"What about Jackson and Chambers? When did you see them last?"

"I ain't seen either one of 'em in years. I'm tellin' you the truth. I'll swear it on my poor old mother's grave."

"You do that," Lance mumbled, turning to leave.

"Wait!" Randy called. "When are you gonna break me out? Hell, I ain't got much longer. They're hangin' me in the mornin'!"

"I'll have to think about it," Lance said, going to the door and knocking. Randy, believing Slade had lied, hurled curses at his departing back.

Lance thanked the sheriff for his cooperation, left, and went straight to the saloon. Buying a bottle of whiskey, he ambled to a back table and sat down. There were only four customers in the place, including Lance. There was very little noise, affording him the quietness he needed to sort out his thoughts. He poured a drink and took it neatly. He refilled the glass, and downed this one as quickly as the first. He had so much on his mind that he didn't want to take the time to think about Sharla. But he seemed to have no choice—she burst into his thoughts and stubbornly remained there. She was in serious trouble and he wanted to help her. Wanting to help her was easy—finding a way to do so would be a lot harder. Damn! Why did she have to come into his life now? He had set his future on a one-way course, which didn't include falling in love.

He grinned, as though he were laughing at himself. In a way, he was. He had been a fool to believe that he could control his own destiny. Fate had slapped that lesson in his face without warning. Sharla was certainly a part of his future; the magnetism between them was too strong. They had been destined to meet, fall in love, and . . . and . . . And what? he wondered. Live happily ever after? At the present time that prospect didn't look too promising. He was filled with vengeance, and she was wanted for murder. He had no intentions of relinquishing his long-awaited revenge; however, he hoped to help Sharla and hunt down his family's killers simultaneously.

He took another drink, wondering how the hell he or anyone else could prove Sharla's innocence.

Sharla's possible innocence was on Constable Woodson's mind as he stopped his buggy in front of the home that had sheltered Sharla for seventeen years. Under Albert's care, the grounds were immaculate, and sweet fragrances from the flower gardens filled the air as Woodson made his way to the back of the house. He knocked on the kitchen door, guessing that was where he'd find Agnes.

He guessed correctly, and the door was opened almost immediately.

"Constable Woodson!" Agnes said, surprised. She waved him inside, wondering why he had come back. After his last visit, she hadn't expected to see him again. He had thoroughly searched Claudia's room and had come up empty-handed.

"Good afternoon, Agnes," he said politely, removing his hat and placing it on the kitchen table. "I'd like to see Claudia's room again."

"But you already searched it and didn't find anything."

"Maybe I overlooked something."

She regarded him keenly. "Does your coming back have anything to do with Maxine's death?"

"Why would you think that?"

"Maxine's death is the talk of the town. Some people are saying that it wasn't an accident."

"Why would they say that?"

"Because you've been asking a lot of questions to a lot of people."

He smiled. "But I haven't gotten any answers that could make me believe it was murder and not an accident."

"You suspect Claudia, don't you?"

"Well, she did know Maxine. But I certainly don't have any foundation for thinking she killed her. I'm probably letting my imagination play games with me."

"I'll take you to her room," Agnes replied, leading the way.

They climbed the stairs to the third floor and went to Claudia's former quarters.

Again, Woodson investigated the small room. Nothing had changed since his last visit. He drew aside the curtain where Claudia had hung her clothes. The two uniforms she had left behind were still there. He started to close the curtain, but Agnes stopped him.

"Wait a minute," she said, moving to his side. Looking at the two uniforms, she mumbled, "That's strange."

"What is?"

"There's only two uniforms. I didn't notice that the last time you were here. There should be three uniforms. The maids are always issued three changes. Claudia must have taken one with her when she left."

"Or else she had it on when she killed James Rayfield. She would have to dispose of it; it'd be splattered with blood."

Agnes's eyes lit up. "You aren't so sure that Sharla is guilty, are you?"

He answered honestly. "I don't know. If I could find that missing uniform, and if it had blood on it . . . ?" He shrugged heavily. "Claudia could have hid it a hundred different places."

"Not if she hid it here in the house."

"Maybe she didn't hide it at all, but burned it."

"Maybe," Agnes agreed. "But let's assume that she hid it. I'll help you search the house. Where do you want to start?"

Woodson wasn't sure, and was considering the matter when soot trickled down the chimney and landed in the hearth. Reacting to the sound, he looked at the small fireplace.

"Birds," Agnes explained. "This time of year, birds check the chimneys for building nests. I suppose they are drawn to chimneys because they seem an ideal place to hide their nests from predators, such as cats."

Or the police, Woodson thought, wondering if the chimney had afforded Claudia a place to stash a bloody uniform. "You know, Agnes, you might have stumbled on to something."

"What do you mean?"

He went to the fireplace, knelt, and reached up into the flue. His arm was elbow-high when his fingers touched the prize he had hoped to find. He grasped the material and jerked it free from its prison.

Standing, he shook out the fabric, sending sooty particles flying about the room. He held his find out in front of him, looking at it gleefully, as though it were a hidden treasure.

To Agnes, it was a hidden treasure, for it proved that Sharla was innocent.

"The missing uniform," Woodson remarked. Despite its filthy condition, it was quite obvious that it was stained with blood; a lot of blood.

"Thank God you found it!" Agnes exclaimed. "When are you going to arrest Claudia?"

"That won't be so easy. The morning after Maxine's death, I went to Dexter's home to question her and learned that she and Dexter had left town. The butler said they were going to San Antonio, but would return within a few weeks."

"San Antonio!" Agnes exclaimed. "Why did they go there?"

"I have no idea."

"Can't you send someone after them?"

He shook his head.

"Then notify every law officer between here and San Antonio."

"I'd rather not do that. Claudia might elude an attempted arrest and go into hiding. Hell, I might never find her. No, there's only one way to guarantee she pays for Rayfield's murder. I'll have to go after her myself. Legally, I can't arrest Claudia once she's out of my jurisdiction. But once I find her, I'll have her taken into the local sheriff's custody, then have extradition papers drawn up. Don't worry; she'll stand trial for Rayfield's murder."

"When are you leaving?"

"In the morning."

She touched his arm. "Be careful. Claudia's as shrewd as she is evil."

"And twice as dangerous," he added, thinking of her violent insanity, for he didn't doubt that she had also murdered Maxine.

Twenty-one

Sharla stood on the Jordans' front porch, her eyes looking down the road to town, hoping to spot Lance. Dusk had fallen, casting murky shadows that played tricks with her eyes. More than once she thought she saw someone, only to realize that she was mistaken. Nothing moved on the road, except the ever-creeping darkness.

She sat on the top step, placed her elbows on her knees, cupped her chin in her hands, and sighed wistfully. She almost wished she had never met Lance Slade. She had enough problems without adding him to the list. They hadn't been alone since the night Mary interrupted their kiss. Sharla longed to be back in his arms again, but he seemed more determined than ever to keep her at a distance. He treated her impersonally, even brusquely on some occasions, but she often saw a pained expression in his eyes that conflicted sharply with his outward display of indifference. She knew he cared about her, that he wanted her as badly as she wanted him! Why he fought his feelings was a total mystery. A mystery that tried her patience.

The front door opened, and Mary came outside. She sat beside Sharla. "I don't think he's coming," she said softly.

"Wh-what?"

"Lance. I don't think he'll be here. Not tonight, anyhow. But I'm sure you'll see him tomorrow."

"What makes you think I'm waiting for Lance?"

She smiled kindly. "Aren't you?"

"Are my feelings that obvious?"

"I'm afraid so."

"He might stop by. It isn't that late."

"You heard what Wyatt said at supper. Lance refused Wyatt's invitation to join us."

Sharla remembered very well. She also remembered Wyatt had said that Lance had been in his saloon all afternoon and that he had rented one of his rooms for the night.

Mary spoke gently: "Sharla, I like Lance Slade. I think he's a good man, but there's a darkness inside him that makes him very dangerous."

"Surely you aren't implying that he's evil!"

"Of course not. That's not the kind of darkness I'm talking about. There is no word to describe it. After the war, I saw a lot of men like Lance—infested with bitterness, rage, and memories they couldn't put to rest."

"But Lance was too young to have been in the war."

"There are different kinds of war. He's at war right now with an enemy we know nothing about. Maybe this enemy actually lives and breathes, or maybe Lance's war is with himself."

"I think I understand what you're saying."

Mary reached over and held Sharla's hand. "Will you take some advice?"

"I might."

"Be careful. Be very, very careful. You must withhold your love until Lance's heart is at peace, otherwise, he will break your heart time and time again."

"If I only knew what troubles him so. Maybe I could help."

"When he's ready for you to know, he'll tell you. Men like Lance can't be rushed. They do things in their own good time." She smiled encouragingly. "Shall we go inside and visit with Emma and Steve?" Wyatt had returned to his saloon.

"You go inside; I think I'll take a walk."

"You're going to him, aren't you?"

Sharla rose to her feet, looked down at Mary and said with brimming tears, "I can't help myself. I love him."

Standing, Mary replied, "I understand. I might be old, but I haven't forgotten how it feels to be in love. But I am afraid for you. I fear Lance isn't free to make a commitment."

"What do you mean? Are you saying that he's married?"

"He's married, all right. But not to a woman. That man's totally committed to his private war, or to his private hell. But I guess war and hell are the same things."

"Maybe you're wrong about Lance," Sharla replied, but without much conviction.

"I hope so, for your sake."

"I won't be gone long," Sharla told her, starting down the steps. She was anxious to find Lance. Love could work miracles, and her love would surely heal whatever was bothering him.

She walked quickly while trying to avoid puddles left behind from an earlier downpour. When she reached the heart of town, a wooden structure located at the end of the street caught her eye. She hadn't seen it when she and the others arrived, for they had entered Madison Creek from the opposite direction. Curious, she headed toward the shadowy shape, puzzled by its strange dimensions.

The moon peeked out from beneath a cloud, and like a beacon in the night, it cast its aureate glow upon the hastily erected structure. Sharla's steps came to an abrupt stop as she gazed wide-eyed at the object of her curiosity. It was a gallows, and the mere sight of it sent a cold chill up her spine. Tomorrow's hanging had slipped her mind.

Whirling about, she put the horrible sight behind her and started back down the street. Was there a gallows in

St. Louis waiting for her? Was this flight of hers in vain? Was she simply running from the inevitable? That Maxine could clear her name seemed next to impossible. Someday the law would surely catch her, and she'd be taken back to St. Louis and tried for murder. Dexter would do everything within his power to ensure a conviction.

She didn't want to turn around and look back at the gallows, but driven by a force she couldn't control, she stopped, turned, and stared at what she feared was her own fate.

A hand suddenly touched her shoulder. Startled, she turned around, her eyes filled with fear, as though she were expecting to confront her impending executioner.

"Lance!" she cried happily, flinging herself into his arms.

He held her closely. "When I left the saloon, I happened to glance down this way and saw you. Sharla, what the hell are you doing here? You don't need to be looking at a damned gallows."

"I didn't realize what it was until I got close enough to make it out."

He released her gently. She wished he hadn't—she wanted to stay in his arms.

"I'll walk you back to the Jordans'," he said, putting an urging hand on her elbow.

She fell into step beside him. "I don't want to go back. Not yet."

"Where do you want to go?"

"I want to be with you."

He paused, and gazed down into her face. The pained expression had returned to his eyes. "Sharla, I don't think that's a good idea."

Now that her nerves had settled, she became aware that he carried a whiskey bottle. "Drinking again?" she asked, disapproval in her voice.

"I've been drinking all afternoon."

"Are you drunk?"

He grinned wryly. "Pretty damned close to it. Let me put it this way, my innocent beauty, I've had too much to drink to trust myself alone with you."

"If that threat is supposed to dissuade me, then you'd better think of something else. I don't consider your intentions a threat, but a hope for the future—our future." She held out her hand for the bottle. "May I have a drink?"

He was taken aback. "You can't be serious."

"Apparently, you drown your problems in whiskey, so why shouldn't I? Or have you forgotten that I will probably hang for murder?"

"I'd never let that happen."

"I don't think you could stop it." She took the bottle from his hand, opened it, and helped herself to a generous swig.

He watched her closely, expecting her to make a face or visibly shiver from the taste of whiskey. However, she swallowed it without any noticeable effects, waited a moment, then took a second drink. She closed the bottle and handed it back to him.

He continued to study this lovely woman who had come into his life so unexpectedly. Her long hair, as golden as the moonlight, cascaded past her shoulders in lustrous waves. He gazed deeply into her sapphire eyes. As always, they perfectly mirrored her feelings. Her adoration was obvious; it filled him with joy, yet, at the same time it deeply troubled him. His future was too unstable to support a relationship. The men he hunted were experienced killers and that he might fall to their hands was a distinct possibility.

Lance, however, was capable of only so much self-control, and his eyes raked hungrily over Sharla. The fullness of her breasts was clearly defined beneath her shirt, and her trousers adhered tightly to her womanly hips. Surrendering to his emotions, Lance placed the bottle on the ground, pulled her against him and kissed her with a passion so demanding that she trembled in his arms.

He took his lips from hers, held her at arm's length, and said very seriously, "I'm giving you one last chance. Do you want me to walk you back to the Jordans' home, or do you want me to take you to my room?"

Her heart seemed to stop beating, as though it were waiting for her answer.

"I want to be alone with you," she murmured, and her heart began to pound with the wonder of it all. She knew sex before marriage was terribly wrong, but there was a murder charge hanging over her head, and it might prevent her from ever getting married. She swallowed heavily, as though an invisible rope had suddenly wrapped itself about her neck.

He picked up the bottle, took her hand, and they headed toward the saloon. The rented rooms were above the establishment and accessible by an outside stairway.

Lance's conscience attempted to intrude, warning him not to take Sharla's innocence without first placing a ring on her finger. But he thrust his conscience aside. Right and wrong no longer mattered to him. Perhaps it was the whiskey that had weakened his resolve, or maybe it was something much stronger: love! He had a feeling it was probably a mixture of both.

They completed the walk to the saloon without speaking. Their hands, clasped tightly together, was all the contact they needed.

Lance guided her up the stairs and into a narrow, dimly lit hall. He went to the second door, took a key from his pocket and unlocked it. Inside was a bed, chest of drawers, a hard-back chair, and a table holding a ceramic bowl, pitcher, towel, and a lamp.

Leaving the door open to light his way, Lance went to the lamp, lit it, then turned the wick down to a warm glow.

He closed and locked the door, then removed his gun belt and hung it over the back of the chair.

Sharla looked about the room and saw that the furniture was old, and that the curtains were faded and threadbare. But everything was very neat and clean.

A couple of glasses sat atop the chest of drawers, and Lance poured two drinks. He handed one to Sharla. "Here's to us," he toasted.

She didn't want to drink any more whiskey. Earlier, when she had so boldly tipped the bottle to her mouth, she had found the taste disgusting. Defiance had kept her from letting Lance know how much she disliked it, for he would surely have found her reaction amusing.

He was waiting for her to respond to his toast, so she braced herself for the whiskey's foul taste, touched her glass to his, then downed the contents. The taste was still unpleasant, but she was getting more used to it. She was not yet aware of the whiskey's physical influence.

Lance put the glasses away, returned to Sharla and drew her into his arms. He kissed her deeply, and the touch of his lips was as intoxicating as the whiskey. Sharla's head began to swim, and her knees weakened. She clung to Lance as though she needed his support to stay on her feet.

His lips moved to her neck and down to the hollow of her throat, his warm breath sending delightful chills through her entire being.

Sharla felt as though she were adrift on a sea of passion, as waves of desire washed over her, drowning all semblance of reality. She and Lance were alone, wonderfully lost in their own Eden. Yesterday was gone and tomorrow was a blur on the horizon. This night, this moment, was time eternal.

When he began unbuttoning her shirt, she was quick to help him. She removed the garment with a flourish, letting it fall to the floor as though it were a rag to be discarded and forgotten. Beneath she wore a thin, lacy chemise that had belonged to Trish. It left little to the imagination, and Lance's gaze admired her silky flesh and the tempting cleavage between her breasts.

She unlaced the undergarment, dropped it, and stood before Lance without a shred of modesty. However, such boldness suddenly stunned her back to her senses. What was she doing? But the whiskey she had consumed and her passion were much stronger than rationality, and she was soon hopelessly lost in the power of Lance's kiss, the strength of his arms, and the feel of his body pressed tightly to hers.

He carried her to the bed, sat her on the edge and removed her boots. He then took off her trousers slowly, enjoying her beauty as it was revealed to him inch by inch. The sight of her long, shapely legs, and relishing what awaited him beneath her cotton drawers, set fire to his passion. He discarded the final article of clothing with eager hands, eased her back on the bed, and stretched out beside her.

"You're so beautiful," he murmured huskily. "I want you, Sharla. I want you more than I ever thought it was possible for me to want a woman."

His confession was thrilling, and she adored him so desperately that she interpreted his words to please herself. Her love was indeed working miracles; he'd forget this so-called war Mary spoke of and fully surrender to their deep feelings for each other.

Trusting in his love, she pressed her lips to his and wound her arms about his neck, presenting him her body, heart, and undying loyalty.

Lance's passion could no longer be denied. He left the bed and began to disrobe hastily. Sharla's modesty was still overshadowed by desire and whiskey, and she watched him intently. His masculine frame was flawless, and such virile perfection unleashed a hunger in Sharla that was as primitive as it was exciting. She beckoned his nude body into her arms, arching her hips to his as he settled upon her.

Keeping most of his weight on his arms, he gazed lovingly down into her face, which was beautifully flushed— the result of passion and too much whiskey. He smiled tenderly, his heart filled with sweet emotion for this caring, sensitive woman who was about to give him her most prized possession: her innocence.

"I've never met anyone like you," he whispered. "But I know I've been waiting for you all my life."

"I know what you mean," she murmured. "I feel the same way. Maybe it's destiny."

"If that's true, then it's the first time destiny has rewarded me." He kissed her, his mouth taking hers with a breathless urgency.

Sharla responded fully, wishing this moment could last forever. "I love you, darling," she murmured as his lips left hers.

Lance moved to lie beside her, holding her body close to his. Kissing and touching, they explored each other's flesh, their senses throbbing with the feel and scent of each other.

When Lance moved over her, she was not only ready for his penetration, but was looking forward to it as though she were an experienced woman and not a virgin.

He entered her carefully, and when he encountered the proof of her virginity, he aggressively plunged deeper, sparing her prolonged discomfort.

The sharp pain passed quickly for Sharla, supplanted by a feeling of ecstasy. His hardness, deep inside her, felt so right, as though she had been born for this moment, this man, and the future that awaited them.

Lance kissed her tenderly. "Are you all right, darlin'?"

"I'm fine," she whispered. "But I've never felt so . . . so . . ." She couldn't find a word to adequately define such perfect rapture.

He smiled. "My sentiments exactly. What I feel right now is beyond explanation. But let's not analyze it; let's just enjoy it."

"Forever," she murmured, pressing her lips to his.

He moved against her, and she arched her hips, instinctively understanding love's rhythm. As she was inundated with wave after wave of unspeakable desire, she felt she would gladly drown in the pleasure of such physical intimacy. She was soon totally consumed by passion and her love for Lance. Everything else ceased to exist.

Later, Sharla basked in the afterglow of their passionate union. Snuggled close with her arm across Lance's chest and her head on his shoulder, she felt wonderfully fulfilled. For the first time in her life, she understood the true meaning of love between and a man and a woman. It filled her with joy, expectations, and hope for the future. Somehow, they would be together always. She dared not believe otherwise, for imagining life without Lance was too distressing to even consider.

He gave her a quick kiss on the lips, then suggested that they get dressed. "If you don't get home soon," he explained, "Mary and the others are liable to start worrying about you—if they aren't already."

She knew he was right and that she must leave. But she vacated his bed with a tearing reluctance. She loved him completely and felt her place was at his side.

Lance filled the ceramic bowl with water so that he and Sharla could wash. That she and Lance, remaining nude, shared such intimate washing didn't embarrass Sharla in the least. It seemed the most natural thing in the world.

They were soon dressed and on their way to the Jordans' house. Lance withdrew into silence during the short walk, and Sharla wished she could read his mind. She hoped he was contemplating asking her to marry him. Tonight had been too beautiful and too perfect not to end in a marriage proposal. Young love was ruling Sharla's thoughts; all of Mary's warnings were conveniently disregarded. That she was wanted for murder was too sobering to think about. She was drunk on love and wanted to remain under its blissful influence forever.

They reached the front porch, and Lance kissed her tenderly. "Good night, Sharla."

His abrupt dismissal was unexpected, and, for a moment, she stared at him with mute astonishment. She finally found her voice, "But Lance . . ."

"I gotta go," he cut in quickly. Turning, he moved away and was soon swallowed up by the dark night.

Sharla was left struggling with disbelief, anger, and heartbreak. She sat on the top step and fought back stinging tears. Lance's behavior was as confusing as it was infuriating. But maybe she was judging him too rashly. He might need more time to come to grips with his feelings. She would be patient and not press him. He loved her; she was sure that he did!

Or was she? He hadn't told her that he loved her. He had spoken of desire, need, and passion, but he hadn't uttered the three words she wanted so desperately to hear.

At that moment, Steve came out onto the porch. "I was just about to go look for you," he said. "I was getting worried."

She bounded to her feet, forced a carefree smile, and replied, "There was no need to worry. As you can see, I'm fine. It's late. I think I'll go to bed. Good night, Steve." She moved past him and into the house.

Meanwhile, Lance had reached the livery, where he saddled his horse and the one he purchased for Randy. He didn't foresee any problem breaking Severs out of jail, for security was lax. He had planned to get a couple of hours' sleep before carrying out his plan, but his encounter with Sharla had made that impossible.

As he led the horses out of the livery and toward the jail, he pushed thoughts of Sharla to a far corner of his mind. Retribution now controlled his every thought and move. There was a stalking, purposeful intent in his walk, his demeanor alert, dangerous, and unrelenting.

Twenty-two

The Jordans and their guests were sleeping soundly when a loud rapping sounded at the front door. The sheriff's voice could be heard above the knocking, demanding that Wyatt let him in.

Wyatt got out of bed and put on his trousers. Steve, using the room down the hall, simultaneously donned his own trousers. The women had also been awakened, and they quickly drew on their robes. All three bedrooms led into a narrow hallway, and their occupants came piling out at the same time, almost colliding in the cramped space.

Wyatt, holding a lit lantern, headed for the front door. The others followed close behind.

The sheriff was still pounding and yelling.

"Keep your britches on, Langley!" Wyatt called. "I'm comin'!" He unlocked the door, and the sheriff barged inside. "What the hell's goin' on?" Wyatt demanded, waving the officer into the parlor. He quickly lit a lamp for more light.

"Lance Slade broke Severs out of jail!"

Sharla was absolutely stunned.

"I don't believe it!" Steve exclaimed. "Why the hell would he do that?"

Langley regarded the younger Jordan suspiciously. "I thought maybe you could tell me. After all, he's your friend."

"Lance isn't exactly my friend; I barely know him. And I sure don't know why he freed Severs." He turned to Sharla and Mary. "Do either of you have any idea?"

"None whatsoever," Mary replied.

Steve's gaze settled on Sharla. "Why do you think he did this? You know him better than we do."

"I don't know Lance Slade," she replied slowly, as though in a daze. "I thought I knew him, but apparently I was wrong."

Wyatt asked the sheriff, "How did Slade manage a jail break?"

Langley looked slightly embarrassed. "It was my fault. I was negligent. Slade came to the jail tonight. I didn't think anything of it. He visited earlier, and he didn't do or say anything to make me suspicious. So when he stopped by tonight, I offered him a cup of coffee. While I was pourin' it, he snuck up behind me and took my gun. I was tied and gagged. Stayed that way for hours until my deputy came on duty to relieve me. The deputy's rounding up a posse. You're welcome to ride with us."

"You're damned right I'm comin'!" Wyatt's eyes flashed angrily. "Severs killed my little girl! When we catch up to 'em, we oughta lynch Slade for helpin' that murderer!"

"They'll be no talk of lynchin'," the sheriff said firmly. "The circuit judge is due back in a couple of weeks. Slade will face him, not a mob with lynching on their minds."

"I'm going with you," Steve decided.

Langley moved to the open door. "We'll meet in front of the jail in thirty minutes."

The sheriff left, and Steve and Wyatt went to their rooms to dress. Emma accompanied her husband.

Sharla moved numbly to the sofa and sat down. Joining her, Mary placed a consoling hand on her granddaughter's arm. "I'm sorry, honey," she murmured, wishing she could do more to comfort her.

"Why would Lance do such a thing?" Sharla murmured aloud.

"I'll fix a pot of coffee," Mary decided. "I don't think anyone will be going back to bed." She glanced at the wall clock above the mantel. "It'll soon be dawn," she said, getting up to go to the kitchen.

Sharla leaned her head against the sofa's high back, and stared vacantly across the room. She clasped her hands tightly, for they had begun to tremble. The numbness was starting to pass, leaving confusion, anger, and pain in its wake.

Lance was gone. He had used her as he would use a prostitute! She was nothing to him. Nothing!

He was a heartless cad! That was obvious, but his reason for helping Randy Severs escape went beyond the scope of her imagination. There, she was at a total loss.

She tried to hold back threatening tears, but her efforts were in vain, for the need to cry was much stronger than her willpower.

The posse didn't return until midday, and they came back without any prisoners. Lance had covered their tracks so thoroughly that the sheriff and his men might as well have been on a wild-goose chase. They had wandered the countryside aimlessly, looking, searching, and coming up with nothing.

Finally, giving up and far out of his jurisdiction, Langley decided to return to Madison Creek.

The women were in the parlor when Wyatt and Steve entered the house. The men were tired, covered with trail dust, and bitterly disappointed. They gave the ladies an account of their failed search, amazed that two riders could seemingly disappear from the face of the earth without leaving behind some kind of trace.

A part of Sharla sympathized with the Jordans, for Severs

had murdered a member of their family, and they deserved justice. But another part of her, the one she seemed unable to control, was relieved that Lance had gotten away. Imagining him in prison brought her no pleasure. She didn't seek revenge, she merely wanted to find a way to stop loving him.

Determined to move forward, she told Mary and the others that she wanted to leave right away. There was no reason to remain here any longer.

"Are you sure you want to leave now?" Mary asked.

"Yes. The sooner the better." Dexter's wanted posters preyed heavily on her mind. If they were to catch up to her, Sheriff Langley's jail would have a new prisoner. She knew it was vital that she keep on the move.

Mary, understanding, agreed that they should leave.

Steve was not about to let the women travel without a man's protection, and he offered to accompany them to San Antonio.

His offer was gratefully accepted.

Lance and Randy were surrounded by foliage so dense that they had to lead their horses through the heavy vegetation. Trees, bushes, and clinging vines covered the area—a habitat for wild animals, snakes, and a multitude of insects.

"There's a small clearing up ahead," Severs told Lance. "That's where we'll find Walker's cabin. He don't always use it. I think it belonged to a relative of his. Anyway, he stays there when he's avoidin' the law. He's probably there now, him and Shark."

Lance didn't say anything. He simply stayed close behind Randy, who was leading the way. Severs had asked Slade for a gun, but had gotten an angry scowl instead. Lance had no intention of arming Randy, nor did he plan to set him free. He would take him back to Madison Creek, dead or alive.

Five years ago, Randy Severs had worked for Lance's family. He had been one of several wranglers. He was hired by Lance's father. A few weeks later, he asked his boss to employ three of his friends. These men were given jobs, for it would soon be time to take a cattle drive to Kansas, and extra hands were badly needed.

Randy had been in town the night his three friends killed Lance's family. He swore he didn't know they were going to kill and rob the Slades. The sheriff believed him. If he had been in on it, he wouldn't have been at the saloon, and later in a prostitute's bed, where he had spent the remainder of the evening.

Now, as Randy made his way through prickly bushes, he said to Lance, "All this time you ain't never stopped lookin' for Chambers, Jackson, and Walker, have you?"

"I'll look for them until I find 'em or die, whichever comes first."

"Well, Walker, he's kinda dumb. And he ain't all that good with a gun. Killin' him will be easy. But Chambers and Jackson, they won't be so easy. I ain't never see men any better with guns than they are. I reckon they're also good at evadin' you."

"Someday their luck will run out."

Randy stopped and chuckled. "Maybe you're the one who's been lucky. I bet one of 'em has a bullet with your name on it."

"Just shut up and keep moving."

"No reason to go no farther," he said. "We done reached the cabin."

Lance moved to Randy's side to get a better look. A row of bushes stood between them and the clearing. A log cabin, in dire need of repair, faced their direction. Smoke billowed from the chimney, and two horses were inside a lean-to that was located south of the cabin.

"Walker and Shark are inside, all right," Randy said. "Them horses are theirs." He turned to Lance. "Now that I brung you here, I reckon I honored my part of our bargain. I guess I'll just hightail it out of here."

"Not so fast."

"But I done what I promised," he whined. "You said you'd set me free if I took you to Walker."

"I said I'd break you out of jail."

"What the hell does that mean?"

"I never said I wouldn't take you back." Drawing his pistol with lightning speed, Lance sent it crashing against Randy's head. The potent blow knocked him unconscious. Lance knew he'd be out for a long time, if he wasn't dead.

Stepping to his horse, Lance slipped his Winchester from its leather case. Moving quietly, he walked a wide berth, which brought him around to the rear of the cabin. Remaining hidden in dense shrubbery, he considered his next move. There didn't seem to be very many options open to him, and he decided his best course was to take the occupants by surprise.

He slipped up to the cabin and peeked inside a rear window. The pane was partially covered by a tattered curtain. The two men were sitting at the table eating. Lance gave the interior a close look. The cabin consisted of one room, the furnishings meager and in poor condition. From Lance's position, he could see the front door. A plank of wood sufficed as a latch, and it was securely in place. It wasn't very thick, and Lance was fairly sure that a couple of direct shots would sever it.

His gaze returned to the men, who seemed totally engrossed in their meal. They spooned beans into their mouths as though they were racing to see who could eat the most in the least amount of time. Lance studied the man called Shark. He was skinny, clean-shaven, and appeared to be in his late twenties. A gun was strapped to his hip. He wondered how fast he could draw that gun.

He didn't waste time thinking about it, for he knew he would soon find out.

He looked at Walker. The man was heavyset, bearded, and like his comrade, he was armed. The expression in Lance's eyes was hard, pitiless, and filled with revenge. He had waited a long time for this moment. Retribution was now within his reach; it sent his heart pounding and his adrenaline flowing. A vision of his murdered family flashed across his mind as he moved away from the window. The vision was as wounding as a stab in the heart, and he forced the memory from his mind. His life depended on a clear head, quick reflexes, and a predator's instincts.

He made his way to the front of the cabin, aimed his rifle at the door and leveled the barrel where he knew the center of the latch was located. He got off two quick shots, then slammed his foot against the door that was now hanging obliquely. By the time it crashed to the floor, Shark and Walker were on their feet and reaching for their pistols. Betting his life that Shark was quicker, Lance took him out first, sending a bullet plowing into his chest. The powerful impact knocked him backward, and he hit the floor with a solid thud.

By now, Walker's gun was unholstered and aimed at Lance. An instant before Walker fired, Lance dropped his rifle and dove to the floor, drawing his pistol as he went down. As Walker's discharged bullet whizzed harmlessly over his head, he fired his Peacemaker before the man could get off a second shot. Lance didn't miss. Walker dropped his gun, and sank slowly to his knees. He keeled over limply, and lay on the floor with care, as though he had chosen this spot for a nap instead of a place to die.

Lance went over and knelt beside him. Walker was still alive, and he stared up into Slade's face with cold hatred. "You bastard," he managed to gasp. "Five years . . . Five years, you hunted me like a goddamned crazy Indian. We should've made sure you were dead that night."

There were times when the memory of his family's slaughter was so unbearable that Lance wished Walker and his friends had indeed killed him. But they had mistakenly left him alive.

"Where can I find Chambers and Jackson?"

"I don't know," he groaned. "But I hope someday you find 'em, 'cause this time they'll finish the job. They'll make sure you're good and dead."

"You're the one who's dead, Walker."

Death then descended upon Walker, as though it had been waiting for Lance's permission before striking.

Slade hurried over to Shark and saw that he was alive. The wound was serious, but it was possible that he would live to confront a hangman's noose.

As Lance was preparing for the trip back to Madison Creek, miles away in St. Louis, Agnes was admitting Hattie into her kitchen. She had sent Albert to fetch the woman, for she preferred to see her in Olivia's home. Going to a house of ill repute made Agnes very uncomfortable.

Agnes served coffee at the kitchen table. The women passed a few moments with small talk, then Hattie asked her hostess why she had wished to see her.

Agnes gave her a detailed account of Constable Woodson's two visits. She then told Hattie that the officer planned to apprehend Claudia himself.

A large grin spread across Hattie's face. "Thank goodness that murderin' Jezebel's gonna get caught."

"Where is Sharla? Do you know?"

"She's on her way to San Antonio. When she arrives, she's supposed to contact a woman named Jenny. She used to work for Maxine, but she now lives in San Antonio."

"Good Lord!" Agnes suddenly groaned. "The constable told me that Dexter and Claudia left for Texas. Somehow, Dexter must have learned where Sharla was going."

Hattie sighed gravely. "Lord, I hope that man doesn't catch Miss Sharla before the constable can find him and tell him that Miss Claudia is the real murderer."

Agnes voiced similar misgivings, then, refilling their coffee cups, she asked with genuine concern, "How have you been, Hattie? I know losing Maxine had to be terribly hard for you."

"I'm managing," she replied. "My grief gets a little easier with each passing day."

"What will happen to Maxine's business?"

"Maxine's will stipulated that it was to be sold to the highest bidder. Her lawyer is taking care of that." A trace of tears misted Hattie's eyes, as she continued, "Maxine left all her assets to me. I'm now a very wealthy woman. She entrusted her lawyer with a letter to me that I was to read upon her death. In the letter, she asked me to give half of the inheritance to Sharla. Anonymously, of course, for she didn't want Sharla to ever know that she was her mother. I plan to honor half of Maxine's request. I'll give Sharla her inheritance, but I intend to tell her the truth. She should know that Maxine was her mother, and she should know how much she loved her."

"The truth will be difficult for Sharla to accept."

"Maybe so, but I'm gonna tell her anyhow. You know, there's nothin' keeping me here. Maybe I should just pack up and move to San Antonio."

"To be with Sharla?"

"No. I was thinking of Mary Simmons."

"Who?" Agnes asked, baffled.

Hattie told Agnes about Maxine's estranged relationship with her parents. She explained that she and Mary had corresponded for several years. She also let her know about the telegram that she had sent to Mary, asking her to help Sharla.

"I'm sure Mary left for San Antonio when she got my wire," Hattie continued. "I'm not considerin' moving there because of Miss Sharla. She barely knows me, and I don't imagine she needs me. But Mary does. We've been friends a long time."

"Only through letters."

"That doesn't matter. We couldn't be closer friends if we saw each other daily."

"I wish you luck and a safe journey. When you see Miss Sharla, give her my best."

"If I see her," Hattie murmured, worry etched on her face. "With Dexter Rayfield in pursuit, there's no tellin' what might happen to that child."

Claudia hated the tedious journey she was compelled to endure. Riding horseback was uncomfortable, and she loathed all the inconveniences that came with camping out. They had spent a few nights at roadside inns, and although she found the establishments crude, they were certainly better than sleeping on the hard ground.

Claudia's constant complaining was the deciding factor that convinced Dexter to take a short detour to a small town, where Chambers and Jackson had assured him there was a hotel. He was hopeful that a bath, a decent meal, and a good night's sleep might improve Claudia's disposition. He was beginning to regret his decision to bring her along, for her nagging was nerve-wracking.

The town's hotel didn't look very promising; it was small, rundown, and didn't have a dining room. Dexter, ignoring Claudia's grumbling, took her inside and rented a room for himself and Claudia, and one for his bodyguards. He led Claudia upstairs, deposited her in their room, then left the hotel with Chambers and Jackson.

They went to the sheriff's office, where Dexter showed the lawman a wanted poster on Sharla.

The man studied it without comment. Despite Dexter's

efforts to have the posters widely distributed, they had failed to make it to this sheriff's town.

"Well?" Rayfield questioned impatiently. "Have you seen Sharla Matthews?"

The sheriff gave the poster back to Dexter. "This is the second time I've seen that poster. A bounty hunter who said his name was Clem Emerson came through town last week askin' if I'd seen Miss Matthews. I'll tell you the same thing I told him. I saw a woman who might be her. It's hard to tell."

"When did you see her?"

"A few days back. She was traveling with an elderly woman. They came here lookin' for a man who stole their money. They found him at the saloon, and got their money back at gunpoint. I told them they needed to stick around and press charges, but they refused to stay."

"You say she was traveling with an elderly woman. Was it just the two of them?"

"I ain't sure. I heard when they left, a stranger was ridin' with 'em. Probably the same stranger that followed 'em out of the saloon. The women knew 'im because I saw the younger one talkin' to 'im."

"Thanks for your help, Sheriff," Dexter said, turning and motioning for his bodyguards to accompany him outside. "I wonder who the hell the stranger is?" he pondered aloud.

"I can ask around town and see if anyone recognized him," Jackson offered.

"You do that, and, Chambers, you go with him."

Dexter returned to the hotel. About an hour later, his men knocked on the door and informed him that no one they had talked to had recognized the stranger.

He dismissed them for the evening, closed the door, and turned to Claudia. "It doesn't really matter who's helping Sharla escape," he told her. "When I catch her, one man's not going to stop me from taking her back to St. Louis. Not with Jackson and Chambers working for me."

Claudia didn't approve of Dexter's bodyguards. They were always leering at her. "Jackson and Chambers!" she uttered distastefully. "Those two give me the creeps. I don't like them, and I don't trust them."

Her opinion didn't matter to Dexter. He brushed her complaint aside with a wave of his hand, told her to get undressed, and into bed. The trip limited their time alone, and Dexter was not about to waste this night talking about Chambers and Jackson.

Twenty-three

Sheriff Langley was in his office, and was talking to Wyatt when his deputy threw open the front door, poked his head inside, and exclaimed, "You ain't gonna believe what's comin' down the street!"

The sheriff, with Wyatt close behind, hurried outside. The sight that greeted them was so unexpected that it rendered them speechless. The townspeople were just as shocked. Some of them gathered in groups to watch the strange procession, others chose to stand in their doorways, but a few spectators, mostly youngsters, ran into the street for a closer look.

Slade and his entourage rode slowly toward the sheriff's office. Lance seemed relaxed, as though his returning to town with three murderers was an everyday occurrence. Randy Severs rode meekly at his side. Walker's body was slung over his horse. Shark, badly wounded, could barely stay in the saddle. He sat slumped over, his body so limp that his head bobbed in time with his horse's gait.

Reaching the jail, Lance dismounted, looked at Langley, and said calmly, "Here are your three bank robbers. One could use an undertaker, and the other one needs a doctor. But Severs is still healthy."

Langley told his deputy to take the wounded fugitive to the doctor. It wasn't necessary to fetch the undertaker, for he was one of the nearby spectators.

The sheriff asked Wyatt to escort Lance inside the jail. He then jerked Severs from his horse. He led his prisoner through his office, opened the door that led to the cells, and put him behind bars. He returned to his office, where Lance and Wyatt were waiting.

Stepping to Lance, the sheriff held out his hand. "Give me your gun."

He turned it over, offering it to Langley butt first.

Moving to his chair, the sheriff sat down and placed Lance's weapon on his desk. Another chair faced the desk, and Langley gestured for Lance to use it.

He took the indicated seat, reached into his pocket and removed a cheroot.

Langley watched him thoughtfully. He acted as though he didn't have a care in the world as he lit the small cigar, blew out the match and dropped it in an ashtray. Leaning back in his chair, he removed his wide-brimmed hat and placed it on the desk. His eyes met Langley's without a flinch.

"Give me one reason why I shouldn't lock you up," Langley said.

"Walker was one of the men who murdered my family. I told Severs I'd break him out of jail if he took me to Walker. I never told him I wouldn't bring him back."

"I suppose Walker is the one who's dead."

"I was willing to bring him in alive, but he didn't leave me that choice."

Although Langley was skeptical, he didn't press the issue. He didn't give a damn that Walker was dead. If Walker and the other two hadn't robbed the bank, Wyatt's ten-year-old daughter would still be alive. Slade had simply saved the town the trouble of hanging him.

"The circuit judge is due back in a couple of weeks. If that bastard you brought in doesn't die, he'll stand trial for murder. I'm wonderin' why you shouldn't be tried for breaking Severs out of jail. You broke the law, Slade. I realize why you did it, and I even sympathize with you. In your place, I might have done the same thing. But the law's the law, and I was elected to enforce it."

"Hell, Langley!" Wyatt spoke up. "This town oughta thank Mr. Slade. He did what we couldn't do! He apprehended the men who murdered my Rebecca! There's no harm done; Severs will still hang!"

The sheriff was reluctant to arrest Slade, for he completely agreed with Wyatt. But he had abided by the law for so many years that it wasn't easy for him to make an exception; however, if any case ever warranted it, this one did. He conceded, surprisingly with a clear conscience. "You're free to go, Slade." He gave him back his gun. "By the way, how many men murdered your family?"

Standing, Lance put on his hat and holstered his pistol. "There were three," he replied.

"Was Walker the last?"

"The first. The other two are still out there somewhere."

"I suppose you aim to keep lookin' for 'em."

"Wouldn't you?"

Langley nodded. "Yeah, I reckon I would. I wish you luck, Slade.

"Thanks, I'll probably need it."

Wyatt moved to Lance and shook his hand. "I appreciate you bringing in the men who killed my little girl." He added somewhat sheepishly, "When I learned you broke Severs out of jail, I was ready to hang you from the nearest tree."

"I don't blame you for feeling that way. I suppose the others are pretty upset. I'll go to your house and explain everything."

"They aren't there," Wyatt replied. "The ladies left, and Steve went with them."

"When did they leave?"

"Early this afternoon."

"If I ride through the night, I can catch up to them by

morning. I left some belongings in my room. Are they still there?"

"Everything should be as you left it. You're welcome to share supper with Emma and me before you start out."

Lance, anxious to see Sharla, declined the invitation, said his good-byes, and left the jail. He hurried to the room above the saloon, got his carpetbag, then headed out of town. He maintained an easy gallop, for his horse had gone all day without rest. But the strong steed was bred for endurance, and it cantered across the terrain as though its stamina was endless.

As Steve tended to the horses, Sharla and Mary cooked supper over an open fire. They were camped in an area bordered by trees and high shrubbery. Shortly before dusk, Steve had left the main road in search of a place to stop for the night. He hadn't ridden very far before finding this location.

No one seemed especially hungry, and the travelers merely picked at their food. Trivial talk prevailed, as though any reference to Lance and what had happened in Madison Creek was taboo.

Following dinner, Mary claimed fatigue and went to the wagon. Steve helped Sharla clean the dishes. She thanked him for his help, and bade him a pleasant good night.

"Stay and talk to me," he said. "It's still early."

She sat beside him. "I guess it is too early to retire. I wouldn't be able to sleep. I'd just toss and turn."

"Thinking about Lance?"

She looked at him sharply, as though by mentioning Lance he had crossed a forbidden line. "I don't want to talk about that skunk!" she snapped.

"I understand," he replied. "Actually, I don't want to discuss him either. Let's talk about you. Tell me about yourself, Trish."

She flinched, as though Steve's calling her Trish was physically wounding. In a way, it was. She was sick and tired of pretending she was someone else. She hated lying to people like Steve and his family.

"Is something wrong?" Jordan asked. "You look very troubled."

She sighed wearily. "Yes, I am troubled. And everything is wrong—more than wrong. It just keeps getting worse."

"Do you want to talk about it?"

His kind eyes invited a full confession. She was sure she could trust him. As she confided in Steve, the fire slowly burned down to a reddish glow, and full night descended, covering the surrounding shrubbery in total blackness.

Steve detected no self-pity in Sharla's voice as she told him about her life, James Rayfield's murder, and her flight from the law. But she didn't stop there; she also told him how she had learned that Mary was her grandmother.

"Quite a lot has happened to you in a very short time," he said, holding her hand. "But you seem to be coping remarkably well."

"I'm not sure how much more I can take. Lance's breaking Severs out of jail was almost the last straw. I thought I could trust him."

He squeezed her hand gently. "You can trust me, Sharla. I'd never betray you or do anything to hurt you."

His amorous implications gave her reason to pause. It hadn't occurred to her that Steve might harbor those kinds of feelings.

"You look surprised," he said. "Is it so hard to believe I could fall in love with you?"

She drew her hand from his. "I like you Steve, but—"

"But you're in love with Slade," he cut in.

"Why do you say that?"

"It's in your eyes every time you look at him. Your beautiful blue eyes will always betray you, Sharla."

"Whether or not I love Lance, doesn't matter. He's

gone, and I'll probably never see him again. Besides, I have more important things to think about. Like a murder charge hanging over my head."

As they discussed Sharla's chances of clearing her name, far back in the dark shrubbery, a shadowy figure moved stealthily through the heavy foliage. He had left his horse behind, for he wanted to advance on foot. His steps were as silent as an Indian's stalking an unsuspecting foe. Dressed all in black, the ebony night provided a perfect shield as he slowly approached the low-burning campfire.

The moment he spotted light from the glowing embers, he crouched behind a bush, parted its branches and studied the pair sitting at the fire. He looked closely at the woman, smiled, and considered his next move.

Clem Emerson was a notorious bounty hunter; no fugitive had ever eluded him for very long. However, finding Sharla Matthews had been relatively easy. He had passed through St. Louis shortly after Dexter had posted the three-thousand-dollar bounty, along with Sharla's picture. Such a huge amount caught his attention, and he hoped to collect the reward. He didn't change his original course, but continued westward, figuring if the woman had escaped the city she'd head in that direction. Inquiring at inns and towns along the way, Clem soon picked up Sharla's trail.

The huge bounty was on his mind as he left his hiding place to make his way to the wagon. With three thousand dollars added to his savings, he could quit his dangerous profession, buy a piece of land and turn it into a profitable ranch.

Moving furtively, he slipped up to the rear of the wagon and drew his gun. A stepladder afforded an easy entry. The darkness inside didn't prevent him from making out Mary's form as she lay asleep on her pallet.

He knelt beside her, and clamped a hand over her mouth.

She came awake instantly. His face was so close to hers that she saw him clearly, despite the dark night.

"You make a sound, and those two outside are dead. Do you understand?"

She nodded.

Emerson was bluffing. He planned to take Sharla alive. He removed his hand from Mary's mouth, held her at gunpoint, and ordered her to get up.

Mary did as she was told, wondering if she should warn Sharla and Steve. One loud scream would do the job. But the man had threatened to kill them if she made a sound. Afraid he would kill them anyhow, she decided to cry out. Clem, sensing her intent, again clamped a hand over her mouth.

He took her to the rear of the wagon and down the small ladder. He placed the barrel of his pistol flush to her temple, then forced her to walk with him to the fire.

Sharla and Steve saw them at the same time, and they jumped to their feet in unison. Jordan was wearing a gun, but he knew drawing it might cause the man to shoot Mary.

Clem released Mary and pushed her in Steve's direction. She stumbled into his arms.

"Are you all right?" he asked, releasing her carefully.

"I think so," she replied.

"Unbuckle your gun," Clem told Jordan. "And don't try anything stupid." He hoped to avoid bloodshed.

Steve considered himself a fast draw, and he questioned if he could take the stranger by surprise. He moved a hand to the buckle as though he had every intention of cooperating. Then, within the blink of an eye, he grabbed for his pistol.

But he wasn't quick enough, and his opponent opened fire. The bullet slammed into Steve's shoulder, sending him spinning to the ground. Clem could have killed him just as easily as he had wounded him. But he was a bounty

hunter, not a cold-blooded murderer. He never killed unless he deemed it necessary.

Sharla started to kneel beside Steve, but Clem's hand
on her shoulder stopped her. "Saddle your horse," he ordered gruffly. "Try anything, and my next bullet will be
in your friend's head, instead of his shoulder."

"Why are you doing this?" she cried. "What do you
want?"

"There's a bounty on you, little lady. I aim to collect it."

She glared at him hatefully. "You're a bounty hunter!"

"Do as I said, and saddle your horse!"

"I'll have to go inside the wagon, that's where my saddle
is stored."

He looked over at the horses; Steve's saddle lay nearby.
"Use that one," he told her.

She whirled away angrily and went to her mare. The
term "bounty hunter" screamed through her mind as she
threw on the saddle. First Lance, and now this evil man!
She despised the term as much as she despised the two
men who lived by it.

She thought about her Winchester. If only it wasn't inside the wagon with her saddle. Steve's rifle was beside his
bedroll, which was in the bounty hunter's vision.

Clem, keeping an eye on Mary and Steve, went to Sharla
and took the mare's reins. "Head straight for the shrubbery," he told her. "I'll be right behind you."

She obeyed. Leading the mare, the bounty hunter followed her into the dense vegetation.

The moment they disappeared, Steve struggled to his
feet and stumbled to his rifle. "I'm goin' after them," he
said weakly. He was bleeding badly, his strength failing. He
dropped to his knees and keeled over.

Mary rushed to his side. "You're so weak you couldn't
catch a kitten." She examined his wound. "That bullet's
gotta come out. It's a good thing I brought my medicine
bag with me."

"Have you ever dug out a bullet?" he asked, hoping this wouldn't be her first time.

"I've done it before," she replied. "But it's been a long time."

"I hope you haven't forgotten how."

"Don't worry, I know what to do. But it's gonna be mighty painful for you."

"Just do it and get it over with. I still intend to go after Sharla. I'll leave in the morning."

"You called her Sharla."

"She told me everything."

Mary wasn't surprised to learn that Sharla had confided in Jordan. "I'll help you inside," she said, aiding him to his feet.

As they started toward the wagon, Mary pushed Sharla's abduction to the back of her mind; she would need a steady hand and a clear head to extract the bullet from Steve's shoulder without injuring him worse. Later, she would have plenty of time to worry about her granddaughter.

Clem and his captive traveled at a brisk pace, quickly putting a good distance between them and the campsite. They rode without talking. Sharla had attempted to communicate with him, but he had refused to cooperate. Finally, he had ordered her to remain silent.

Sharla was more apprehensive than afraid. She didn't think this man would kill her as long as she didn't try anything. Escape didn't seem very probable; at least not any time soon. She was unarmed and totally under his control. However, she didn't intend to simply submit to a journey back to St. Louis. Surely, somewhere along the trail, a chance to flee would arise. She must stay alert and grasp the opportunity; otherwise, it might pass her by.

It was after midnight before Clem decided to stop and

rest the weary horses. They left the frequently traveled road and headed into the woods. Finding a partially clear area, Clem reined in, gesturing for Sharla to do likewise.

With rope in hand, he led her to a tall oak, told her to sit, then bound her securely to the tree's trunk. The rope was tied about her chest, pinning her arms to her sides. The position was uncomfortable, and she dreaded spending the night bound in such a restricting fashion.

She was surprised when her captor apologized for her discomfort. "I'm sorry about tyin' you up like this, but I gotta get a few hours of sleep. This way, I know you'll still be here when I wake up."

He took a rolled blanket from his horse, spread it on the ground close beside her, and lay down. He lay on his back, his arms folded beneath his head. Earlier, clouds had covered the heavens, but they had moved westward, leaving behind a clear sky.

Sharla studied the bounty hunter. She could see him quite plainly, for the night was bathed in moonlight. The man wasn't handsome. His eyes were too close set, his nose too broad, and his face was deeply seamed. However, it wasn't an ugly face, but an interesting one—even an attractive one in a rugged sort of way. A full, dark-brown mustache shadowed his upper lip. It was hard for Sharla to estimate his age, but she guessed him to be in his late thirties or early forties.

He was average height, lean, but obviously strong, for muscles clearly bulged beneath his tight-fitting shirt. Suddenly, as though he had sensed her scrutiny, he turned his head and looked at her.

She quickly lowered her gaze.

"My name's Clem Emerson," he said, as though an introduction was called for. "Considerin' you're from St. Louis, I don't suppose you've heard of me."

"No," she replied. "And I wish I hadn't heard of you now."

He smiled. "Spunky, aren't you?"

She merely glowered at him.

"You know, I've collected a lot of bounties through the years, but you're my first female."

"Lucky me," she grumbled.

"Did you really commit murder?"

"If I said I didn't, would you turn me loose?"

"Not with a three-thousand-dollar bounty on your head. Besides, it's not my job to determine your innocence or guilt; that's up to a judge and jury. My job's just to bring you in."

"Your line of work is despicable."

He chuckled softly. "What do you know about bounty hunters?"

"I know more than I care to know!" A vision of Lance flashed across her mind.

He rolled to his side, presenting her his back. "I gotta get some sleep. Be quiet and I won't have to gag you."

She was more than willing to oblige, for she had nothing more to say to her captor. Claiming her innocence and pleading for her release would be a waste of time. Apparently Clem Emerson didn't care about innocence or guilt; the three-thousand-dollar reward was all that mattered.

Her spirits tumbled. She tried to keep them bolstered by reminding herself that she might escape, but she knew the possibility was so slim it was next to impossible. She must face the truth: Clem Emerson would most likely hand her over to Dexter Rayfield.

Twenty-four

Lance decided to stop and give his horse about an hour's rest. He veered off the road, dismounted, sat beneath a tree, and leaned back against its trunk. Bright moonlight pierced its way through the gaps in green branches that slowly swayed back and forth, their motion propelled by a gentle breeze.

Lance closed his eyes, relaxed, and told himself he might as well take a nap. He was on the verge of dozing off when a faint sound brought him wide awake. He wasn't able to clearly define the noise, for it was too far away. It could have been a horse's neigh, or just the wind whispering through the treetops. He looked at his stallion; its ears were pricked. It suddenly snorted, as though it were warning its master that they were not alone.

Lance got quickly to his feet. Again, the stallion snorted loudly, then stamped a hoof against the turf. Lance silenced it with a firm command, took the reins, and led the horse farther into the woods. He wasn't sure from which direction the sound had originated. However, he opted to move straight ahead. If the sound was a horse's whinny, then its rider was probably a traveler who had left the road to camp for the night. There would be no reason for him to meander through the woods. He'd most likely take a direct path.

Lance didn't walk very far before deciding to tie his

horse to a tree limb. From here on, he planned to move silently.

As he continued onward, he didn't question his reason for slipping up on an unsuspecting traveler. His motive was instinctive. For the past five years, caution had been his constant companion.

Moonbeams, lancing through the treetops, afforded ample light. A short distance ahead, the golden rays fell across two saddled horses. Slade advanced furtively, but an innate warning suddenly sent him spinning on his heel, drawing his Peacemaker so quickly that it seemed to fly into his hand. Lance confronted a man dressed entirely in black, his own gun drawn and aimed. But neither man pulled a trigger, nor did they try to disarm the other one. Instead, they smiled and holstered their weapons.

"How the hell did you know I was here?" Lance asked in a friendly tone.

"Remember me teachin' you how to sense that ticklin' at the back of your neck? Well, I got that feelin' and decided to have a look around."

Lance chuckled. "Ticklin', hell. The wind's at my back. You probably got my scent. Your Comanche blood can smell a white man a mile away." He shook the man's hand. "It's good to see you again, Clem."

"What are you doin' in these parts?"

"I'm on my way to San Antonio. Are you headin' that way?"

"No. I'm goin' to St. Louis." He waved a hand toward the campsite, which was located behind dense shrubbery and scattered trees. "Let's have a smoke and talk for a while."

Lance walked at his side. "Who's traveling with you?" he asked, for he had seen two horses.

"You'll see," he replied. He wanted to surprise Slade with his female fugitive who was worth three thousand dollars. In their profession, such a huge amount was practically unheard of.

Lance spotted Sharla the moment they emerged from the shrubbery. He stopped, turned to Clem, and demanded angrily, "What the hell are you doing with her?"

He was taken aback by his friend's unexpected ire. "She's wanted for murder, and I'm takin' her to St. Louis."

Meanwhile, Sharla stared at Lance with astonishment, his presence almost more than her mind could grasp.

Lance usually carried a knife in his boot; tonight he had it with him. He withdrew it, hurried to Sharla, and cut her loose. Offering her his hand, he helped her to her feet.

"Hold it right there!" Clem ordered, his gun drawn and aimed at Slade. "She's my prisoner. There's a three-thousand-dollar reward for her return, and I intend to collect it."

"You'll have to kill me first," Lance replied.

An entourage of emotions swirled through Sharla: confusion, shock, anger, and even joy at seeing Lance again. She had believed that he was gone forever, that he had callously left her as though their relationship meant nothing to him. Yet, here he was, risking his life to protect hers! She wondered why he was here, and where was Randy Severs?

"Damn it, Slade!" Clem grumbled. "I never thought you'd stoop to stealin' another man's bounty!"

"Sharla's innocent; I don't intend to collect the bounty. And I'll kill any man who tries."

"So you know the lady, huh?"

"Yes, I know her."

"If you care what happens to her, then how come you aren't travelin' with her?"

"I was, but something came up and I had to leave."

Emerson's pistol remained aimed at Lance. "I like you, Slade. Hell, you and I have shared a lot of good times. I even took you under my wing and taught you everything

I know. But there's a limit to friendship. Three thousand dollars is awfully close to that limit."

"Then kill me, or holster your gun and give me a fair chance."

"Think you can out draw me?" he asked, a twinkling challenge in his dark eyes.

"There's one way to find out."

Clem actually considered Lance's proposition. He was curious to see if his friend was faster. However, he couldn't quite bring himself to go through with it. He liked Lance too much. He holstered his gun, and said with a wry grin, "What the hell; three thousand dollars is higher than I can count anyhow."

Lance returned his smile. "I appreciate this, Clem. I hope someday I can repay you."

"Hereafter, you better stick close to that lady," he said, moving to his blanket. He knelt and began to roll it so that it would fit behind his saddle. "I'm not the only bounty hunter who's liable to be lookin' for her. You wanna keep her safe, then stay with her. Leavin' her with an old woman and a fool isn't much protection."

"A fool?" Lance questioned, wondering why he'd describe Steve in such a way.

"He was fool enough to try and draw his gun against mine. Hell, I even had my gun unholstered and aimed straight at him. In my book, that makes him a fool."

"You didn't kill him, did you?"

"I guess I have a weak spot for fools. But he won't be usin' his shootin' arm anytime soon." He went to his horse and attached the rolled blanket. He turned and looked back at Lance. "I guess I don't have a right to call someone else a fool, when I just forfeited three thousand dollars." His gaze went to Sharla, and, tipping the brim of his hat, he told her, "Sorry for the inconvenience, ma'am, but I was just doin' my job."

Her eyes flashed resentfully. "Your job is disgusting!

Bounty hunters have no compassion, understanding, and are totally insensitive!"

Clem, grinning, spoke to Lance, "I don't think the lady has a very high opinion of either one of us. Good luck, amigo; you're gonna need it." He started to mount up.

"Wait," Lance said. "I need to get my horse. Why don't you come with me? It'll give us a chance to talk."

Clem agreed.

"I'll be right back," Lance told Sharla.

Emerson, leading his horse, accompanied Lance into the woods.

"What's troubling you?" Clem questioned. He knew Slade well enough to sense something was on his mind.

"I found Walker," he said.

"Did you kill him?" Clem asked, his tone flat, as though his inquiry was no more important than asking about the weather.

"Yeah, I killed him."

"I suppose you're gonna keep looking for Chambers and Jackson?"

"Why not? Nothing has happened to make me change my mind."

"What about Sharla Matthews?"

"What about her?"

"Where does she fit in? You can't court the lady and hunt down killers at the same time."

"I know that."

They reached Lance's horse.

Clem, watching his companion closely, asked, "Which comes first? Miss Matthews or revenge?"

"The night my family was murdered, I swore I'd find the men who killed them, or die trying. I have one down and two to go; I can't stop now."

Clem, understanding, smiled. "No, I don't suppose you can." He shook Lance's hand. "I hope you stay alive,

Slade. Chasing Jackson and Chambers is living dangerously. They're liable to kill you."

"I know," Lance replied. There was no fear in his voice.

Clem mounted his horse. "See you around," he said.
His eyes, meeting Lance's, were filled with respect and
friendship. He rode farther into the woods and was soon
out of sight.

Sharla was fuming. Lance and his despicable friend had
treated her as though she was a piece of property. Furthermore, their male-minded attitudes were infuriating. She
was a woman, therefore, her opinion didn't matter.

As she awaited Lance's return, she paced furiously, her
anger increasing with each step. Lance's gall was unbeliev-
able. How dare he break Randy Severs out of jail, disappear
without a word, then suddenly reappear!

By the time Lance returned with his horse, Sharla had
worked herself into a fury. She greeted him with heated
words. "You contemptible skunk! Why did you help Severs
escape? How could you do such a thing to Steve's family?
Is Randy Severs another one of your despicable friends—
like Clem Emerson? If he was in jail, I suppose you'd break
him out, too!"

"I probably would," he replied calmly.

Hands on hips, she eyed him fiercely. "How could I have
been so wrong about you? I thought you were a man of
principles. Apparently you're nothing but a crook!"

"Is your tirade about over?"

"Don't talk to me like I'm a child!"

"Then stop acting like one." He stood before her, his
demeanor totally disarming. "Randy Severs is back in jail.
I returned him to Madison Creek, along with the other
two bank robbers. One of them is barely alive and the
other one's at the undertaker's."

Sharla was astounded. "I don't understand. Are you saying you broke Severs out of jail so he'd take you to the other two men?"

"That's about it."

"But why would he do such a thing? And why did you even suspect that he would?"

"Severs used to work for my father. Five years ago, three of his friends murdered my family. Walker, the one at the undertaker's, was one of the killers." He took her hand and led her to the tree where earlier she had been tied. Urging her to sit beside him, he continued, "I should have told you about my family before now, but you have so many problems of your own that I didn't want to saddle you with mine."

His sincerity, the pain in his voice, washed away her anger.

"My father hired Severs's friends: Walker, Chambers, and Jackson. In a couple of weeks we planned a cattle drive to Kansas, and we needed extra hands. The night of the murders, an annual barn dance was held in town. Crystal Pass is a very small town, and populated with some of the nicest people you'll ever meet. Sometimes, however, killers come to town. In this case, they pretended to be cowhands. My family and I always attended the barn dance, and we planned to go this time. But my sixteen-year-old brother came down sick. There was still no reason why my sister and I couldn't go, but I'm not much for dances, and she didn't seem all that interested. We decided to stay home. My cousin, Bill, was living with us." He arched a brow, and a faint smile touched his lips. "You remember Bill; he's the man you were supposed to marry."

She frowned petulantly. "I don't need to be reminded who Bill is. And I was never supposed to marry him, as you very well know!"

Taking her by surprise, Lance leaned closer and pressed his lips to hers. It was a light kiss, but a tender, lingering one.

"That night, Bill went to town with the wranglers," Lance continued, as though there had been no interruption. "The wranglers were given the night off.

"My father didn't trust banks, and he kept his cash in a safe at home. I tried several times to talk him into depositing his money in the bank, but Dad was as stubborn as a damned mule. He turned a deaf ear to every argument I presented.

"About nine o'clock that night, I was in the office bringing the ledger up to date. A side door led outside; the cowhands used it when they needed to come to the office. That way, their dirty boots didn't track up my mother's house. There was a knock on the door, and I answered it. Chambers, Walker, and Jackson were on the other side. They said that they had decided to quit and wanted their wages. I told them I'd pay them in the morning. I was a fool not to suspect something, but back then I trusted a man until he gave me a reason not to. Hell, I wasn't even armed. I never wore a gun in the house; Mom didn't allow it.

"Chambers drew his pistol and shot me. He aimed for my head, but the bullet merely grazed me. It hit with enough force to knock me out cold. Leaving me for dead, they went on a murdering rampage.

"I came to about an hour later. My father's body was in the office. It was in front of the safe, which had been opened and emptied. He was shot in the back. I found my mother in the parlor. Her sewing basket was beside her body. She was strangled with the shirt she had been mending. Upstairs, I found my brother dead in his bed. He was shot in the chest. I went to my sister's room. She was in bed, nude, bleeding, but still alive. The bastards raped her before shooting her! She died in my arms."

"How old was your sister?"

"Fourteen," he murmured.

Lance had told his story quickly, almost mechanically.

But Sharla was sure she understood why. Talking about that night brought it back too vividly, which necessitated finishing the story as quickly as possible. However, despite his efforts to keep his voice controlled, she had detected his rage and heartache. She placed a comforting hand on his.

He drew his hand away. "I don't need your sympathy; I need your understanding."

"Why can't I give you both?"

"It happened five years ago, Sharla. The time for sympathy has passed. I've learned to accept their deaths. But I'll never learn to accept their killers going free. Never!"

"Which means, there's no place in your life for love."

He grimaced. The truth hurt. Nevertheless, he was irrevocably bound to his quest. "It's not that there's no place in my life; there's no time. Maybe someday . . . ?"

A future with Lance now seemed even more unlikely. Her heart ached as she fought back tears. Crying would only make everything worse. Tears would destroy her pride, and put Lance in a very uncomfortable position. She was determined to preserve her pride, and at the same time avoid a discomfiting scene. She wanted Lance's love, not his pity.

"What happened after your family was murdered?" she asked, her heartache concealed behind a calm expression.

"I went kinda of crazy," he replied. "Following the funerals, I returned to the ranch, paid off the wranglers, and told them to leave. Bill was stunned. He wanted to know what the hell I was up to. Although my father's cash was gone, his assets were worth a lot of money. I gave the cattle and half the land to Bill. He objected, of course, saying it was too much. But I insisted. I told him that I was leaving, so he might as well take what I was offering. I then told him to pack his things and get out of the house. He didn't want to leave, but I didn't give him any other choice. Hell, I tore into him like a deranged maniac. As soon as he was gone, I went through every room in the house and collected certain items I couldn't bear to lose. Like my mother's Bible, my father's pocket watch, and some personal things that belonged to my brother and sister. There were objects in the house that were handed down from my grandparents, and their parents before them. I carried everything I wanted to keep outside and piled them in the front yard. Then I torched the house and watched it burn to the ground."

"But why?" Sharla exclaimed. "Why would you destroy your home?"

"Home?" he questioned harshly. "It was no longer a home, but a standing reminder of the carnage that took place there. I never wanted to walk into that house again. The night of the murders, I promised myself that I'd find the men responsible, and I set out to do just that. I failed miserably, and a few months later I returned to Crystal Pass. For weeks I stayed drunk. I was so plagued with guilt and failure that I couldn't live with myself unless I was in a drunken stupor."

"Why did you feel guilty?"

"I blamed myself for letting the killers into the house, for not protecting my family. I wasn't thinking rationally; I realize that now. But at the time, I was still too grief-stricken to think or act reasonably. My days were spent drinking or sleeping off a drunk from the night before.

"Then one afternoon, Clem Emerson came to town. For some reason, he decided to befriend the town's drunk. He gave me the initiative to sober up, to stop drowning in guilt, and to do something with my life. He told me where I had gone wrong chasing my family's killers. I was a rancher, not an experienced hunter or gunfighter. Don't misunderstand me; I was a good shot, but it takes more than that to confront the men I wanted to find. It takes a predator's instincts, an innate sense of survival, and a deadly determination. I didn't know it at the time, but I

already had those traits; they just needed to be trained
and honed. I left town with Clem and traveled with him
for nearly a year. During that time, he taught me everything he knew. When I felt I was ready to be on my own,
Clem and I parted company. We saw each other a few times
after that; our friendship remained intact. I became a
bounty hunter because that was the only way I could support myself without staying in one place."

"Why has it taken you so long to find your family's murderers?"

"The West is immense; sometimes it seems boundless.
It's too much territory for one man to cover. Also, I had
to spend a lot of my time hunting bounties because I
needed money. You can't survive without it. I got quite a
few leads on Chambers and Jackson. Chambers stole my
palomino the night he killed my family. That horse is quite
magnificent, and people take notice of it. Riding it is like
leaving a calling card behind. The last reliable information
I got on Chambers and Jackson led me to believe they
headed into Mexico. Following them into a vast country
like Mexico would have been a waste of time. A couple of
months ago, I heard they were back on this side of the
border. I knew all I had to do was bide my time and eventually they'd show up again."

"What about Walker?" Sharla asked. "You never got a
lead on him until you talked to Randy Severs?"

"I got a few leads here and there, but none of them
ever panned out."

Sharla started to say something, even took a deep
breath, but suddenly changed her mind.

"What is it?" Lance asked. "What were you going to
say?"

She was obviously hesitant; she knew speaking her
thoughts would probably lead to an argument. However,
not expressing her views was like agreeing with his, and
she didn't want him thinking that she approved of his way

of life. She believed revenge was wrong, and she detested his chosen profession.

She took a deep, bolstering breath, then voiced her true feelings, "Dedicating your life to finding and killing your family's murderers makes you as violent as they are. And becoming a bounty hunter is even worse. You should forget Jackson and Chambers, quit your line of work, and do something productive with your life. You said you gave Bill half the land, that means you still have the other half. Build a house, buy some cattle, and return to ranching."

The argument she thought would ensue didn't come about. To her surprise, Lance didn't respond angrily. Quite the opposite. With a disarming smile, he murmured, "I didn't think you'd understand." Then, surprising her even more, he put an arm about her shoulders, drew her close, and asked, "Do you want to leave, or would you rather stay here and make love?"

Twenty-five

"Wh-what?" Sharla stammered, even though she had heard Lance clearly. There was nothing wrong with her ears; she was simply too stunned to respond any other way.

A sensual smile curled his black mustache, and his gray eyes gazed deeply into hers. "I asked, do you want to make love?"

She bounded angrily to her feet. In an instant he was beside her, his arms about her waist. She forcefully pushed him away.

"How dare you!" she cried. "You made it quite clear that you have no time for a lasting relationship, then you actually have the nerve to propose that we make love! I'm not your harlot, Mr. Slade!"

"I didn't say that I would never have time for us. Someday, things might be different."

"Someday!" she lashed out. "I'll not gamble my heart on 'someday'!"

"Life holds no guarantees, Sharla."

"I'm fully aware of that!"

"I don't blame you for not trusting me. But now that I've explained everything—"

"Trust you?" she cut in. "After the way you deceived me?"

"I never deceived you. At least not intentionally."

"Just because you didn't do so intentionally, do you think that makes it all right?"

"I know you're the only right thing that has happened in my life in a long time. I need you, Sharla."

His declaration tore into her heart with a force that immediately weakened her defenses. She suddenly felt helpless, as though her armor had been stripped away, leaving her vulnerable to Lance's sexual intent. If only she wasn't so desperately in love with him! Her love, it seemed, was an emotion she was incapable of controlling.

Sharla's thoughts were reflected in her sapphire eyes, and moving closer to her, Lance drew her into his arms. When he bent his head, she didn't turn her face away; instead, she accepted his kiss without hesitation. His mouth, claiming hers, was wonderfully overpowering.

He lifted her into his arms and laid her gently upon a bed of grass. Positioning himself at her side, he brought her body flush to his. As his mouth possessed hers, his hand caressed her breasts, but her shirt barred him from feeling her bare flesh. He was tempted to strip away her clothes and then his own—to feel her naked body pressed tightly to his. But they were not totally safe here; there were no protective walls or locked doors. He would have to settle for partial nudity. His hand moved to the belt securing her trousers.

But a warning signal suddenly penetrated Sharla's mind, and it successfully pierced its way through the passion that was ruling her every thought—her every move. She stiffened and pushed Lance's hand away. She mustn't make love to him. She had let him use her this way once before; it must not happen a second time!

"What's wrong?" he asked, puzzled by her sudden reluctance.

"I can't do this!" she cried. "I won't let you make a fool of me!"

"Is that what you think this is all about?"

"Isn't it?" she retorted sharply. Her anger, however, was directed primarily at herself. She had no patience with this weakness inside her that Lance controlled so effortlessly.

He spoke patiently, his eyes never leaving her face. "My goal in life is not to make a fool of you. I only want to love you."

"I am fully aware of your goal, and it has nothing to do with me. I'm not that important to you. Chambers and Jackson mean more to you than I do. You don't want to love me; you want to use me."

His patience wavered. Why couldn't she understand? "Are you giving me an ultimatum? Do you want me to choose between you and finding the men who butchered my family? My God, Sharla! If you really loved me, you'd be willing to wait until I'm free."

"You are free!" she returned. "The only bars that hold you are the ones you built for yourself. You can tear them down as easily as you put them up. I am the one who will end up behind bars that are real!"

"Not if I can help it."

She laughed bitterly. "When the time comes, you'll probably be off somewhere chasing Chambers and Jackson!"

"No," he said quickly. "I won't let that happen." He knew he must put his revenge aside temporarily. Sharla's freedom took precedence over anything else. "I'm not going to leave you."

"Never?" she pressed.

"Never is a long time. I don't think I could live with myself if I completely gave up on finding Chambers and Jackson. Sharla, I can promise you my love and my protection, but I can't promise you that I'll stop looking for my family's killers."

"I appreciate your honesty, Lance. I don't understand the revenge that drives you, but I guess I have to accept that it's more powerful than my love."

"Not more powerful—more demanding."

Sharla struggled with her emotions. A part of her insisted that she receive a full commitment from Lance, but another part was willing to concede to his terms. A part of Lance's love was better than none at all. It seemed that she could literally feel her defenses crumbling, like a wall too fragile to withstand the slightest opposition. She had no dominance over her feelings for Lance; he was in control. She was too much in love to defend herself.

Her arms went about his neck, and she pressed her lips to his in total surrender. Their tentative future fled to a dark corner of her mind. Tomorrow no longer mattered; it was too obscure and too dangerous to dwell upon. A gallows in St. Louis was pending her return, and two armed killers were out there somewhere waiting for Lance. They must live for the moment, and relish this time together, for their futures might suddenly end with a gallows, or from a killer's bullet.

This time, when Lance's hand moved to her belt, she didn't push it away. He quickly removed her boots, trousers, and undergarment. She watched through love-glazed eyes as, resting on his knees, he unbuckled his gun belt, placed it within easy reach and drew down his own trousers. He lay carefully upon her, keeping most of his weight supported on his arms. She opened her legs for him, wanting and needing his hardness deep inside her.

He joined their bodies in one quick thrust. She moaned with pleasure, arched her hips and accepted his full length.

Lance kissed her deeply, then murmured, "I love you."

"I love you, too," she whispered. She clung to him, her hips moving in perfect time to his.

Lance made love to her demandingly, almost desperately, as though he needed to possess her wholly—to make her a part of him that could never be taken away. Sharla responded with equal aggression, her hips grinding into his with such fervor that her heart pounded with exhaustion, as well as passion.

Fulfillment, fathomless and all-consuming, came to them at the same time. Complete rapture overwhelmed the lovers, as the tide of ecstasy crested and then ebbed, leaving them blissfully satisfied and totally spent.

Lance kissed her tenderly, then lay beside her. She snuggled close, her head on his shoulder, a leg slung over his. They didn't speak, and the only sounds in the night came from the woods' nocturnal residents, the soft wind whispering through the treetops, and the periodic neighing and snorting of the horses.

Sharla's thoughts swirled, as though her mind was caught in a spinning funnel, mixing and confusing her senses beyond her control. She tried desperately to settle her emotions—to understand why she had succumbed so easily. Did love really make one so weak? She supposed it did, for there was no other logical explanation. She loved Lance completely—unequivocally! Fighting her feelings was a losing battle. She might as well give up, come to terms with her love for Lance, and accept defeat. She had no defense against him.

Lance's thoughts were as unsettling as Sharla's. That she was wanted for murder worried him a great deal. Proving her innocence wasn't going to be easy. Easy, hell! It was probably next to impossible. He questioned if he should take her back to St. Louis, hire a reputable lawyer, and depend on a jury to find her innocent. He quickly dashed that idea, for a picture of Sharla standing on a gallows suddenly flashed across his mind. No, he would not entrust Sharla's life to twelve jurors if he could help it!

His thoughts drifted to the passionate union they had just shared. He supposed he should curse himself for taking advantage of her vulnerability. But, like Sharla, he had no control over his love. He needed her as desperately as a drowning victim needed a lifeline. In a way, she was his

lifeline. For the past five years, he had merely been existing. He had turned his back on life and had lived only for
revenge. The night his family was murdered, he had fallen
into a dark abyss, and was hopelessly entrapped in its endless pit. Hate, retribution, and violence were trapped in
there with him. These three vices controlled his very existence. They were the forces that drove him, and his reasons for never giving up his quest. But Sharla's love had
thrown him a lifeline; he had grabbed on and was now
leaving that place of darkness. He wasn't quite ready to
surrender his revenge, but it was no longer the center of
his life. Sharla came first, for he loved her with all his
heart.

He leaned up, smiled wistfully, then kissed her with deep
devotion. "It won't always be like this. Everything will be
all right."

She wasn't so sure. She seriously doubted that Maxine
could ever prove that she didn't kill James Rayfield. And
she didn't dare believe that Lance could relinquish his
revenge. If she let herself believe that, she'd only be disappointed. However, she didn't reveal these doubts. Instead, she responded lightheartedly, "Did you know that
grass makes an itchy bed?"

Grinning, he turned her onto her side and gently patted
her bare behind. "I guess grass isn't very comfortable
against such delicate flesh. Next time we'll use a blanket."

"Next time we'll use a bed," she retorted with a pert
smile.

He sat up, reached for her things and handed them to
her. As she stood and slipped them on, he straightened
his clothes and buckled on his gun.

"We'd better leave," Lance said. "We need to get to the
wagon and check on Jordan."

Sharla suddenly felt guilty that she hadn't considered
Steve's injury. But Lance's presence had obliterated everything except the need to be in his arms.

"I don't think Steve's wound was too serious," she said. "But you're right, we should hurry and check on him. If he needs a doctor, we'll have to go back to Madison Creek."

"That could be risky, you know. All these delays mean those wanted posters are liable to catch up to you."

"I know," she replied softly. "But if Steve needs a doctor, I don't have any other choice. I'll just have to take my chances."

"We won't stay a moment longer than necessary. It's too important that you keep on the move." She had told Lance that upon her arrival in San Antonio, she was supposed to contact a woman named Jenny. He knew who she was, for he had frequented her place of business. She owned a saloon, but drinking wasn't the main attraction of the place, for she had four prostitutes working for her.

As they went to their horses and mounted, Lance said what was on his mind. "Sharla, maybe you shouldn't go to San Antonio. I don't know where the hell Jenny can hide you, except in a room above her saloon. That's no place for you. I think you should let me take you to Bill's ranch. You'll be safe there."

"Will you be there with me?"

"I told you that I won't leave you—not now."

"And later?"

"I can't make any promises. But if I do leave, I'll come back to you."

"You can't come back if you're dead. Chambers and Jackson are liable to kill you. Dear God, Lance! Why must you risk your life for revenge? Is this what your parents would have wanted?"

He shook his head. "No, it isn't. They were gentle, caring people who tried to live by God's rules."

She looked at him closely. "Is there nothing I can say that will change your mind?"

"Let's not worry about me; let's worry about you. Your problems are a lot more urgent than mine."

The subject was thereby dismissed. Lance had ended it abruptly, and the expression in his eyes told her that it was not to be reopened. She conceded, but only for the present. He would not get off that easily, for she had every intention of bringing it up again.

Shortly after Mary had extracted the bullet from Steve's shoulder, he had fallen asleep. He slept soundly, despite the constant ache that ran the full length of his arm. Mary had encouraged him to take several swallows of whiskey before and after she had tended to him. The liquor had numbed his pain and had eased him into a deep slumber.

Now, as the morning sun crested, its bright rays lighting the wagon's interior, Steve slowly awakened. He was first conscious of the pain in his shoulder. It felt like a red-hot dagger was lodged in his flesh, and he quickly checked his wound, as though he expected to find that there was indeed a dagger causing his pain. Shirtless, he could clearly see his shoulder. It was neatly bandaged, and no blood had seeped through. Apparently, Mary had done a professional work of surgery.

He sat up gingerly, and glanced about the wagon. Mary was on her pallet. She was lying very still, and he assumed that she was asleep. He still intended to find Sharla; he wasn't about to be deterred by a shoulder wound.

He found his shirt, and using his good arm, he slung it over his shoulders. Getting to his feet proved precarious, for he was still very weak. He nevertheless managed, and getting his balance, he moved over and knelt beside Mary's pallet. He was reluctant to awaken her, but he had to let her know that he was leaving to find Sharla. He placed a hand on her shoulder, and shook her gently.

She didn't respond.

He then noticed that her brow was wet with perspiration. Her skin appeared pale and clammy. "Mary!" he said strongly. "Mary, can you hear me?"

Her eyelids fluttered open. "You don't have to yell; I can hear you."

"Are you ill?"

"I've been feeling poorly for the past couple of days. But last night after I got through tending to you, I started feeling worse."

"If you've been sick for the past couple of days, why didn't you let us know?"

"I didn't want to worry anyone, or be a burden."

"I'm taking you back to Madison Creek. You need a doctor."

"No," she said, gripping his shirtsleeve. "You must find Sharla."

"I can't leave you here. Not like this."

"I'll be all right."

He stood, the sudden motion causing his head to start spinning. The dizziness was so severe that he almost passed out.

"We make a fine pair," Mary said weakly. "I don't know who's worse off, me or you."

"Don't worry. I can manage to get us back to Madison Creek."

"Please. Go after Sharla. I don't matter."

"You matter very much. I'm taking you to a doctor and that's final."

He left to hitch up the wagon. Despite his injury, he forced himself to hurry. He wanted to get Mary to a doctor as quickly as possible, for he was worried that she was seriously ill.

Twenty-six

Steve had the team hitched to the wagon and was ready to leave when Sharla returned with Lance. Steve was shocked and overjoyed that Sharla had escaped her abductor. He supposed Slade was responsible for her release, but that didn't lessen his anger—he would never forgive Slade for helping Randy Severs! He was torn between welcoming Sharla or turning to Lance and venting his rage. The latter possibility won out, and as Slade dismounted, Jordan went to him and said angrily, "You sorry bastard! I oughta kill you for breaking Severs out of jail!"

Lance's eyes turned hard, and his body went rigid. However, he spoke calmly. "You should watch your language, Jordan. I don't take kindly to bein' called a bastard. I don't like threats much either."

"Steve!" Sharla exclaimed, placing her body between the two men. "Lance did break Severs out of jail, but he took him back. He also captured the other two bank robbers. The men responsible for your niece's murder have been apprehended, thanks to Lance!"

"This is all very confusing," Steve replied. "Do you mind explaining?"

"Later," Slade answered. "Right now, we need to know how you're doing?" He looked closely at Steve's bandaged shoulder.

"Mary took out the bullet," Jordan said. "She did a marvelous job."

"Do you need a doctor?"

"I don't think so, but I'm afraid that Mary does. She's pretty sick. I was planning on taking her back to Madison Creek."

Sharla hurried to check on Mary, her heart pounding as she climbed inside the wagon. Fear for Mary's life hit her with a startling force. Until this moment, she hadn't realized how deeply she cared for the woman.

Mary appeared to be asleep, and Sharla moved quietly to the pallet, sat down, and looked at her grandmother through a teary blur. The woman's face was damp with perspiration, and her complexion was entirely too pale.

As though she sensed Sharla's presence, Mary opened her eyes and gazed up into her granddaughter's face. A smile touched her lips. "Thank God you're back. But how . . . ?"

"Lance found me," she said.

"Lance?"

Skirting the more complicated details, she gave Mary a hurried account of what had happened.

"I kinda figured Lance had a reason for breaking Severs out of jail; I just couldn't imagine what it was."

"We're taking you back to Madison Creek. You need to see a doctor."

"Let Steve take me back. You and Lance must move on. It's dangerous for you to stay in one place too long."

"I'm not leaving you," Sharla said. "And don't waste your strength arguing with me. My mind's made up."

Her hand clasped Sharla's. "I don't deserve such kindness from you. God forgive me for deserting my own flesh and blood. I failed you and your mother."

"It's not too late. You and Maxine can find your way back to each other." She had purposely omitted her own name.

"Yes, but I pray you'll make the journey with us. Your mother needs you."

Sharla stiffened, and let go of Mary's hand. She didn't want to be cruel, but more importantly, she was against giving Mary false hope. "I don't want a relationship with Maxine. She forfeited that right when she gave me away."

"Don't be so bitter."

"I'm sorry, but I can't help how I feel."

Mary closed her eyes, and remained silent for so long that Sharla thought she had fallen asleep. She was about to see if Lance and Steve were ready to leave when, suddenly, Mary looked up at her. Her face was strained, and she had a strange expression in her eyes.

Sharla froze. Dear God, was she dying?

Again, Mary's hand found Sharla's. She spoke hesitantly, as though she had to force the words from her mouth, "I . . . I still have this feeling that . . . that something has happened to Maxine."

Sharla sighed with relief, thankful that it wasn't impending death but concern for Maxine that had brought about such a change in Mary. She gently patted the woman's hand, and said consolingly, "I'm sure Maxine is fine. But if it'll make you feel any better, when we get to Madison Creek, I'll ask Lance to send her a wire. There's no risk involved. The law isn't looking for Lance. There's no reason why a wire from him to Maxine should arouse suspicion."

"But that means we'll have to wait for her to answer the wire."

"We'll have plenty of time to wait. I'm sure the doctor will order you to bed, and will insist that you stay there for quite some time."

"Three days," Mary replied. "I won't stay in bed longer than three days. Even three days is putting your freedom at risk."

Sharla didn't argue, for she knew Mary was right.

* * *

Time was also on Dexter Rayfield's mind as he and his companions stopped to eat lunch. He considered time his enemy, for he believed it lessened his chances of apprehending Sharla. If he didn't catch her soon, then he might never find her. The vast West could hide a fugitive forever.

He ordered Chambers and Jackson to build a fire, heat two cans of hash, and brew a pot of coffee.

Although they carried out his instructions, they did so reluctantly and somewhat angrily. Rayfield's arrogance was starting to get to them. They weren't used to obeying orders. In fact, they were more familiar with robbing and killing men like Dexter Rayfield. They had accepted this job because it seemed an easy way to make money and return to Texas at the same time. But they were beginning to question if it had been such a good idea. In their opinion, Dexter was a smug bastard, and smashing a fist into his aristocratic nose was a constant temptation.

Dexter had no inkling that his bodyguards disliked him, nor did he realize that he couldn't trust them. He paid their wages, so he assumed he not only had their loyalty but also their full cooperation. Growing up in St. Louis, protected by wealth and social prominence, he had never encountered men like Chambers and Jackson. Therefore, he had foolishly entrusted his life, as well as Claudia's, to a pair of killers who were about as trustworthy as two rabid dogs.

Dexter joined Claudia, who was sitting beneath a tree. He stretched out on the grass, shaded his eyes with his hat, and decided to take a nap.

This was fine with Claudia. She didn't care to carry on a conversation. She was too miserable and disgusted. She hated traveling in this fashion, and she almost wished she hadn't inveigled an invitation. She sighed deeply, and told herself that she must endure. They would soon catch

Sharla, and then she could put this terrible trip behind her. Dexter would buy her a beautiful home, shower her with expensive jewelry, and give her a generous allowance.

A complacent smile curled her lips. Yes, she would soon live in grand style! She knew her house would not be as elegant as Olivia's, but she was willing to settle for less. As her thoughts lingered on her former employer's home, she recalled the little bedroom where she had spent so many nights. She had often lain in bed, unable to sleep, her mind filled with dreams of marrying James Rayfield.

She didn't want to think about the night she killed him, but she couldn't seem to stop herself from remembering. Against her will, it all came back to her in a flash: the letter opener—the shock on James's face when she plunged it deeply into his chest—her flight to her room—stripping off her bloody uniform—searching for a place to hide it, then shoving it into the chimney.

She suddenly sat straight up with a start. The blood-spattered uniform. My God, it was still in the chimney! How could she have forgotten it? She had intended to remove it, cut it into shreds, then sneak downstairs and burn the evidence in the kitchen stove.

Her heart was pounding so strongly that she put a hand to her chest, as though she could slow its rapid beat. She actually felt sick to her stomach, and her brow beaded with nervous perspiration. If Agnes or Albert were to find the stashed uniform, they would certainly realize the stains on it were from dried blood. They would hand it over to the constable, and then she would become his prime suspect.

Panic rose inside her, sending her head swimming and her body trembling. How could she have made such a huge mistake? The thought that she had forgotten to destroy the bloody uniform was almost more than she could cope with. The panic inside her increased, and, for a moment, she thought she might faint. She forced herself to take deep, calming breaths. She must not give in to fear. More than likely, the uniform was still safely hidden in the chimney, and would stay that way for a long time. Dexter had closed the house, and there was no one living there except for Agnes and Albert. Also, winter was months away. The fireplace in her room would remain unlit for a long time. When she returned to St. Louis, she would find an excuse to revisit her old room, get the uniform, then permanently dispose of it.

Her nerves settled, and she felt a little foolish for panicking so easily.

Chambers announced gruffly that lunch was ready. Dexter had dozed off, but the rich timbre in Chambers's voice awakened him. He and Claudia went to the fire and filled their plates. The group ate without dinner conversation. Following the meal, Rayfield ordered his two bodyguards to clean the dishes and break camp.

Jackson frowned harshly. "How come your woman can't tend to cookin' and cleanin'? Hell, it's woman's work, ain't it?"

Rayfield stiffened. He wasn't accustomed to an employee balking at a direct order. "I pay your wages," he said firmly. "And you'll do as I say!"

Chambers, listening, resented Rayfield as much as Jackson did, but he wasn't sure if this was the time to do anything about it. In fact, he hadn't decided yet if a rebellion was necessary. Rayfield was an arrogant son-of-a-bitch, true, but he was also very rich. Chambers hoped to convince Rayfield to part with some of his money—three thousand dollars to be exact. The reward posted for Sharla Matthews should belong to him and Jackson. After all, without their help, Rayfield wouldn't stand a chance in hell of finding her. When the time was right, he intended to point that out to Rayfield. But, for now, he figured he might as well tolerate the pompous ass. He turned to Jackson. "Stop your complainin', and do as you're told," he ordered.

Jackson cast him an angry glare, but he saw a subtle plea in his friend's eyes that cooled his dander. He bit back a retort, and started on the chores.

Chambers left to water the horses. A minute or so later, Dexter followed him. Admiring Chambers's impressive palomino, he said, "That sure is a magnificent stallion. Where did you find him?"

"I caught him wild," he lied.

"You should take better care of him." The animal's neglect was sadly obvious.

"I ain't got time to pamper no horse."

"Would you consider selling him? I'll give you a fair price."

Chambers shook his head. "Naw, he ain't for sale. He might be gettin' on in years, and I sure as hell don't coddle him, but he's the strongest and most dependable horse I ever owned. This here beast has gotten me out of more than one jam, 'cause he's fast and always rarin' to go."

"Well, if you change your mind, let me know." Dexter returned to Claudia.

Chambers watched as his boss sat close to the woman, as though he couldn't bear to be more than a few inches from her. He laughed under his breath. Rayfield was totally smitten with his harlot. However, he didn't really blame him, for the woman was exceptionally attractive. He wouldn't mind getting in between her legs himself! The thought alone was arousing, and he moaned with discomfort as his manhood swelled. He quickly turned away, and made himself concentrate on watering the horses.

Sharla waited in the Jordans' parlor as Dr. Williams tended to Mary. Upon their return to Madison Creek, they had gone straight to Wyatt's house. As Lance was fetching the doctor, Sharla and Emma had put Mary to bed.

Sharla's nerves were tightly strung. She would sit for a

few minutes, then get up and start walking back and forth. She seemed unable to choose between sitting or pacing.

Steve and Lance shared the parlor with Sharla. Wyatt was at the saloon, and Emma was in the kitchen.

Lance was sitting on the sofa, but he got up, went to Sharla and placed a halting hand on her arm. "Relax, darlin'. Tiring yourself out pacing isn't gonna bring the doctor in here any sooner."

"I know, but I'm so worried that Mary is seriously ill. She should never have made this trip. It's all my fault. She left the farm because she wanted to find me."

"You can't blame yourself. You didn't send her a wire; Hattie did."

"That reminds me," Sharla said. "Mary and I want you to send a wire to Maxine."

"Why do you want me to do that?"

"Mary has this crazy notion that something has happened to Maxine. I don't care what you say in the wire, just word it so that she'll know to send a reply. Hearing from Maxine will put Mary's mind to rest."

"All right," he agreed. "I'll take care of it now. Or would you rather I stayed with you until you talk to the doctor?"

"No. I'll be fine."

He kissed her lips softly, grabbed his hat from the sofa, and left the house.

A feeling of warmth filled Sharla. She believed in Lance again, and trusted him fully. Their future was uncertain, but she had every confidence in their love.

Dr. Williams came into the parlor, bringing Sharla out of her reverie.

"How is she," Sharla asked at once.

The doctor, portly, and middle-aged, smiled at Sharla. He had a kind smile, and gentle, caring eyes. "Mary will be much better after a few days rest. The woman is worn out. She's seventy-four years old, you know."

"No, I didn't know," Sharla replied.

Dr. Williams raised a questioning brow. "Isn't she your grandmother?"

Sharla admitted that she was.

He didn't delve into Sharla's reason for not knowing her grandmother's age. He didn't consider it any of his business. "Mary said you're traveling to San Antonio. That's a long, tiring trip for a woman of her age. Young lady, if you want your grandmother to live to see San Antonio, then you better make sure that she doesn't work too hard, and that she gets plenty of rest."

"I'll certainly see to that."

The doctor turned his attention to Steve. "Now, I'd better take a look at that shoulder. Bullet wound?"

"That it is," he replied. "My very first." His demeanor was cocky, as though the wound was something of which to be proud.

Williams humphed. "If you don't change your ways and settle down to a decent, God-fearing life, that bullet wound may be your first, but it won't be your last."

"May I see my grandmother?" Sharla asked the doctor.

"Yes, but don't stay too long. She needs her rest."

The moment Sharla left, Steve asked Williams, "How bad is Mary . . . really? You can tell me."

He sighed heavily. "Mary made me promise not to say anything to her granddaughter. She's more concerned with not worrying her granddaughter than she is with her own health."

"Is her condition serious?"

"She has an irregular heartbeat and a touch of congestion in her lungs. At her age, that's very serious."

"I'm sorry to hear that," Steve replied. "I admire Mary Simmons. She's quite a woman. Is she going to . . . ?"

"Die?" Williams completed. "Sure she will. We're all going to die."

"You know what I mean."

"I can't tell you how much time she has because I don't know. Now, I need to take a look at that shoulder."

Lance sent the wire to Maxine, left the telegraph office and decided to stop at the sheriff's office.

Langley, seated at his desk, rose and shook Slade's hand. "I heard you were back in town."

"Steve and Mary Simmons needed to see the doctor."

"How are they?"

"I don't know about Mary, but I'm sure Steve will be fine."

"What happened to him?"

"He was shot in the shoulder."

"This sounds interesting," Langley remarked. He always kept a bottle of whiskey handy, and he now withdrew it from his desk drawer and poured two drinks. He gestured for Lance to take a chair, handed him his glass, then returned to his own seat. "How did Steve get shot?" he asked.

Lance suddenly found himself in a jam. He couldn't very well explain Clem Emerson without revealing Clem's reason for abducting Sharla. He wasn't about to tell the sheriff that the woman claiming to be Trish Lawrence was really a wanted fugitive.

"I can't talk about it," he decided to reply.

"Why not?"

"Let's just say, it's personal."

Langley was disappointed; he had been anticipating an exciting tale. For the most part, his life was as boring as his job, and he had hoped to experience a little second-hand excitement.

"Is Severs still alive?" Lance asked.

"Nope. We hung the bastard this mornin'. He went to the gallows screamin' and a kickin'. He's buried in a far corner of the cemetery among the weeds and brambles. If you ask me, that's where he belongs."

"What about Shark?"

"He's locked up. The doctor said he'll probably live to stand trial. In a couple of weeks, this town will have another hangin'."

Lance finished his whiskey, stood, and thanked Langley for his hospitality.

"How long are you stayin'?" the sheriff asked Lance, who was nearing the front door.

"A few days," he replied.

The afternoon sun was extremely warm, and its heat struck Lance full force as he stepped outside. Summer was quickly approaching. He hoped the temperature would stay fairly moderate for the remainder of the journey, for he hoped to make the trip as pleasant as possible for Mary.

He started walking toward the edge of town, where Wyatt's home was located. Across the street, three men came out of the saloon. Lance, his thoughts on Mary's condition, was not aware of their presence.

Two of these men, however, were very aware of Lance. For a tense moment, they stared at the bounty hunter as though they couldn't believe their own eyes. Then, avoiding the chance that he might glance in their direction, the pair went back into the saloon, followed closely by the third man.

Going to a rear table, they drew three chairs and sat down. The youngest man, who, along with his brother, had recognized Slade, now stared silently at his brother, as though he dared not speak before he did. The other man's eyes darted back and forth from one brother to the other. He was confused and had no idea why his comrades were acting so strangely. He didn't know the men all that well; he had only been riding with them for a little over a month.

The two Canton brothers were thieves. Mostly, they rustled cattle, or robbed stagecoaches. On some occasions their crimes resulted in murder. There were no wanted posters on the Cantons. So far they had managed to break the law without revealing their identities. That is, except for Ben, the third and youngest brother.

Rebelling against his brothers, who always told him what to do and treated him like he wasn't yet a man, Ben had angrily struck out on his own. At the age of twenty, he was hot-headed and bent on making a name for himself. He wanted to be as famous as Billy The Kid.

Six months ago, Ben had stopped in Laramie and had stayed a few days. He got into an argument with the town's blacksmith over a livery fee. Unable to control his temper, Ben shot the man in cold blood. The blacksmith's twelve-year-old son witnessed the shooting and Ben turned his gun on the frightened lad and sent a bullet into his chest, ending his young life. He then rode quickly out of town, but the blacksmith lived long enough to identify Ben to the town's sheriff.

Wanted posters on Ben were widely distributed. The two Cantons, having seen the posters, set out to find their youngest sibling to hide him from the law. However, Lance found Ben before they did. Lance tried to take the fugitive in alive, but Ben foolishly drew on him, leaving Lance no choice but to defend himself. Ben died instantly.

When they learned of their brother's death, the Cantons swore revenge. That Slade had shot in self-defense didn't matter. He was still responsible for Ben's death. A few weeks after the shooting, they found Lance in San Antonio. The sheriff thwarted a confrontation, and siding with Lance, he arrested the Cantons and kept them in jail for days. By the time they were released, Slade's whereabouts was unknown.

Now, the Cantons could hardly believe that Lance was within their reach.

The oldest brother turned a steely gaze to his sibling.

"This time, ain't no sheriff gonna protect that bastard. We're gonna grab him and get him out of town."

"What's goin' on?" their friend asked.

"That man we seen was Lance Slade, the son-of-a-bitch who killed Ben."

The man knew all about Ben and the way he had died. The Cantons talked about it all the time. He was as unsavory as his companions and was more than willing to help them achieve their revenge.

"You got a plan in mind?" he asked the oldest brother.

"Not yet, but I'll think of something." His gaze was cold, hard, and without mercy. A murderous smile crept to his thick lips and curled itself like a snake about to strike. "Slade's as good as dead!" he hissed. "I guarantee it."

Twenty-seven

Sharla's spirits were high, for she was hopeful that Mary would make a full recovery. Twenty-four hours of complete bed rest had already made quite a change. Mary's color had returned, and she was feeling much better. She even claimed that she was strong enough to continue their journey, but Sharla insisted that she remain in bed at least two more days.

Sharla was alone in the parlor when Lance knocked at the front door. Steve was at the saloon with Wyatt, and Emma was in the kitchen. She went to the door and saw Lance standing on the porch. Glancing over his shoulder, she was surprised to see her mare tied at the hitching rail, along with Lance's stallion.

"Are we going somewhere?" she asked with a smile.

"I thought you might like to take a ride. It's a beautiful day."

Spending the afternoon with Lance sounded heavenly. "Let me tell Emma that I'm leaving. I'll be right back." She hurried to the kitchen. Changing clothes wasn't necessary, for she was wearing her trousers.

She returned quickly, and she and Lance mounted their horses and rode out of town. Sharla, wanting to feel the wind in her hair and experience the thrill of speed, coaxed her mare to run as fast as it could. Lance's powerful stallion stayed alongside the mare; it could have easily left the smaller horse far behind, but Lance held a tight rein.

Back in Madison Creek, the Cantons' friend, Chester Thorton, walked hastily toward the saloon, where he had left his horse. He had followed Slade to the Jordans' home and had seen him leave with the woman. The Canton brothers were no longer in town but were camped nearby. Last night they left Madison Creek for fear that Slade might spot them. Chester had remained to keep an eye on Slade.

Now, as he hurried to get his horse, his thoughts were flowing. He figured Slade would be preoccupied with the woman, which would make him vulnerable and careless. He hoped to catch up to them, capture the bounty hunter, then take him to his comrades' campsite. He couldn't leave the woman behind, of course, for she would notify the law. He planned to take her, too. After they killed Slade, they could enjoy the woman. He didn't care if she lived or died; he'd leave that decision to the older Canton, for Bert was always in charge.

Reaching his horse, Thorton was about to swing into the saddle when Langley, making his rounds, strolled past the saloon. He stopped and regarded Thorton suspiciously. He knew the stranger had ridden into Madison Creek with two other men. These two had apparently left, but for some reason, this one had stayed behind. The sheriff was curious, as well as distrustful.

"What's your name, stranger?" he asked.

"Chester Thorton," he replied, stepping away from his horse.

"Were you goin' somewhere?"

"Just for a ride," he mumbled.

Langley's eyes raked the man thoroughly. He looked to be in his early thirties, was somewhat unkempt, and had a dangerous aura about him that put Langley on his guard. "What's your business in Madison Creek?" he asked.

"No special business, Sheriff. Just takin' a few days' rest before headin' out. I'm on my way to Arkansas to visit my family." He lied easily, and fairly convincingly.

"What happened to your two friends?"

"They headed north. I think they got kin folks up that way."

"How long you plannin' on stayin' here?"

"A day, maybe two." He held up his arms, as though warding off Langley's suspicions. "I ain't lookin' for no trouble, Sheriff. I'm just a wrangler; I ain't no gunfighter."

"Did I say you were?"

"No, but you sure are actin' like I am."

Langley forced a smile. "Well, to show you there's no hard feelings, let me buy you a drink."

"You ain't foolin' me, Sheriff. You just want to keep question' me."

"If you ain't got anything to hide, then you shouldn't mind the questions."

Thorton was trapped. He had no choice but to let the sheriff buy him a drink and at the same time satisfy his curiosity. Simmering inwardly, and forced to give up his plan to pursue Slade, he followed the law officer into the saloon.

Lance and Sharla raced across the pastoral countryside. Above, the sky was cerulean blue, and quick-moving clouds skimmed toward the horizon, as though they were racing with the two horses far below. The landscape spread out in a green tapestry. Here and there tall trees stood like sentinels protecting the unblemished land. Wildflowers grew in abundance, their sweet nectar drawing several hummingbirds. The tiny creatures hovered above the colorful petals, their wings moving faster than the eye could see.

The Eden-like terrain was emotionally soothing, as well

as uplifting. Therefore, Sharla and Lance were relaxed and feeling wonderful as they stopped to rest. Letting the horses graze nearby, they went to a tree and sat down beneath its leafy umbrella. They welcomed the shade, for the weather was quite warm.

"I'm glad you asked me to ride with you," Sharla said. "I needed to get away for a while."

He kissed her tenderly. "I'm sure you did. I just wish I could do more, like take away all your problems."

"I do have more than my share, don't I?"

Her question didn't really call for an answer. "How's Mary?" he asked.

"She's much better. We'll leave in two days."

"Are you sure she'll be up to traveling?"

"I can't be sure, but I do know that it's risky for me to stay here much longer. Leaving Mary behind is out of the question; she's determined to stay with me."

"She loves you," Lance said softly.

Sharla sat rigidly. "Loves me?" she questioned somewhat bitterly. "Isn't it a little late for that?"

"At the risk of sounding corny, there is an old adage that comes to mind: Better late than never."

She relaxed. "I know I shouldn't be so bitter. But it's hard for me to accept this new family of mine. Sometimes I want to scream out to Mary and Maxine: Where were you for the past twenty years? I just don't understand their kind of love."

He held her hand. "Maybe you should stop judging them. I'm sure they have suffered enough. And they apparently love you. Maxine was there for you when you really needed her. Mary, despite her age, set out to find you. That sounds an awful lot like family love and loyalty to me."

She snuggled into his arms. "I don't want to discuss my problems. This afternoon is too perfect."

"What would you like to do?" he asked with a sensual smile.

Her eyes twinkled saucily. "I think you know what I have in mind."

"Wanton little minx, aren't you?"

"If I am, then it's your fault. You made me this way."

"Good for me," he chuckled.

"But, Lance, do we dare? I mean, we aren't exactly secluded, and it is broad daylight."

Lance looked about the immediate area. High shrubbery grew a short distance behind the tree, blocking an unexpected rider's approach from that direction. He leapt to his feet, smiled down at Sharla, and said, "Yes, we do dare. But this time, we'll use a blanket."

She faked a pout. "If I remember correctly, I said we would use a bed next time."

He quirked a teasing brow. "Do you want to change your mind?"

Desire for Lance was flowing hotly through her veins. "I certainly do not! Get that blanket, Mr. Slade. You are in love with a wanton minx, remember?"

"As if I could forget," he replied, smiling expansively. He hastened to his horse, retrieved a rolled-up blanket and returned to Sharla. Taking her hand, he led her behind the tree's massive trunk, and spread out the blanket.

There, they made love beneath the foliage-covered branches, where they were well hidden by the powerful oak and the dense shrubbery. Sharla, her passion as fervent as Lance's, gave herself to him fully—relishing each kiss, every whispered endearment, and the forceful thrusting that dipped his hardness further and further into her moist depths. She loved the feel of him deep inside her, their bodies joined in perfect rapture. She felt she could make love to him for a hundred years, and still be greedy for more. She couldn't get enough of him. Not now, not ever!

Lost in their devotion and need for each other, they pushed all their troubles and problems aside and surrendered completely to the power of their love.

Later, they lay snuggled in each other's arms, luxuriating in the aftermath of their fiery union. They talked, kissed, promised each other their undying loyalty, then as their passions were reignited, they made love again.

Chester Thorton's disposition was cranky as he rode into the Cantons' campsite. That Sheriff Langley had thwarted his plan to follow Lance had his temper riled. Even though the lawman had dismissed him nearly an hour ago, his anger was still boiling.

Expressing his ire through hand gestures and wide sweeps of his arms, he told the Canton brothers what had happened.

Bert Canton responded with a loud guffaw.

"What's so damned funny?" Thorton snapped.

"Hell, Langley probably saved your ass. You try to go against Slade one-on-one, you'll end up six feet underground."

The other Canton agreed. "Chester, you ain't that damned good with a gun. Why, Slade could unholster his gun, shoot you, and reholster it before you hit the ground."

"Shut up, Wesley!" Thorton grumbled, finding the younger man's belittling offensive.

"Don't tell me to shut up!" he said angrily.

"Both of you shut up!" Bert demanded. "This ain't no time for us to be yellin' at each other." He turned to Thorton. "Where's Slade stayin'?"

"He has a room above the saloon."

"Does he spend much time there?"

"He spends most of his time at Jordan's house. Last night, he didn't go to his room until late."

"Where does he keep his horse?"

"At the livery."

"Tonight, when he returns to his room, Wesley and me are gonna be waitin' for him."

"Where am I gonna be?"

"You're gonna get his horse from the livery. I want it to look like Slade decided to pack up and leave town. I don't want Langley gettin' suspicious and roundin' up a posse."

"Once we got Slade, where are we gonna take him?"

"We're gonna go about a day's ride from here. Just in case Langley doesn't believe Slade left on his own accord, I intend to put some miles between us and Madison Creek."

"Can I be the one to kill him?" Wesley asked his brother.

"We'll both kill him," he replied with a generous smile, as though his offer was not only noble, but magnanimous as well.

Dusk was less than an hour away when Sharla and Lance returned to town. Leaving Sharla at the house, Lance took the horses to the livery. He planned to check at the telegraph office, then clean up and have dinner with Sharla and the Jordans.

A wire was waiting for Lance, but it wasn't from Maxine. Her lawyer had sent the reply. He read the telegram, then went directly to the Jordans' home. He was filled with dread as he knocked on the front door. It was opened by Steve.

"I didn't expect you this soon," he said, waving Lance inside. "Sharla said you wouldn't be here until about seven."

As they went into the parlor, Lance explained, "I received a wire from Maxine's lawyer. Maxine is dead."

"My God!" Steve groaned. "Then Mary's intuition was right."

"Where is Sharla?"

"She's with Mary."

"Will you tell her I'm here?"

Steve left to send Sharla to Lance. A few moments later she came into the parlor.

"My goodness, Lance," she said happily, going to him and kissing him soundly on the lips. "I thought you were going to clean up. I wanted to take a bath, too, and change clothes. Why did you hurry back? Can't you stand being away from me for more than a hour or so?"

"Sharla . . ." he began hesitantly.

She suddenly became aware that he seemed distraught. She hadn't noticed it before, for she had still been too wrapped up in the warm glow of their perfect afternoon.

"Lance, what's wrong?" she asked.

The telegram was in his shirt pocket. He took it out and unfolded it. "This is from Maxine's lawyer."

Sharla tensed. "What does it say?"

"It's bad news."

"Please, read it."

He read the short missive aloud: "Maxine Reynolds is dead—Death under investigation—Murder or accident not yet confirmed."

Lance folded the paper and placed it on the table in front of the sofa. He turned back to Sharla, wondering how she was going to take Maxine's death. She was a little pale, and a trace of tears misted her eyes; otherwise, she seemed calm and in control.

"Claudia," she murmured so softly that Lance barely heard her.

"What about Claudia?"

"She killed Maxine."

"You can't be sure."

"No, not logically. But deep in the pit of my stomach, I just know she killed Maxine. Somehow, she learned that

Maxine was trying to help me. Maybe Maxine was on to something, and Claudia murdered her to silence her."

"Maxine's death is under investigation. If Claudia is responsible, maybe this time she'll get caught." Lance moved closer to Sharla, and placed his hands firmly on her shoulders. "Let's put Claudia aside for the moment. We need to talk about you."

"Me?" she questioned. "I'm all right."

"Are you?"

"I'm not about to fall to pieces, if that's what you're worried about. I barely knew Maxine. I'm sorry that she's dead. I'm more than sorry; I'm crushed. She probably died because she was trying to help me. But I don't feel a daughter's grief."

"I understand," he replied kindly.

"Mary!" she suddenly moaned. "What will this do to her? Maybe I shouldn't tell her until she's stronger."

"Tell me what?" Mary asked, coming into the parlor. She had donned a robe, and was wearing soft-sole slippers, which had silenced her steps.

"You shouldn't be out of bed," Sharla told her.

"Nonsense!" she scoffed. "I feel fine. I'm not an invalid; at least not yet. Now, what is it that you're hesitant to tell me?"

Sharla motioned to the sofa. "I think you should sit down."

"It's Maxine, isn't it?" she asked, remaining on her feet. "Has something happened to her?"

Sharla moved over to her grandmother, and told her as gently as possible, "Yes, it's about Maxine. Lance received a telegram from her lawyer. I'm sorry, but . . . but . . ."

"Is my daughter dead?"

"Yes," Sharla murmured.

Mary tottered, but only for a moment. She quickly regained her balance. Her face blanched, and her heart ached as though it had been hit with a sledgehammer; nevertheless, she kept her emotions under control.

"How did Maxine die?" she asked. A quaver in her voice exposed her grief.

"We don't know," Lance answered, handing her the telegram.

She read it, wadded it into her hand and kept it there. "I . . . I think I'll go back to bed," she said, turning and leaving the room as quietly as she had entered.

"I should go to her," Sharla said.

"Maybe you should wait awhile," Lance suggested. "She probably needs some time alone. She has a lot to cope with."

Sharla agreed. "Yes, I suppose you're right."

Sharla, wanting to give Mary ample time alone, took a bath and changed clothes. She put on one of the riding skirts that Maxine had given her. She didn't want to wear the immodest blouse that matched the skirt, so she borrowed a blouse from Emma. It fit fairly well, for Emma had worn it when she was much slimmer.

Sharla's emotions were jumbled as she went to check on Mary. She was terribly sorry that Maxine was dead. However, she didn't feel like she had lost a mother; more like she had lost someone she liked but didn't know all that well. That Claudia might be responsible for Maxine's death made Sharla feel that she, too, was somehow to blame. If Maxine hadn't been trying to help her, she would probably still be alive.

Sharla found Mary sitting in a chair beside the bed. The room was lit by one small lamp, its wick turned down low. Sharla sat on the edge of the bed, faced her grandmother and waited for her to speak first.

A minute or so passed before Mary murmured, "I don't know how much longer God intends to let me stay on

this earth, but I do know that for the remainder of my
life, I'll be haunted by those thirty years that stood between Maxine and me. It's so strange; now that she's
gone, I keep remembering her as a small child. She was
such a beautiful, delightful child." A sob caught in her
throat, and she clasped her hands together to control
their trembling. "I know I'm not entirely to blame. Maxine is also to blame. When she embraced prostitution,
she knew it would destroy her father and devastate me.
I'll never understand why she turned her back on us, and
on God's teachings. But she was my daughter, and I never
stopped loving her."

Sharla didn't comment. She had already made it clear
to Mary that she didn't understand her family, or their
definition of love.

"Dinner is done. Would you like me to bring you a tray?
You should eat; you'll need your strength."

Mary shook her head. "I'm not hungry—maybe later."

Sharla stood, moved to her grandmother and placed a
consoling hand on her shoulder. "I wish I could help you,
but I don't know what to say."

She patted Sharla's hand. "Just knowing that you care
helps more than you realize."

Sharla kissed her grandmother's cheek, then quickly left
the room, as though she suddenly needed to flee this
woman who was so strongly related to the mother she never
really knew, and now would never know! A part of her
longed to cry deeply for Maxine—to release, through tears,
this bitterness she harbored toward the woman for denying
her a mother's love. But the willful side of Sharla refused
to surrender to these kind of tears. Crying wouldn't change
anything, for the past was beyond vindication.

Lance didn't leave directly after dinner, but stayed and
visited with the Jordans and Sharla. Although the telegram

and Mary's grief was very much on their minds, the evening was pleasant and everyone enjoyed each other's company.

When Lance was ready to leave, Sharla walked him to the front porch. He immediately drew her into his arms, and kissed her with passion.

"I love you," he whispered in her ear, holding her extremely close.

His kiss, followed by his endearment, was thrilling to Sharla. "I love you, too," she murmured, clinging tightly.

He released her reluctantly. "It's late; I'd better go. I'll see you tomorrow."

She eyed him pertly. "Maybe we can take another ride. The countryside is so beautiful that I'd love to see it again."

He grinned, and quirked a brow. "I know what you mean. I'd like to see the countryside again myself. I'm especially fond of that area beneath the tall oak."

"Yes, it is a breathtaking spot. We must visit it again."

He kissed her lips softly. "Until tomorrow, my passionate little minx."

"Good night, Lance."

She watched through love-glazed eyes as he walked away and headed toward the center of town. She was happy, despite all the problems that plagued her. She trusted Lance, and no longer doubted his love. She believed she could depend on him. He'd never abandon her again, or ride out of her life without a word!

As she went back into the house and locked the door behind her, the Canton brothers were prying open the window in Lance's room. They had slipped up the outside stairway. Lance's room faced the street, and using a knife, they successfully pried the window open. They quickly climbed inside, and waited for their victim.

Twenty-eight

Sharla monopolized Lance's thoughts as he unlocked the door to his room and stepped inside. The interior was dark, but moonbeams shining through the window lit a path to the bedside lamp. He started toward it when, all at once, a shadowy figure caught his eye. At the same time he heard footsteps behind him. His hand was halfway to his holstered gun before the barrel of a pistol slammed against the back of his head. The hard blow knocked him to the floor, leaving him too dazed to stop Bert Canton from taking his gun. Bert handed the Peacemaker to Wesley, then bent over Lance, grabbed him by the shoulders and forced him to his feet.

"We meet again, Slade!" he uttered gruffly.

Lance's head was pounding, and his vision was temporarily blurred. He stared at his attacker as he tried to make out his identity. Gradually Bert's face, which was illuminated in the infiltrating moonlight, became clear to Lance. He glanced over the man's shoulder and recognized the younger Canton, who was standing close behind his brother. Lance, filled with anger, stood rigid. He figured he was as good as dead, and he was enraged with himself for letting the Cantons take him so easily. For the past five years, he had stayed alive by staying alert. But the perfect afternoon he had spent with Sharla, coupled with thoughts of repeating it all tomorrow, had caused him to foolishly let down his guard. For the first time since becoming a bounty hunter, he had neglected his survival instincts, and he was sure the mistake would now cost him his life.

Bert was disappointed that Lance's face showed anger and no fear. He wanted to see the man humbled, beaten, and begging for his life. "I'm tempted to kill you right now and be done with it," he told Lance. "But when I'm havin' a good time, I like it to last as long as possible." His beady eyes glinted with anticipation, and a demonic grin spread across his bearded face. "We're goin' for a long ride, Slade. Wesley and me, we wanna enjoy your company for a while. No sense in rushin' things, is there?"

Lance preferred to die here—quickly and mercifully. He doubled his hand into a fist and swung at Bert, hoping to incite Wesley into shooting him. As his knuckles smashed into Bert's chin, knocking him backward, Wesley, standing behind Bert, moved just in time to avoid his brother's body from plowing into his. Taken off guard, and somewhat panicked, he was about to shoot Lance, but Bert managed to grab his arm.

"You idiot!" he grumbled. "Don't you realize Slade wants you to shoot him?" He turned to Lance, his expression furious. He wiped a hand across his chin. Lance's knuckles had cut his flesh, and a trickle of blood had oozed into his thick beard. A chilling laugh emanated from deep in his throat, and before wielding his gun and knocking Lance unconscious, he uttered, "You ain't gonna die fast, you son-of-a-bitch! I'm gonna kill you piece by piece, inch by inch!"

The next morning, Sharla awoke in good spirits. Because Mary was ill, Steve had given his room to Sharla, and he had spent the last two nights sleeping on the sofa.

She lay in bed, remembering the wonderful afternoon she had spent with Lance. A warm tingle coursed through her, and it brought a delightful smile to her lips as she looked forward to sharing another romantic interlude with Lance. This interlude would be as perfect as yesterday's. She was certain that it would be, for she no longer doubted Lance's love and loyalty. She actually felt a little giddy, and wondered if all women felt this way when they fell in love. She laughed softly at herself; she supposed she was acting like a silly schoolgirl, but she didn't care. She intended to relish the thrill of being in love! A happy sigh escaped her lips, for she considered herself very fortunate to have found a man like Lance. He was not only devilishly handsome, but strong, sensitive, and dependable. If only . . . if only he would set his revenge aside and forget pursuing Chambers and Jackson! She sighed again, only this time it was a sigh of discontent. Lance would never completely discard his vengeance, regardless of how much he loved her. She knew she must find a way to accept that fact and learn to deal with it.

She fought against her plunging mood, but she seemed to have no control over it. Her problems were too real and too serious to be pushed aside as though they were merely trivial annoyances to be solved at her leisure. She was a fugitive wanted for murder! Her arrest was probably inevitable. She couldn't foresee escaping the law indefinitely. Sooner or later, she would most likely be caught. Lance would be powerless to save her; he would have no choice but to witness her trial and . . . and her ultimate execution? A chill crept up her spine, for she knew if Dexter had his way, she would pay with her life. He was very prominent in St. Louis and had a lot of political connections, and he would do everything within his power to guarantee she received the death penalty.

She had hoped and prayed that Maxine would somehow prove Claudia's guilt, but that possibility had died along with Maxine. She didn't really want to think about the woman who had been her mother, but her mind willfully

lingered on Maxine. She remembered Maxine's face, and
the image made her throat ache with bitter pain. She bore
a strong resemblance to her mother. She recalled a painting of John Matthews; it was a huge piece and hung over
the fireplace in the den. It remained there even after Olivia
married James Rayfield. Seeing the painting in her mind,
Sharla realized she also bore a likeness to her father. It
wasn't as striking as her resemblance to Maxine, but the
family similarity was noticeably detectable. She tried to
imagine how many times she had really looked at John
Matthews's portrait during the seventeen years she had
lived in his home. She had mostly taken the painting for
granted; it was just one of many pieces of art that had
decorated the walls. But she had looked closely at it a few
times. She supposed if she had been searching for a resemblance between herself and John Matthews, she would
have found it. However, that he might be her father had
never entered her mind. In the beginning, she had gazed
at the picture with a child's interest, so she had not given
it much thought one way or the other. As she grew into a
young lady, though, she realized the man in the painting
was very handsome and distinguished-looking.

A petulant frown furrowed her brow. How could she
have been so innocent? That she had seen only a handsome, distinguished gentleman instead of her father now
seemed terribly naive to Sharla. The likeness between father and daughter had been caught on canvas, but she
had been too guilelessly blind to see it.

She threw off the covers, and got out of bed. Her earlier
feelings of elation had dissipated; she was now consumed
with anger and bitterness. All her life she had wondered
about her parents. When she was very young, she had often
cried herself to sleep, wishing she had a mother and father
like everyone else. As the years passed, she stopped crying
for the parents she never knew and began to resent them.
They hadn't wanted her, had chosen to give her to the

orphanage. She could think of only one plausible reason for their desertion: she had been born out of wedlock!

"Well, I was right on that account!" she said aloud. "Not only was I born out of wedlock, but my father was a rich aristocrat and my mother was his paid lover!"

Some of her anger drained, and she sat wearily on the edge of the bed, as though her strength had ebbed along with her anger. Now, at long last, she knew her parents' identities. But she had learned the truth too late, for her father and mother were dead. She could never attempt to build a relationship with either of them, even if she wanted to—which she quickly told herself she didn't. But she was deluding herself. That she would never know her parents was disheartening, but it was a sadness she wasn't quite ready to face. Therefore, she adhered to bitterness, for it was her strongest defense.

Determined to better her mood, she successfully cleared her mind of depressing thoughts and returned to thinking about Lance and their afternoon date. By the time she joined the Jordans for breakfast, her disposition was cheery. Her spirits remained high as she helped Emma with household chores and visited with her grandmother. Mary's health was still improving; for that, Sharla was grateful. She had been worried that Maxine's death might bring on a relapse. But, apparently, Mary Simmons had an inner strength that was indestructible.

Sharla was sitting beside Mary's bed reading to her when Steve knocked on the bedroom door. "Come in," Sharla called.

He opened the door, but didn't cross the portal. "May I see you for a moment?" he asked Sharla.

Steve seemed upset, and she quickly marked her place in the book, then placed it on the bedside table. She told Mary that she'd be back later, then followed Steve into the parlor.

"Is something wrong?" she asked. "You look troubled."

He spoke haltingly, for he was a bearer of bad news. "Sharla . . . I just came from town. I looked for Lance . . . and when I couldn't find him, I went to his room. I don't know how to tell you this but . . . but Lance is gone."

"What are you saying?" she cried.

"He left town. He took his belongings, his horse, and rode out. He must have left some time last night, or early this morning."

"No!" she remarked desperately. "He wouldn't do something like that to me. Not again! He promised."

"I'm sorry, Sharla," Steve said gently. "But you have to face the truth. He's gone, maybe for good this time. But if you want me to go after him, I will." He despised Lance for hurting Sharla, and considered him a cold-hearted bastard.

"No," she replied, her voice controlled, despite her pain and shock. "I don't want you to try and find him. I don't ever want to see him again!" Against her will, her chin quivered, and tears filled her eyes. "I hate him!" she lashed out, anger mingling with heartache. "He's a liar! He's also despicable and totally insensitive to anyone's feelings but his own! He doesn't care about me! The only thing he cares about is finding Chambers and Jackson! That's where he is, you know. Chasing after them. Last night or this morning, he must have gotten a lead and off he went. To hell with me! To hell with our love!"

Her ranting stopped suddenly, for she knew her emotions were very close to the edge. Not wanting to break down in front of Steve, she fled the parlor and went to her room.

There, she fell across the bed and cried until there were no tears left to shed. Her sobs ceased, and she lay perfectly still, as though she were afraid that even the tiniest movement might cause her wounded heart to shatter beyond repair. She remained on her stomach, her face pressed into the tear-dampened pillow. That Lance had ruthlessly deserted her was almost more than she could bear. Her life seemed to be drowning in wave after wave of tribulations. She wondered how much more she could take before giving in to hopelessness and despair.

A profound sense of loneliness bore down upon her. She was alone—Olivia was dead, and so were the parents she never knew. For a few wonderful days she had believed that Lance loved her and would always be there for her, but that had been a fantasy spun in the foolish webs of her mind.

She had never felt so rejected or so terribly alone.

The bedroom door opened, but Sharla didn't bother to sit up and greet whoever was coming into the room. She felt the mattress give as someone sat on the edge of the bed. A gentle hand touched her shoulder.

"Steve told me what happened," she heard Mary say. "Honey, I am so sorry."

Her grandmother's kind voice touched a chord deep inside Sharla, and she found herself admitting, "I've never felt so alone."

"Your pain is my pain, Sharla. You aren't alone."

She sat up and gazed at Mary through eyes that were again turning misty.

"You're my granddaughter, and I love you. You probably find that hard to believe, considering I also deserted you. If I could change that part of my past, I would. But it's a burden I must carry for the remainder of my life. It's our sin—mine, Ezra's, and Maxine's. For some reason, God, in his wisdom and mercy, has granted us this time together. He knows you need me, and I certainly need you." She held out her arms to Sharla. "Let me share your pain. You aren't alone."

She went gratefully into her grandmother's embrace, where she was held, consoled, and loved as she cried again for the man she believed had manipulated her, lied to her, then left her as though her feelings didn't matter.

This time, when she dried her tears, she promised herself that she was through crying over Lance. He wasn't worth it! Drawing upon what was left of her emotions and pride, she told Mary, "We'll leave in the morning. If Steve wants to travel with us, he's more than welcome. But we're heading for San Antonio with or without him."

"I'm sure he'll decide to go with us." She regarded her granddaughter closely. "Honey, are you sure you're up to leaving so soon?"

A mask of indifference fell across Sharla's face. At the same time, she was filled with an inner rage that took precedence over her pain. She buried her love for Lance deep down in her heart, where she hoped it would eventually wither away and die.

"Of course I'm up to leaving," she told Mary, her chin raised bravely. "It'd take more than a skunk like Lance Slade to break my spirits."

Mary patted her hand, and said with an encouraging smile, "Good for you."

Dexter Rayfield and his entourage made camp at sunset. They were very close to the Arkansas-Texas line, and planned to cross the border late tomorrow morning.

Following supper, as the travelers sat about the campfire, Jeff Chambers looked across the flames and said to Dexter, "We're gettin' low on food. Tomorrow, we need to stop at a town called Madison Creek and buy up some more grub. Goin' there will take us out of the way, but we won't lose too much time."

Rayfield grunted. He hated wasting time, regardless of the reason why. He was certain Sharla wasn't losing any time. Quite the contrary, she was probably fleeing to San Antonio as though the devil himself was at her heels. Well, it wasn't the devil closing in on her, but retribution. She could run, she could hide, but sooner or later, he would find her. Then she would pay for killing James!

Chambers rolled a cigarette, lit it, looked again at Dexter, and broached the subject that had been preying on his mind. "Mr. Rayfield, Lou and me . . . Well, we've been thinkin'. When we catch that woman you're lookin' for, Lou and me oughta get the three-thousand-dollar reward."

Dexter eyed him sharply. "You and Jackson were hired as bodyguards. I'm paying you well to keep me alive, and that's the only money I intend to give you. You and Jackson have a lot of gall asking me for the reward. You're not getting it, so you might as well stop thinking about it!"

Dexter stood, reached down, grabbed Claudia's hand, and drew her to her feet. "It's time to turn in," he said gruffly. Taking Claudia with him, he headed for their bedrolls, which were located a good distance from the fire, and even a farther distance from where the other two planned to sleep. At this time of night, Dexter preferred to keep Claudia segregated from his bodyguards. He considered Chambers and Jackson too uncouth to sleep in close proximity to Claudia; such closeness might arouse their sexual urges. Restraining such urges might be too much for them, for their self-control was probably as weak as their mentality.

Chambers and Jackson remained at the fire. That Rayfield had refused to promise them the reward money had Chambers dangerously riled, and his large hands were balled into fists, for he was itching to send them plowing into his boss's arrogant face. He despised Rayfield and was ready to part company with him.

Jackson's feelings coincided with his partner's. "We oughta punch that bastard in the nose, take what money he has on him, then hang him by his neck until he's dead."

"We'll smash in his face and take his money, but we ain't gonna kill him."

"Why not? Seein' that weasel kickin' at the end of a rope would be real entertainin'."

"We gotta leave him alive. If we kill him, there won't be no three-thousand-dollar reward. You and me, we're gonna find that Matthews woman, then we'll get someone else to claim the reward. If some sheriff notifies Rayfield it was us who turned her in, he'll refuse to pay up."

"Who are we gonna get to claim the reward money?"

"Miguel," he said.

Jackson smiled. "Hell, yeah! Good ole Miguel will do it for the price of a puta and a tequila bottle." Miguel was the ideal man for the job. An old crony of theirs, he could be trusted. Furthermore, he would never cross them, for he'd know that they would hunt him down and kill him.

"When we find the woman," Jeff continued, "we'll take her to El Paso. Miguel will be there, he always is. We'll hand her over to him, and he'll turn her in to the sheriff. Then we'll just bide our time and wait for all that money."

"You reckon Rayfield will come to El Paso to get her?"

"Hell, no. He'll send someone after her. Once we leave him behind, he'll hightail it back to St. Louis. That lily-livered bastard is too afraid to go into Texas by himself." Chambers paused, took a drag off his cigarette, then put forth a second plan: "That Matthews gal ain't the only woman Rayfield will pay money for. We're gonna take his whore with us, then return her to him for ransom. I ain't got no details worked out yet, but we got plenty of time to figure out how we're gonna trade her for the money."

"How much ransom should we ask for?"

"Hell, his whore should be worth as much as the Matthews gal. We oughta get another three thousand."

Greed placed a large smile on Jackson's face. "We're gonna end up with six thousand dollars! I ain't seen that much money since we killed old man Slade and cleaned out his safe. Hell, we had to share part of that loot with Walker, but this time it'll only be a two-way split!"

"Keep your voice down," Chambers warned. He waved a terse hand toward Dexter and Claudia. "We don't want them overhearin' us." He put out his cigarette and got to his feet. "We might as well call it a night. We'll settle up with Rayfield in the mornin'."

Jackson chuckled. "That pompous ass better sleep good tonight, 'cause he ain't gonna be sleepin' so good tomorrow night."

Miles away from Dexter's campsite, Constable Woodson was sitting alone at his own fire. He cursed softly under his breath, berating himself for chasing after Claudia and Dexter. At his age, he should be home in bed, not camped outside, exposing his rheumatism to the elements. He began to question his own judgment. This journey to seek justice was probably the most foolhardy thing he had ever undertaken. His wife certainly thought so. She had pleaded with him not to leave.

His joints ached from being in the saddle all day, and he groaned as he stretched his tired legs. They felt cramped, as though he were still astride his horse. He actually considered turning around and going back to St. Louis. This kind of work was a job for a much younger man. He should contact a U.S. marshal and let him find Claudia. He gave the possibility serious thought, but as his thoughts drifted to Sharla, he discarded the notion. Finding an available U.S. marshal to track Claudia would take time. Time, he believed, was against Sharla, for Dexter Rayfield was in pursuit.

He didn't trust Dexter. He was too overbearing and too hot-headed. If he caught Sharla, and she tried to escape, Woodson believed Dexter was capable of using extreme force to prevent her from leaving. Then there was Claudia to consider. He suspected Claudia preferred that Sharla not live to stand trial, and was afraid that she might do everything within her power to make that happen.

His conscience demanded that he forget about going home, for it was partly his fault that Sharla had felt compelled to run away. He had been too quick to lean toward her guilt. His sense of right and wrong obligated him to find Claudia, then clear Sharla of the charges against her.

He gazed thoughtfully into the flickering flames and wondered where Sharla was spending this night, and how she was faring.

Sharla was lying in bed, staring up at the dark ceiling, wide awake. Sleep was important, for she planned to leave at dawn. Although her body was tired, she couldn't put her mind to rest. Lance's betrayal was like a powerful stimulus, keeping her emotions aroused and her anger stirring. Her heart ached, but she refused to dwell on that aspect of her feelings. If she didn't think about it, maybe it would mercifully go away!

She had given her love and trust to a man who had cruelly thrown them back in her face. He had stolen her pride and her innocence, but she was resolved to holding on to her dignity. She would go on with her life, and with God's help, prove that she didn't kill James Rayfield. Clearing her name was now her only goal, and she would dedicate her every waking moment to that achievement. Lance Slade no longer had a place in her life. He was a bad memory she was determined to eradicate!

Twenty-nine

Chambers and Jackson waited until after breakfast to make their move. The food had been eaten and the dishes put away before Chambers gave his comrade a secret nod, which meant it was time to deal with Rayfield.

Dexter had saddled Claudia's horse and was saddling his own when Chambers walked up behind him; meanwhile, Jackson kept an eye on Claudia, who was still sitting at the campfire, even though it had been doused some time ago. Whether or not there was a fire didn't matter to Claudia. She had remained seated, for she never helped with the camp chores.

Dexter kept a sheathed rifle on his horse, but he didn't wear a holstered gun, so Chambers didn't bother to draw his own pistol. Considering his fists all the weapons he needed, he clamped a hand on Rayfield's shoulder and forcefully spun him around. Chambers's knuckles struck against Dexter's chin, and the potent blow knocked him backward.

Dexter fell heavily against his horse, the sudden impact causing the animal to whinny and prance skittishly. Dexter regained his balance, wiped blood from his chin, then gaped at Chambers as though the man had taken leave of his senses.

"Are you crazy?" Rayfield demanded. "Why the hell did you hit me?"

" 'Cause you're an arrogant son-of-a-bitch, and if I didn't have plans for you and your woman, I'd kill you."

Claudia had jumped to her feet the moment Chambers struck Rayfield. She now made a move to rush to Dexter's side, but Jackson read her intent, darted in front of her and grabbed her arm.

Rayfield's initial shock was turning into fear, and his voice quivered slightly as he asked Chambers, "What do you mean, you have plans for Claudia and me?"

"Lou and me are leavin', and we're takin' your whore with us. If you ever want to see her again, then you better do exactly what I say."

Chambers reached into his shirt pocket, withdrew a piece of paper and handed it to Dexter. "This mornin' before anyone woke up," he continued, "I drawed this map. I want three thousand dollars delivered to the spot I got marked with an X. And I want it delivered exactly on the noon hour; not a minute before and not a minute after. If you're thinkin' about bringin' the law with you, then you'd better forget it. The spot I picked out is open land for miles around. You don't come alone, or send someone else who don't come alone, the woman dies! You cooperate, and I'll send her back to you."

"My God!" Dexter exclaimed. "This is absurd! You can't be serious!"

Chambers mimicked Rayfield, his impersonation going so far as to raising his chin in a smug fashion. "This is absurd! You can't be serious!" was his echo, his voice an octave higher than normal. Then he suddenly broke into harsh laughter.

Dexter was not amused. "Your humor is not only pathetic, but totally unnecessary. I'll give you three thousand dollars not to kidnap Claudia. Naturally, I don't have that kind of money on me, but I can go to the nearest bank and arrange a transfer from my bank to that one."

"And what's Lou and me supposed to do while this

transfer is goin' on? Wait like sittin' ducks until the law finds us?"

"I won't say anything to the law. You have my word."

"To hell with your word! We'll do it my way, or I'll kill you and your woman just for the hell of it. It's your choice. You wanna live or die?"

There was a cold frankness in Chambers's threat that left no doubt in Dexter's mind that he would indeed kill him and Claudia. He surrendered to reason and said, "I'll cooperate."

"I figured you would," Chambers gloated. "I realize it'll take time. That's why I ain't givin' you no specific day to deliver the ransom. But startin' two weeks from now, every day at noon I'm gonna be at the spot where I marked the X. If the money ain't delivered within two months, the woman will die. I ain't gonna give you no more time than that."

"It could take longer than two months. I'll probably have to return to St. Louis, then hire someone more experienced than I am to deliver the money. I'm not familiar with Texas. How am I supposed to find this area where you put the X?"

Claudia, who was listening raptly, blurted out to Dexter, "Don't you dare waste time returning to St. Louis! Have the money transferred to the bank in Madison Creek or some other nearby town. Then deliver the ransom yourself!"

Chuckling, Chambers told her, "Rayfield's a lily-livered greenhorn. He'll hightail it back to St. Louis and hire someone to deliver the money."

Dexter didn't deny Chambers's accusation, for he was indeed considering returning to St. Louis and combing the city for a man qualified for such a dangerous job. He knew this kind of man would cost him a great deal of money, even more than the ransom he would ultimately deliver. He began to question if Claudia was worth such

an enormous expense. But as he looked at her, he was
deeply moved by the fear in her eyes, and touched by
her helplessness. He remembered her sexual zeal, the feel
of her velvety flesh, and his own unsatiable desire for this
young woman who had bewitched him with her beauty
and passion. Yes, she was worth whatever it would cost to
ensure her safe return. A pang of guilt coursed through
him. If he were a man and not a coward, he would deliver
the ransom himself. Dexter had never considered himself
a coward, and was stunned to find himself thinking that
way now. However, until today, he had never faced real
danger; therefore, his courage had never been tested.
That his bravery was lacking was hard for Dexter to accept, and he tried to bolster the nerve to assure Claudia
that he would personally save her from the clutches of
her kidnappers. But the words remained stuck in his
throat.

Meanwhile, Claudia was waiting intensely for Dexter to
soothe her fears and to denounce Chambers's accusations.
Her hopes plunged along with Dexter's silence.

Chambers was now impatient to leave, and he told Jackson to take Rayfield's rifle and to untie the packhorse.

But Jackson had something he wanted to take care of
before leaving. He moved over to Dexter, and his upper
lip actually snarled as he verbally released his pent-up rage:
"Rayfield, you're a pompous ass! You ain't done nothin'
but boss me around since the day Jeff and me went to
work for you." He doubled his hands into fists. "I've been
wantin' to do this for a long time!"

Attacking with the quickness of a striking snake, Jackson
smashed one fist into his victim's jaw, then jabbed the second fist into his stomach. As Dexter doubled over with
pain, Jackson finished him off with a powerful uppercut.

Rayfield dropped to the ground, where he lay writhing
as shudders began to wrack him. Suddenly, Jackson's boot

slammed into his stomach, almost choking off his breath. Rayfield heaved violently before vomiting.

Amused, Jackson said to his comrade, "He don't look so arrogant and almighty important no more, does he?"

"Looks kinda pitiful," Chambers grinned. "All puke-covered and squirmin'."

Claudia's nerves erupted, and she cried out to her abductors, "Please don't take me with you! Dexter won't pay the ransom. I'm nothing to him!"

Chambers went to Claudia, picked her up and carried her to her horse. He put her in the saddle, then said gruffly, "Woman, I'm awarnin' you—keep your mouth shut unless you're spoken to! I ain't gonna listen to no bitchin' and no complainin'! I ain't nothin' like Mr. Rayfield. You start whinin' like you've been whinin' since we left St. Louis, and I'll slap you around until you learn to keep quiet! You understand me, woman?"

She managed a feeble nod.

He turned back to Rayfield, who was still on the ground, twisting and groaning with pain. "Two months! You got two months to pay the ransom. You don't pay, and I'll cut out your whore's heart and send it to you in the mail!" With that, he mounted his horse.

Jackson looked through Dexter's saddlebags and found some money. He handed the loot to Chambers, then got on his horse. Taking their captive and the remaining supplies, they rode out of camp, leaving Rayfield lying in his own vomit.

As Claudia and her kidnappers were heading southwest, a covered wagon was on the same course. The wagon, which was a short distance ahead, was driven by Sharla. Jackson and Chambers were much closer to their bounty than they could possibly realize.

The time lost in Madison Creek was very much on

Sharla's mind as she sat thoughtfully, the reins wrapped loosely about her fingers. The horses' pace was slow, and the well-traveled road was fairly straight; so there was really no reason to hold a tight rein. The team plodded onward on their own accord.

Mary was resting in the back of the wagon. Steve, who had insisted on accompanying the ladies, was riding horseback. He had ridden ahead to look for a good place to stop and eat lunch.

So much time had been lost since leaving St. Louis that Sharla feared this trip had now become very dangerous. She wondered how many bounty hunters were looking for her, and how many wanted posters had already reached the towns ahead. She suddenly wished Lance was there, for she felt safer in his presence. But she quickly thrust that wish from her mind. She didn't need him, and told herself that she would rather face an arrest than lay eyes on Lance Slade! She could hardly believe that she had let him make such a fool of her. She had blindly believed in him, had trusted him completely, and had given him her unconditional love. In return, she had received lies, betrayal, and rejection. She wanted to forget him—to cast him from her mind and heart. But she knew that would take time. First, she had to find a way to stop loving him.

She gazed vacantly over the team and into the distance, her mind refusing to relinquish thoughts of Lance. She found herself wondering where he was at this very moment. Was he thinking about her?

"Of course he isn't thinking about me," she muttered aloud. "I was nothing to him except an easy conquest!"

"Did you say something?" Mary suddenly asked, climbing over the seat and joining Sharla.

"I was just mumbling to myself."

"Where's Steve?"

"He rode ahead to find a place to stop for lunch."

"Good, because I'm getting hungry."

Sharla smiled. "That's a good sign."

"Physically, I feel fine. But my heart needs a lot of mending."

Sharla patted her grandmother's hand. "I understand, but I'm here to help you."

Mary's eyes filled with heartfelt tears. "God bless you, child. You are indeed a treasure. And remember, Sharla, that I'm also here to help you. I know Lance has hurt you and that you are terribly depressed."

She raised her chin defiantly. "Depressed? I hardly think so! I'm much wiser, thanks to Lance Slade. But I refuse to be depressed. Lance is a low-down, lying skunk! I never want to see him again. Wherever he is; I hope he stays there!"

Lance, his hands tied behind him, stood his ground and watched his captors without a waver of fear. They had ridden through the night, for Bert wanted to put a safe distance between them and the sheriff in Madison Creek. Lance had regained consciousness a few miles out of town. He had awakened to find himself slung over his horse, his wrists and ankles tied. An hour or so after midnight, Bert had decided to halt and give the horses a short rest. Following the brief stop, Lance was allowed to ride astride, his hands securely tied.

They had stopped in this area a few moments ago, and Lance had been pulled from his horse, then left to face his intended killers, who were debating exactly how they wanted to go about killing him. Thorton had no real interest in the procedure, but the Cantons wanted their victim to suffer greatly before succumbing to death.

"Why don't we start by beatin' the hell out of him?" Wesley suggested.

Bert wasn't opposed to his brother's motion; in fact, he

agreed completely. "First, we'll beat him to a bloody pulp, then we'll use him for target practice."

"I saw a man do that once," Thorton said. "He tied his victim on the ground, spreadeagle. Then he stood a distance away and practiced shooting off the poor devil's fingers. Then he aimed for his arms, his legs, and finally put a bullet right between the man's eyes. But before he finally died, he sure enough suffered. I ain't never heard a man scream like he did."

Bert smiled gleefully; when he had suggested using Slade for target practice, he hadn't really considered the best way to go about it. The idea had no real substance; it had simply sounded good. Bert decided Thorton's account had sealed Lance's fate.

"Sounds like a lot of fun," he said to Thorton. He then turned to Lance. His cruel grin was enough to evoke fear from the bravest heart. Nevertheless, Lance's demeanor remained stoical, as though his impending torture was of no concern. Bert had expected to see stark terror on Lance's face, and the man's refusal to cower before him inflamed Bert's rage to an even higher degree.

Anxious now to mete out his first form of punishment, Bert told Wesley and Thorton to hold Slade.

They moved quickly to Lance. Poised, one on each side of him, they held him so that he couldn't fall to the ground.

"After I get through," Bert told his brother, "you can deliver some punches. Just don't hit him hard enough to kill him. We want him alive and conscious for target practice."

Bert's huge fists plowed strongly into his victim, striking Lance's chin twice, then landing once above his right eye before finishing with a severe blow to his ribs. The last blow sent blinding pain streaking through Lance, for Bert's powerful jab had cracked a rib.

Ready now to let his brother in on the fun, Bert was

about to tell him it was his turn when, all at once, they were interrupted by a deep voice.

"Unholster your guns," said the voice. "Then raise your arms above your heads."

The intruder was at Bert's back, but he was so well hidden in the nearby shrubbery that neither Wesley nor Thorton could see him.

Then, preferring to show himself to his enemies, the man emerged from the shrubbery. The Cantons and Thorton were astonished to see that the man's gun was holstered. They considered him a fool to confront them in this fashion. After all, they were three against one.

Wesley and Thorton released Lance, and as he sank to his knees, he got a good glimpse of the intruder. Despite the excruciating pain gripping his ribs, a smile actually touched his lips. The man's gun was holstered, true, but if the Cantons and their friend didn't cooperate, he knew they would die.

The intruder was Clem Emerson, and drawing against these three men was child's play for a gunslinger with his expertise. Actually, he was hoping his holstered weapon would goad them into drawing their guns, for he wanted a legitimate excuse to send them to hell.

Lance's captors reached for their guns at the same time. Clem drew his Peacemaker with lightning speed, shot Bert before his hand even touched his gun; then as Thorton's fingers were gripping his pistol, Clem fired a bullet into his chest. Wesley, the last to die, had time to free his gun halfway from its holster before falling to the ground and drawing his final breath.

Clem checked the three men and made sure they were dead before holstering his gun. He then went to Lance, who was still on his knees, an arm held tightly across his ribs. He got to his feet somewhat shakily, the simple feat wracking him with more pain. Lance's chin was bleeding, and an ugly bruise was already forming above his eye.

"You look like hell," Clem remarked lightly, but with an undercurrent of concern.

"I think I have a cracked rib; or at least I hope it's just cracked and not broken."

"How did you get mixed up with these hombres?" Clem asked, waving a terse hand toward the three bodies.

"I'll tell you about it on our way to Madison Creek. That is, if you want to ride there with me."

"That's where I was headed. Besides, I reckon I should take these bodies to the sheriff for buryin'." He suddenly grinned wryly. "By the way, where's Miss Matthews? Don't tell me you've lost her again."

"I hope she's still in Madison Creek. But wherever she is, she's probably madder than hell. I'm sure she thinks I ran out on her again. If she's not in town, I'll have the doctor wrap my ribs, then I'll catch up to her."

"Ridin' with a cracked rib is gonna be mighty uncomfortable."

"I don't dread the pain nearly as much as I dread trying to explain myself to Sharla before she can grab her grandmother's shotgun and fill me full of buckshot."

Clem chuckled. "You could try waving a white flag."

Lance smiled. "I just might take your advice." He shook his friend's hand. "Thanks for saving my life. You were the last person I expected to see. I thought by now you'd be a long way from here."

"I have an uncle who lives close by. I visited with him for a couple of days. I was on my way to Madison Creek to buy supplies when I happened to come upon this gathering, where you were obviously the guest of honor."

Lance grimaced as a sharp pain suddenly reminded him of his injury. "Let's put these bodies on their horses and start back to Madison Creek."

"You're in no condition to lift dead men. I'll take care of that."

Although Lance watched as his friend slung the bodies

over the horses, his thoughts were elsewhere. Sharla probably believed that he had betrayed her, and knowing she
felt that way bothered him a great deal. He knew she must
be hurt and upset. He was anxious to see her and explain
what had happened.

Chambers and Jackson spotted campfire smoke, and
they reined in abruptly. Claudia, riding between the two
men, stopped without being told to do so. Although she
was tempted to coax her horse into a fast canter and head
toward the distant camp for help, she never seriously considered going through with it. Her captors would stop her
if they had to shoot her horse out from under her. Her
disobedience would only bring Chambers's wrath down
upon her.

"Stay with the woman," Chambers told Jackson. "I'm
gonna ride ahead and have a look around."

He headed in the direction of the smoke that was bil-
lowing upward into a clear blue sky. He returned a few
minutes later and reported his find: "Two women and a
man are camped a short distance from the road. They got
a covered wagon, which means they probably are equipped
with supplies. Considerin' we're low on grub, we'll take
theirs. And any money that got on 'em. We'll tie and gag
the whore and leave her here."

Chambers dismounted, stepped to Claudia and lifted
her to the ground. He quickly tied her to a tree, secured
a bandanna across her mouth, and said with a chuckle,
"Don't worry, sweetheart. We won't be gone long." He
reached out a hand and squeezed her nipple. "While
you're awaitin', you might think about the fun we're gonna
have later on. Once we're a safe distance from these parts,
we'll stop for a couple of days and play 'poke her.' " He
laughed at the confusion in her eyes, for he knew she was
wondering why he wanted to play poker.

Finding his pun hilarious, he laughed even harder as he turned away, went back to his horse, and swung into the saddle. He and Jackson started toward the nearby campsite.

Thirty

Lunch was over, but Sharla and the others sat about the campfire as though they were in no hurry to leave. Such leisure was merely a pretense on Sharla's part, as well as Steve's. They knew it was important not to waste time, but they had secretly conspired to travel slowly for the first few days of their journey. Worried about Mary's health, they didn't want her to become overly tired so soon after her illness.

They were still at the fire when two riders leading a pack-horse approached their camp. Jordan bounded to his feet, a hand resting cautiously on his holstered gun.

"Howdy, folks!" Chambers called, his tone friendly. "We spotted your fire and thought you might have some coffee for two weary travelers."

Steve remained cautious, and as the men drew closer, he ordered, "Stop right there. I don't mean to be inhospitable, but we were just about to break camp. Besides, the coffeepot's empty, so you two might as well move on."

Chambers faked a disarming smile. "Sorry to have bothered you. You folks have a good day." With that, he began to turn his horse about as though he were leaving. The ploy worked, and Steve foolishly moved his hand away from his pistol.

Chambers drew his Colt 45. with a blurring speed, aimed it at Steve and fired. He seldom missed, and he didn't miss this time. Steve fell to the ground, clutching at his chest as he went down. Blood flowed copiously from a gaping wound beneath his heart.

A scream echoed in Sharla's ears; it took a moment for her to realize that the blood-curdling cry was coming from her own throat. She rushed to Steve's side and knelt beside him. She didn't check his wound, nor did she try to talk to him. Her mind was now working instinctively. She drew Steve's gun from its holster, leapt to her feet, and was about to fire if necessary, but the sight confronting her compelled her to drop the pistol.

As Sharla was hurrying to Steve's side; Chambers, dismounting, had grabbed Mary. He now had his gun pointed at her head.

Jackson went to Sharla and picked up the weapon. He glanced down at Jordan, then turned to Chambers and said as though he greatly admired his friend's skill, "You shot real good. The bastard's done seen his last sunrise."

"No!" Sharla cried, dropping to her knees beside Steve, hoping that he wasn't dead. She felt desperately for a pulse, but there was none. Her friend was gone. Grief tore into her heart with a rending force, as sobs shook her shoulders.

But Jackson didn't allow her time to mourn, for his hands gripped her arms, forcing her roughly to her feet. He slapped her face soundly and demanded that she stop bawling.

The stinging blow forced her grief to the far recesses of her mind. Her sorrow was quickly supplanted by anger, and she stared at Jackson with barely controlled rage.

Chambers released Mary, and started toward the wagon to steal supplies when he suddenly hesitated. He turned back and looked closely at Sharla. He wasn't sure why he wanted a closer look; his response had been brought on by a compulsion he didn't fully understand. He walked over to Sharla and eyed her thoughtfully. He found her face familiar and tried to recall where he might have seen her. The solution to his puzzle came to him all at once. The face he was studying was the same face that was on Rayfield's wanted posters.

"Well, I'll be damned!" he uttered aloud. A large smile spread across his face. "Lou, you know who we got here?" he asked, pointing a finger at Sharla.

"A good-lookin' gal who needs a little lovin'?" Jackson guessed, eyeing Sharla lewdly.

"Hell, this woman's worth more than a pokin' session. This here is Sharla Matthews. We done got us three thousand dollars. I thought we'd have to comb the countryside lookin' for this gal, but I'll kiss your ass if she didn't just drop right into our laps!"

Jackson hastened to his horse, withdrew a wanted poster from his saddlebags, then, standing before Sharla, he compared her face to the one on the poster. "It's her, all right!" he exclaimed, barely containing his excitement. "If this don't beat hell! I reckon this is our lucky day!"

Chambers clutched Sharla's arm and drew her forward. "Stay with the old woman," he told Jackson. "Me and this valuable little gal are gonna go to the wagon and pack some grub. While I'm gone, look through the man's pockets and see if he's carryin' any money."

Keeping a firm hold on Sharla's arm, Chambers took her to the wagon. The footstool was placed outside, and she used it to go inside, her companion right behind her.

Grabbing a folded blanket, Chambers handed it to her. "Here," he said, "wrap the grub in this."

She spread out the blanket and began filling it with canned food. The stored cans were lined flush against one side of the canvas, so Sharla worked with her back facing Chambers. As she carried out her task, a length of shiny metal suddenly caught her eye. A butcher knife, its handle covered by a napkin, lay within her reach. She knew a knife didn't afford much protection against two armed men, but it was better than nothing. She continued to gather the cans, for she didn't want to arouse Chamber's suspicions. As she wondered where she could possibly hide the weapon, she remembered that Lance sometimes carried a knife in his boot. Slipping a knife into her own boot would be relatively easy, for she always stuck the legs of her trousers inside her high-top boots. She was grateful that she had decided to wear trousers today and not a riding skirt.

Moving quickly, but stealthily, she drew the napkin up over the entire knife. She wrapped it snugly, left it where it was and picked up three cans. She dropped them intentionally, and as she had hoped, they rolled across the wagon floor.

Cursing her clumsiness, Chambers turned away from her to retrieve the stray cans. Sharla, using his preoccupation to her advantage, grabbed the wrapped knife and hastily slipped it into her boot. It lay against her ankle snugly but not uncomfortably.

Putting the retrieved cans with the others, Chambers said, "We got enough grub." He wrapped the food, gestured for Sharla to take the lead and followed her outside.

Chambers attached the bundle to the packhorse, then asked Jackson if Steve had been carrying any money.

He showed his companion some bills in his hand, stuffed them in his pocket and replied, "It ain't a lot, but more than I expected to find."

"What about you women?" Chambers asked. "You got any money?"

"Of course not," Sharla lied without hesitation. "Steve took care of our expenses."

Chambers believed her; if he were traveling with two women, all the money would be in his care. Therefore, judging others by himself, he accepted her explanation. He waved a hand toward Steve's saddled horse and told Sharla that it was time to leave.

When she didn't move, he said harshly, "Get on that damned horse 'fore I throw you on it!"

Sharla was afraid, not for herself but for Mary. "Wh-what about my grandmother?" she asked Chambers. "Please don't hurt her!"

"I ain't worried 'bout no old woman!" he grumbled. "I don't reckon she'll be achasin' us!"

Sharla breathed a sigh of relief.

However, her relief was quickly tested, for Jackson disagreed with his comrade. "Hell, we oughta kill the old woman. She'll go to the sheriff!"

"So what? You think that pompous ass we left behind ain't gonna hightail it to the nearest sheriff? Don't matter none! Ain't no posse gonna catch us. Not if we start puttin' some miles between us and them."

Grabbing Sharla's arm, Chambers forced her to Steve's horse. As she swung into the saddle, she looked over at Mary, who was standing beside the ebbing fire, watching her. Sharla saw the worry and fear on the woman's face. She summoned a brave smile for her grandmother and mouthed the words, "I love you."

Jackson and Chambers mounted their horses. Leading the pack animal carrying their stolen goods, and keeping their captive between them, they galloped away from the campsite.

Sharla was surprised when they suddenly rode off the main trail and headed into the surrounding woodland. They didn't go very far before coming upon a woman tied to a tree. Sharla recognized Claudia instantly and stared at her with mind-numbing shock.

Sharla's presence, however, wasn't all that shocking to Claudia. For days, Dexter had felt that they were drawing closer to Sharla. Evidently, she had been much closer than Dexter realized. Sharla's arrival filled Claudia with mixed emotions. Her misery welcomed company, and she was

glad that she was no longer a lone prisoner. But she wished
her partner in misery was someone else.

Chambers dismounted, removed Claudia's gag and untied her. He told her to get on her horse, then, ordering
the women to ride directly in front of him and Jackson,
they returned to the road.

Claudia's nerves were tightly strung as she waited for
Sharla to speak first. Her silence had Claudia completely
baffled, for she had been expecting an immediate confrontation.

Sharla had a lot to say to Claudia and several questions
to ask, but she preferred to wait until her shock had waned
and her rage was under control. When she finally felt she
could deal calmly with Claudia, she asked her, "What are
you doing with these men?"

"Dexter met them in St. Louis. He hired them to accompany us to Texas."

"What's your relationship with Dexter?"

Claudia smiled cattily. "He's in love with me."

Sharla seriously doubted if that was possible. "Why did
Dexter want to come to Texas?"

"To look for you, of course."

"How did he learn I was here?"

She raised her chin smugly. "He has his way of learning
anything he wants to learn."

"Where is Dexter?"

"These men he hired to keep him safe, turned on him.
They left him behind."

"Why are you with them?"

"They are holding me for ransom."

Sharla paused for only a moment before blurting out,
"Why did you kill Maxine?"

The question startled Claudia. "How did you know she
was dead?"

"Like Dexter, I have a way of learning what I want to
learn."

"What makes you think I killed her?"

"Oh, you killed her all right! Just like you killed James!"

"You should have proof before making such accusations."

"I'll find the proof, Claudia. One way or another."

"I hardly think so. You can't find what isn't there. By the way, what connection do you have with Maxine? I can't imagine what you would have in common with a woman like her."

"She was my mother." The words spewed forth on their own accord, surprising Sharla. That she had so readily admitted her kinship to Maxine was quite startling. A faint smile brushed her lips, for she considered her admission a positive sign that she was learning to deal with her past. There had been no ring of bitterness in her voice, but resignation mingled with a touch of . . . love? Pride? She wasn't sure, she only knew admitting the truth was painless.

Claudia, staring wide-eyed at Sharla, found her news incredible. "Your mother!" she exclaimed. "Well, that explains everything."

"What do you mean?"

"Maxine gave me a job so that she could spy on me."

"Did she get too close to the truth? Is that why you killed her?"

Claudia wasn't about to confess, even though she knew there was no danger, for it would merely be her word against Sharla's. Dexter and the law would believe her, of course, for a fugitive's word certainly wasn't very credible. Her refusal to make a full confession stemmed from the fact that she had to travel with Sharla; therefore, she didn't want to completely alienate her.

"I didn't kill Maxine," she replied. "Nor did I kill James. I know you think I did, but I swear I had nothing to do with his death."

"You two bitches shut up!" Chambers suddenly ordered. He couldn't overhear their conversation, and suspected they were plotting an escape. "Don't say nothin' to each other again, or I'll stuff gags in your mouths! Slap them reins against your horses; we're movin' too damned slow!"

The women coaxed their mounts into a faster pace. Afraid Chambers would carry out his threat, they said no more to each other.

Dexter rode into Madison Creek a few hours after dark. He had used a map to find his way. He went straight to the sheriff's office, dismounted, and walked inside.

Langley was sitting at his desk, drinking a cup of coffee. He regarded the stranger curiously. Dexter had changed into clean clothes, but his bruised and lacerated face attested to a possible surprise assault; or maybe he had simply gotten the worse of a fair fight.

Dexter gestured toward the chair facing the sheriff. "May I sit down?"

"Please do," he replied.

"My name is Dexter Rayfield. Two men have kidnapped my . . . my . . ." He wasn't sure how to address Claudia; mistress was too inappropriate. "My . . . my fiancée," he decided to say.

Having gained Langley's undivided attention, he gave him a full and detailed explanation.

When he finally finished, Langley told him with a heavy sigh, "I'm sorry, Mr. Rayfield, but there's nothing I can do now. Picking up their trail at night is impossible. However, I'll round up a posse in the morning. But I must warn you that I can't pursue them once they are out of my jurisdiction."

"I don't want you to pursue them," Dexter replied testily. "If they suspect a posse is chasing them, they're liable to kill Claudia."

"If you don't want my help, then why are you here?"

"I had planned to go back to St. Louis, draw the money

from my account, and hire someone to deliver the ransom. But as I was riding into town, I noticed that your town has a bank. If there is a man in this town who would be willing to deliver the ransom, then I can have the necessary funds transferred to this bank. It would save a lot of time."

"Then you're willing to pay the ransom?"

"Of course."

"There's a man in town who might be interested. I doubt if he'll agree to be a sittin' duck and deliver the ransom, but he might agree to hunt down the kidnappers and permanently dispose of them."

"But what about Claudia?"

"Mr. Rayfield, men like these two don't keep their word. The only way to save your fiancée is to kill the kidnappers before they can kill her."

"Where is this man?"

"I think he's at the saloon."

"What's his name?"

"Clem Emerson. Believe me, he's the man for the job."

"Does he live in Madison Creek?"

"Nope. He's just passin' through. In fact, he just got to town a couple of hours ago. Brought three dead bodies in with him."

"Why did he kill three men?"

"They were about to kill a friend of his."

Dexter rose to his feet. "I hope I can trust Mr. Emerson. The last two men I hired proved quite untrustworthy."

"I'll personally vouch for Emerson. He can kill without blinkin' an eye, but he's got enough Indian blood in him to make him a man of his word."

"Indian blood?" Dexter gasped. "Good Lord! I hope he isn't too uncivilized!"

Langley chuckled. Greenhorns like Rayfield should stay back East where they belong. "I think he stopped scalping his victims some time ago," he said jokingly.

Dexter saw no humor in the man's remark, and grunted

accordingly. He was about to leave when he remembered that he hadn't shown the sheriff the wanted poster on Sharla that he carried in his shirt pocket. Removing it, he unfolded the paper and handed it to Langley. His earlier explanation had included his reason for coming to Texas; thus, the sheriff was not confused when Dexter said, "This is the fugitive I'm looking for. You may already have received one or more of these posters."

"Nope; I ain't ever seen it before."

Dexter frowned impatiently. "Have you seen the woman?"

Langley looked closely at the face on the poster. "I've seen a woman who looks a lot like her. But her name ain't Sharla Matthews. It's Trish Lawrence."

"An alias," he grumbled. He remembered Trish Lawrence and knew she had worked for Maxine; more than once, he had paid for Trish's favors. For some reason, Sharla had taken her identity.

"When did you last see this woman who calls herself Trish Lawrence?" he asked Langley.

"She left town this morning. If you want to know more about her, ask Emerson to introduce you to Lance Slade."

"Lance Slade?" he repeated. "I met him in St. Louis. What does he have to do with Sharla Matthews? Furthermore, he knows she's a fugitive. How dare he not turn her over to the law! Some bounty hunter he is! When I see him again, I'll certainly tell him what I think of him!"

"I wouldn't do that if I were you."

"Why not?" he huffed.

"Let me put it this way, Mr. Rayfield—there's only one man I can think of who's as dangerous as Clem Emerson, and his name is Lance Slade. In fact, now that I think about it, it might be in your best interest to avoid him."

"I hardly think so! If he has information on Sharla, then I intend to hear it, even if I have to bribe him." With that, Dexter strutted to the door and left.

He went across the street to the saloon. Wyatt was tending bar, and Dexter asked him about Clem Emerson.

"That's him over there," Wyatt said, gesturing toward a man sitting alone at a back table.

Dexter could see Clem clearly, for he was facing in his direction. There was something about the man that exuded a threatening aura. Dexter supposed his dark complexion and high cheekbones were a result of his Indian heritage. However, it wasn't his inherited looks that made him seem so dangerous, it was his stoical demeanor. Dexter noticed he had a whiskey bottle and two glasses; he was apparently expecting somebody.

Buying his own bottle of whiskey, and taking it and a glass with him, Dexter moved over to Clem's table. "Excuse me for disturbing you," he said, "but the sheriff suggested that I talk to you."

Clem regarded the stranger as though he were nothing more than a nuisance, like an annoying insect he might swat at any moment.

"May I sit down?" Dexter asked.

Clem used his foot to scoot a chair away from the table and toward Rayfield.

Although Dexter resented the man's rude behavior, he didn't show it. He eased into the chair, opened the bottle and filled his glass. "I need to buy your services," he explained.

Clem arched a brow. "What makes you think I got any services to sell?"

"The sheriff said . . ."

"To hell with what he said," Clem butted in. "Listen, mister, I'm not a hired gun. I don't go around killin' men just to settle some damned dispute." He eyed Dexter's bruised face, suspecting his recent beating was his reason for being here. "If someone's got you riled, then kill him yourself."

"My situation isn't what you think. You see, my fiancée

has been kidnapped. The men who abducted her want three thousand dollars for her return."

"Do you know who took her?"

"Yes, I do. Jeff Chambers and Lou Jackson."

Clem was suddenly very interested. "I've heard of Chambers and Jackson," he said. "If they have your fiancée, you'll never see her alive. Paying the ransom won't make any difference; they'll still kill her."

"That's what the sheriff said."

"What do you want from me?"

"I'll pay you five hundred dollars to save my fiancée." Dexter intended to start with a low offer and work his way up if necessary. "Chambers and Jackson abducted her this morning; if you leave at dawn, they'll only be a day ahead of you." He had Chambers's map, and he handed it to Clem. "The X is where the ransom is supposed to be delivered. The map is so badly drawn that it's barely legible. I hope you can decipher it better than I can."

"The X is about ten miles north of El Paso."

"Good! You know where they're heading. That will make it easier for you to find them."

"Before I decide whether or not to take this job, I want you to tell me who you are."

"My name's Dexter Rayfield."

Clem didn't twitch a muscle, though he was familiar with his companion's name; the man had posted a three-thousand-dollar reward for Sharla Matthews. He didn't let on that he knew anything about the reward, instead, he asked, "How did you get mixed up with Chambers and Jackson?"

Dexter took a drink of his whiskey, settled back in his chair, and drew a long breath. Only minutes before he had related the lengthy story to the sheriff, and now he had to do it a second time. He sighed somewhat tediously, then began a full explanation.

* * *

As Dexter's story was unfolding, Lance was leaving Dr. Williams's house. Fortunately, Chambers's punch had only bruised a rib. However, the injury was painful, and the doctor told Lance it would remain that way for some time. He also advised him to wait a week or more before riding horseback. That, of course, was out of the question. Sharla had put herself at risk by leaving town. Although Jordan was traveling with her, his presence did little to ease Lance's apprehensions, for he didn't think Jordan was capable of protecting her. The man was a gambler, not a gunfighter.

Lance headed toward the saloon, where he knew Clem was waiting for him. He intended to have a couple of drinks with his friend before leaving to find Sharla.

Earlier, when he had returned to town with Clem, he had left Clem at the sheriff's office to explain the three bodies and had ridden straight to Wyatt's home. As he had feared, Sharla was gone, and so were Mary and Steve.

Reaching the saloon, Lance pushed open the bat-wing doors and went inside. The establishment was crowded and most of the tables were filled. Glancing about, he spotted Clem, who was sitting in the back of the room with another man. Lance had actually taken a couple of steps toward their table before recognizing the person talking to his friend. His steps faltered, but only for an instant.

The men caught sight of Lance, and Clem drew out a chair for him.

But Lance didn't take the chair, instead, he grabbed Dexter by the front of his shirt and jerked him to his feet. "You stupid bastard!" he uttered harshly. "Your damned wanted posters are gonna draw scum out of their hellholes to look for Sharla! And when they find her, they aren't gonna care what kind of condition she's in when they collect the reward. As long as she's still breathing they'll figure you owe them three thousand dollars! You crazy son-of-a-bitch! So help me God, if anything happens to her because of those posters, I'll hunt you down and kill you!''

Thirty-one

"Unhand me!" Dexter demanded, mustering courage he didn't realize he had.

Lance released his hold, then shoved Dexter back into his chair. "Sit there, and don't try to get up."

Clem edged the empty chair toward Lance. "You better sit down, too, amigo. I just heard something you'll be very interested in learning."

"What's that?" Lance asked, sitting, and pouring himself a glass of whiskey.

"It seems Rayfield hired a couple of bodyguards before leaving St. Louis. He didn't use very good judgment. This mornin', they beat him up, stole his money, then kidnapped his fiancée and are holdin' her for ransom. You know these two bastards—Chambers and Jackson."

Every nerve in Lance's body tightened.

"Rayfield wants to hire me to save his woman," Clem continued. "If he's willin' to up the ante, I just might take the job."

Lance didn't say anything, for he was too emotionally torn. His family's murderers were somewhere in the vicinity—the odds of finding them were certainly in his favor. If he wanted them, all he had to do was choose chasing them over following Sharla. He could try to confront Chambers and Jackson, then when that was taken care of, go in search of Sharla. The revenge inside him demanded that he find his family's killers, but his love for Sharla was much stronger. Too many risks awaited her on the road to San Antonio, and she needed his protection. He would not abandon her.

He looked at Clem. "I hope you take the job. I can't go after Chambers and Jackson; not now. I'm sure you know why. I don't guess it really matters if I catch those bastards or you do. Justice is the only thing that matters."

Clem smiled warmly. "It seems love is more powerful than revenge. That's good. It's time for you to lay down your guns, marry, and start a family. You also have a ranch to rebuild."

Dexter, impatient with their conversation, butted in: "Mr. Slade, why have you protected Sharla? You know where she is, don't you? What's your price? How much will it cost me to learn her whereabouts?"

"Go to hell" was Lance's response.

"Don't you realize the woman is a murderer? She killed my brother out of greed because she didn't want to share Olivia's estate."

"Sharla didn't kill your brother, you stupid ass!"

Dexter, offended, sat stiffly in the straight-backed chair. "Obviously, the murdering chit has you completely fooled. You are the one who is stupid, Mr. Slade." He quickly turned his attention to Clem. "Well, are you going to take the job? Time is wasting. Every minute you spend trying to make up your mind, those men are taking Claudia farther and farther away."

"Claudia?" Lance asked. "Is she your fiancée?"

"You say her name as though you know her."

"I don't know her, but I certainly know of her. And I take back what I said. You aren't stupid, you're a complete idiot! You've been sleeping with your brother's murderer!"

"That's ridiculous! She didn't murder James. Sharla's been filling your head with malicious lies."

"Not only did she kill James, but I bet she also killed Maxine Reynolds."

"Maxine is dead?" Dexter gasped. He and the others had left St. Louis the morning after Maxine's murder, so Dexter knew nothing about it. "When did she die?"

"I don't know exactly when."

"Well, I can assure you that Claudia had nothing to do with it. She's been on the road with me." Again, he turned to Clem. "Apparently, five hundred dollars isn't enough. I'll give you a thousand."

"Make it three thousand and I'll take the job." Actually, Clem had every intention of pursuing Chambers and Jackson with or without Dexter's reward. He intended to go after them for Lance's sake. But he saw no reason not to make money at the same time.

"Three thousand!" Dexter exclaimed. He was genuinely surprised, for he had misjudged Clem. He thought a thousand dollars was the man's top price; in fact, he doubted if Emerson had ever seen a thousand dollars. Clem's buckskin shirt and pants were well worn, his boots were badly scuffed, and his hat, lying on the table, was weather-spotted, and the wide brim somewhat tattered. Judging the man by his appearance, Dexter had figured he would be happy to agree to a thousand dollars.

"If you want me to go after your woman," Clem said, "it's gonna cost you three big ones." He smiled secretly at Slade, then added, "Besides, it'll make up for the three thousand dollars I forfeited to a friend."

"Very well!" Dexter conceded. "Tomorrow morning I'll have funds transferred to this bank. By the time you return, the money should be here. However, there is a stipulation."

"What's that?"

"If Claudia isn't returned to me alive, there's no payment."

"You got a deal," Clem replied, pouring a round of whiskey.

At that moment, Sheriff Langley entered the saloon, said a few words to Wyatt, who threw off his apron, told his assistant to tend bar, then left for home.

Langley ambled over to the men's table to speak to Lance. "I got some disturbin' news for you," he said. "Mary Simmons just rode into town. She told me two men approached their camp, killed Steve and abducted Miss Lawrence—or should I say Miss Matthews?"

Lance bounded to his feet. "My God! Jordan's dead?"

"Mary said they shot him in cold blood. She wasn't strong enough to put his body in the wagon, or drive the team. So she had to leave Jordan and the wagon behind. She rode into town on horseback. They were camped about five hours from here. I'm gonna get a couple of men to ride out there with me. I'll be back tomorrow with the wagon and Jordan's body."

"Is Mary at Wyatt's house?"

"Yeah, I just left her there." Langley spoke to Dexter, "Mary said one of the men called the other one "Lou." Didn't you tell me the men who took your fiancée are Lou Jackson and Jeff Chambers?"

"Yes, that's right."

"Describe them."

He gave the sheriff an accurate depiction.

"They're the ones, all right. Mary described them the same way."

"They probably took Sharla for the ransom," Dexter said. "They would recognize her from the wanted posters."

Lance spoke to Clem: "I'm going to check on Mary; while I'm doing that, buy some supplies and extra ammunition. We'll leave tonight."

"I'll meet you at Wyatt's house," Clem replied.

Lance then turned a steely gaze in Dexter's direction.

"I'm bringing Sharla back to Madison Creek. It's time she stopped running. In the meantime, you have Langley call in all those damned posters." Lance whirled about, walked out of the saloon, and headed toward the Jordans' home.

He was deeply worried. Convincing Sharla to stop running and fight the murder charge against her might be a terrible mistake. However, he knew she couldn't run indefinitely; sooner or later the law would catch up to her. Running would only prolong the inevitable. But Lance had renewed hope. It wasn't much, but was certainly worth holding on to. His hope was Claudia, and that he would somehow get a confession out of her.

He knocked on the Jordans' door. Wyatt let him in and showed him to the parlor.

"I'm sorry about Steve," Lance said. "I didn't know him all that well, but I liked him."

Wyatt held no grudge against Lance for leaving Steve to travel alone with the women, for he had learned of Lance's abduction. "I suppose you're here to see Mary?"

"If she's up to it."

"She's in her room with Emma. I'll get her for you."

A few moments later, Mary entered the parlor. She lashed out at Lance angrily: "You heartless devil! Do you realize how deeply you hurt Sharla? Or do you even care?"

Lance held up a hand, warding off her verbal attack. "Apparently, no one has told you what happened." He quickly recounted his run-in with the Cantons and Thorton.

"I'm sorry," Mary apologized. "I shouldn't have jumped down your throat without giving you a chance to explain."

"Your apology is accepted," he replied, summoning a warm smile. "Clem and I are leaving in a few minutes to find Sharla. I think you should know that I've decided to try and convince her to stop running."

"Do you think that's wise?"

"I don't know; I only know she can't evade the law forever. By the way, Dexter Rayfield's in town. The men who took Sharla also kidnapped Claudia."

"So Rayfield and Claudia are in Texas!" she exclaimed. "But those men didn't have Claudia with them when they attacked us."

"They probably left her tied nearby."

"Is Claudia the reason you think Sharla should stop running? Do you think you can get the truth out of her?"

"I'm sure as hell gonna try."

"Maxine tried, and lost her life." Sudden tears filled Mary's eyes, overflowed, and rolled unabated down her face.

Lance moved to Mary and gently drew her into his arms. He held her close.

"I failed Maxine, and I also failed Sharla," she sobbed. "I left the farm to protect Sharla, to keep her safe from harm. But all I accomplished was to bring more harm down upon her. If I hadn't fallen ill, those men wouldn't have found us, and Steve would still be alive."

"You can't blame yourself for any of this. If you want to put the blame somewhere, put it on Claudia and Rayfield: Claudia for murdering James, and Dexter for distributing those damned wanted posters."

Mary moved out of Lance's embrace, took a handkerchief from her dress pocket, and dried her eyes. "You're right, of course." She managed a small smile. "I thank God that Sharla has you. You're a good man, Lance Slade. My prayers are with you, and I have faith that with God's help, you and your friend will save Sharla from those two murderers."

Lance felt he and Clem would need her prayers, for Chambers and Jackson were specialists at their trades. They were master gunmen, successful robbers, and expert killers. They were no ordinary, run-of-the-mill criminals: Chambers and Jackson were a force to be reckoned with.

Lance knew that their skills were as well honed as his and Clem's. The impending confrontation could be deadly!

It was well after midnight before Chambers decided to stop. He ruled out a campfire, and the tired travelers ate their food cold. The area was surrounded by dense shrubbery, and Chambers allowed the women to step into the bushes for privacy. To prevent an attempted escape, he insisted that they sing or talk the entire time, for if one or both fell silent, he would come after them.

Subsequently, the women's hands and ankles were tied: They received one blanket to share, and were left to spend the night beneath a tall pecan tree. Chambers took the first watch, and Jackson retired to his bedroll, where he promptly fell asleep.

Sleep, however, evaded Sharla, as well as Claudia. Although the women were fatigued, they were too upset and worried to put their minds to rest.

Sharing such close proximity to Claudia was difficult for Sharla. She truly believed that Claudia had killed James, and might very well have killed Maxine. Now, their closeness was almost more than she could bear. Because of Claudia, she was a fugitive on the run, her life had been turned upside down, and she had found her mother, only to lose her to Claudia's evilness.

The women were lying side by side, their backs facing each other. Claudia turned over, and asked softly, "Were you alone?"

"Alone? What do you mean?"

"When you were captured, was there anybody with you?"

"Yes. There were two people traveling with me. One was a good friend; he's dead now."

"And the other person?"

"Why all these questions?"

"I was just wondering if there might be someone following you, someone who could rescue us."

"There's no one," she murmured, her thoughts racing to Lance. He could have saved them, but of course he had abandoned her in favor of chasing after two ghosts from his past!

"I wonder where they are taking us," Claudia pondered aloud. "Chambers gave Dexter a map—"

"Chambers!" Sharla cut in. That these two men might be the ones who murdered Lance's family seemed too far-fetched to be true. "What is the other man's name?"

"Jackson," Claudia answered. "Jeff Chambers and Lou Jackson."

Sharla sat up with a start. "My God!" she cried softly.

"What's wrong with you?" Claudia asked. "You look like you've just seen a ghost."

"I have," she answered. "Two ghosts to be exact." She lay back down, and gazed up at the myriad of stars lighting the night sky. She had a sudden urge to laugh, and if the situation wasn't so serious, she might very well laugh herself into hysterics. Lance was off God only knew where looking for Chambers and Jackson; how ironic that she had found them instead. *Well,* she told herself, *I didn't exactly find them; they found me is more like it.* Regardless, she was their prisoner, and Lance was out there somewhere chasing shadows.

"You know something you aren't telling me, don't you?" Claudia asked, watching Sharla closely.

"I've heard of Chambers and Jackson," she replied. "They are cold-blooded murderers. They'll keep me alive because that's the only way they can claim the three thousand dollars." Sharla turned and met Claudia's questioning eyes. "However, once they collect the ransom money, I doubt if they'll let you live."

"You're only saying that to scare me."

"Scaring you isn't on my mind. I want you to live. If you die, then I can never prove that I didn't kill James."

"How do you know so much about Chambers and Jackson?" Claudia was still skeptical, and thought Sharla was trying to frighten her out of spite.

"I know someone who is well acquainted with Chambers and Jackson. They killed his family: his parents, brother, and sister. These two men aren't humans, but demons straight from the fires of hell!"

A chill crept up Claudia's spine. She was suddenly very afraid, but she was also angry, her rage aimed directly at Dexter. He was a fool to hire men like Chambers and Jackson. She hadn't trusted the two men from the very beginning and had tried to warn Dexter. If only he had listened to her!

Sharla turned onto her side, presenting her back to Claudia. "Let's try and get some sleep," she murmured. It was a little chilly without a top blanket, and Sharla considered asking Chambers for extra cover, but she quickly discarded the notion. If he had wanted them to have two blankets, they would already have them. Withholding comfort from his prisoners was probably his way of putting them in their place.

Sharla's thoughts drifted to Steve. His death was hard for her to deal with; he had been a good friend, and was genuinely warm, considerate, and compassionate. That his life had been snuffed out by these two demons filled her with rage. For the first time in her life, she craved the taste of revenge, and knew she would not rest until Chambers and Jackson paid for killing Steve. She now fully understood the retribution that had driven Lance for five, long years. Men like Chambers and Jackson had to be stopped!

Meanwhile, as Sharla was thinking of revenge, Claudia was contemplating using her sexual powers to inveigle Chambers. She chose him because he obviously controlled Jackson. Jeff gave the orders, and Lou followed. Seducing

Chambers was a repulsive ploy, but seemed to be her only
option. Given a choice, she would much rather sleep with
Chambers than lose her life. She wasn't sure when she
should make her move. She considered it for a few moments and decided the sooner the better.

Chambers's vigil had placed him somewhere in the
nearby shrubbery, and Claudia wasn't sure of his exact
location. She sat up and called softly, "Chambers? Where
are you? I must talk to you."

"What are you up to?" Sharla asked sharply.

"Stay out of this!" Claudia snapped.

Chambers's huge shadow emerged from the thick foliage. Claudia's heart began to beat nervously as he came
and knelt before her.

"What do you want?" he asked gruffly.

She conjured up one of her most enticing smiles. "I
need to talk to you alone. Untie me, please?"

Taking her by surprise, Chambers threw back his head
and roared with laughter.

"Stop that!" she spat angrily, her seductive ploy taking
second place to her wrath. How dare the crude man laugh
at her!

Chambers's humor died as fast as it had erupted. "You
stupid bitch!" he grumbled. "What did you have in mind,
huh? Were you plannin' on spreadin' your legs for me?
Did you think a little lovin' would make me treat you better? Woman, don't you realize you ain't got no bargainin'
power. What you got I can take any time I want to. And I
aim to do just that. But not until the time's right. I can't
take no chances right now, 'cause there might be a posse
on our tail. But later, when I know it's safe, you and me
are gonna play a little game called 'poke her.' When I get
through pokin' you, I'm gonna poke this other gal."

Chambers was again amused, and chuckling under his
breath, he returned to the shrubbery.

"You fool!" Sharla said harshly. "Did you really think you could cajole that bastard?"

"It might have been a foolish plan, but at least I was willing to try something. Unlike you, I'm not afraid to try and save my life. But then, of course, your life isn't in danger, is it?"

"Not as long as I cooperate with them," Sharla replied. "Dexter's posters state that I must be returned alive. Ironic, isn't it, that I may owe my life to Dexter?"

Claudia frowned hatefully, and turned away from Sharla.

Chambers's words had instilled a fear in Sharla's heart that she had refused to reveal. True, she didn't believe her life was in all that much danger; however, she felt she could handle certain death easier than a sexual assault on her body. Just imagining such horror sent a icy shiver rippling up her spine.

She thought about the knife hidden in her boot, and it gave her a small measure of comfort. If necessary, she would use it on herself before submitting to Chambers's abuse.

However, Sharla had an inner strength that wasn't easily shaken by Chambers's intimidation. She was determined to stay alert and grasp the first opportunity to escape. She was not about to meekly succumb to her captors' dominance; the moment they made a mistake, she would pounce on it. She could only hope and pray that a chance to flee would arise before Chambers considered it safe to carry out his sexual threats.

Knowing a rested mind was essential, she closed her eyes. Sleep eluded her for a long time, but it finally fell over her like a black cloak, blocking out grim reality.

However, her repose didn't last very long, for she dreamt of Lance, and awoke with his name on her lips. It took almost an hour for exhaustion to lead her back into sleep; this time, she didn't dream.

Thirty-two

The next day, Chambers set a strenuous pace. In case a posse was following, he took several twists and turns to throw them off the track. Sharla tried to keep her bearings, for if she managed to escape, she would need to find Madison Creek. However, after hours of Chambers's meandering course, she wasn't sure which direction led back to town.

They made camp a few hours after dark. The spot was well camouflaged, for it was located in the midst of overgrown shrubbery and tall trees. Although the clearing was small, it served its purpose, for there was enough room for the travelers to lay out bedrolls and herd the horses. Again, Chambers decided against a campfire, and supper was eaten cold.

Following the meal, the women spread their shared blanket as far away from the men as possible. However, considering the camp's narrow dimensions, the distance was only a few feet.

Sharla and Claudia were extremely fatigued, and were close to falling asleep when Jackson's words brought them wide awake.

"Ain't it time to poke the women?" he asked Chambers.

The man yawned, then stretched lazily, as though a sexual assault was no big deal. "Yeah, I reckon we might as well have a little fun."

"Which one do you want?"

Claudia was no longer Chambers's first choice, for he found Sharla more desirable. "I'll take the Matthews woman," he said. "The other one's a whore. Hell, humpin' a whore ain't nothin' different; I do that all the time. But I ain't never had me no . . . gen-u-wine lady."

Jackson was disappointed, for he had wanted Sharla. "Tomorrow night, can we switch women?"

"Sure," Chambers agreed. He chuckled heartily. "We're partners, ain't we?"

The men were sitting on their blankets; they got to their feet in unison and moved over to their prospective victims.

Chambers reached down, grabbed Sharla's arm and jerked her to her feet. Leaving Jackson with Claudia, he forced Sharla to his own blanket and shoved her to the ground. He removed his gun belt, and placed it aside. Then his huge body plowed on top of hers, and his weight nearly knocked the air from her lungs.

Chambers's mouth found hers, and his slobbery kiss was so repulsive that Sharla's stomach actually heaved. But she quickly closed her mind to the lips ravaging hers, bent her leg, and slipped her hand down to the boot concealing the knife. She would not submit to this horrible man, but would escape or die trying!

Her fingers found, then grasped, the knife's handle. She withdrew the weapon cautiously, for Chambers's mouth had now moved down to her neck, his wet tongue licking her skin. Sharla gritted her teeth, mustered her courage, and girded herself to carry out what she must do. Sinking a knife's blade into someone's flesh sickened her, but Chambers's assault sickened her more.

She slid the knife up the side of her leg, and as Chambers's hand groped at her breasts, she drew up the weapon, plunged it into his side, and left it there.

He howled with shock, as well as pain. Jackson was so engrossed in his own assault that his comrade's yell totally escaped him. Chambers got to his knees and was about to remove the embedded knife when Sharla's foot caught him square in the face. The strong kick sent him sprawling onto his back. Crawling on her hands and knees, she reached his gun belt and freed his pistol a second before his hand could grab her arm.

Suddenly, Chambers withdrew the knife from his flesh. He intended to hurl it into Sharla's heart, but his adversary was quicker, and before he could throw the weapon, Sharla hit him across the head with the pistol. The powerful impact knocked him unconscious. He lay motionless, the knife still clutched in his hand.

Sharla turned her attention to Jackson and Claudia. The man was still completely involved in his attack. Like Chambers, he had removed his gun belt. Sharla moved quietly, although Claudia's cries were loud enough to muffle her steps. Reaching Jackson's holster, she kicked it out of his reach.

His body was covering Claudia's, and his hands were bruising her breasts as Sharla's placed the barrel of Chambers's pistol to the back of his head.

Jackson froze as he heard the unmistakable click of a gun's hammer being cocked.

"I should do the world a favor," Sharla uttered, "and blow your brains out!" That she could feel such violence actually startled her. She stepped back a safe distance, then told him to get slowly to his feet.

The moment Claudia was free of his weight, she squirmed off the blanket and crawled half the distance to Sharla before finding the strength to stand. However, her knees were so shaky that she feared she might collapse.

Jackson's gaze darted to Chambers, and he wondered if he was dead. Blood had soaked his shirt and he was lying deathly still.

Sharla read Jackson's mind. "He isn't dead. At least not yet. But he might bleed to death."

"You bitch!" Jackson raged. "If Jeff don't kill you, I will!"

"I wouldn't make such threats if I were you. After all, I'm a woman, and women frighten easily. I might decide to shoot you out of fear." Keeping her eyes on Jackson, she spoke to Claudia: "Get his gun belt and the horses." Sharla had decided not only to take their weapons, but also their horses. She wasn't about to leave them the means to recapture her and Claudia.

Picking up Jackson's gun belt, Claudia asked harshly, "You aren't planning on leaving them alive, are you?"

"Shut up and do as I told you, or I'll leave you here with them!"

For a moment, Claudia considered drawing Jackson's gun and killing the men herself, but considering it was as far as she got. Besides, murdering Chambers and Jackson served no purpose, for they were no longer a threat to her life. Furthermore, such an act would alienate Sharla, and she needed her, for she was not only lost, but too scared to travel alone. Conceding to Sharla's order, she hurried to the horses and led them back.

The women mounted; Sharla managed to swing into the saddle and at the same time hold Jackson at gunpoint.

Taking the men's steeds, along with the packhorse, they rode out of the small clearing, through the thick shrubbery and onto open land.

Sharla suddenly reined in.

Halting beside her, Claudia demanded, "Why did you stop? We need to keep moving!"

"I'm trying to get our bearings."

Claudia sighed testily. "Oh this is great! You're just as lost as I am!"

"We should head north," Sharla decided.

"Which way is north?"

"We've been traveling south, therefore, all we have to

do is turn around. That should be simple enough for even you to understand."

They turned the horses about and took off at a steady gallop. Sharla knew going straight north wouldn't lead them to Madison Creek, but they were heading in the general direction. For now, that was enough.

At dawn, Chambers and Jackson left the campsite, made their way through the heavy foliage, and began walking northeast. An isolated town, twenty-odd miles away, lay in that direction. When they arrived, they planned to buy a couple of horses and guns. The money they stole from Dexter was in Chambers's saddlebags, which had been on his horse. But Jackson had stuck the money he took from Steve into his pocket, so they were not without finances.

Chambers's head still pounded from Sharla's hard blow, and the wound to his side ached with each step he took. That he had been bested by a woman was infuriating. He swore revenge: Somehow, someway, he would even the score. Collecting the bounty on Sharla no longer concerned him; he was only interested in killing her!

They had been walking about an hour when two riders approached. The men reined in and regarded Chambers and Jackson curiously.

"We're in luck," Chambers whispered, as he and Jackson moved slowly toward the two strangers. "They look like easy pickins' to me."

Jackson, agreeing, feigned an amiable smile, and called out to the men, "Good morning. I guess you're wonderin' why we're afoot. Yesterday, we were bushwhacked out here in the middle of nowhere by desperadoes. They stole our horses, guns, and wounded my friend."

These riders were indeed easy prey for Chambers and Jackson, for one was a farmer and the other a doctor. Neither sported a holstered weapon; their only protection were sheathed rifles. The doctor lived in the small town ahead; the farmer had fetched him because his young son was ill.

"Why don't you two mount up behind us?" the physician suggested. "We're not far from this man's farm. After I tend to his son, I'll have a look at your friend's wound."

"That's mighty kind of you, Doc," Jackson replied.

Chambers, pretending to be so wounded that he could barely maneuver, stepped clumsily to the doctor's horse. The man offered him a helping hand, for Chambers appeared too weak to swing into the saddle without aid.

As Chambers grasped the doctor's hand, he drew Sharla's butcher knife from his belt and thrust it into his victim's stomach. Before the shocked farmer could react, Jackson unsheathed the doctor's rifle, aimed it at the man and fired two rapid shots. The farmer fell off his horse and hit the dirt road with a deadly thud.

As Jackson was carrying out cold-blooded murder, Chambers jerked the doctor from the saddle and slung him to the ground. He was still alive, but Chambers took care of that with a second stab, this one straight into the heart.

The men quickly mounted the horses.

"Those bitches have gotta be headin' north," Chambers uttered, hate in his eyes. "Leadin' three horses will slow 'em down. We oughta be able to catch them by mornin'. We'll keep the whore alive until we collect the ransom, but that other bitch is gonna die!"

"But what about the bounty?" Jackson asked.

"To hell with it!" Chambers bellowed. "That god-damned woman stabbed me and knocked me unconscious! That damned bitch is gonna die!"

Sharla set a steady tempo that was not only tiring to herself and Claudia, but tiring to the horses as well. But she was anxious to reach Madison Creek, so she forced a complaining Claudia and the weary animals to travel through the night and until sunset of the next day.

Claudia wanted a cooked meal and hot coffee, but Sharla opposed a fire.

"Why must we eat cold food and do without coffee?" Claudia asked crankily.

"A fire would give away our location. We don't know who might be in the vicinity. Do you think Chambers and Jackson are the only rapists or killers who travel these roads?"

Claudia conceded, although begrudgingly, for her mood was hostile. She hated riding with Sharla, and if she wasn't so scared of traveling alone, she'd kill Sharla here and now. She could always blame her death on Chambers and Jackson. The idea came to her without warning, but she didn't cast it aside; quite the contrary, she savored it. Her main reason for riding to Texas with Dexter was to find an opportunity to get rid of Sharla; then Dexter would put his revenge to rest, buy her a home, and shower her with expensive gifts. Now, the opportunity to permanently dispose of Sharla was within her grasp. She could hardly believe that it would be so easy. She smiled to herself. As soon as they were close enough to Madison Creek for her to find her way there alone, she would kill Sharla. The packhorse carried the gun belts and rifles belonging to Chambers and Jackson. Sneaking one of the pistols and using it to end Sharla's life would not be a problem. Today, Sharla had kept a rifle across her lap, ready to use it at a moment's notice. Claudia, however, intended to shoot Sharla in the back.

The women spread two blankets, sat down, and as they ate a cold meal, the setting sun kindled the sky before slowly disappearing over the far horizon. Gradually, dusk gave way to full night. The sky was cloudless, and a golden moon, sharing the heavens with a multitude of glittering stars, bathed the land in an aureate glow.

Sharla was thankful that the sky wasn't overcast, for pitch blackness would certainly have been scary and nerve-wracking. She had Steve's rifle at her side, and she placed a hand on it, as though she needed to reassure herself that it was still there.

Meanwhile, Claudia was again contemplating Sharla's death. The more she thought about it, the more her excitement grew. Soon, she would be rid of Sharla, she and Dexter would be back in St. Louis, and James's murder would be a closed case. The happy prospect put a large smile on her face and a pleased giggle in her throat.

"Is something funny?" Sharla asked, for she had heard Claudia's soft giggle.

"I was just thinking," she replied, a lilt in her voice.

"About what?"

"Oh, just things," she lied. "You know, a hot meal, a bath, and clean clothes." She brushed a hand across her dust-coated skirt.

Sharla had recognized Claudia's riding attire, and knew it had come from her own closet. She hadn't bothered to comment on it; until now, "Why are you wearing my clothes?"

"It was Dexter's idea, not mine. Believe me, I take no pleasure from wearing someone else's clothes."

Sharla didn't really care about the clothes; she was more interested in Claudia and Dexter's relationship. "How did you become involved with Dexter?" she asked.

"The very same day I went to work for Maxine, Dexter came to see me," Claudia explained. "He's been with me ever since. He's totally infatuated with me, and loves me so much that he'll give me anything I desire."

"Loves you?" Sharla questioned. "Surely, you don't believe that. If he loved you, he'd marry you."

Claudia smiled complacently. "You are so unbelievably naive. I don't want Dexter's name; I want his money. And

I intend to get as much of it as I can before he moves on to someone else."

"Is that what you wanted from James? His money?"

Claudia was taken off guard, but only for a moment. She saw no reason to deny the truth. There was no one to hear what she said, except for Sharla, and she would soon be dead. Even if something happened to prevent her from killing Sharla, what was said tonight could never be proven. It'd merely be her word against Sharla's.

"No, I didn't want money from James," Claudia said candidly. "I wanted him to marry me. I loved James; he was everything to me?"

"Did you kill him because he refused to marry you?"

A murderous frown crossed Claudia's face; Rayfield's treatment of her still had to the power to enrage her senses. "Not only did he refuse to marry me, but he treated me like I was dirt! I gave him my heart, my body, and my soul; in return, he planned to cast me from his life as though I was nothing more to him than a cheap harlot!" Insanity, its fury spine-chilling, flared in Claudia's eyes as she now ranted in a voice filled with unforgotten rage, "He wanted me gone so he could find another lover. I couldn't let that happen! I loved him too much. I knew I'd rather see him dead than in another's woman's arms. That's why I killed him! Sometimes, I'm glad I did it, then other times, I wish he were still alive! Maybe it wasn't really over between us. Maybe I could have convinced him to take me back! But he's gone, and nothing can change that. But I'll always love him. Not Dexter or anyone else can take his place. I'll always love James . . . always! I . . . I guess I loved him . . . too much!"

Shock held Sharla captive, and she was riveted, as though powerless to move so much as a muscle. Until this moment, she hadn't realized that her companion was so completely and dangerously demented. She had always thought of Claudia as a killer, but not as a woman who was violently insane. She suddenly needed to move farther away from Claudia, for her proximity was bone-chilling, as though they were surrounded by icebergs instead of green shrubbery. Forcing movement back into her limbs, Sharla picked up her rifle and got somewhat shakily to her feet.

"Where are you going?" Claudia asked.

"I need to make sure the horses are properly secured. Then I'll stand watch. You get some sleep."

Claudia's rage was now under control, and she regretted having lost her composure. She hoped her ranting wouldn't cause Sharla to take extra precautions against her. If only . . . if only she could learn to subdue her temper. She feigned a smile and offered to take the second watch.

Sharla didn't respond; she simply moved away. But she knew she wouldn't wake Claudia to stand guard, for she wouldn't put it past the woman to kill her in her sleep. However, staying awake was not the solution, for she needed rest to remain alert. She would get a few hours sleep, but she'd move her blanket close to the horses, for they might whinny and awaken her should danger, in any form, approach. She would also sleep with two companions: a rifle and a pistol!

Sharla slept fitfully and awakened at dawn. Although she had a natural instinct for handling dangerous situations, she was no match for men like Chambers and Jackson. Slipping up on Sharla and Claudia was not even a challenge to their professionalism, for they were too competent at this kind of work. They knew to stay downwind, which prevented the horses from picking up their scent. They also knew how to move silently through the surrounding shrubbery, their steps not even disturbing the birds still ensconced in their nests. Skilled trackers, finding the women had been easy, and they were certain that recapturing them would be a simple feat.

Sharla was kneeling beside her blanket, rolling it, when Chambers and Jackson, armed with their stolen weapons, bolted from the shrubbery. The men were indeed expert ambushers, but they were poor judges of women. They carried their rifles loosely, for they didn't think either woman had the ability to fire a weapon before they could stop her.

Sharla stared at the men with anger, as well as fear. Claudia, on the other hand, panicked. She screamed, and her shrill cry drew the men's attention. Sharla reacted at once, and grabbing Steve's Winchester, she leapt to her feet, took quick aim and shot Jackson, who was the closest target. Chambers, though, was too quick for Sharla, and before she could turn the gun on him, he cocked his weapon and fired. The bullet merely grazed Sharla's shoulder, but the glance was so powerful that it knocked the rifle from her grasp and threw her to the ground. She managed to sit up, but retrieving her weapon was not possible, for Chambers was already there and he had kicked the rifle aside. He now leered down into her face with unadulterated hate.

Her shoulder ached as though it had been hit with a brick, and blood from the wound trickled down her arm. But Sharla was not really aware of the pain or the blood, for the murder in Chamber's eyes blocked everything from her mind, except for her own impending death. She knew without a doubt that this man was going to kill her!

"You goddamned bitch!" he growled, pointing the rifle's barrel at her face. "It's gonna give me a lot of pleasure to blow that pretty face of yours into a bloody mess!" He recocked his weapon, and Sharla confronted death bravely, believing the metallic-sounding click of a gun's hammer would be the last thing she would hear on this earth.

Thirty-three

Sharla closed her eyes, for darkness was less frightening than staring down the barrel of a rifle. A gun blast sounded, but it took a second for her mind to grasp that the shot hadn't come from Chambers' weapon. Her eyes flew open, and she saw that Chambers was on the ground, his hands clawing at a gaping chest wound, as though he could somehow repair his torn flesh. The wound was fatal and he was dead before Sharla had time to get to her feet.

She heard steps behind her, turned, and was stunned to see Lance and Clem Emerson entering camp. They were leading their horses, as well as the two stolen horses that Chambers and Jackson had left in the shrubbery. Both men carried rifles, and she wondered which one had shot Chambers.

As Clem checked Jackson, Lance went to Chambers and saw that he was dead. He turned to Sharla, and despite the pain in her shoulder and her harrowing brush with death, she met his eyes without a waver. Lance was impressed with her courage, but certainly not surprised by it; he had always known that Sharla Matthews was an extraordinary woman.

Becoming aware of her injury, he stepped to his horse and took a clean bandanna from his saddlebags, along with a flask of whiskey. He then went to Sharla and said gently, "I need to tend to your wound."

She didn't say anything. She wondered about his bruised face, but didn't bother to ask. The less she said to him, the better!

He grasped her shirtsleeve and tore it away from her shoulder. "This is going to burn," he said, opening the flask. "But the pain won't last very long."

She wished the pain in her heart could go away as quickly. But seeing Lance again had hit her terribly hard, and she knew that no amount of time could completely heal her heartache. She loved him too deeply.

He poured whiskey over her wound, and she bit down on her bottom lip to keep from crying out. By the time Lance had the bandanna tightly wrapped, the pain had lessened considerably.

"As soon as we get back to town, you need to see the doctor," he told her.

With a slight lift to her chin, she answered coolly, "I am perfectly aware that I should see a doctor. I don't need you to tell me the obvious. In fact, I don't need you at all."

He grinned wryly. "That's a hell of a thing to say to a man who just saved your life."

"So it was you who shot Chambers. I was hoping it was Clem Emerson. I would much rather owe my life to him than to you."

"Sharla, I understand your hostility, but I can explain . . ."

"I'm not interested in your explanation."

"Well, you're going to hear it whether you want to or not. However, this isn't exactly the best time. We'll talk later."

"Not if I can help it!" she snapped, determined to preserve her pride. After all, it was all she had left—Lance had already stolen everything else!

Slade let her retort pass, and gestured toward Claudia, who was coming toward them. "Is that Claudia?"

"Yes, but how did you know?"

"Rayfield's in Madison Creek."

Claudia was now close enough to overhear Lance's remark. She smiled brightly, and exclaimed, "Thank goodness Dexter didn't go back to St. Louis!" She paused beside Lance; his bruised face didn't mar his good looks, and her gaze was admiring. She favored Slade with an enticing smile, and murmured in a sugar-coated voice, "I want to thank you for rescuing Sharla and me. You're as brave as you are handsome. Did Dexter hire you to find me?"

"No, he didn't." Lance waved a hand in Clem's direction. "He hired Emerson for the job. I came along for only one reason."

"Oh?" she prodded. "What reason was that?"

"To save Sharla."

Fire flashed in Sharla's eyes. "I'm not the reason why you're here! You lying skunk! You're here because of Chambers and Jackson. You came here for revenge. Well, you can finally put your revenge to rest! Chambers and Jackson are dead, and so is our relationship!" With that, she brushed Lance aside, picked up her rifle, and went to her horse.

Lance followed quickly. Sharla was about to swing into the saddle, but Lance clamped a hand on her arm. "Where the hell do you think you're going?"

"I'm not sure, but I can't go back to Madison Creek. Not with Dexter there."

"You have to go back."

"I'm sure he's shown the sheriff a wanted poster. Langley will arrest me the moment I return."

"I don't think so. But that's not the issue. This may be our only chance to prove you're innocent. We have the real murderer here; we just have to find a way to entrap her."

"Claudia's too shrewd for that."

"Sharla, you can't keep running. Sooner or later, the law's gonna catch up to you. You've got to stand and face this."

She knew he was right: She had always known that eventually she would have to confront the charges against her; she had only been prolonging the inevitable. But knowing this didn't make it any easier. Dexter Rayfield was powerful, and in a court of law, she wouldn't stand a chance against him.

She sighed heavily. "All right, I'll go back to town. I know I can't keep running. But I don't think justice will prevail; I'll spend the rest of my life in prison, or else face the gallows."

"I won't let that happen."

She laughed bitterly. "Surely, you don't expect me to depend on you! I trusted you for the last time, Lance Slade! I don't want to discuss this any further. However, I do need to know about Mary. Did she make it back to Madison Creek?"

"Yes, she did. I was sorry to hear about Jordan."

Tears threatened, but she held them in check. If she started crying, she might not stop for a long time.

"Why was Chambers about to kill you?"

As she gave him a full account, Lance was deeply impressed with her bravery and, determination. He was also somewhat taken aback to hear that she was competent with a rifle. Evidently, he didn't know Sharla Matthews as well as he thought he did.

"I never wanted to kill anyone," she finished sadly.

"Jackson was a heartless murderer. Try not to be upset." Lance was anxious to leave. "Time's wasting," he said. "If we leave now, we can reach Madison Creek late this afternoon."

He started to turn away, but her question stopped him, "Lance, how did you and Clem find us?"

He smiled lightheartedly. "It took a little skill and a lot of luck."

She had a feeling it was the other way around.

Clem was lifting Jackson's body to put it on a horse; Lance hurried over and gave him a helping hand. As they moved toward Chambers, Clem asked, "Now that your family's murderers are dead, how does it make you feel?"

"At peace," Lance murmured. "But I still have another fight facing me, and this one can't be settled with guns. It might have to be settled in a court of law."

They lifted Chambers's body and placed it over a horse. Lance then moved to the palomino that Chambers had stolen from him the night he had killed his family. He was pleased to note that the animal was still in fairly good condition, despite the obvious signs of neglect. He patted the horse's neck, and murmured gently, "It's time to go home; we've both been away too long."

Glancing over at Sharla, who was mounted and ready to leave, Lance knew he couldn't go home without the woman he loved. "We'll make it back," he said, speaking his thoughts to the palomino, "but it might take awhile."

They rode into Madison Creek an hour before sunset. Sharla went to the doctor's house before going to the Jordans'. Meanwhile, Lance visited Langley, for he needed to hand over the bodies and explain what had happened. He also intended to let Langley know that Chambers and Jackson had apparently stolen two horses; more than likely they had killed the owners. He knew Langley would investigate the matter.

As Lance was taking care of that, Clem located Dexter and returned Claudia to his care. Rayfield assured him that the transfer of funds from his bank to this one should be completed sometime tomorrow.

Lance had asked Clem to meet him at the Jordans', and

after delivering Claudia, he rode to their home. Wyatt was at the saloon and Emma was shopping. He was admitted by Sharla, who showed him into the parlor. Mary was sitting on the sofa, pouring tea. Although the bounty hunter's presence was somewhat unnerving, Mary offered him refreshment, which he declined.

Clem had a habit of minding his own business, but he decided to make an exception. At the campsite, he had overheard parts of Sharla and Lance's argument. During the trip back to town, they had barely spoken to each other. He was certain that Lance intended to straighten everything out with Sharla, but Clem supposed a little help from him might make it easier.

He cleared his throat, for he was not comfortable with the subject matter he was about to broach. "Miss Sharla, ma'am, I think you should know what happened to Lance."

"I already know," she replied. "Mary told me about the Cantons. I misjudged Lance, and for that I owe him an apology."

"You owe him an apology for something else, too."

"What's that?"

"You think his reason for coming after you was to find Chambers and Jackson. You're wrong, ma'am. Before he learned of your abduction, he knew Chambers and Jackson were in the area. He chose not to go after them, but to find you instead. You came first, ma'am. I've known Lance for five years, and that's the first time anything meant more to him than findin' the men who killed his family."

Sharla was overjoyed. At the same time, however, she was terribly upset with herself for having accused Lance unjustly. If only she had given him a chance to explain! She cursed her own stubbornness.

"That's all I got to say, ma'am," Clem continued. "I told

Lance I'd meet him here, but I think I'll go find him and see if he wants to have a couple of drinks."

Sharla thanked him and showed him to the door. Returning to the parlor, she smiled at Mary and exclaimed happily, "Lance does love me! Above all else!"

"Lance is a good man, and he'll make you a fine husband."

Sharla's happiness was short-lived, and as her joy plunged, she murmured sadly, "Lance and I have no future together. Dexter will make sure of that." She bolstered her spirits, and refused to give in to defeat. "I'm not about to go down without a fight!" she remarked willfully. "I intend to have a talk with Dexter Rayfield. He's arrogant and self-centered, but he's not completely unreasonable. Maybe I can convince him to at least consider Claudia a suspect. Where's Dexter staying? Do you know?"

"Wyatt rented him a room above the saloon. But don't you think you should wait and have Lance go with you?"

"I can handle this alone," she replied, already heading for the door. "But if Lance arrives before I return, you can tell him where I've gone."

Dexter was elated that Claudia was alive and unharmed. Not that he loved her; he was merely obsessed with her lovely body and her sexual enthusiasm. Still, despite his elation, he was upset that Sharla was at the Jordans' house instead of behind bars. He knew where she was staying, for he had visited the sheriff's office, and Langley seemed content to leave Sharla where she was. On his way back to his room, he had spotted Emerson and Slade going into the saloon. He suspected Slade had talked the sheriff into letting Sharla remain free.

While he was gone, Claudia had ordered a bath and was immersed in water when he unlocked the door and stepped inside. She was a seductive sight, and his loins were immediately on fire. But he suppressed his desire, for she seemed to be thoroughly enjoying relaxing in a hot tub. He decided to be considerate and make love to her later. However, if he remained much longer, he might not be able to control his passion; her nude body beneath the water was too tempting.

He went to a standing wardrobe, opened a drawer and withdrew a newly purchased pistol. He placed the gun on the small table beside the bed. "I'm going to the saloon and have a couple of drinks, but I'll leave this pistol with you . . . just in case." He moved to the tub, bent over, and kissed her lips softly. "When I return, I hope to find you in bed, ready to please your man."

She smiled agreeably, took his hand and placed it between her legs. "Think about this while you're gone."

"That's all I've thought about since the first night I made love to you," he replied, his voice husky with passion. He left, promising to be back soon.

Langley was about to lock up the office and go home for dinner when a stranger walked through the front door. The middle-aged gentleman, dressed in eastern attire, was average-looking, and there was nothing about him that would make him stand out in a crowd. Nevertheless, Langley's second sense told him that this man was a law officer.

"Good evening, Sheriff," the man said, removing his hat. "My name's Woodson, and I'm from St. Louis." He reached into his pocket and handed Langley his badge and credentials.

"Won't you have a seat, Constable?" Langley asked, returning Woodson's property.

He took a chair. Langley sat in his own chair, and watched Woodson across the span of the desktop, waiting for him to state his reason for being here.

"I'm looking for two people," Woodson began. "They

might have passed this way. Dexter Rayfield and a woman named Claudia."

"You're in luck, Constable. They're here in town."

Woodson was surprised. He believed that Rayfield and Claudia were still days ahead of him. However, he had traveled strenuously for the past two weeks, surviving on three to four hours sleep each day, and often eating his meals on horseback.

"Where is Rayfield staying?" he asked Langley.

"He rented a room above the town's saloon."

"Do you know the room number?"

"There's only four rooms; he's in number three. Do you mind telling me why you're after Rayfield and the woman? It must be real important for you to chase after 'em all the way from St. Louis."

"It's very important," Woodson replied.

"I'm kinda confused. I thought you'd be lookin' for Sharla Matthews. She is wanted for murder, isn't she?"

"Yes, she is. But why do you ask about Sharla Matthews? Do you know her?"

"No, not really. However, she's in town, too. Actually, I've been tryin' to decide whether or not I should place her under arrest. If you'd explain why you're here, it might help me make up my mind."

"If you don't mind, I'll explain everything at another time. Right now, I'm very anxious to talk to Dexter Rayfield. Later, though, I will need you to make an arrest, and then I'll have extradition papers drawn up."

As Woodson was conversing with Langley, Sharla was moving quickly up the outside stairway that led to the rooms above Wyatt's saloon. She didn't know which room was Dexter's, so she knocked on each door as she made her way down the narrow corridor. She received no answer until she reached the third room.

The door opened, and she came face-to-face with Claudia.

Claudia had finished her bath and was wearing a robe. The garment was new: Dexter, preparing for her return, had purchased a few things from the mercantile. The robe was unbecoming and a size too large.

"Is Dexter here?" Sharla asked.

"He's at the saloon, but he'll be back soon."

Sharla brushed Claudia aside and invited herself in. "I'll wait for him."

Closing the door, Claudia replied, "I know why you're here, and it won't do you any good. Dexter will never take your word over mine."

"Maybe not," Sharla admitted. "But I'm going to try my best to convince him."

Another knock sounded at the door. "That's probably Dexter," Claudia said, her expression smug and self-assured. "He'll take you straight to jail and insist that the sheriff put you behind bars. He told me he has already notified a U.S. marshal. He'll be here day after tomorrow to escort you back to St. Louis." With a pleased smile, Claudia turned to the door and opened it. Woodson was on the other side, and his shocking presence caused the smile to freeze on her lips.

Sharla was as stunned as Claudia, for she had never imagined that Constable Woodson would personally pursue her. She felt sick inside, for she believed this man was here to arrest her, and then escort her back to St. Louis.

Woodson entered the room, and was disappointed to find that Dexter wasn't there. He had hoped to talk to him before having Langley arrest Claudia. He looked at Sharla, and her bleak expression touched him deeply. He decided not to wait for Dexter, for he owed it to Sharla to ease her mind without further delay. He offered her an encouraging smile, before turning to Claudia.

"Miss Wilkens," he began, "I'll have to ask you to get

dressed, then accompany me to the sheriff's office. I intend to take you back to St. Louis to stand trial for James Rayfield's murder."

Sharla's heart suddenly pounded with joy.

Claudia's heart was also pounding, and, for a moment, she was paralyzed with fear. She forced life back into her body, neglected the partially open door, and moved slowly toward the bedside table, where Dexter's pistol lay. The gun was mostly obscured behind a ceramic basin; its presence had escaped Woodson, as well as Sharla. Claudia's mind, though unhinged, was shrewd, and her thoughts were running fluidly. She paused in front of the small table, her body blocking the pistol.

Her mind had conjured up a hasty plan, but she had to make sure that it would work before carrying it out. Forcing her voice to remain calm, she said to Woodson, "I suppose you told Sheriff Langley that I'll be his prisoner."

"I told him there would be an arrest, but I didn't say who would be arrested. Why do you ask?"

She shrugged, as though indifferent. "I'm just a little curious. I imagine he was very surprised to learn that Sharla is no longer a suspect."

"Miss Wilkens, I didn't discuss this case with the sheriff. Later, I'll give him all the answers he wants. But for now, my priority is putting you behind bars. I'll have Miss Matthews hold up a sheet, you step behind it and get dressed."

"Why do you think I killed James?"

Woodson was not about to offer more information. "Let's just say, I'm mighty suspicious."

Claudia smiled inwardly; the man had no credible evidence! "Very well, Constable Woodson. I'll do as you say." As she spoke, however, she slipped a hand behind her back and found the pistol. Moving with exceptional speed, she aimed the gun at Woodson.

"Don't be a fool!" he said strongly. "You can't get away with killing me!"

"Of course I can! It's simple. You came here to arrest Sharla, and she grabbed this gun and shot you. Then, she and I fought over the weapon; it went off and poor Sharla was dead."

Lance followed Dexter out of the saloon. He had decided to talk to him—to try to get him to listen to reason. He caught up to him as he was about to climb the stairs to his room.

"Rayfield," Lance began, "I'd like to talk to you."

"About Sharla, I suppose."

"And Claudia."

Dexter raised a concerned brow. "Did something happen to Claudia that Emerson didn't tell me?"

"Not that I know of. I just rented a room from Wyatt; we can talk there."

They climbed the stairway and started down the corridor. Dexter was surprised to find that the door to his own room was standing partway open. By now, Claudia had worked herself into a frenzy and was ranting almost incoherently. The men paused in the open portal.

Claudia was totally oblivious to their presence, and her raving continued, the pistol still aimed at Woodson, who had goaded her into confessing, "Yes; I killed James!" she ranted. "And I would kill him again if I had the chance! He treated me like I was dirt under his feet. I loved him; I would have died for him. Don't you understand? He drove me to killing him! It was all his fault!"

Dexter's presence didn't escape Woodson, and wanting him to hear more from Claudia, he continued his baiting, "Before you shoot me, blame it on Sharla, then shoot her, would you mind telling me if you killed Maxine Reynolds?"

"Of course I did! She found out that my father died in

an insane asylum, and she was going to take the information to Dexter. I couldn't let her do that!"

"Before you fire that gun, I think you should know that I found the bloody uniform you had on when you killed James Rayfield. You stashed it in the chimney in your room. It's now at the police station, and there is a warrant for your arrest. Killing Miss Matthews and me serves no purpose."

"No!" Claudia panicked. "You're lying!"

"You know I'm telling the truth. If I was lying, I wouldn't know where you hid the uniform."

Dexter stepped all the way into the room, his movement catching Claudia's attention. She looked away from Woodson, and as she did, he lurched forward and grabbed the pistol from her hand.

Claudia sank to her knees, buried her face in her hands and wept hysterically.

Dexter stood over her, looking down at her with disgust instead of rage. He did feel anger, however, but it was aimed at himself. He had been totally hoodwinked by this woman, thinking with passion instead of common sense! He rubbed his hands together, as though he were washing them clean of Claudia. He turned to Woodson, his expression as cold as stone, "Take her to the jail and out of my sight. A U.S. marshal is on his way to town; he'll help you escort her back to St. Louis."

"You don't plan to ride with us?"

"No. I'll travel alone. I don't want to be in this woman's company." A set of Claudia's clothes were hanging in the wardrobe. Dexter gave them to Woodson. "Take her as she is; she can dress in her cell!"

Woodson went to Claudia, who was still crying. He grasped her arm and urged her to her feet. He coaxed her toward the door, but she drew away, clutched Dexter's sleeve, and moaned pathetically, "It's not my fault. James and Maxine plotted against me! Dexter, help me . . . please!"

He pried her fingers from his arm, throwing her hand aside as though touching her was repulsive. "Get her out of here!" he told Woodson.

Gripping her arm firmly, the constable led her to the door, but before leaving, he looked back at Sharla. "Miss Matthews, I'd like you to know that I personally came after Claudia because I felt so bad about wrongfully accusing you."

She smiled warmly. "I appreciate your dedication."

The moment they were gone, Dexter, obviously sheepish, said to Sharla, "I . . . I don't know what to say. I've done you a terrible injustice. Maybe someday, you can forgive me."

Lance was standing beside the door; Sharla looked at him, smiled brightly, then said to Dexter, "In a strange sort of way, I'm grateful to you. If you hadn't accused me of murder, I would never have met Lance Slade." She went to Lance's side, took his hand and led him through the door. She paused, glanced at Dexter over her shoulder, and added, "I harbor no bitterness. I am too happy, too much in love, and too excited about the future to let an ass like you put a damper on my elation."

She and Lance moved down the corridor, and descended the stairway. As they headed toward the Jordans' home, Lance squeezed her hand gently, and asked, "How does it feel to be free?"

"Free?" she questioned pertly. "I hardly think so. I hope to be permanently tied by the strings of matrimony. You will marry me, won't you?"

Lance drew her into his arms and hugged her tightly. "Just try and stop me."

"Never," she whispered. She put a hand at the nape of his neck, raised her lips to his and kissed him ardently.

"You've obviously forgiven me for deserting you." He smiled hesitantly. "But, Sharla, I didn't really desert you."

"I know," she replied. "Mary told me about the Cantons, and Clem filled me on the rest. I'm sorry that I didn't trust you. I promise it will never happen again."

They walked hand in hand. "Let's leave in the morning. I'm anxious to restore my ranch and build us a home. In the meantime, we can stay with my cousin. I'd like for us to get married in Bill's home, if that's all right with you."

"Sounds fine to me. Lance, what about Mary? I'd like to invite her to live with us."

"She's more than welcome. However, I don't have a lot of money, and we'll have to start off with a small home. But we can always build on to it."

"Money isn't a problem," she said offhandedly. "I'll soon be twenty-one. Then I'll receive my inheritance from Olivia. It's a very substantial amount."

Lance brought their steps to an abrupt halt. "But, Sharla, I don't want . . ."

"I know what you're about to say, Lance Slade. You don't feel right about taking money from your wife." With hands on hips, she eyed him willfully. "For years, I have dreamed of owning a ranch. Your male pride is not going to rob me of my dream. However, I will settle for owning half of a ranch." She smiled and offered him a handshake. "Well? Are we business partners?"

Instead of shaking her hand, he kissed it. "Business partners?" he questioned, smiling handsomely. "Very well, we're business partners, life-long partners, and best of all, bedroom partners."

"Oh, I do like that last part," she murmured seductively, and despite her shoulder wound, she slipped her arms about his neck. "Let's seal our agreement with a kiss, shall we?"

He kissed her with deep devotion. That they were

standing in the middle of the street, their kiss drawing gawking onlookers, didn't matter a whit to either of them, for they were completely oblivious to everything except each other.

Epilogue

Sharla rode to the stables, dismounted, and handed her mare over to a wrangler. She was feeling extremely happy as she walked away from the stables and toward her home. She paused and studied the white adobe ranch house as though seeing it for the very first time. She loved her home. Its beauty lay in its simplicity. The one-story, sprawling structure was designed with a large family in mind, for she and Lance wanted four or five children. The spacious rooms were tastefully decorated with expensive furnishings from San Antonio, and as far away as New Orleans and St. Louis. One room had been set aside for a nursery, but it had remained unoccupied. Sharla, wanting a child desperately, had begun to despair.

Now, however, as she thought about the nursery, a smile brightened her face and put a twinkle in her eyes. She had just returned from visiting the doctor, who had confirmed her suspicions. She was pregnant! She could hardly wait to tell Lance.

He was working on the range with the wranglers, but she knew he'd be home earlier than usual, for they were having dinner guests, and Lance would need time to wash and dress before company arrived.

Sharla hurried into the house, where she was greeted

by her housekeeper, Maria. The woman helped Sharla run the huge home, and her husband, Juan, tended the manicured lawn, the flower garden, and took care of minor repairs.

Sharla wanted a bath, and with Maria's and Juan's help, the tub in the master bedroom was filled with warm water. Left alone to soak and savor her thoughts, Sharla lay back in the mammoth tub and sighed dreamily as memories ruffled through her mind.

The past three years had been nearly perfect—the only flaw, her failure to conceive a child. Despite that disappointment, she and Lance had built a happy marriage and a prosperous ranch. Sometimes, she found it hard to believe that so much time had passed; it seemed like only yesterday that she was a fugitive on the run. Remembering that time filled her with mixed emotions. A part of her treasured the memory, for that was when she met Lance and fell in love. But that time in her life was marred with sadness: Maxine's death, and also Steve's.

She didn't often allow herself to think about Claudia, for remembering her was too painful. However, this day seemed to be a day of reflection, so she let the woman enter her thoughts. Claudia never stood trial for James Rayfield's murder, for she hanged herself in her cell while waiting for the trial to begin. The jail custodians found her dead. Sharla learned the news from Agnes, for they corresponded regularly. She also learned that Dexter took an extended vacation in Europe and returned a year later, married to the daughter of an English nobleman. Agnes and Albert now worked for Dexter, for he and his bride moved into Olivia's home. Agnes wrote that Dexter was still somewhat arrogant, but that his young wife was very nice and had a positive influence on her husband.

Sharla's thoughts drifted aimlessly for a while, finally coming to rest on Mary. For months after their long journey from Missouri to southern Texas, Sharla had worried about her grandmother's health. But she eventually stopped worrying so much, for Mary seemed quite hearty for her age—swearing she would live to spoil her great-grandchildren.

Although Mary didn't reside with Sharla and Lance, they weren't concerned about her care, for she was in Hattie's capable, loving hands. The two women lived in a modest but elegant home at the edge of town. Maxine had left Hattie financially secure, and having no family of her own, she was happy to settle close to Sharla, and share a home with Mary.

Sharla had been shocked to learn that she had inherited part of Maxine's estate. She didn't invest this money in the ranch, for she and Lance didn't really need it; also, she knew Lance would balk at taking more money from his wife. Therefore, she entrusted the inheritance to her lawyer's care; someday it would belong to her children. However, as the years passed, leaving her childless, she wondered if there would ever be any children to reap the benefits of Maxine's generosity.

Sharla smiled, and placed a hand on her stomach. It had taken three years, but finally she and Lance had started a family.

The bedroom door opened, startling Sharla out of her reverie. Lance came inside, and observing his wife, naked, submerged in a tub of water, placed an appreciative gleam in his eyes. Sharla's long tresses were pinned into an up-sweep, crowning her head with golden curls. Her blue eyes were shining brightly, and her cheeks were becomingly flushed. Her beauty never failed to amaze him; in his eyes, she was perfect.

"It seems I'm just in time for a bath," he said with a smile. "I hope the water's still warm."

"It is," she replied. "I'll be out in just a moment."

"Take your time. That tub's big enough for both of us."

"Then get undressed and join me."

He stripped hastily, and Sharla watched his every move. Marriage hadn't cooled her passion, nor had it caused her to take Lance's striking virility for granted. His masculine presence still had the power to send her pulse racing with desire and love.

He came to the tub; she moved over and gave him room. He eased into the water and sat down facing her.

She sudsed the cloth, then began to wash, a smile on her face and a special gleam in her eyes.

Watching her, Lance said, "There's something you aren't telling me."

"What makes you think that?"

"Darlin', you look like the cat who just swallowed the canary."

"Do I?" she asked pertly.

"You do know something, don't you?"

"Yes, I certainly do."

"Does it have something to do with Mary or Hattie?"

"Why them?"

"They're having dinner with us, and I just thought . . . ?"

He suddenly chuckled. "I know why you look so pleased. Women always get that look when babies are involved."

She was taken aback; how could he have guessed the truth so easily? However, as he continued, Sharla realized her secret was still safe.

"It's Trish, isn't it?" he was saying. "She and Bill are also coming for dinner. Are they expecting another baby? Do they plan to make the announcement tonight?"

Trish and Bill were married; in fact, they had taken their marriage vows while Sharla was still a fugitive. When Trish had left Maxine's establishment without an explanation, she had gone to Bill to plead with him not to cast her aside. When Sharla and Lance had arrived at Bill's ranch to find him and Trish married, they had been taken completely by surprise. Last year, Trish had given birth to a son. Sharla had been very happy for her, but she had also been a little envious.

Now, her smile expanding, Sharla replied, "I don't think Trish is expecting again. She hasn't said anything to me." She handed Lance the washcloth, got out of the tub, and wrapped herself in a towel.

Lance was still eyeing her suspiciously. "Sharla, will you please explain why you're . . . you're . . ." He sighed impatiently. "Damn it, you're actually glowing!"

"Hurry and wash, then I'll let you in on a secret."

He did so quickly, dried, and tucked a towel around his waist.

Moving into his embrace, she slipped her arms about his neck, and gazed adoringly into his gray eyes. "There will be an announcement tonight," she murmured. "But you and I will make the announcement, not Trish and Bill."

"Exactly what are we announcing?" he asked, suspecting the truth, but almost afraid to believe it.

"We're going to have a baby, darling."

"Are you sure?"

"Yes. I saw the doctor this afternoon."

Lance was more than happy; he was elated. He kissed his wife with love, then swept her into his arms and carried her to the bed. He placed her gently on her feet, and drew back the covers.

"What are you doing?" she asked.

"We're going to celebrate."

"In bed?"

"Can you think of a better way?"

"I certainly cannot," she said eagerly, removing her towel with a flurry. She lay on the bed, and held out her arms.

Letting his own towel drop to the floor, Lance went into his wife's beckoning arms.

"I love you, Mrs. Slade," he whispered, placed a hand on her stomach, and added, "I also love our baby."

"Will you be disappointed if it's a girl?"

"Of course not."

"If we do have a daughter, I'd like to name her Olivia Maxine. Would you mind?"

"Not at all," he replied; however, he arched a questioning brow.

"What are you thinking about?"

"Does this mean all your bitterness is gone? You harbored some hard feelings toward Olivia and Maxine."

"I no longer feel that way. Olivia was a loving person, and I will always remember her that way. Maxine gave me away because she wanted me to have everything in life that she couldn't possibly give me. When I needed her, she was there for me."

Lance kissed her lips tenderly. "And if we have a boy? What do you want to name him?"

"He'll be named after his father." She snuggled against him, pressed her thighs to his, and purred seductively, "Didn't you say something about a celebration?"

"I think I did," he replied, his brow furrowed, as though he wasn't sure.

She nudged him playfully. "Lance Slade, if we're going to celebrate, then I suggest that we get started. Otherwise, our guests will be here and we'll still be in bed."

"We can't let that happen" was his reply, his lips coming down on hers.

Lance and Sharla were deeply, passionately in love, and their desire for each other was quickly kindled. Fiery kisses, stimulating fondling, and whispered endearments soon ignited their passion into a raging flame that demanded complete fulfillment.

Their bodies came together as one; and lost in their wondrous unity, they were transported to another plane—existing solely in their Utopian paradise.

Afterward, they lay cuddled in each other's arms, taking a moment to bask in the afterglow of their perfect union.

"I love you so much," Sharla murmured, "that I can't imagine life without you. I'm so glad we found each other."

"You can thank destiny for that," Lance replied. "I do believe that we were destined to meet, fall in love, and spend the rest of our lives together."

Sharla couldn't have said it better.

BOOK YOUR PLACE ON OUR WEBSITE AND MAKE THE READING CONNECTION!

We've created a customized website just for our very special readers, where you can get the inside scoop on everything that's going on with Zebra, Pinnacle and Kensington books.

When you come online, you'll have the exciting opportunity to:

- View covers of upcoming books

- Read sample chapters

- Learn about our future publishing schedule (listed by publication month *and author*)

- Find out when your favorite authors will be visiting a city near you

- Search for and order backlist books from our online catalog

- Check out author bios and background information

- Send e-mail to your favorite authors

- Meet the Kensington staff online

- Join us in weekly chats with authors, readers and other guests

- Get writing guidelines

- AND MUCH MORE!

Visit our website at
http://www.zebrabooks.com

ROMANCE FROM FERN MICHAELS

DEAR EMILY   (0-8217-4952-8, $5.99)

WISH LIST   (0-8217-5228-6, $6.99)

AND IN HARDCOVER:

VEGAS RICH   (1-57566-057-1, $25.00)

SPINE TINGLING ROMANCE
FROM STELLA CAMERON!

PASSIONATE ROMANCE
FROM BETINA KRAHN!

HIDDEN FIRES   (0-8217-4953-6, $4.99)

LOVE'S BRAZEN FIRE   (0-8217-5691-5, $5.99)

MIDNIGHT MAGIC   (0-8217-4994-3, $4.99)

PASSION'S RANSOM   (0-8217-5130-1, $5.99)

REBEL PASSION   (0-8217-5526-9, $5.99)